Totally Bound Publishing books by Ellen Mint

I0645760

Coven of Desire

VEIL

ELLEN MINT

Veil
ISBN # 978-1-80250-592-4
©Copyright Ellen Mint 2024
Cover Art by Kelly Martin ©Copyright Month 2023
Interior text design by Claire Siemaszkiewicz
Totally Bound Publishing

VEIL

Dedication

Who's hottest in a tux — Cal, Daniel, Garavel, Raul or Ink? Read on to find out.

Chapter One

Layla

The box hit the floor.

The men's voices drifted in and out, bubbling with worry and confusion as the kitten batted at the flimsy brown paper. All I could do was stare, my mouth frozen as I held it up.

When the dim yellow light struck it, a rainbow burst into the air. It didn't follow the path of the light. Instead, the entire room transformed into pulsing color. The unicorn skin was more beautiful than I had ever imagined.

"He came through," I said.

"Babe?" Cal scooped a protective hand around my waist and plucked the stone from my fingers. The light died, revealing the same blotchy brown and black surface that'd been visible when I'd opened the box. "It's a rock."

"It's the final ingredient," I cried in both joy and terror. A week had passed since the witch-hunter-turned-elf had vanished. I'd tried to not dwell on where he'd gone or if I'd ever see him again. None of that mattered now. With this stone, I could cast Valerie's spell and bring Daniel back to life.

What if I fuck it up?

"What has you in such a state?" Ink asked, oozing into the room. "Calvin, did you place another shackle upon her finger?"

"No." He groaned, looking at my finger where the amethyst pressed against my pinkie from the ring slipping. Taking my hand in his, he chided Ink. "Why are you an ass all the time?"

Ink shrugged with his usual cheeky grin. "It would be cruel to deny the world this perfection." He twisted like he was snapping his spine and curled a hand around his butt, then gave it a slap.

"That isn't what I—"

Cal's complaint was interrupted by Ink plucking the rock from his fingers. Once again it lit up with the rainbow, but the colors didn't fill the whole living room. Ink tossed the unicorn skin back and forth from one hand to the other. "So the stain in the rug is to become permanent. Well, fifty or so years permanent."

Ignoring his dig, I jerked my chin to the stone. "Raul came through."

Ink tossed the rock up high and ignored it to face me. "Your concern lies in defending the honor of a witch hunter and not crying out to the ghost?"

All my focus was on the falling stone. It looked like a garden rock, but for all I knew, it was as fragile as glass. "Ink..."

I leaped for it when he snatched it out of the air and clenched his fist around the stone. The rainbow vanished. "Interesting."

"Daniel?" I called before remembering the other ingredients I needed. "Garavel?"

My angel arrived with a bowl in tow. "My lady?" he asked before glancing at Ink and Cal. "Are we to have another orgy?"

Ink snickered, but was cut off by the man of the hour phasing through the air. The August heat chilled to frostiest December. The blue halo around his body was unavoidable now.

"You called?" he asked, his voice echoing not like he was in the living room but in a huge, empty hall. Time was running out.

"We've got it," I said, approaching Daniel. He lifted his chin, his eyes a ghastly pale.

"Got what?"

I reached back for the stone, but Ink dug his claws in, his lip quirked into a near sneer. Smacking my hand into his forearm, I tried again. He sighed like a fainting dowager and finally opened his hands. As I held the unicorn skin, the light show erupted, colors shifting around in a wave. The wandering eyes of the ghost slowed and focused. As he stared, Daniel's irises darkened to a sharp brown.

"Is that...?"

"We're bringing you back." Tears choked me and I held out the stone like it was the world's biggest diamond. Daniel placed his hands, ethereal and cool, just above mine. Soon they'd be warm and solid. I could touch him. I could touch all of him.

"Because raising the dead has never been an ill omen," Ink grumped.

"Babe, when are you...? When are we doing this?"

As I stared into the achingly handsome face, at his sculpted lips and chiseled cheekbones, my heart raced.

Something that hot, that beautiful, needed to be brought back to this world. "Now."

* * * *

I dusted off my hands, spreading green chalk across my jeans. Out of habit, I held Valerie's spell up to Daniel. "How's it look?"

An answer didn't come. I turned, expecting him to be behind my shoulder scrutinizing every line. Instead, he lingered by the couch we'd shoved back against the fireplace.

The other guys stood at various points of the drawn ward. Not because they needed to, but because I didn't know where to send them. Cal held my spell book open for me. He kept trying to take a peek even though the pages were blank to him. None of them knew I'd opened it to a spell that'd protect us from a zombie's curse. No one but Daniel.

"It's almost ready," I said, approaching him. He should have been jumping for joy. For thirty years, he'd been trapped in this unending purgatory. I was about to free him. His head hung to the side and he peered at the circle with wariness.

"Barring the feather of an angel and blood of a demon. Two of the most powerful magics plucked from obscurity put to use to resurrect a single mortal. I can't decide if the Celestials would find this hilarious or depressing."

"Ink." I'd known he'd be a pain, but I hadn't expected him to start tightening the screws before I even cast the spell.

He met me eye to eye, lips pulled back so his demon fangs were exposed. I braced myself for a derisive snort, but he softened. His teeth flattened and his eyes drooped. With a shiver, he turned away from me to focus on Cal. "Wolf, your posture is atrocious. Shoulders back, arms straight."

"Daniel?" I eased closer, extending my palm upward. He broke from his crossed stance to caress his hand over mine, only the cold touching me. "What's the matter? Why aren't you excited? You're going to be alive again."

He closed his eyes. "This spell is half-baked, from a witch who, for no known reason, helped you escape. What is her plan in all of this? Why did she send you this incredibly rare and powerful spell, and how did she possess it in the first place?"

"Is it Valerie's motives that are bothering you or...?" I gulped hard, my cheeks burning. "Or is it me?"

His eyes opened wide and he jerked back. "Layla, no, it isn't—"

"I could say the wrong word, the wrong syllable. Get the letters all messed up."

"Babe, come on," Cal said. "You're not gonna do that."

"I could banish you by mistake. Or destroy the house. I don't know."

"With this level of power, you might raze the whole of the neighborhood to ash."

"For moon's sake, Ink. Shut it," Cal fought back. "Layla, you're not going to destroy my house, or all the other houses or banish Daniel. You know that."

"The wolf..." Garavel gritted his teeth at that. "Speaks truly. Your magics never waver. Only your faith in yourself does."

Their opinions, while sweet, didn't matter. They weren't the ones whose very existence rested on my fingers. "Daniel?"

"I'm...I'm scared." Panic choked him. His face flushed. He tried to clench his fingers around mine, but they sailed on through. I braced myself for a trademark cutting incubus remark, but Ink stayed silent. All of them did while Daniel fell apart.

"My faith in you is as strong as ever. I believe you can do it, but at what cost? What if this...if there's a trick or a trap and you're hurt? My life's not worth that."

"At last, something we agree upon," Ink said, but his signature smirk was gone. He sounded sincere as hell. The rest of the men nodded solemnly with Daniel.

"You're wrong. All of you. You're worth it, Daniel, because...you'd do the same for me."

He gasped, hunting for the air he didn't need. "I love you."

Placing my hand over the golden heart at the top of my chest, I said, "I know, and it's time to make you whole again. Garavel?"

"Yes?"

"Bring out the feather," I said.

The angel reached behind his neck where he somehow stored a massive sword. "Ah..." He fished his hand out where the ten-pound kitten had dug her nails into his forearm. What I cared about was the massive feather pinched between the tips of his fingers. He seemed terrified to touch the reminder of his creator who he'd killed to save me.

I lightly brushed my palm over the shaft, so white it nearly blinded me. I didn't look at the feather but focused on Garavel. At first, he didn't let go. I traced my hand around the curve of his cheek and held him tight.

"Promise me..." Garavel stuttered. "That it will be for a worthy purpose."

"Daniel knew something that terrifies Conquest. We'll find it and stop him."

"Good." He opened his fingers and I caught the feather.

"Now the blood. Ink?"

Daniel scoffed. "You gave it to the demon? I thought you said you put it in a safe place."

Snickering, Ink reached into his pocket and lifted the glass vial to the light. "Clench your sphincter, ghost. There was no safer place to store the destructive power of demonic blood than in the clutches of a creature that cannot use it."

He held out the vial to me with no fuss, but as I went to take it, he had to say, "I would ask if you think it is worthwhile to expend such power, but when have you ever acted sensibly?"

"I am fucking an incubus," I said and clenched the distressingly cold vial. Ink smiled and bowed his head. As if he had nothing more to give, he stepped back.

"One feather of an angel, one drop of demon's blood, one unicorn flesh to unite the two." Holding the feather out, I was about to tip the vial of blood when my hands began to shake.

I'm gonna drop it. It'll shatter at my feet and I'll lose my only chance to hold him.

Warm fingers swept behind mine, steadying them to a surgeon's level. Cal pressed in tighter behind me to whisper, "You've got this," before kissing me on the nape of my neck.

With his help, a single drop of blood beaded on the lip of the glass and plummeted toward the blinding white feather. The moment the blood hit the downy spines, the feather hardened to a rock, like a feather fossil but heavier than a bowling ball. I struggled to keep it upright, tears rising.

What happened? Was the angel not good enough? Did the feather lose its magic because he's dead?

The fossil crumbled first to gravel, then sand in my palm. Just as I held my breath, the angel's feather burst into dust which began floating away.

"Is it supposed to do that?" Cal voiced what I was too terrified to say. We had another feather, but who was to say the same thing wouldn't happen? "It's gone."

The heavy dust faded from the light, the feather taken as quickly as Daniel had been.

"Look again," Ink instructed. I fought to blink away the tears and stared. The air was no different than before with the house dust dancing in the sunlight. I focused on a single mote twirling like a dirty snowflake. As it spun, worlds appeared. A giant green marble with purple waters cascading off the edge. A black volcano with hissing red veins of lava exploding from its cracks. Skies of orange with blue sunsets. Every possible impossibility formed in a second, then folded into another.

"You've reduced the feather and blood to the base ingredients of creation. We are tinkering in the Celestials' toolbox now. Be wary."

Ink's warning was like a fire alarm blaring in my head. If he was worried, shit was about to get real. But I couldn't stop, not when we were so close. "Now I add the unicorn skin."

Kissing the rock for good luck, I cupped it in my hands and threw it. Rather than rebounding off the wall and hitting the TV, the stone landed dead center in the middle of the floating bits of creation. It began to rotate as, one by one, every color peeled off. First red, then orange…the room lit up to the solitary hue tearing off the stone. The light grew brighter, burning with every falling shift until purple pierced straight through my brain—and blackness fell.

"Layla?"

"Can anyone get a light?"

"Where are you?"

"Ink? Is that your hand on my—?"

A soundless explosion and light came into being. A single, pinprick-sized ball floated in the middle of the ward, casting both light and heat.

"Did you just make a sun?" Cal asked.

"There is no life without light," Ink mused, then squeezed my ass.

I fought to tear my eyes away from the source, not just of light and heat but magic. It shivered inside of me the way no other magic had—wild and young. Ink stared at the same micro-sun and rapture dawned on his face.

"Don't even think about it," I ordered.

"To sip from the dawn of creation would be a most exquisite meal," he murmured, his face slack with awe. Then he snickered. "And also my last. Shall we chuck the bones of the dead inside and see what slithers out of the universe's birth canal?"

I shivered at his metaphor and turned to Daniel. "Are you ready?"

He bowed his head. "Layla, promise me that if...if something goes wrong, if this doesn't work—"

What? Does he have a backup plan? A way to bring back a ghost that he's found in one of the books?

Wafting his chilled fingers above my cheek, Daniel stepped closer. He placed his palm over the locket and whispered, "You do not blame yourself."

"I can't—"

"Promise. Or this ends here."

Everyone went silent save the low hum of the universe birthing itself before us. "Daniel, I…" Clenching around the locket through his hand, I gazed into his eyes. "I promise." I pulled open the golden heart and lifted the single fragment of finger bone.

Facing the storm, I held the piece of the lost. *There's a very good chance this will fail. I won't just lose the opportunity… I'll lose him. But if I don't do anything, I'll lose him anyway.*

"Daniel, I love you," I cried out. Then I tossed the bone into the primordial fire. Nothing happened. Daniel remained beside me, his cool form competing against the heat of the micro-sun.

Now for the hardest part, reading gibberish and getting it right. Shaking, I unrolled the scrap of paper we'd been working on. Daniel had written it phonetically for me.

Raising my head, I stared at the incoherent mix of vowels and consonants. I took one last look at him and spoke. "Rise."

A bong echoed through the room and I slapped a hand over my mouth. "I didn't say that. I said this…whatever this is."

"You are speaking the language of creation," Garavel explained. "Nonsense is impossible when sense does not yet exist."

"From the ashes of Celestials, the fires of their veins, I command you to rise…Daniel Lu. Return from the darkness and enter the light."

The room exploded, blinding white rays shooting out of the sun. We hit the ground as one, power rampaging above us. Daniel opened his mouth and threw his head back. The light pierced him, burrowing tiny holes in his body that began to chew him apart. He swiveled his head to me, his mouth still strained as if he were screaming.

What did I do?

I reached for him, and he smiled. "Layla," he whispered just as the light burned him to ash.

Darkness fell.

Scrambling to my feet, I fought to catch fire on my fingers, when Ink grabbed my hand. "That is most unwise right now. You might set the entire planet aflame." I pulled to get my arm back, needing to find a flashlight and a passage to bring Daniel back.

"Cal? Garavel?"

"I am here, lady witch. A cushion softened my fall."

"That'd be me." Cal moaned. Manic shuffling told me the two were trying to get untangled, no doubt uneasy in this pitch darkness. I reached for any of them, knocking my palm into an arm and trailing down to a hand. Garavel's.

"We have to fix this. Find a way to…"

"Lady witch, look."

He pointed, though he didn't have to. A single mote of dust glowed. It appeared five feet in the air, then floated down to the ground. More appeared, each taking the same path, but as they fell, they built outward as if creating something…or someone.

"Is it working?" I cried out.

"Appears to be," Cal said. In the near darkness, he held up two thumbs for me.

Ink sauntered closer to watch and mused. "A thought occurs to me. Are you certain he shall be returned to you as he had been?"

"What are you talking about?"

"Or will he be revived as a babe, and you shall have to raise your future lover from infancy? How de Sade of you."

"Ink." I groaned, not ready to face those fucked-up repercussions.

I didn't have to wait long to see if Ink was right. The magic picked up speed, forming the outline of a fully grown man. It moved like a 3D printer, laying out a layer before moving higher. I couldn't see any details, the light blinding them away, but in the shadows I spotted toes and fingers, the crook of an elbow, a person. A man. Daniel.

Holding Garavel's and Ink's hands, I watched in near silence. Hours must have passed, but I was terrified to blink. If I looked away, he could vanish. With every layer of light, it grew harder to see. My eyes watered. I couldn't fight it anymore and closed them tight just as creation vanished.

The darkness receded as the house lights took over. Blinking away my tears, I faced my creation.

My god, he's beautiful. It hit me that in my months of knowing him, I'd never seen Daniel sleep. I couldn't. There he was, his arms at the side, his soulful eyes closed, his lips parted — deep in the throes of slumber. So deep it could almost be confused for…for…?

"Is he breathing?"

"I'm not sure. Dan? Hey, Daniel?" Cal shouted.

The hands holding me fell away. I crossed the line of creation without realizing it was there and dove for his still lips. "Daniel?" I cried, my voice beating against the darkness. "Breathe. You have to breathe. Fight. Come back to me. Please."

Chapter Two

Daniel

In the beginning, there was pain.

Not the usual pounding-in-the-head, creaking-in-the-chest kind of pain. This burned me inside and out, every vein in my body bursting with lava, every organ seizing in a vise, every inch of my skin sizzling like fat on spare ribs. I couldn't survive this. No one could.

Images flickered in my mind. A mess of books. The stench of fireworks. Scarlet dripping off my hand. A face in shadows. Darkness swallowing me whole.

"Daniel? You have to breathe."

I gasped. Oxygen tore apart my sinuses and throat, but once my body got a taste, it took another sip.

"Holy shit, he's breathing."

"Babe."

"My bond, be wary."

My dying mind flickered awake. The still images began to move. A gun, smoke rising against the backdrop of a library and the man standing behind it as my ribs split and heart burst from the bullet.

"You shot me, you bastard!" My tongue flailed about, the words garbled in my cottony ears. With each syllable, my muscles remembered what it was to be alive.

My eyelids shot open and I lashed out, prepared to rip off the head of the fucker who had tried to murder me. Big brown eyes gazed at me, their edges crinkled with worry. Heat blasted up my palm from the warmth of her body.

Her fucking hot body. *Holy shit, I wouldn't mind being shot a few times if I got to wake up to those breasts in my face.*

"Layla." A blond man scooped her up from behind, pulling her away. Then another dark-haired man dressed like a waiter moved into place. He waved a flaming log at me.

"We do not yet know if he hungers for human flesh," he said, whipping the log back and forth.

"What the shit is going on?" I tried to scurry away from the man about to burn off my eyebrows, but my arms were as soft as rice pudding and I slumped back to the floor. "Who are...?" My chin hit my bare chest and I kept staring down. "Why the fuck am I naked?"

"Hm." The man with the log cupped his hand over the fire. Steam strained between his fingers as he mused, "The undead rarely concern themselves with modesty. He is unlikely to be a zombie."

I was in a crazy house. Some cult had kidnapped me, stripped me naked and were about to sacrifice me. I tried to crawl away again, my arms working better than before, but still practically worthless. Did they drug me?

"Whatever you want, I don't got it. My parents aren't rich." Oh, Jesus, I didn't even see the other guy, the biggest of them all. He crossed his arms tight and...wings sprouted off his back. Did they mix LSD in with the kidnapping sedatives?

I needed to get out of here. Find a payphone and call the cops. My scrambling picked up enough speed that I managed to ram my shoulder into the door. The men didn't move, only watching as I strained my hand up for the handle to freedom.

Then she walked forward.

"Babe, are you...?" the blond man asked, somehow the least intimidating of them despite having the frame of a Terminator.

God, she's beautiful.

Aesthetically, she was gorgeous with an oval face and huge eyes, the thickest lips that could make men do stupid shit and a cute wide nose. But it was more than that. Sure, her tits were amazing and I wondered how they'd look naked. Weirdest of all, somehow I knew the heart below was the kindest, sweetest one to ever beat. How?

"Daniel?" She said my name again, but instead of panic, I felt elation. "It's okay. You're safe. You're..." Tears welled in her chocolate eyes and I wanted to kick myself for causing them.

She bent down, extending a hand toward me. Instinctively, I pressed back, terrified of being trapped. As she landed on her knee, a gold necklace swung out from her cleavage. It spun in a circle, the open heart locket hypnotizing me.

"Daniel, it's me. Layla."

Her hand brushed against my skin. Thirty years of purgatory gushed into my head. Loneliness. Guilt. Regret. Confinement. Abandoned. Forgotten. Fading.

Then a light. An anchor in the never-ending sea — a hand reaching for me, pulling me back to shore. The once treacherous waves faded and I no longer feared drowning with her at my side.

"Layla?" fell from my lips. The skin on my mouth tightened and relaxed, my tongue tapping the roof of my mouth with each syllable. Flesh and bone formed that word and not the lingering shell of what remained.

Her eyes lightened as if the whole world had been plucked from her shoulders and her lips slid into a smile. Those lips I'd watched from afar, that the others could taste at their pleasure.

With all the strength in my new body, I dug my fingers through her hair and pulled her to me. Every kind word that fell from them, every promise, every sweet affirmation meant nothing compared to the rush of her kiss. Those lips I'd traced with her finger more times than I could count caressed and softened against mine. The deep cupid's bow pressed into my bare upper lip and I moaned.

Thirty years of celibate agony faded to a dull ache as Layla's kiss swept through me. I had to break off, my body pleading for oxygen. But as I pulled away, she smiled, her face brightening like the sun.

"I love you," I whispered, then kissed her again.

* * * *

Layla

It was cliché as hell, but I needed someone to pinch me. Daniel was real, tangible and lying under me with a pleased smile. I turned my head, letting him talk, when two palms curved around my ass and dug in.

Daniel chuckled. "I told myself I'd be a gentleman once I got my body back. Take it slow with a little romance." He pinched the waistband of my jeans and pulled my hips lower. "You make that impossible," he whispered, his nose beside mine before he kissed me. He wasted no time digging under my tank top and rubbing my bare skin. I sighed and Daniel slipped his tongue into my mouth.

After six months of nothing but his ghost kisses, just the tip of his tongue drove me mad. I moaned like I'd never been touched and he caught me under my chin, pinning me in place. "My god, that sound... I want to live inside of it."

Daniel's wild eyes hunted mine and he pushed my hips lower. There was no mistaking the hard rod prodding up my stomach and then some. I gulped, trying to figure out where the crown started and the base ended as Daniel brushed back my fallen hair to hold my face.

"Well..." Cal's awkward voice brought me back to reality. I slipped off of Daniel to catch my werewolf standing behind me armed with a fireplace poker. He returned it to the jangling iron set. "Seems everything went off without a hitch. Uh, what do we —? We should go. Right?"

"Should there not be a celebration of this momentous occasion?" Garavel asked. "It is rare for one to have a second birth."

"I'm sure they've got a 'welcome back from the dead' cake at the grocery store," Cal said with a laugh, but Gravel stared at him as if he were dead serious.

"Would that also require ice cream?"

"Sure, fine. Ice cream. And a cake. We'll go get that and leave them to...ya know." Cal patted Garavel's shoulders, the two showing a level of solidarity I had never expected. My werewolf and angel were getting along, my ghost was alive. Could everything in my life finally be going right?

"You do not intend to stay and witness his performance?"

I groaned, forgetting the prickly thorn in my rose bush.

Ink dragged a chair across the floor, the sound causing me to flinch, and sat down in it. He crossed his legs and tented his fingers like a birder watching a pair of songbirds mate.

"Surely after all this time and the ex-ghost's never-ending boasting, it shall be a bedding for the ages. I should take notes." He plucked a small notebook from his breast pocket and clicked open a pen.

"Here I thought you'd give your jealousy at least a five-minute break," Daniel fought back.

"Only a fool would be jealous of a newborn."

"Not if he thinks his place is about to be usurped."

"Okay." I waved my hands to try to break up this impending fight. "This is… It's a big deal. A big change, I know. For all of us."

"Mostly for you," Cal said, confusing me. He said it with a snicker then turned away, the back of his neck bright pink.

"Can we give Daniel a little time before we all battle over the new pecking order?"

"She means she wishes to determine if his pecker is in working order."

That was not fucking helping. "Ink?" On my knees, I stared up into his eyes. If I wasn't afraid of tipping over, I'd have clasped my hands together, too. "Please?"

He sighed dramatically, stuffed away his notebook and stood. "Very well. I shall leave you two alone for…what? Ten minutes? I assume that's as long as he'll last."

"For god's sake."

"His flesh is brand new," Ink said and Cal grimaced in agreement.

"Yeah, that plumbing's just been hooked up, so..."

"Not you, too."

Cal walked over to scoop his arms around me, pulling my chin against his lower belly. There were so many abs, it was like hugging the Himalayas. "Just saying, babe, don't get your hopes up. First times go quick," he whispered and kissed the top of my head. "Also the backup lube's in the end table drawer behind the remote."

Backup lube? I needed it with his monster, sure, but...

Holy hell.

It'd looked normal, maybe a bit above average when he was lying there unconscious. But as Daniel stared down my shirt, his cock pierced the sky like the tower of Babylon. "Is that ten inches?" I cried out, not meaning to say it aloud.

Daniel beamed and shrugged his shoulder with pride, then Ink leaned closer and held out an extended thumb. "Eight and one quarter, actually."

"It's bigger than yours," Daniel argued back but Ink chuckled.

"Size means little when the owner cannot control it. Enjoy your three and half minutes, my bond." Smirking, Ink vanished to god only knew where. Cal stumbled to his feet, then caught Garavel by the arm.

"We should get going too."

"How do you keep that from prodding out of your trousers?" Garavel asked, reaching closer as if to flick it.

Cal tugged hard, not giving the angel an inch. "Cake? We were gonna get cake."

"Oh yes, and ice cream. Do you prefer chocolate or cherry nut? We shall get both." Garavel's cries faded as Cal pulled him into the kitchen. I'd never heard the door slam so hard in my life.

"Well?" Daniel skirted the tips of his fingers up my arm before rubbing across my shoulder. "Where were we?"

Smiling, I pivoted my chin to look at him. "Why didn't you tell me you had…that?" I gestured to his cock, still in slightly-terrified awe. It twitched but had so much torque the crown swayed clear across his thin hips like a metronome. I couldn't look away.

"Would you have believed me?" he asked.

"Yes," I admitted, then frowned. "Unless you were fighting with Ink, then all bets are off."

Daniel cupped my cheek and brushed the tip of his pinkie against my lips. I parted them out of habit, expecting it to be my finger. But instead of rounding to the other side, he slipped his digit into my mouth. I puckered my lips and traced around his pinkie with my tongue.

His groan was so guttural and feral, I half expected him to sprout fur. Right. He had just come back from the dead. Anything seemed possible. I leaned back so his finger fell free and asked, "How are you feeling?"

"I am…" Daniel crowed. "Fingers, toes…" He darted his eyes down his body and smiled slyly. "Everything is feeling, touching, experiencing. Do you have any idea how scratchy oxygen is rushing into your nose?"

"Uh…no?"

"Neither did I until I spent thirty years without it." He breathed deep, expanding his chest. Then he put his lips together and whistled. "Fuck." Tears beaded in his eyes and he collapsed his arm over them.

"Daniel?" I slid closer on my hip. "What is it? What's wrong?"

"It's stupid. I should be losing my shit over tasting dumplings again, or…" He dropped his arm and raised his head off the floor. "Or being able to touch you. But it's the damn whistling that's got me bawling. I hate whistling," he declared and gave another one.

"I can't even do it," I said.

"Sure you can. All you have to do is put your lips together" — he pushed against my cheeks until I puckered up — "and blow."

I prepared a puff of air when Daniel surged forward and kissed me. I leaned closer, trying to meet him when a hand curled around my waist and pulled. There wasn't much force in it, but it was enough to teeter me off balance. I yelped in surprise and shifted my knee until I straddled his thigh.

Daniel's eyes blazed as he stared up at me. "Layla?" he breathed, cupping both his hands against my cheeks and pushing back my hair. Everything we'd been through was for this. To touch him, to taste him, to hold him in my arms and listen to his beating heart.

"Yes?"

He lifted the hand that'd been a part of my body but never touched me. The fingers that'd composed thousands of words of love and romance, but couldn't run through my hair. I waited, anticipating him to cup my cheek and declare his affections as only Daniel could.

His free-flying palm landed on my shoulder. "You're wearing far too much clothing," he declared and wrapped the spaghetti straps of my cami around his fingers. They bulged as he tightened his hold. Tugging the strap down, Daniel exposed my bare shoulder and kissed it.

He drew his leg up my inner thigh, pushing it out. Daniel pulled both straps straight down, pinning my upper arms tighter to my chest. I wobbled closer, terrified I might fall and crush him, but he didn't care. He kissed across my exposed skin, dotting every errant freckle with his tongue while raising his knee higher until it brushed against me.

Even with spandex and cotton in the way, the heat of his new body and the pressure of his real knee flared right through me. I ground against him, my soaked lips seeping through the cheap yoga pants to his naked knee.

Daniel paused in kissing the top of my cleavage. A low, ominous chuckle rumbled in his chest and he whispered, "Good girl."

Fuck. From anyone else, I'd have fought back, but Daniel's praise melted my spine and left my brain floating on a pink cloud. He swept the tips of his fingers across the swell of my breasts bulging out of the top of my cami. Heat and a cascade of goosebumps trailed that light but erotic touch as he stared me in the eye.

"Now," Daniel ordered. "Take them off."

I immediately sat up to reach for my waistband before sense clobbered in between us. He hadn't been alive for more than five minutes. Was it really smart to do this now?

"I don't know if—" I said when he rose, pressing his forehead to mine.

His voice stilled, the steady pant of need gone in an instant. "Are you questioning me?"

The unassailable tone caught me. I tried to look down, but there was no escaping Daniel's gaze. "I'm worried that you're—"

He laughed. I'd heard him laugh hundreds of times before, but never like this. It darkened in this throat like a shot of espresso at two a.m. "I'm here so you don't have to worry," Daniel declared, then he dug his hands under my pants.

I expected him to pry them off, but he scraped his nails around my hip and bent low. Teeth bit the top of my bare breast just as he clamped onto my ass. I shivered, a full-on tidal wave taking out my yoga pants. A moan broke free as he tongued down my cleavage and my elastic waistband snapped below my buttocks.

Daniel pulled my shirt lower until my nipples peeked out of the top. He drew his bottom teeth across the edge of one, threatening to bite down, before swiveling and lapping at my nipple. Meanwhile, he pried at my ass, drawing his fingers under the curve and up, teasing me in a way that made me want to scream.

All the while, that huge cock pointed slightly northwest. I wanted to hold it, to smooth my palm over the pink crown and jerk off the tan shaft. I began to shift, hoping to take all my weight on one hand. But as I moved, I realized too late that he'd trapped me. The camisole straps pinned my arms so tight to my body, I couldn't move my hands. I was trapped on my hands and knees at his pleasure.

"Daniel?" I gasped.

"You're worrying again," he mused before softly pinching my nipple between his teeth. *Fuck.* I shivered on my hands, wanting to thrust myself onto his teasing fingers. He brushed them against my taint and the bottom edge of my vulva. "I don't want you to. Forget your worries, your concerns. Stop thinking as I fuck you to oblivion."

He thrust his thumb deep inside me and pushed my ass down. I cried out, "I want that."

"I know you do," Daniel responded. "I know every touch that excites you. Every nip and pinch you ache for. How badly you want to have every obligation stripped from your mind until you're heaving for air in a puddle on the bed." He plunged two fingers inside of me and toyed with my clit, brushing over the hood with a gentle swipe.

I moaned and tried to jerk my hips to match his movements. Daniel clamped onto my ass to stop me, forcing me to live in the pink haze of his touch—forever on the cusp of an orgasm. He'd studied me for six months, used my body to learn all my secrets. With his fingers teasing me below, Daniel held on to one of my breasts and sucked my nipple into his mouth.

The burn in my wrists began to fade. All I knew was his tongue and touch, sucking and flicking across my skin. Everything vanished—my upcoming semester, clinicals, Conquest, planning my wedding. My whole world collapsed to Daniel fucking me slowly on the floor.

"It's not fair," I cried. I couldn't give in to the eternal bliss, my mind fighting back. Daniel slipped his fingers away and stared up at me.

Sense flooded my brain, along with the pain in my arms. I fumbled closer, trying to shake off the strain, but I wobbled and collapsed against his chest.

Daniel brushed back my hair. "What's not?"

Panting, I struggled to weave my turbulent thoughts into a coherent sentence. "You. You know how to play my body."

"Better than a bass," he bragged.

"But I don't have a fucking clue how to touch you." Did he like his nipples being flicked? His hair pulled? Was he into jerking his shaft hard? Teasing the crown? Rimming? I was alone in the dark.

Daniel chuckled. "That's what's got you worried? My beloved, I'm a man. I like fucking you. That's it. No big mystery."

Bullshit. All of them were different. Cal liked to be collared and ordered to his knees. Garavel was sweet and gentle—unable to so much as pinch me. Ink was down for anything, but seemed to really love letting his demon side out. And Raul—

Daniel hooked his hand around the nape of my neck. "I'll show you what I want, and you...you will stop worrying, stop thinking and be fucked. Understand?"

I gulped and nodded, feeling way too wide-eyed for a woman with four cocks in the pantry. Daniel cupped my chin, sweeping his thumb back and forth over my bottom lip. "Here's what's going to happen. First, either you take off your clothes, or I rip them off." He backed that up by plucking the strap of my cheap camisole and pulling until the five seams were at the breaking point.

I knew how they felt.

Placing the strap back rather than snapping me, Daniel soothed his hands up my arms and leaned closer. With his warm, living breath, he whispered in my ear, "Then I'm going to put you on your back, throw your ankles over my shoulders and lose my mind as your eyes roll back with each thrust of my cock."

"Missionary?" I squeaked, trembling at the promise, but unable to stop my tongue. "After all this time, that's what you want?"

"What I want, what I've dreamed about since the first day we met is to watch you and your gorgeous face as I enter you again, and again" —he scooped a hand under my shirt to take a breast in his palm—"and again. What do you say?" Daniel pulled on the strap, his eyebrows peaking with the question.

I scrambled like a dropped egg. It was my pants I went for first, having to roll my hands down my sides to reach them. Daniel watched while propped up on his elbows as I gracefully sat back on my knees, tugged down my pants, then realized I'd trapped myself. Again.

All the while, his cock ticked back and forth as he watched me—the weirdo with her shirt under her tits and pants at her knees. I didn't care what Ink said—that thing had to be ten inches. Eleven! It was huge, the crown past his belly button.

No wonder he walked around with the confidence of a tiger even while dead.

Daniel cocked his head, his longer black hair sweeping across his face. "Are you having second thoughts?"

"Only in that I can't afford to buy a new top."

He chuckled and sat up. I watched his eyes, anticipating the strain without realizing it. His body had just been built out of the cosmos. Muscle atrophy seemed likely. But Daniel moved smoother than a silk ribbon. Rising to his knees, he met me like the dashing knight assisting the helpless princess.

"Allow me," he said, reaching for my hips. Instead of yanking my pants the last of the way, he took control. With one hand hooked around the small of my back and another circling behind my neck, he guided me to the floor. Daniel came with me, pressing his chest to mine and his cock riding up to the bottom of my tits.

In one quick motion, he removed the offending yoga pants and paused. Head bent, he smoothed his palms up my thighs while staring at me in pieces. A voice quieter than the AC whispered, "In death, you were beautiful like a sunset. A raindrop on a flower. The crash of lightning in the stormy clouds. Bounding breasts that enthralled me. A steamy, welcoming pussy daring me to explore."

Trying to keep my tone level, I asked, "And now?"

"Now I can feel the heat of your lips, the slick arousal sucking my fingers in for more, the give of your tits and the tightening of your nipples as I pinch them. I was frozen in the darkness. Now I'm burning in the light. Layla." Daniel clenched tight to my calves, then guided them up. My ankle dug into his shoulders, pressing into the sharp bones and tendons as he flexed.

"All I want is to fuck you." He panted. Taking me by the hips, he pulled my ass flush to his thighs, cupped his foot-long at the base and stared into my eyes.

Smiling, I nodded.

Daniel circled his sleek crown around my lips, bathing it in the arousal he'd caused and gearing up my body. My skin trembled and I bit my lip. Daniel thrust himself inside.

The first push caught my breath. My lips slackened and rounded into an O. I curled my toes, catching them in his silky black hair, and Daniel kept going. The first inch became three, then five.

I'd been near to bursting from Cal but had never felt so full. It couldn't be all of him. Right? I focused up at Daniel, his face stern but dewy with sweat.

Slowly, he cracked a smile. "Believe me, my love, there's so much more to come."

My legs slipped lower, my knees clenching on his shoulders as Daniel thrust himself balls deep. Holy shit, I'd been speared clean through. I expected the crown of his cock to poke into the back of my throat. Gulping in air, I stared up at Daniel sitting perfectly still.

"Well?" I asked, raking my nails down his trim chest. "What are you waiting for?"

He snapped his ass far enough back that the first thrust felt like he was entering me a second time. From my chest down to my thighs, my body buzzed in anticipation, growing more ravenous with each jerk of his cock. Daniel started slow, teasing me. He reached back to clamp around my ankles, pinning both in place, then he grunted. "Touch yourself as I would."

With most other guys I'd feel a twinge of self-consciousness as if I was breaking some taboo. But not with Daniel. My fingers traipsed across my clit before my ears processed his order. Rubbing the nub up and down, then back and forth, I squirmed on his huge cock.

Daniel cried out. "Fuck, Layla. This is… Fuck." His gentle thrusting became manic and I kept teasing myself just to the point then backing off. I doubted Daniel could last much longer, but I wanted to match him. I wanted to come at the same time he…

Come with…

Fuck.

"You can't come in me!" I shouted, nearly sitting up before I slipped back onto my ass.

"What? Why?" His voice crackled as if he were about to blow. I tried to wiggle off in time, but Daniel had enough control to pull himself out. It felt like a sword swallower pulling out a claymore, but he held his throbbing red cock just above my belly. It shined bright as he bent closer.

My legs tumbled off his shoulders as he lay above me. Balancing on one hand, he jerked his cock against my stomach and kissed me. I rounded around my clit fast, chasing the orgasm I'd been denying for too long.

This one hit so sharp and fast, I cried out as if I'd been struck. My yelp burst against Daniel's lips and he gasped. I fought the urge to slip off into my own pleasure to watch as his mouth crinkled into a long E, his shoulders slackened and his cock spurted warm cum up my shirt and down my cleavage.

"Lay…la." He sighed and collapsed on top of me.

Chapter Three

Daniel

I slid to the floor, giving her breathing room. A dull thud radiated up my hip and down my leg. I couldn't shake it, the sensation pinching my thigh into the bone below. Was my body breaking down? Had we failed already? Trying to escape, I rolled onto my back, and it hit me.

Pain. Thirty years I'd never felt so much as a hangnail or a pimple. The press of my hip digging into the hard ground was enough to send me into a panic.

"Jesus." I moaned, digging my head back into the floor. Before I could contemplate the complications of living again, warm breasts pooled across my lower chest and Layla nestled on my pec. I swept my arm around her, holding her close.

Holding her. I was actually touching her skin, caressing her spine, running my knuckles against that swoop of her ass. *Holy shit.*

"It's gone." Her surprise caught me. She was running her fingers through my hair, her lips pursed tight. "The blue."

I tried to roll my eyes back to see my own forehead. "Thank fuck for that." I sighed. She kept teasing the streak as if all it needed was a little encouragement to dye itself back. "I didn't want to do it in the first place. All four of us in a cheap-ass motel bathroom trying to smear bleach in without burning our faces off was not my best hour."

The memory came in an instant. It didn't fight from the depths of time to be dragged out and unspooled like crumbling microfiche. The stench of chemicals, of cigarette smoke caked onto the mirror, my friends laughing and squirting the blue dye at each other hit me like it was last Tuesday and not thirty years ago.

I struggled to tamp down the memory and the grief bubbling inside my new heart. Living again was going to take some getting used to. I couldn't blame Frankenstein for freaking out. "Don't tell me you're going to miss the streak," I said. I wasn't in a rush to do it again, but if she wanted it, I'd glob on the bleach right now.

She dropped my hair back up with the rest and snuggled tighter to me. "Not as long as I can hold you."

I squeezed tighter, listening to her breaths and counting her heartbeats. She was alive, I knew that, but I couldn't stop trying to live through her. I raised my hand, wanting to touch her — those breasts, her hip, pull her leg in between mine. I'd done it all and so much more a minute earlier, but suddenly I grew unsure of what to do. The wet stain seeping into her shirt began to flake across my skin. I frowned at the reminder of her request.

Placing my chin against her forehead, I tried to find out without looking her in the eye. "Can I ask why you didn't want me to come inside of you?"

"Um...well."

"You have no problem letting the werewolf shoot his shot, generally like a firehose."

She stifled a laugh, even if it was true. There was marking his territory and then there was treating it like a Banksy. "It's different with Cal, and the other two. Oh, god, I should have told them. I should have told you."

Her voice drifted away like she was mentally fleeing from an argument I didn't even realize we were having. I tried to sit up, only for my strength to collapse. *Living is exhausting.*

Layla breathed deeply, circling her hand back and forth over my stomach. "Apparently, and I just learned this from my mom right before I fell into elf land..." She took another steadying breath and I braced myself for the worst.

She's cursed.

Semen can kill her.

She's wigged out by the idea of me coming in her.

The damn demon broke something inside of her.

Layla clenched her fingers, scraping her nails over my skin, and gasped out, "I'm super fertile."

My mind went to a box of Miracle-Gro. *Did she get turned into a plant? No, that makes no damn sense.* "What does that mean?"

"I guess it's a witch's job to get knocked up like ASAP. Get the magic, get a fetus. You'd think they'd put that in the book on page one."

Pregnant? A baby...? "I...I saw no mention of this in my research."

"Me either. And I asked my book. A lot. It gave me this shifty 'I don't want to talk about it' feeling and slammed shut. I didn't get a lot from my mom beyond 'have baby now' but it sure made it sound like those old scared-abstinent PSAs. Have sex, make baby, ruin life, die in gutter."

"Layla." I scooped her closer, trying to reassure her. But as I opened my mouth to assure her we'd never let her die in a gutter or ruin her life, my heart constricted. A baby? I hadn't even taken *my* first step and I nearly... I could have...

Okay. Panicked breaths sputtered from my lips.

"See. It's... I don't know. I'm doing my best to avoid my magical destiny. It was easy with the rest of them. They can't make babies in my belly. Sorry, blastocytes in my fallopians."

"And I can."

She slipped off of me and buried her head onto the sweaty floor. "I'm sorry," Layla mumbled as if any of this could be her fault.

"Beloved, this isn't... We can work around this. Birth control."

"I've got an IUD, plus I started birth control pills once I got back. But..." She extended her fist, unfolding her fingers so purple light cascaded inside of it. "I don't think a little piece of copper and a handful of hormones will slow magic down."

Condoms. Pulling out. Shit the rest of them didn't have to worry about sat on my head. Rebellion burned hot inside my veins until Layla turned her head. That single wary eye peering below her scattered hair doused the impertinent youth in thirty years of wisdom. "My heart," I assured her. "I'll wear a garbage bag if it means I can be with you."

She snickered, her cheeks pinking at the idea.

"A Hazmat suit? Mylar? Just dip my dick in wax like a birthday candle."

Layla finally turned to me and I lay on my side beside her. Holding her close, I brushed back her hair and kissed the tip of her nose. She smiled at the touch, then tumbled into my arms. "Please, can we keep this between us? Just for now. I'll tell them all eventually. I'm too exhausted to deal with Ink's snarky responses."

"If he had to change a diaper, he'd probably toss the baby into the trash instead."

"All I want to focus on is nursing studies, stopping the end of the universe and you — "

I gazed into her eyes, the whole world reflecting back. She was my everything and I was her…

" — guys," Layla finished.

I was one of her many. Reaching around behind, I brushed my hand over hers and knocked into the rock on her finger. "What about Cal?"

He'd gotten down on one knee, begged her for forever and they were getting married. None of us knew where that left us. The angel didn't understand, the demon didn't care. I didn't have a say until now. I could marry her too, or instead. She gave up everything to bring me back, after all.

"Shouldn't you tell your future husband that he'll be raising someone else's child?"

Her eyes opened wide and she gulped.

"We're back!" The enthusiastic call of the werewolf caused Layla to spin around in place. I could only see a hint of feet and ankles as two pairs of jeans walked into the room. "We're not interrupting, are we?" Cal asked.

"No." Layla scattered, reaching for her pants. She managed to slip them on without any struggle, then attempted her shirt. "I should probably change."

"Wait, babe." Cal swung an arm out to catch her and pulled her close. She melted in his strong grip and he boldly stared at her exposed tits. "You're so moon damn hot like that." He whimpered and kissed her. As she clung tight to his massive biceps, I struggled to turn my chin enough to look away.

A bellow that'd shake the heavens themselves erupted from the giant angel. Heaving both hands out wide, he shouted, "We have cake."

* * * *

Cal

"Try this." I tossed one of my shirts at Daniel. He reached up to catch it just as the gray fabric hit his head. With the same pickled expression I got to enjoy when he was dead, the man rolled the tee over his head and it plummeted down his body.

"Thanks. I guess." He groaned, tugging on the loose belt to keep up the loaned jeans. "How's it look?" He aimed it at Layla, who held a hand over her mouth.

"You are the plague-ridden urchin mere moments from coughing out an organ and expiring on the street," Ink called out.

"I wasn't talking to you."

My phone buzzed. Needing an excuse from the commotion, I gathered up the plates — all but one licked clean of frosting — and slipped into the kitchen.

"You look as if you're being devoured by a worm made of textiles and it's regurgitating your head."

"You're just jeal—"

The kitchen door swung closed and I fished out my phone. I couldn't miss this call. "Hey, Mom." With the phone pressed to my ear via my shoulder, I dropped the plates in the sink and turned on the water.

"Just doing dishes."

"Every time I call you, you're washing them. You'd think with so many hands in that house, you wouldn't be the one who keeps having to do them."

I frowned. Ink would flat-out refuse. I'd already lost some of my favorite bowls to Garavel's inability to understand his strength and that metal didn't go in microwaves. As for Daniel... "Well, I might have some help soon."

"Oh, so you heard already?"

"Heard? Heard what?" Was something going down on the pack boards? I hadn't had time to check them in ages.

"Hang on. My food's here."

I put my phone on speaker and left it beside the sink. I planned to dive elbow-deep into the soapy water when she walked into my life.

"Ink, play nice," Layla shouted back through the open door.

"I am. Your newest chew toy wouldn't survive me playing otherwise."

She shook her head in a far too familiar exhaustion, then smiled at me. A look of "what can you do?" crossed her face and she shrugged.

"Thank you, for the cake." Layla wrapped her arms around me from behind, crushing her cheek against my back. I breathed deep, smelling the new lotion, the fabric softener on her pants and the smear of Daniel's semen. "I can't believe you found one with 'Congratulations on being alive' on it."

I laughed. "I asked and no one seemed to care. I think they'd have put anything on it. Well, anything other than 'Fuck me slowly with a chainsaw'."

Layla swept around beside me and grimaced. "I don't want to go to that party."

"Can you imagine the birthday clown?" I laughed at the idea and she rested her head on my shoulder, watching me rinse off the first plate.

"Sweetheart, you don't have to do the dishes. Here, let me." She reached for the brush but in doing so, her body swayed.

I caught her, smearing soapy water across her thin shirt, which turned translucent. Layla placed a hand on her forehead. "Sorry, I don't know what that was."

"You just brought someone back from the dead. I think that would exhaust anyone."

"Maybe. I felt fine before." She frowned as if something was bothering her and I smelled the evidence of another male on her.

"Could be that Daniel wore you out," I said diplomatically.

"Oh, no," she said fast and I smiled down to my toes. Smug in my prowess, I placed two plates on the drying rack with a little flourish.

"I did warn you."

"Warn me about?" She stopped massaging her forehead and looked at me.

With a finger covered in white sludge, I pointed to Layla's chest. Her face turned red and she tried to slap a hand over the evidence as if that could fool a werewolf. Even if she'd taken two showers, I'd still smell him on her. "First times are like trying to ride a rocket car built out of an old missile. Everything's going great, then boom." The chances of him even getting it in her seemed low.

She frowned deeper and slipped away. *Crap.* Was she blaming herself for his lack of endurance?

Abandoning the suds, I reached a hand out to her. "Babe?"

Lightly, Layla placed her fingers in my palm, but she didn't step any closer. "There's something I've been meaning to talk to you about."

"I'm all pointed ears," I said.

"Okay, so—"

"Calvin? You there?" My mother's voice rang out in the kitchen.

I winced and plucked my phone up toward my mouth. "Hi, Mom."

"Um, hi Mrs., uh, Catherine."

"Is that Layla? How are you, dear?" My mom caught on right away. "You can call me Cat."

Layla awkwardly laughed and tucked into her shoulders. "Things are well."

"Clinicals are going good? Calvin's been doing wonderful in pediatrics."

"For moon's sake, Mom. She knows that."

"You're in the ICU, right?"

Poor Layla's face drained and she jerkily nodded. "Yeah, yes, I am. Mrs.—oh, for…"

I took the phone off of speaker and placed it to my ear. "What were you calling about?"

"I heard from your brother."

Mark? Without thinking, I pulled my phone from my ear and scrolled through my messages. I had to go down a long list to find his name with all of mine unanswered.

"What'd he say?" I must have sounded panicky because Layla perked up.

"He wanted to know if I was in your area."

"And…?"

"And that was it. I said no and didn't get anything else back. Have you—?"

"No." Mark was a pain in the ass who prided himself on being a lone wolf. He'd often make himself scarce for months at a time, only showing up for a holiday or two, then vanishing at three in the morning. I shouldn't have blamed myself for his disappearance, but I did.

"Well, I just wanted you to know. How are things between you and Layla? Set a date yet?"

I beamed at my love and slipped a hand over hers. "Not yet. We're both focused on school."

"You should do it soon. Packs have to schedule around hunting seasons. I'm gonna go dig into my tacos. I'll call you usual time tomorrow."

"Okay, Mom. Love you."

"Love you too. Be well."

Layla watched me hang up the phone with focused clarity. "What was that all about?"

Pain stung in the back of my eyes. I should tell her about Mark. About how I was feeling gutted at him shunning me. That I was worried that if I didn't warn him about Conquest he might get swept up in this mess. Or that I might not get to tell him about my wedding.

"She wanted to know if we set a date for the wedding," I said, slapping on my easy smile. *Layla has enough stress already. She doesn't need my whiny mess on top of it.*

"Are we supposed to do that?"

"Well, eventually. Bit hard for the bride and groom to throw themselves a surprise wedding." I tried to laugh it off, but dread thundered in my chest. "Or are you having second thoughts?"

"No," she said fast. "Not about marrying you, anyway. It's more planning a wedding. With everything going on, I just...it seems like it'd make sense to wait until we're out of school. And the world isn't a crater filled with monsters."

"We're going to stop him," I assured her, pulling her into my arms.

Layla hung on to me, needing me to take more of her weight than I expected. She'd really worn herself out with that spell. "I know. Hope, anyway."

"And you're right. We should wait until after school, when we'll be bogged down with our nursing jobs instead of our nursing studies."

She kissed me quickly, but I tightened my grip and guided her back. Layla's lips softened as she fell into me. They parted and I drew my tongue with hers, feasting upon her scent dancing with mine.

"For shit's sake, demon!"

Layla slipped away from me, her pliant lips knotting up. "Hopefully a year or two will give them time to adjust to it, especially Daniel."

Right. Daniel mattered in this, too. So did the once-temporary demon, and the angel. *Which I'm fine with. The more the merrier.*

"My bond, your newest meat sack has tumbled to the floor. Should I kick him out of the way of heavy traffic?"

Layla groaned and turned to shout at Ink when her phone notifications blew up. "Ah, shit. I forgot Dana and Fariah wanted to see me. I'll cancel. There's too much…"

"Babe." I kissed her forehead to stop her from texting. "I'll take care of Daniel. Get him up to bed. He's only a few hours old, he probably needs sleep. You should go see your friends."

"Really? God, I feel awful skipping out on you like this. They're—"

"I've got it. Go."

She gave me one last kiss, then plucked her purse off the hook over the door. "Thank you. I love you." Layla gave a little wave of her fingers and dashed out of the door.

I leaned against the sink, soapy water seeping into my jeans. "I can't live without you."

Chapter Four

Layla

Damn it, Dana. This doesn't make any sense.

I stared at her last text telling me to meet her behind the abandoned Taco John's on Eighth. Instead of my friend up to some new scheme, I found a tipped-over dumpster and a pile of construction barriers. She couldn't be late. I was the late one.

Something was off. I dialed her number and placed my phone to my ear.

A thick glove stinking of leather slammed against my mouth. My first instinct was to bite down when a whole ass arm locked around my stomach. *Son of a...* I swung my elbow back, trying to clobber whatever chest I was being pressed up to.

Lightning spilled into my closed fist. I spun it around, palm flat, and slapped it to the thigh of my attacker. *Enjoy this, asshole.* The electricity sparked off my fingertips.

"Ah, not so fast."

What the fuck?

The hands keeping me hostage fell slack. Even still, I kicked my heel into a shin and got a few feet away before turning to face him. Black suit, black sunglasses, skinny-ass tie—a witch hunter.

Magic roiled inside of me, begging to be unleashed on my enemy. He held his hands up and the glasses shifted off that long nose far enough to reveal the green of his eyes.

"Stone?" sputtered from my mouth and the lightning bit my fingers.

"I'm not Stone anymore," he said, his voice ragged like he'd just gotten over a cough.

Right. He'd abandoned the witch hunters because of what they had done to him and his birth family. Of course, he then showed up dressed just like them. "Are you sure about that? Wait. Where's the green? You're back to human?"

Instead of the long bat-like ears and pea-green skin of the elves, he was his usual Latino self. He narrowed his eyes, vanishing the only hint of his changeling truth behind the black shades. "No, not exactly. Not yet, anyway." He peered down the alleyway as if he expected to find anyone other than pigeons. Then, he pinched the bridge of his glasses and tugged them off.

The imposing agent shimmered for a second, and the tan skin melted into the elven green. In his witch-hunter getup, he looked like a complete tit, the paragon of dickhead authority just looking for a skull to crack. Without the glasses, somehow the tight suit changed, looking more like the garb for a lord of the manor. His posture shifted too, his chin rising and his wide cat eyes staring with purpose.

I hated myself for shivering.

"What are you doing here?"

He slipped the glasses back on, returning to the bureaucratic bastard. It was harder to remember that Raul was below. "I needed to speak with you."

He found me at random in a back alley behind a taco joint? "How the hell...?" My jaw dropped and I clenched tighter around my phone. "Are you tracking my phone?"

"No, not precisely." He should have looked remorseful, but that all-too-familiar smugness radiated from his gorgeous face. "I am tracking you, of course."

"Of course. You sound like a psychopath."

"In this case, I intercepted your text messages and used them to bring you here."

I stared at my screen, my phone turned traitor because of his hunter tricks. An overwhelming urge to drop my phone on the ground and smash it with my shoe bubbled inside. I stopped and traced my thumb over the broken screen I couldn't afford to repair. It didn't matter if I could buy a new phone. He'd just tap that, too.

"So you're saying you know my number but rather than, I don't know, use that, you thought hacking my messages and sending a false one to me was a better use of your time?"

He snorted as if I was the unreasonable one. "If I easily downloaded your data, so can Zimmerman and the rest of the witch hunters."

I missed the stench of smoke at first, all my focus on trying to escape him. His voice wasn't scratchy from a cough. His long hair was tucked up higher than usual, the ends crisp and melted together. He'd just escaped a fire.

"So, your friends are hunting you, too? How's that feel?"

Raul glared. "You're being trite."

"No, I'm enjoying the heaping bowl of *schadenfreude.*"

"You should care."

"Oh, I care. It's just also nice to see you knocked down a peg or two. God knows you need it."

He threw his hands up in the air in peak dramatic fashion, but I crossed mine and glared. What did he want from me? To fall at his feet in gratitude? He upheld his end of the bargain. Big deal. Oh, the witch hunters are after me? No shit.

"I don't have time for whatever this is." I pulled my purse tighter to my chest and walked past him.

Raul wrapped his arms around me, both palms pressing against my belly. "Stop," he commanded. I'd have flung a fireball at his face and run for it, but the bastard kept pulling me across the blacktop until my ass landed right against his crotch.

My heart thundered in my chest as his cock less-than-innocently stirred. He stared down at me and goosebumps rose on my bare shoulders. I tried to fight off the shiver, but that made it worse. With Raul, every burst of adrenaline seemed to go straight to my panties.

"What." I panted, ignoring his hands — one resting above my waistband, the other just below my bra. "Do you." That damnable cock thumped its way to full staff, the crown nestling against the small of my back.

Taking back control, I turned in his grip and glared into the soulless shades. "Want?"

He was the first to blink, metaphorically. His throat trembled and he lifted his hands off my hips as if he wasn't thinking about fucking me on the trash right now. "Unlike you, I've been busy."

"Screw you." I laughed in his face. "I'm busier than you'll ever know."

"Have you contacted any other covens? Scouted Conquest's newest ventures? Formed inroads with potential allies?"

Was I supposed to do that? I looked away, which was all the opening he needed.

"I see, you've been busy with…" Raul took my left hand and raised it. He ran his thumb over the ring and sneered. "Stupid things."

"Fuck you. Why are you so…? Gah!" I wrenched my hand away and stumbled out of his grip. Without the overpowering stench of smoke and the heat of his lithe body, I was able to breathe. "For your information, I've been busy collecting an informant against Conquest. So…piss up a rope."

"I see." His mighty perch must have taken some damage as Raul crossed his arms and pouted. That luscious Latino elf bottom lip jutted out to the point I wanted to flick it just to see what he'd do.

"Is that it? You're here to brag about all the stuff you've been up to since you ran away. Congrats. I don't have a gold sticker, so how about one off of a banana?"

"Why are you so insufferable?"

"Why are you a hypocritical asshole?"

He crumpled his hands like he wanted to choke the life out of me, and I walked closer, daring him to try. He looked about to reach out and grab me by the arms when he dropped his hands and turned away. The tension didn't vanish, but it took a breather.

"I'm here to warn you."

"About Conquest? About the witch hunters? About all the shit I already know about?"

"About...!" Raul argued back before he sighed. "I knew this was a mistake. Expecting to find an ally in a woman who beds demons is delusional."

"There's that pompous ass I beat with a horseshoe."

"As I remember it, you went for my face. Seems you didn't want to damage my ass." His voice that'd been on the urge of breaking plummeted to a deep bass that shivered down my spine.

"Don't flatter yourself," I mumbled, losing the high ground. "I hit what was available."

Raul smiled as if he got what he wanted. Had he come here to see if I was still attracted to him? That if he pushed enough of my buttons I'd tear off his clothes and either fuck him or murder him? Possibly one, then the other.

"Miss Leeland."

"Are you kidding me?" We were back to that again?

"I've been using my time to infiltrate the agency and, with it, I've made contact with employed witches."

"You mean the ones you threatened and beat into employment."

He didn't even blink. Either he was coming to accept it was wrong, or he had decided to ignore the truth in favor of pretending he was right. "That is to say, I would, except I can't find them."

"Oh no, your stable of slave witches have broken free. Whatever will you do?"

"Even if they were no longer working for the agency, I should still be able to track them with their genetic markers."

I didn't understand, but dread gurgled in my stomach. "What does that mean?"

"That while you waste your time with dresses and flowers and painting mason jars" — he scowled at my hand as if my engagement ring had cursed him out — "witches are vanishing across the world." With that, he turned on a dime and began to walk away.

I fiddled with my ring, twisting the silver band back and forth while staring at the man who was and wasn't my enemy. "What do you want me to do about it?"

He paused but didn't look at me. "Take this threat seriously, before the threat takes you." A flash of light blinded me and by the time I blinked it away, Raul was gone.

"Why are you always such a cryptic asshole?" I shouted, causing a nesting pigeon to fly out of the roof and right over my head.

Only the beeping of my phone answered me.

Where are u?

Dana's text looked enraged, as if I'd planned this whole mess. I looked around once more for Raul, hoping for him to explain without the acrimony or sexual tension. An old taco wrapper rolled on the wind.

Something happened and I missed your text. Can you tell me where you are?

Chapter Five

Layla

I didn't realize where I was going until I walked through the door and was greeted by soft piano music, carpet, long curtains and chairs huddled around a small dais. "You've got to be..."

"There she is!" Dana shouted, leaping out of the padded armchair so fast it nearly pitched to the side. She ran to me and took my hand, lifting it into the line of sight of a woman in a black turtleneck. "This is the bride."

The clerk stared at my ring as if she expected it to be made of sugar, then her face brightened. "Wonderful. I'm Sheila, and I am excited to help you on this journey. If you'd please follow me to your private room."

I tugged my hand away and nervously pushed the band. Dana beamed, slipped a hand over my shoulders and guided me after the sales clerk.

"Fair, she's here," Dana called to our other friend who'd had enough sense to cram in some studying while hiding in one of the chairs. Fariah quickly bundled up her books and chased after us.

I stayed silent, letting Sheila fuss over me and ask all the wedding questions I had no answer for. "Well, what kind of dress are you looking for?"

"One that fits," I pleaded, unprepared for this.

The sales clerk laughed, telling me she worked on commission. "Why don't I pick out a few options and we can go from there? Back in a few. Please, enjoy the complimentary refreshments." She waved her hand to the bottles of room-temperature water and the stand of plastic flutes before slipping out through the curtains.

Dana wasted no time in picking up the champagne bottle and pouring a full glass. The room tightened with the foreboding omen of hundreds of broken dreams. I looked at the ceiling-tall mirrors for a second, frowning at the crumpled mess in them. I hadn't even put on real pants. It was a wonder they didn't chase me out with a broom.

"Wedding dress shopping? Really?"

Dana dropped the first glass into my hand, then poured one for herself. "Yes, really. Fariah, you still…?"

Our friend picked out one of the water bottles.

"Never hurts to ask," Dana said, taking a long drink.

"We haven't picked a date. This is pointless."

"No, it ain't. You're a bride. Brides need dresses for their weddings. Also showers. Engagement parties. Bachelorette parties. Ooh, Fair, you got any ideas yet for that?"

"A few," Fariah said before taking a sip of the water.

As my friends dashed around the little area repositioning the chairs, I stared into my glass. Tiny bubbles rose to the surface, unable to stop their trajectory even if it ended in them popping. God, I was empathizing with fake champagne. I tipped the glass back, trying to not imagine every bubble on my tongue was a micro-scream.

"Besides, all the articles say you need to get your dress early."

"We're thinking of waiting until we graduate. That's not for... I don't want to think how much school is left."

"Still a chance to look, wear big dresses, drink champagne and take a break." Dana fell back into her chair with an exhausted grunt.

"Where's Angelo?" I asked about her nephew.

"With his father for the weekend." She frowned and reached for her glass. "Forget all of that. Fariah, put away the damn books. Layla." Dana leaped to her feet and caught me by the hand. She pulled me onto the little stage where countless other brides had stood. "For god's sake, smile. You're marrying Calvin Rollin, a ridiculously hot, hopelessly devoted, home-owning man who cooks. That's winning the billion-dollar scratch-off."

Yeah, I was. I clasped my hand over my heart, watching the light play off the amethyst. Cal could have picked anything, and I'd have loved it because I loved him. But he found this beautiful ring with a purple stone just for me. I sighed to myself when I looked behind to catch Dana flipping through a catalog of dresses.

"Are you sure you aren't using my engagement as an excuse for you to try on wedding dresses?"

"Psh," Dana snorted and showed something she found to Fariah. "As if I'd want your life, sleeping with two hot guys without the other one caring."

"Three," Fariah said softly.

"There's another one?"

"Yes, I met him at your cousin's cabin. Here." She scrolled through her phone and showed an image of Garavel holding the go-kart above his head.

Dana whistled loudly, took the phone and held it to my face. "Are you climbing this ebony mountain?"

"It's less scaling, more being cradled in his arms."

"And again, your fiancé, the man you're gonna walk down the aisle with, is cool with that?"

"Yes. Yes, he knows about Garavel and Ink and Daniel."

Damn it.

Her eyes lit up and she looked to Fariah who shrugged. "I know about Tattoo, but who's Daniel? Another beefcake brother?"

God, why did I say anything? *Because he isn't a secret anymore. He's flesh and bone, and my friends will get to meet him.* "No. He's more angsty punk rock in a lithe Asian body."

"Holy…" Dana clasped her hands to her face and pulled down her cheeks. "You know what, yes. I want your life. Maybe not forever, just a week or two to properly break them in. Any chance your girlfriend can make that happen?" she asked Fariah, and I frowned.

Not at Dana's question, I knew she was kidding. Hoped, anyway. It was the reminder that Fariah was still involved with a dangerous djinn.

"She doesn't grant wishes," Fariah said.

"Are you sure about that, Fair?" Dana asked, causing Fariah's delicate face to burn red. She tried to pull the edge of her hair scarf down over her eyes as she ducked lower in the chair.

Coughing, Fariah said, "Besides. I thought you didn't like Ink."

"Oh yeah, he's an asshole prick, but damn if they aren't great lays. Right, Layls?" She turned her devious grin on me, and I nodded.

Ink prided himself on two things—being able to piss anyone off in ten seconds, and his sexual prowess. He'd probably be more than happy to show off his skills with Dana, or anyone else that asked. The only thing keeping him in line was being bound to me.

I lifted my wrist, expecting to see the tether. Without it, Ink would be free to do whatever he wanted, whoever he wanted. And I'd have no way to stop him.

"Layla." The sales clerk burst through the door, her arms bulging with piles of white dresses in bags. "What do you think about mermaid dresses?"

* * * *

An hour later and I had to have tried on every single dress in the damn place. Mermaid dresses made me look like a walrus, empire cuts made me look pregnant and the weird-ass cutouts that revealed nearly all of my indecent skin seemed like something Ink would choose. I grimaced, struggling to keep my nipples hidden behind a handful of crystals on the bodice. Those chocolate areolas were not easily contained.

"Maybe something more modest?" I asked, struggling to get a breath in as Sheila tugged the too-small dress together behind me. She hadn't been able to zip up any of the dresses.

"Why not a dress with lace sleeves? They'll help to disguise your..." She gestured to my arms and I crossed them hard.

"My what?" Sure, I'd been putting on stress pounds lately thanks to the world ending, but that extra weight had also snagged me five men, so fuck her.

Sheila's eyes worried but her face remained static. "Um...I'll go see what I have in back."

"Just for that, I'm going sleeveless," I declared as she slipped out of the curtain. Then I stared at my breasts hoisted up to my chin from the corset she'd clapped on. "Might need some straps for these though."

The atmosphere shifted and the strike of a match burned down my throat. I turned to hunt it out when the curtain drew back. Instead of the judgmental Sheila, a face hidden behind her mass of black hair peered inside. Fariah leaped to her feet and rushed for the creature posing as a woman.

"*Ya hayati*," she greeted her, taking her hands and pulling the djinn into the private room. It wasn't obvious to the naked eye, but in the mirror's reflection, tiny tufts of smoke wafted off of Maram's head. As Fariah leaned in close to brush her nose against the djinn's, the smoke turned pink along with her cheeks.

"Oh god, you're both so cute it makes me sick. My blood sugar can't handle this." Dana groaned and pretended to roll over, but her smile grew as the two whispered together.

"Hello, Dana, and..." Maram's eyes dropped to the ground. "Layla. Am I interrupting? I can go...?"

"Don't be silly. You're welcome," Fariah insisted before darting a warning look at me.

"Sure, bring your girlfriend along. Why not? Hey Dana, you got a guy you want to stop by and watch me prance around in wedding dresses?"

"Fuck, I wish. You know, a male strip club plus wedding boutique is not the worst idea ever." Dana was trying to soothe the tension, but it wasn't working.

Hunched over, the constricting dress angering me, I reach for my purse and the spell book inside. Maram watched — not as the shy, sweet girl she pretended to be, but the dangerous ifrit she really was. "You're tracking in mud," I said, pointing to Maram's shoes. She lifted the simple flat and inspected the heel. "Did you climb out of a fresh grave?"

"Layla," Fariah clipped in a warning. Her voice never raised above a pleasant librarian, but she could hone it sharper than a razor.

Maram dropped her foot. "I should go. This is not my place."

"No." Fariah clamped onto her hand, or was that the ifrit influencing her to do it? "I don't know what your problem is with Maram, or me, but she doesn't have to stand for this. She's a delightful, kind person who's only treated you with—"

"*Ya amar,*" Maram spoke gently to Fariah. "It is all right. I'd be a fool to expect a witch to befriend me. I only stopped in to say hello. I'll be going now."

Fariah cupped her cheek and kissed the tip of her nose. "I'm leaving too." With a stern grit and keeping a lock on Maram's hand, she stuffed her bags into her arms. "Layla."

Silence stretched between us, much as it had the last time I'd tried to get her to see what Maram was. I was the one to break away from Fariah's fierce stare.

"Go on, love," she said to Maram, guiding her to the exit. I clenched my fingers, tempted to cast a spell and rip away the pretty illusion disguising Maram's reality. Sighing, I slumped my shoulder, letting my purse swing away from my hand.

"Fair, come on. We were gonna get pizza after..." Dana tried to reach for their retreating friend.

Fariah did pause but only to look at the dirt, then stare daggers at me. "For your information, she's a gardener." With that, she threw open the curtains and walked away. Dana swiveled her head to me, her eye twitching and finger raising for a waggle. I was saved by the return of the sales clerk and another dress.

"Is the other one in the bathroom?" she asked while helping me into a whole ballet company's worth of tulle.

"No. She had to leave."

"I see," Sheila said, then stood. "Let me check on something. You enjoy the dress."

"Probably worried Fariah's gonna blow up a toilet," Dana muttered, her arms crossed as she glared at me in the mirror.

I tried to focus on the god-awful dress that had made me look like a Barbie cake. All I needed was a blonde wig and a mess of pink rosettes. That would have made Dana laugh, but I knew better than to say anything.

"Are you gonna let this go? She's happy."

"She's in danger. You don't know djinn like I do. They're liars."

"All djinn? You've met every single one in the universe?"

Damn it, why couldn't they understand? The tug of Samuke's greasy fingers prying into my brain snapped through me. He was calculating, a sociopath, willing to work with a Horseman and do god only knew what to people. "The one I did know tried to kill me and carried out the murder of my friend."

Dana's mouth fell open. "Really?"

I hadn't told her the full story, not really. Sure, being a witch sounded fun when it was all fire on my fingers and monsters in my bed. She didn't need to know how close I'd come to death every day since my birthday. Slowly, I dropped my head. Daniel's death had happened before I was even born, and he was back now. But watching him suffer for six months had only stoked my hate for Samuke.

"The only reason he didn't kill me is because I managed to outsmart him. Barely. Fariah could be in danger."

"Or she could be in love with a nice lady who catches on fire sometimes. You don't think you're letting one guy cloud your judgment?"

"Do you know what an ifrit is? According to her holy book, Fariah's dating a demon."

"So? You are too." Dana shrugged.

"He's not a demon."

She laughed and rolled her eyes. "According to him. According to the dictionary, the holy book for nerds, on the other hand…"

I wasn't an idiot. I knew what she was driving at, but comparing Ink—who had admitted he was an incubus the first time I met him—to Maram, who'd been lying since day one, was ridiculous. Incubi wanted one thing, but djinn wanted everything. Why couldn't they understand? "I'm trying to protect her. She's in danger. You don't get it."

Dana sighed. "Maybe, Layls, she doesn't need your protection. Maybe Fariah knows exactly what she's doing."

She'd accepted Maram way too fast. They didn't even argue, just talked and hugged it out. That had to be the djinn's influence. They could snake their fingers inside of minds and hearts, wrench them to their desires like puppets and...

A figure loomed in the mirror. Hunched shoulders and shifty eyes—the villain clenched her fists in anticipation of a fight not realizing she was about to start it. Was this why everyone hated witches?

"Maybe." I turned away from my reflection, unable to handle the hatred in the eyes. "Maybe you're right. But I'm not ready to make nice yet."

Dana stepped closer and twisted her finger so I'd turn around. "At least aim for civil." She reached for the mess of buttons to undo them. "Who knows, you and Maram could be fighting evil monsters together as a magical, butt-kicking duo."

I shot out a laugh at the idea when Raul's words came back to me. He was trying to build an army. What was I doing besides waiting for White to make his move?

"Jesus Christ, you look like a grandmother's doily collection threw up. I'm getting you out of this," Dana said, reaching the end of the buttons and going for the zipper.

As oxygen raced into my freed chest, I eyed up my phone. If I needed people to join me, then I might as well start with the hardest of them all.

Chapter Six

Layla

Four days passed before I had a chance to spend time with anyone that didn't need a catheter. Exhausted and needing a break, Cal suggested we get out of the house — somehow I didn't expect everyone to come with.

Ink started it by catching Daniel in some of Cal's borrowed clothes and asking, "Excuse me, small child, have you lost your mother?"

"One ward and you'd be pinned to this sidewalk for eternity." Daniel waved a piece of chalk under Ink's nose, but the motion caused the rolled-up sleeves to undo and flop off the end of his hand. Ink's laugh bounced off of every storefront in the strip mall next to the so-so taco joint. We didn't have the money for the good one.

I slipped out from under Cal's protective arm to get in between the two of them. "Come on, Ink. Lay off, okay?"

He chuckled softly and eyed me down. "Depends upon what you are offering in exchange?" He pressed his forehead to mine, nearly drilling me into the blistering sidewalk. A forearm snaked around my waist and Ink hefted me up onto my tiptoes as he kissed me.

My head swam like I had breathed in too much ether. I grabbed his hair, treating it like the mane of a wild mustang. "The back seat is empty and your waistband is elastic," Ink whispered as he tugged on my scrub's bottoms.

"The demon just takes whatever he wants," Daniel grumbled.

Ink frowned deeply. "I do not take, only appreciate what is offered. A fact that seems to confound you, once-undead." Despite arguing with Daniel, he let me go.

"You can't get over the fact that I'm alive and I can do this—"

"Whoa!"

Daniel plucked me off my feet, one hand around the nape of my neck and the other on my back. I was in a half dip, half swoon when he bent over to kiss me. My toes curled in anticipation of the chill, so his heat overwhelmed me. I parted my lips in shock and Daniel plunged his tongue in. Wrapping my arms tighter around the nape of his neck, I kissed him back harder. He had complete control, my weight balanced on the tips of his fingers.

"Hey," he whispered to me, before helping me back to my feet. "These past four days have been excruciating."

I bit my lip and blushed. I'd been working twelve-hour shifts, only breaking to study. I hadn't had a chance to be with any of them, especially the man who had just got his hot ass back.

A slow swatting of palms caused me to look over my shoulder. Ink clapped three more times before he smirked. "Congratulations, you are as capable as a random mortal. That must fill you with pride."

"You're so fucking jealous, you can't stand it," Daniel said with a laugh.

"The idea anyone could be jealous of a man dressed as if he's dissolving before our eyes is hilarious."

Daniel shoved his sleeves higher and jerked a finger in Ink's face. It was Cal who interceded. "Okay, we're making do. Right. If it bugs you so much, Ink, why don't you get him something better?"

My incubus crossed his arms. "No."

"Then what's your solution?"

"He could wear my robes," Garavel bellowed. He'd taken up the rear to guard our flank, even though I had explained to him the chances of an ambush while in a mega parking lot were low.

Daniel pulled a face and Ink laughed harder. "There would be a sight. The shriveled man in the angel's holy regalia. Yes. Let's do that."

"Fornicate with a rose bush," Daniel argued back.

"Its buds would quiver in anticipation."

Cal tried to play arbiter, but neither Ink nor Daniel would look twice at him.

I do not have the energy to deal with this. I slowed and leaned against Garavel, who was quick to swoop an arm around me. "Have they been like this the whole time?"

"No."

Great. I'd been worried those two would come to blows in some testosterone-fueled cage match to get my attention.

"They do not speak at all when you are in your healing temple."

"That's...uh." I bit my lip, watching incubus and human lob rising threats and curse words at each other. Cal was trapped between, one hand held out to Daniel and the other planted on Ink's chest. That one had his full claws out, his arm rippling with the rising strength of the werewolf.

I massaged my forehead, bouncing the ring's band against my brow. How was I going to get this to work? Five men who couldn't stand each other all competing for me and living in the same house. It was madness.

Four. There are four men. Which is enough. I don't need more, certainly not an asshole like him. We'd fight as badly as Daniel and Ink, and probably burn the house down.

Trying to shake off the dream my sex-deprived body had of a certain elf's vines wrapped around my wrists and ankles, I looked around the strip mall signs. "Hey, there's a thrift store," I called out.

That caught Daniel's attention. "Really?" He hunted for the blue sign in the window. "Thank god, I can finally get out of this yuppie puppy getup."

"Yuppie?" Cal mouthed. "Who the hell says yuppie? You're like talking to a grandpa sometimes."

Daniel shrugged him off and dashed into the store. I trailed after when Ink pressed on the door, holding it in place. "A most excellent distraction, my bond. Shall we abscond to the water closet of the Loco's Tacos where we three may smother you in sour cream?"

"Ink." His comment somehow made me cringe, turned me on and rumbled my stomach. "Let's get Daniel clothes first. Then we can talk about you, Cal and Garavel eating nachos off my body."

I didn't have time to question my life as I pushed away Ink's hand and walked into the land of thrift. The floor, covered in a stain-proof flat gray carpet, rose at a slight five-degree angle. Racks and racks of clothing that somehow smelled dusty and industrially laundered at the same time filled the tiny space. In the back, a thick blue curtain hung in between walls, revealing the full shins of whoever dressed inside.

It was there that Ink looked, his eyes blazing as he took my arm. I patted his hand and shook my head. "Why don't you all look for something here? There's some…" My eyes landed directly on a mountain of garish leggings. Some of those prints had to have been created by the demon of nightmares to induce madness. "Really great stuff here."

"I could use a new pair of jeans," Cal said, my savior diplomat. Before he vanished into the land of denim, I ran my palm up his chest to his shoulder.

"Thank you," I whispered and kissed him.

He brushed his thumb over my cheek and sighed. "I love you."

"Do you expect me to find anything serviceable in this trash heap?" Ink huffed.

"You never know," I said.

"I know that the ghost has been alive for nigh on a week of toiling and you have yet to plunge into his memories."

"Don't start. He's healing. It's…it's traumatic as hell to go back in there. To relieve what killed him."

Ink narrowed his eyes and crossed his arms. "Have you even inquired for his cooperation?"

A few times. That first day, he'd been so exhausted, I felt like an asshole even asking. The next time, when I caught him between my shifts he said he wasn't certain if he'd remember what he saw from Conquest, but he'd tell me when he did.

"It doesn't matter. We have time."

"Your certainty in the face of delusion is unwavering."

I paused in sweeping through the rack of old purses. "Ink, I'm exhausted, okay? Just say whatever pithy thing you need to say."

"Who is this King of Burgers? Does his realm stretch beyond the arctic seas?" Garavel shouted, holding up a promotional T-shirt that'd fit one of his biceps.

I opened my mouth to explain, but it was Ink who swept up beside him. "Allow me." He returned the kid's shirt, then took Garavel by the arm. "You will require the big and large section of this garment market. The mortal is the one who needs the child's clothing."

Boys…

Chapter Seven

Layla

"You're never gonna believe what I found." Giddy, Cal shoved aside hangers to reveal a line of vibrant leisure suits. "There's enough here for all of us." He passed one to Garavel—who obediently accepted the olive and orange one. Daniel held his out by the tips of his fingers. Ink didn't even open his hand, letting the magenta fabric hit the floor.

"Come on, it'll be funny."

"The fever boiling your brains is hilarious," Ink said. "These monstrosities, however..."

"That's the point. They're ugly so it's funny. We can match." Cal held the yellow and brown one with a checkered shirt up to his chest, then he waggled his eyebrows at me. "Babe? What do you think? How badly do you want to ravish me?"

I had to bite my lip to keep from laughing, but that didn't slow Cal down. With one hand pressing the suit to his chest, he caught me with the other. "Aren't you overcome by the sexual magnetism of polyester and chest hair?"

Daniel glared at not just the suit but Cal's behavior. Ink crossed his arms and watched. Only Garavel seemed fascinated as he pulled the suit jacket off the hanger and slipped it around his wide shoulders. I winced at the strain pulling apart not just the seams but the weave of fabric.

"Should I wear this for the wedding?" Cal asked. His voice rang with a laugh, but his eyes... Concern bubbled inside of them as if he was afraid I might call the whole thing off.

"Mm, I don't know if yellow's your color. Maybe if there's a blue one?" I peered to the side, hoping there wasn't, but Cal laughed and scooped me up into his arms. He buried his face against my neck whispering how much he loved me.

"One person to a dressing room," the bored woman at the glass counter said.

My phone jingled and I reached into my bag. Cal returned to them arguing about the suits while I read the text. "Guys, it's my mom."

"What does she want now?" Cal asked.

"No doubt she's drawing lots on which of our throats to slit for her next spell. The ex-ghost's is looking particularly epicene."

Cal scooped a hand under mine. "Babe?"

"She's just down the street at the café. Wants to talk." I could say no. Tell her I was busy with everything else in my life. Even if my mom knew I was lying, so what? She had lied to me for fifteen years. "I should go see her."

"We can come with," Cal volunteered, his silly suits forgotten.

"It's okay."

"Are you certain, my bond? Your materfamilias has shown a propensity for enraging you. Also attempting to abduct you."

"I texted her first. And see, she texted back. I won't be more than ten minutes. We just need to talk about some witch things. She's abrasive but wouldn't hurt me or anyone I love."

Ink coughed loudly and looked to Cal whose head suddenly dropped. His smile froze into place and he shook away whatever hit him. "You're right. But if you need us…"

"You're a shout away," I said and kissed Cal on the cheek. Bundling my phone in my purse, I walked for the door when Ink pressed his palm against it. Before he could begin, I sighed. "Don't worry about her."

"It is not her well-being that is my concern." Ink stared down at me as if he wasn't going to let me out. I squared my shoulders, prepared to point out that I was a grown woman who could handle my own shit. "But if she attempts anything, I will be there to stop it." With that, Ink stepped back.

I gave one last goodbye to my boys and headed to a little café around the corner. Two tables roasted in the August sun, lite jazz pumping out through the open door. There sat my mother on a tall stool at the counter against the window. She wasn't staring at the city but flipping through a blue leather book. Her legs were curled up to the side as if she was ready to drop down at a moment's notice and run. She kept twirling a finger through the hair at the nape of her neck like the rest of the world didn't exist.

After ordering the first iced drink I'd spotted, I walked over to her. She didn't look up. "Hi," I began. Only the twinkling piano and muted trumpet filled the silence. To my horror, steam rose from her cup. "Are you drinking hot coffee?"

"What else would I be?" she asked before taking a long sip.

"It's like a thousand degrees out?"

"So? Don't tell me you get the iced princess froufrou chocolate bombs. You drank Parisian coffee when you were seven."

I blinked at the memory of my mom letting me steal sips from her mugs while we sat outside cafés for hours waiting for her customers. "That much caffeine can stunt a child's growth," I said, struggling to climb onto the tall stool.

My mom watched a moment then sighed. "I'm sorry if I didn't read all of the mommy blogs at the time. There wasn't time to worry about your gluten intake when a Horseman of the apocalypse was beating down our door."

The bored barista walked my drink over to me. As I thanked her, my mother eyed up every clink of ice. I took a long sip, daring her to say anything. The first hit of caffeine revitalized me enough to keep going. I had a lot to tell her and no idea where to begin.

"You cast the spell."

I gulped hard then coughed, sputtering milk and coffee across the counter. "How…how can you tell?"

"That you used an angel's feather and demon's blood? Laylee, you're glowing."

"Thanks?"

"The creation remnants are still in your skin and hair. It's why the scroungers are so thick. Look." She pointed outside the window where horrifying blobs of teeth and organs rolled around the street. Some had legs, others arms to walk, but all used a massive tongue to leech up excess magic. I shivered at the horrific sight.

"Why are they out there? I haven't seen them in months thanks to this." I pulled up the bottom of my shirt, revealing the black ward I'd had placed under my ribs.

"Is that a *tattoo*?" my mother, the witch who faked her own death, shrieked like a WASP.

"Yeah. And it works a ton better than the stupid spell. I never have to see scroungers or touch up any wards on my walls."

My mom pursed her lips in thought and stared out of the window. As I sat in place, they gave me a wider berth, drawn to the magic but also terrified of the ward. "I won't question your methods. Your magic is yours."

I snorted at that response. My mother wasn't a live-your-life-how-you-want parent. *What's she playing at?*

"You mean you can't stop me," I realized.

"I assume you wanted to talk about the resurrection and what your ghost—"

"Daniel."

She sighed. "What Daniel knew about our mutual problem."

Crap. I should have known that was all she cared about. Nervously, I fiddled with my ring, twisting it around my finger with my thumb. It was enough to draw my mom's attention. She watched the flash of purple make one more round, then her eyes lit up.

"Layla Moesha Leeland, what is that?"

I used to imagine what it'd be like telling my mom. How I'd flash her the ring and she'd gasp, ask me how he did it then insist she plan the wedding down to the napkins. Maybe it was that false memory, or a need to pretend everything was normal, but I smiled with pride and extended Cal's ring. "I'm getting married."

She stared at me, her lip curled into a half sneer. "What the hell for?"

"Because I...I love him." My voice rose, my fists bunched so tight the band dug into my palm. Why couldn't she be happy for me just once? "And I want to be with him forever."

"Which one?"

Her dry tone stopped me dead. It wasn't traditional. I wouldn't be signing my body over to one man in exchange for a goat and a sack of grain. I wouldn't be forsaking three others even as I took vows to one. Twisting the pretty amethyst back and forth, I muttered, "Cal." She kicked all the joy out of me, my chin dropping until it hit my chest.

"The werewolf. One of the many you cannot have a child with. You should be focusing on continuing the line and not wasting your time with...weddings."

"Let me get this straight. You're mad that I'm planning to get married and not knocked up? Did I walk through a mirror by mistake?" If so, the coffee shop was the blandest section of Wonderland.

My mother sighed and took a long sip of her espresso. "What society expects of you does not matter. You are a..." She raised her head and glanced around. "You know what you are, and we do not get married."

"Why? Why the fuck am I not allowed to be happy?"

"Will it make you happy?"

"Yes!"

She crossed her arms the same way she had every time I'd asked for a puppy. "How can you be sure?

What if he abandons you? What if you grow weary of him? What if — ?"

"What if we stay in love for a hundred years and die in an old meadow holding each other's hands?" *Gah! What the hell am I doing here?* She didn't care about me. She wouldn't care about my life, about the things that I wanted — it was only about the craft. About protecting that fucking line. Well, screw that. If it died with me, then so be it. It was my choice, my life to live.

I leaped off the stool and yanked my coffee so hard, ice cubes sloshed over the edge, shattering to pieces on the floor. Sneering, I stepped back. "I thought you'd be happy for me. I thought you might even be excited about your daughter getting married."

"I don't know why."

My hand clenched and fire sparked on my fingers. The smoke burned in my nose and I tried to shake it away, but the fire kept climbing higher. I couldn't stay here. I couldn't be near her or I'd burst. After dunking my flaming hand in my iced coffee, I left the cup on the counter and turned to leave.

"Laylee?"

Keep walking. Don't give her the satisfaction of pretending you care. She's never cared about you.

"Witches don't marry."

"Because you're all old hags who'd rather live in shacks in the woods talking about how you're so much better than everyone else."

So much for not letting her know you care.

My mom didn't answer right away. She finished her drink, then placed the cup on the saucer. "Because our lives are dangerous. We make enemies. Enemies who don't play fair. Who will go out of their way to hurt and kill the people we love."

She twisted around in her stool and I gasped. Tears watered in her eyes. "Witches don't marry because our hearts aren't strong enough to endure it."

"You don't know what you're talking about. Cal's a..." I looked around again. "He's strong. He can survive."

I braced for another argument, my mother always having to get the last word in. She returned to her book, the tears evaporated. But in a soft voice, she said, "For your sake, I hope you're right."

Out of habit, I reached for the heart pendant. It no longer contained a piece of Daniel, but I still wore it. Instead of reminding me of the man I loved, now it was a relic from the one I never knew. "If you didn't love my father, then why did you keep his locket?"

"I never said I didn't love him."

"But..." She had told me nothing about him, had made me think that he was nothing more than a ship in the night. I wasn't allowed to ask questions. Yet she loved him?

With her back to me, my mother said, "I'm not telling you this out of hatred for you, or your werewolf, Laylee, but experience. Do not keep the man, the men, you love in your life. Or you will suffer a pain unlike anything you've ever known."

I wanted to be angry, to shout at her that she didn't know what she was talking about. But deep inside my heart, a nugget of fear took hold.

Babe? You've got to see this.

Cal's text gave me the excuse I needed to flee. An image popped up of him in the horrible leisure suit. Another followed of Garavel bursting out of his. After that were two more, the first of Ink threatening to set his horrible suit on fire. The last was Daniel. Instead of playing along, he'd dressed in a black tee, ripped tight jeans, a leather jacket that snapped up the side, and a pair of studded combat boots.

Hot right?

They were a mismatched set. Goofy, sweet, sarcastic and rebellious—I loved them so much it...it hurt. A crash broke from a scrounger waggling its tongue down the inside of a trashcan. It peered over at me, its multitude of eyes boggling. They were a nuisance, one of many that came with being in a witch's life. I raised my fist and said the banishing spell, clearing the street.

I'm strong enough. They're strong enough. We can survive anything.

Yeah. You're hot.

Chapter Eight

Daniel

My fingers slipped down the strings, barely casting a note out of the unplugged bass. It was enough to catch the attention of the angel's cat. She glided her way in, stopped at the edge of the rug and meowed at me.

"Is that your professional opinion?" I asked, testing out a real chord. My teeth gritted at the sour note and I reached up to tune it. The cat spoke at me, sharing her opinion of my rusty skills.

I'd been shocked when Layla had dashed out onto the porch as the delivery driver drove away. She'd tried to pull a heavy box inside, then given up and called me out. A bass with an amp. Sure, it was scuffed up with signs of serious abuse over the years. But the minute the weight of the neck fell into my hands and my fingers pressed down on the strings, I was home.

She could only stay for a kiss, having to head back to the hospital, but she told me she expected a song. I planned to give her so much more once she got home. Any idiot could seduce a woman with a guitar — it took a man with skill to peel all of her clothes off with the thigh-quaking notes of a bass. I tested a riff, then jotted down an idea in my notebook. Fiona meowed and leaped onto the army footlocker I'd snagged at the consignment shop.

"You're right. It's trash," I said and erased the chords.

"Oh, that's what that was. I was afraid the AC unit was about to give out."

Calvin stood in the doorway, his scrub top decorated with childish stickers. I only bothered with a peek to find he also had a gold star painted on his cheek.

"Aren't you supposed to be at work?" I asked, ignoring his comment.

"My round finished a half hour ago." He caught the kitten and scooped her up like a baby. Fiona played along, her purring so loud it beat out my solo. "Have you seen Layla?"

"Why? Worried she's hiding under my bed?"

"What?" Cal was hopelessly lost and I sighed. The demon would have understood right away. Where the hell was he anyway? How did I wind up alone in the house?

"My brave warrior," Garavel shouted from the hallway.

Cal sucked in a breath as the babied cat dug her claws into him to climb his chest and leap off his shoulder into her master's arms. She skittered up to rub her head against the angel's then shot a challenging look at Cal. He was tolerated, as were the rest of us. Garavel was her true king.

"I have finished my sweep of the perimeter," Garavel announced.

"You did it during the day?" Cal asked.

"Do not worry. I was very subtle." He grinned wide and erupted his wings. One stretched down the hallway while the other plowed against the wall, shaking a picture frame.

Cal crossed his arms, his face pinched with worry. "Did you find anything?"

"No. There is no evidence of Conquest moving against our fortress, but I shall remain vigilant."

"I'll do a lap tonight, sniff out the forest. You gonna come along?" the wolf asked. To my surprise, the angel bowed his head in agreement. Were they working together? Since when?

"Now I believe I shall enjoy the fruits of my labors in the land of slumber!" Garavel boomed. He tugged on the pull cord and the attic ladder slammed down. Its legs crumpled the cardboard box the bass came in. I didn't even look up.

It was Cal, the obstinate good host, who winced. "How are you settling in?" he asked me.

The mattress was cheap, the pillows rocks, and I had to share my space with a man that barely fit in any room. I shifted the bass off my lap and rose. "I wanted to speak to you about that."

"Shoot. Anything you need. I mean, in reason. Can't get you a hot tub, though…" His eyes unfocused as he was no doubt picturing Layla naked in the turbulent water jets.

"It's about the sleeping arrangements."

Cal snorted. "Look, I can see about new sheets, but beds are expensive and we're saving up for a —"

"Not that. The bed's...fine. What I want to know is when I get to sleep with her."

His pale face shifted tomato red. "That's, um, that's up to her. So..."

"Not sex. I don't need your permission for that. For the past two weeks, she's slept in your bed and no one else's. Why?"

His jaw dropped and he shrugged. "Because it's her bed too."

"What's wrong with mine?"

"You want her to share a full?"

Her leg draped over me, the other between mine so her thigh nestled under my balls. Her breath caressing my chest as I held her safe in my arms while we both fell asleep. I looked back and smiled. "We'd fit. But she doesn't seem to be given the option. Why not with me? Or Garavel?"

"Yes. Why can I not hold my lady witch in her slumber?"

"Because it's ball-melting hot outside and there's no air conditioning in the attic," Cal argued.

"Oh, yes. Mortals are prone to combusting in the heat. I forgot."

I didn't expect Layla to run up to the attic every other night, but there was no reason for her to be confined to Cal's bed. "You didn't think of it. Understandable. But the dynamic's changed. I'm here, I'm breathing and I think I have as much right to share her as you do."

That easy smile hardened to a steel frown. He was good at pretending to be laid back, but the second Cal ran into something he didn't want to give up, he was a dog with a bone.

"Or are you going to hold her hostage?"

The front door opened and she called out, "I'm home and starting a load of laundry. Get naked."

Her giddy laugh bounded through the house and was answered by no one. Cal glared me down, his hackles up. "Layla can do whatever she wants. If she's gonna spend a few nights a week cramped in a tiny bed with you, more power to her. But I don't think you care."

"That so?"

"I think you're pissed off that I get to marry her first and won't admit it."

"And you're worried that she might choose my long, hard bed over your little wide one."

Garavel hurled himself across the room to bounce on my mattress. "It's not as hard as mine." We both ignored him, Cal staring me down. I gave it back.

The stairs creaked, and he shook his head. As he stepped away, she poked her head into my room. "Laundry?" Layla asked, holding out the basket.

Without pause, the wolf tugged his scrub top over his head. She boldly drooled over his naked torso with far too many unwieldy muscles. "Babe, let me." After tossing his top into the basket, he took the whole thing from her in one hand. With the other, he extended his arm.

Layla scooped hers around it and gripped tight to his biceps with a little giggle. He beamed at her, about to take her down the stairs when she looked back at me. "What about you?"

"I'm good," I said. Let the wolf exhaust himself fucking her on the dryer. I was playing the long game.

"Wait." Garavel bounded up his ladder so fast, I gritted my teeth at the whining hinges. A boulder of socks dropped from above. When it struck, the mass burst, scattering old socks in every color across my room. "I think that's all of them," he shouted.

I calmly picked one out of my guitar case and tossed it toward Cal. He was too busy scooping the rest up to stop Layla from walking over to me. "You owe me," she said. I looked up into her eyes sparkling with mischief when she kissed my cheek. "My song."

The wolf gathered her up while toying with the drawstring on her bottoms. He placed a possessive arm across her shoulder and the two walked away.

I owe you far more than a song.
You deserve my life.

* * * *

Cal

God damn. I knew she was hot and often replayed images of her while I clogged the shower drain. But watching her shrug off her boxy top to reveal her freckled breasts straining against her bra socked me in the gut. I lost my breath and my mind.

"Holy...fuck," I stuttered, staring at her like I'd never seen her before.

"What's the matter?"

"You." I pinned her against the rolling washer without thinking, digging my palms into the cool metal to try to focus. "You are so goddamn beautiful. It punched me in the face."

Layla blushed, the redness blooming from her face down to her hefted tits. I wanted to bury my face in them.

"I am marrying the hottest woman in the world."

"Cal! No, you're not." She squealed and playfully smacked me on the shoulder.

The wolf paced inside of me, not caring that the washer and dryer were in the hall closet and anyone could walk past. It wanted her then and there. I jerked my hips, pinning her ass against the washer then pressing my forehead against hers. "Is that not my ring on your finger?" I asked, running my fingers over her left hand.

"Yes." She bit her lip and giggled.

Fuck. That ruined me. I wrapped my fingers around hers, cinching the ring tight. Brushing my nose against her cheek, I whispered, "Don't you want to be mine?"

"That…" Layla gulped, her eyes wide as if she was afraid of something. "That isn't what I meant."

"Well, it can't be that you aren't the hottest woman in the world." I grabbed both of her hands and pressed them back. Layla strained over the washer, her neck vulnerable as her eyes darkened. I had a vague notion of my cock hardening against the loose boxer briefs. The flesh meant little as the wolf fought for dominance. Her scent invigorated my nostrils, pinging every nerve in my system until I shivered to my toes.

"It's sweet, but…" she started to argue, but I wouldn't hear it. The wolf wouldn't believe it.

I shook away its force prying on my ears and focused on her. Somehow, I'd stretched her to the point I'd mashed her knuckles against the control panel and her naked back splayed against the washer. Damn it all, the unbalanced thump of the agitator swung her breasts, hypnotizing me.

"I want to…the wolf wants to take you right here and now." I gritted my jaw, struggling to keep out the fangs. *Just a little nip to her breast, right above that light brown cup of her bra. She'll squeal in delight.*

Layla didn't slip her hands free. She rested back and studied me with her bottomless eyes. I should let her go. There was something I needed to tell her.

Thinking only made the wolf growl harder. It knew what it wanted and was pissed I fought back.

"Well...?" Layla tipped her head, a disarming smile rising on her beautiful face.

Kiss her, rip away her panties. Sink your tongue and nose inside of her. Breathe deep of her pleasure. Smear it across your face. Take her, make her ours.

Pressure bounded against my balls and up my cock. I was so focused on her, I didn't realize she was teasing me with her foot. Layla managed to sweep her toes back and forth across my girth as she eyed me up. "What's stopping you?"

The last thing I wanted was to hurt the people I loved. To watch their eyes dart, their faces crumple, their lips part in a near-scream — it terrified me. I swore I would never lift a hand in anger. That was an easy oath to follow.

Her toying toe managed to pry apart my fly and my cock thudded out. I reached out to catch it, automatically thinking of stuffing it back in. But Layla bit her lip and swept her hips back and forth, her eyes heavy with need.

My fingers tightened as if I could mold my skin and winnow down that fat girth to something manageable. God, I wished it worked that way. "Babe," I gasped, my ears ringing, my heart pounding, my tongue salivating. All I wanted was to wrap her legs around my waist and fuck her.

"We…we could head upstairs?" *Where there's lube and other tools to keep me from doing any damage.*

Layla tugged on her hands and I let the one I held go. I shifted my heels, prepared to take a step back so she could get to her feet. When she hooked onto the thin strap of her panties, my brain skipped.

Does she need to wash her underwear too?

The purple lace slipped down her thighs and landed on her ankles. I couldn't look away, lost but delighted in the fabric kissing her skin. Then she slipped one foot out and glided her calf around my waist. "I need you." Layla panted, encircling me with her legs. Her naked pussy dripped down to her ass. I wanted to lick it up, but she cinched her hold and pulled me closer.

"I want you to fuck me hard and fast," she commanded.

The wolf's tail wagged, proud and ecstatic to be verbally collared. My fingers tugged on my underwear, sending my cock bounding around like a brick in a dryer.

This isn't smart. This will hurt her.

She won't want to be with me anymore.

She'll be scared of me.

"Babe?" My hips jerked, my cock seeking refuge in the warm, wet comfort before it. The crown spread her brown vulva wide and I moaned. Her heat rose through me, beckoning me closer. I tried to focus on keeping my cool until Layla whispered.

"Cal. I love you."

The mental shackles snapped, the beast broken loose with those three words. I lunged forward, pinning her arms back, my fingers sinking into her wrists. She moaned in surprise and arched her back. My wolf didn't need any invitation and I sank my fangs into her breast. No, teeth. They were human teeth. All the while, I kept working my hips, sweeping the crown of my cock back and forth.

Layla squirmed, her breath hitching as I darted my tongue down her bra. Then she started to thrust back. My history taught me to pull away before she hurt herself. But the wolf had me in its clutches and the promise of that silky, ribbed oasis beckoned me.

"Holy fuck!" Layla cried out.

I snaked my hands away, my body boiling in shame. Suddenly, she launched up, wrapping her arms around the back of my head. "Don't you stop," she shouted and crashed my nose into her sternum.

Whooping and crying, Layla scratched her nails up my back and I fucked her. Not hard like the others would, but the worrying voice vanished to rabid instinct. My hips moved in time with the washer, thrusting my cock deeper until my balls bounded against the metal casing. I dug into her hips, hefting Layla as she cried for more.

It was all she shouted, her words broken up by pants. "More. More. More!"

A fire burned in my brain. I pulled out so fast, her body barely had a second to slip before I dropped to my knees and sucked on her clit. Layla squealed, her thighs molding to my head as I licked and sucked. She went rigid, her eyes locked tight and I recognized that. She was fighting to stay in the zone.

Keep licking. Push her over the edge.

My hand slipped and my palm clenched around my cock. I juggled my balls, thinking of her pussy sucking me in. How badly she'd screamed for it, for me.

In a flash, I spun Layla around and planted her hands on the washer. She shook her head and glanced back at me over her shoulder, just as I lined up my cock and thrust inside.

"Oh fuck, Cal. You never. We never... Yes. Jesus. Don't stop."

Her vagina shivered, rolling around me and clamping onto the already tight flesh. I cried out and plunged my teeth against her shoulder. The orgasm started in my nose—a tickling that exploded as if I breathed, ate and lived sex in one second. Then it hit my cock, bucking my balls up tight and spurting hard.

Layla collapsed to the washer, her cheek hitting the cool metal as she panted. I slipped out of her orgasming pussy, trying to catch the mess before it landed on our clothes. She twisted around to watch me just as a large glob shot out and hit both of our pairs of underwear.

Glistening from head to toe, Layla smiled, bent down and picked up the panties and briefs I'd stained. With a little laugh, she tossed them both into the washer. "I needed that," she whispered, sounding more like she was talking to a bottle of wine. We'd both been running ourselves ragged. Maybe I shouldn't dump all of this on her right now.

"Congratulations." Out of nowhere, Ink wandered past. He lightly pushed me aside without care and pulled out a handful of dryer sheets. "You've managed to prove yourself useful, at least for the moment." Ignoring me, he focused only on Layla who was smiling wide. "Here," he said and handed her a stool cushion.

"What's that for?" I asked, but Layla's bright smile slipped and she pressed her nails into the pillow.

"Give it a moment, I'm certain realization will dawn." Ink tipped his head and walked away.

Shit. I hurt her. I lost my focus and I hurt her. Damn it all...

"Ink?" Layla tossed the pillow back at him. He didn't even bother to catch it, letting it hit his side and the floor. "I'm good."

He opened his goddamn, shit-stirring mouth, then closed it tight. "You do tend to savor the bite and sting. If you will excuse me."

I should have known he was up to his usual tricks. I thought he'd been getting better — at least less of an asshole — but for all of his posturing, he was as jealous as Daniel, just less likely to confront me about it. "Where the hell have you been?" I asked. "Nobody's seen hide nor hair of you in days."

"My hair is upon my head instead of littered over the settee. As for my hide? That is for my bond to discover. Good day." With his usual priggish prance, he waltzed off to do moon knew what.

"Is he up to something?" Layla asked, her eyes narrowed.

"As if he'd tell me, or anyone else for that matter. He's been..." Weird since I'd proposed. Ink had always used his tongue like a straight razor, but the cuts had been to the bone lately. Was I crazy or did he plan to stop the wedding? What about Daniel? Garavel had started out not liking me. I kept waiting for when he'd finally understand what marriage meant and pitch a fit to protect her from the evil werewolf.

"He's Ink," I said. Layla didn't need this. She had so much shit on her shoulders. I could handle three grown men acting like jealous school girls. If it came to it, we could wrestle it out. "How are you doing?"

Layla melted against me, her head tumbling to my shoulder. "Much better now. I didn't realize how stressed I was until you deep-dicked it out of me."

I kissed her forehead. "Always happy to oblige. How'd the meeting with your mom go?"

"She..." Layla bit her lip and darted her eyes away. "She's focused on stopping Conquest. I didn't have a chance to tell her about us."

My love frowned, her heart breaking and taking mine with. It looked like she wanted her mother to be a part of her life again, but I knew better than to interfere.

"There was something I wanted to talk to you about. About the wedding."

"Are you going to make Ink wear frills?" she asked, putting on a laugh.

"Knowing my luck, he'd wear them and nothing else. Actually, it's...maybe it's early, I don't know how these things go. But this guy who I did some work for, nothing major, just building fences and chasing away deer."

"He knows you're a...?"

"His first wife was a werewolf. He's not a part of the pack anymore but is still in the system. Anyway, he owns this little resort in the woods."

Layla's breathing stilled. "By the compound?"

"Fuck no. Other side of the lake. Near the Currants."

"That place is fancy," she said.

"I helped him out years ago, but what I remember is that it's got a big building for conventions and...weddings. Plus some cabins for guests or the couple to honeymoon in."

"Cal?" She smiled slyly at me.

"I was just thinking. I mean, we have to have it somewhere. And since I did him a solid, maybe he'll cut us a deal. Do you…?" Why was I so nervous asking this? I took her hand in mine and cupped my palm over hers. The amethyst poked up between my fingers. "Do you want to check it out as a possible—?"

Layla leaped forward to kiss me. Just as I thought to return it, she said, "I'd love to."

Chapter Nine

Layla

"Wow..."

The older gentleman walked to the middle of the room. "Ignore the long tables and stacks of binders." He pushed one to the side, catching the eye of a man in a suit. A banner for PolyTech Industries dangled off the beam crossing the steepled ceiling. The walls were made of cherry wood so the light streaming through the glazed windows gave the entire room a pink glow.

Cal held my hand tight as he watched me take this place in. The driveway was white rock gravel with snapdragons and bearded irises blooming along the path. Two rosebushes in reds and whites straddled the building's entrance as well as a fountain that belonged in a fairy-tale town's square. I'd expected a cute little cabin in the woods, maybe enough to hold our closest friends with peeling paint and linoleum floors. This was a country club.

"It's gorgeous," I tried to whisper.

"Most couples will hang some flowers here," the owner said, waving his hand across the support beam. "There's also a retractable chandelier. I can let it down if you'd like?"

I spotted a hint of it hiding in the roof's peak. *A fountain and a chandelier? This is insane.* "No, that's... that's okay," I said. "I don't want to mess up their conference."

A printed pasteboard outside had welcomed the tristate leaders. They'd all adjourned for lunch, letting us get a quick peek. It'd been a mess as they all traveled back into the city to eat, forcing us to park back on the side of the highway just to get through. A few businessmen had remained behind to watch over their stuff as if a couple of future newlyweds would nick binders full of sales numbers. I nodded in their direction, trying to wordlessly thank them, but the men turned away.

Cal tightened his hold from excited to protective. "Babe? What do you think?"

"There's room for a buffet back there if you're catering." The owner pointed to a table nearer to the front doors covered in nameplates. "We can also wheel in our bar cart."

"Is that a stage?" Cal prompted. He wasn't gazing around in awe like me. He remembered a lot more of this place than he'd let on.

"Yep." The owner gestured to the obvious dais the business tables faced. An empty easel sat up there, but it was easy to imagine a bunch of instruments or a DJ booth instead. "This place can seat up to three-fifty."

"That…" I gasped, then whispered in Cal's ear, "I don't think I've met more than seventy-five people in my life."

"Don't worry, babe." He cinched his arm around me, holding me safe. The place was exquisite, the kind of venue that'd be featured in magazines and on splash pages for websites. It was so perfect it intimated the hell out of me. Who was I to deserve to get married here?

"Wait, you haven't seen the best part."

"There's more?" I shuddered.

The owner skedaddled past. For looking like a crotchety eighty-something farmer in a pair of overalls and shit kickers, he moved like a hawk. I could barely keep up as he dashed for the door and held it open.

Cal's smile beamed brighter than the sun. He took my hand and damn near skipped out. The August heat hit fast and I closed my eyes against the light. "I assume the main hall's got both heat and air."

"Just put in a new system. This summer's been brutal."

That was putting it mildly. I had spent my summer killing an angel and challenging a Horseman. Even my one vacation had required me to fight witch hunters and open a portal to hell. The less said about my time trapped in the lands of the elves, the better. Anything autumn threw at me would be a breeze in comparison.

"Over here you can see a hint of the cabins." The owner pointed in the direction of two blue roofs prodding through the green leaves. "Bet you remember that one, young pup."

"Laying the floor was hell," Cal complained.

"It's our honeymoon cabin. Way I hear it, there's been a good seventeen babies conceived since you helped finish it."

He said it with a laugh, as if he found it funny, but glanced back at the two of us. I jerked up higher, wanting to run into the forests and never look back. Why was everyone going on and on about babies? Cal patted my hand and beamed. "Good to know my pain brought some pleasure into the world."

"You two planning on…?" This man, a stranger not even five minutes ago, stared at me like I owed him an explanation of my fertility. I tried to not buckle, sweat building on my back. "Ah." He got distracted almost instantly and turned to face another building. "Here we are."

While the main one was shaped more like a barn with a tall loft, this looked like an old west church. The steepled roof was periwinkle blue and held a small tower with a silver bell knocking about inside.

Like a medieval building, the front entrance was rounded at the top, with slatted wood painted the same Virgin Mary blue. Two stained-glass windows sat at either side, bearing an image of rainbow-colored rosettes. The owner pointed to one and said, "The gays love this. They put this place in one of their chat room servers because of it. So much business. Come on and have a look inside." He pulled on the massive brass handle and the door creaked open.

I stepped up the porch stairs and entered, expecting the scent of dust and moldy Bibles to strike. Instead, a peachy floral aroma hung in the air. Much like in the main building, the windows built against the side walls and the roof were all frosted, casting rosy light. Rather than lines of pews, white wicker chairs lined the golden carpeted aisle. Tiny poles marked each row with adorable lanterns dangling from the top.

At the end of the church were three wooden steps up to the altar. Only, instead of a cross or a nearly naked dying man, a giant pair of interconnected hearts hung before the huge window. They would be the centerpiece if it wasn't for the beautiful stained-glass window behind. The mosaics were in shades of pinks, reds and whites, each piece inlaid to form a giant blooming flower. As the sunlight pierced through the glass, a massive rose landed on the steps of the altar where the couple would stand.

"Wow," I repeated, my heart ping-ponging from feeling overwhelmed to minuscule. I had never believed in god, but if there was one, their face would be this beautiful.

"Some couples like to have the ceremony here, then the reception in the meeting hall."

"Babe? What do you think?"

"It's…" Impressive. Awe-inspiring. Terrifying. Expensive. "Beautiful."

Cal beamed and wrapped an arm around me. "Any chance we could hang something off those hearts?"

The owner smiled knowingly and looked at the dangling pieces. "Gonna uphold the old tradition?"

Old tradition? I looked to Cal but he shrugged. "Just curious."

"Well, let me…" The owner jerked and pulled out his phone. Staring at it, he groaned. "Excuse me. I have to take this." He hustled past us and out of the chapel. Just before the massive door closed, he said, "I heard you the first two hundred—"

Now that we were shut up inside, the chapel was quieter than snow. My ears thumped with my heartbeat and my steps echoed against the massive glass windows. "No AC," I whispered, noticing the rising heat.

"Probably don't want to have an orthodox ceremony here. Those can take hours."

"Orthodox?" I asked.

Cal tipped his head. "Orthodox lunar. It's...a lot. A lot of chanting, a lot of sitting, a lot of kneeling and a lot of biting. Don't worry, even if I wanted that, human mates aren't allowed."

I'd never heard of this religion before. *What did he say about biting?*

"What do you think? Honest opinion without Max in the room. You can't disappoint me."

"It is..." I took in the place wishing I could find a single fault in it. "Beautiful."

"Pretty damn perfect, huh?"

"And so expensive. How expensive?" I hadn't thought to ask before. I didn't think he'd take me to a place that could host royal werewolf weddings.

Cal crinkled his nose and ran his hand back through his hair. "I'm not sure, but I know Max'll cut me a deal. And hey, maybe I could work some of it off. He keeps talking about wanting more cabins."

"Sweetie, you shouldn't have to put in hard labor just so we can have a wedding. That's... No. It's too much. We can — we'll find someplace more affordable. I mean, the cost to decorate this place, both places alone... We'll be paying it off longer than our school loans."

I thought he'd be happy or at least relieved he didn't have to spend a fortune for one day. But Cal's shoulders deflated. "What's bothering you? You've looked like a scared deer since we walked through the gate. Do you hate the place? You can tell me if you do. I won't be mad."

"It's not that. It is beautiful. I mean, dukes and princesses probably get married here."

"Only one that I know of, but she was a countess."

Jesus, I was kidding. "It's just…" *I thought there'd be more time. We'd have to struggle to find a place, and picking a date would be far enough in the future everything would be settled. My mom would be happy for me. My schooling would be over. My guys would stop fighting. And the apocalypse would be stopped.*

Cal brushed a hand over my cheek, startling me up into his eyes. He sighed deeply, pain lancing his breath. "Babe?"

"Are you upset I can't have your children?"

We both blinked in shock at what flew from my lips. Cal scrunched his brow. "What are you talking about?"

"You know. You a werewolf, me a…a not wolf. We can't have—any kids I do have won't be…yours."

"Yes, they will," he insisted.

"No. You were the one to tell me. We can't produce viable embryos and…gah, why am I talking about embryos?"

Cal wrapped his arms around me, his face softening as he kissed my forehead. "Babe? Is this what's been eating you up? Aside from me and the demon."

"I have to…" *No, I don't have to do anything. What my mother wants didn't matter.* "You love babies. You tell me about all the kids you interact with at work. And I can't give you your own."

"Do you want to have a baby? I mean, I thought you did."

"I do. Not right now, but in the future. It's just…it won't be yours."

"Layla." He held me tight and brushed his thumbs against my cheeks.

"I love you. I want to be with you. But can I ask you to raise someone else's kid? To never have one of your own just because you marry me? It'd kill most men."

"Most human men. Werewolves... We don't think like that. We don't view a child as owned by one mother and father. They are of the family, so they are ours. Whatever baby grows inside of you is as much mine as it is Daniel's, or Garavel's, or—assuming he suffers serious brain damage—Ink's."

"Really?" That sounded too good to be true.

"I love you. You are my..." He teared up, the stained-glass rose shifting his blue eyes pink. "You're my world. My rock. My... I don't care."

"What?"

"If you don't want to have kids. If you can't have kids. I would rather spend my whole life with you childless than one minute of it without you."

It didn't hit me how badly I needed to hear those words until I crushed myself against his chest. Cal wrapped around me like a blanket, resting his chin on my shoulder.

"Whew." He gasped, slipping away to get his bearings. "I'm glad that that's it. For a minute I was getting worried that... Never mind. It's dumb. Are you fretting over the rest of them too?"

He was worried I was what? I shook my head. "The rest of who?"

"The demon, the ghost and the angel. Ex-ghost. I'm still not used to that."

"Daniel's been... It's okay. I think. I haven't seen Ink around lately." Why hadn't I seen him? He was always there if I so much as thought of him. Usually trying to get into my pants and whispering the dirtiest innuendo in my ear. "I've been busy with the hospital. He's probably sensing my only desires are to get sleep and foot rubs."

God, that sounds good. And no one would be better at it than —

"Well, I know what I'm doing once we get home," Cal offered and I smiled at him, mentally scrubbing away the green face. "Actually, I wanted to talk to you about Daniel. He's been —"

The door flung open and the owner's angry steps slammed into the floor. He glared at us like a hungry dog eyeing up a steak. Instinctively, I shifted behind Cal, who raised a protective hand.

"Young pup, you like this place?"

"Yes?" he said while looking back at me. I nodded. "Very much so."

"It's yours for a song. I've had it up to here with this pushy, demented —"

"Bridezilla?" I asked.

"She's fine. It's the groom and his family. They've been the worst moochers I've ever had to put up with. The rich ones always are. Two hundred bucks and I'll let you have the chapel, the barn and... Fuck it, the honeymoon cabin, too."

"Two hundred..." My jaw dropped. We wouldn't even be able to get a cake for that.

"One catch, though. You'll have to take their date. October thirtieth."

"Babe, that's a day before your birthday. Are you cool with having your anniversary then?" Cal asked as if he wasn't vibrating with excitement. He wanted this place with his whole heart but was too scared to tell me.

"Two days of you spoiling me rotten? How ever will I survive?" I curled my palm around his cheek. Cal pressed his forehead to mine and growled.

A loud "*ahem*" from the owner kept us from kissing. At least he didn't look about to rescind the offer. Cal gazed deep into my eyes. "Do you think we could pull it off?"

"We'll only have a year and three months to plan it, but—"

"Uh, no. Sorry. It's October thirtieth of this year."

This year? We'd have to plan a wedding from scratch in less than three months? No. There's no way.

"That's a bit of a crunch, Max. We haven't started looking at anything else..." Cal spoke up, no doubt trying to cover for me as I fought for air. *Three months?*

"I get it. Let me see." He scrolled through his phone for what felt like twenty minutes before looking back at us. "The next open date is November five years from now. Sorry, pup, this place is popular."

Cal stared down at me, silently pleading that I'd say yes. But he hadn't read the same wedding planning schedules I had. Three months wasn't enough time to send out invitations, never mind book a caterer, a florist, a cake, clothes. We couldn't do it.

"Can we think on it?" Cal asked.

He shrugged. "Sure. No chance in hell I'm giving it back to those snots. They thought I should provide a white stallion free of charge. Fuck that. I hope he slips in horse crap. But, Rollin, as much as I like you, I'll need to know in a few days. I can't leave it open forever."

"Thank you." Cal bobbed his head in gratitude. He slipped an arm around me and carried me. I didn't think to move because my body was still in shock.

October? That's not even ninety days. There's no way. No how.

My shoes hit the white gravel. As a piece sailed through the sun, it sparkled like glitter. "Why don't we head home?" Cal asked me, before waving to the owner once more. "Thanks again, Max."

"Congrats, you two. May the moon shine blessings on your mating."

I didn't think I started walking on my own until we were at the gate. Hundreds of ribbons from previous weddings were wrapped around the iron poles. I cried out, "We can't do it."

"I know." He sounded like the fight was already kicked out of him.

"It's too soon. There's no food. Or invitations. Or stupid little bags of seeds for guests to plant. I don't have a dress. None of them fit me!"

Cal lifted his drooping head. "You went dress shopping?"

"It... Dana said you had to start early. At least a year before the wedding."

His hopeful smile faded and he nodded. "How'd they look?"

"Awful. I refuse to look like a slutty sack of potatoes walking down the aisle."

"Babe. Even if you wore a slutty potato sack, you'd be the most beautiful woman in the world."

God, I wanted to tell him yes. To throw caution to the wind and get married in the most perfect wedding venue I'd ever seen. But I had an apocalypse to stop and clinicals to survive. Surviving our new semester while we were both stressed with wedding cramming? It couldn't be done, as badly as I wanted to.

"I'm sorry," I whispered, my head hanging down.

"No. You're right. I get it. School. Clinicals. Getting the others used to you marrying me."

I didn't even think how they'd react. "Last thing either of us needs is Ink and Daniel getting into a rap battle at the reception."

Cal chuckled. "That's our entertainment sorted." His hopeful tone made me wish I could see a way forward. That was my Cal, always finding the brighter side in things no matter how awful it got. "There's the truck," he said, jerking his head to the old red and silver beast sitting by the side of the gravel road.

"Why don't we stop by Mashewe for dinner? I'm craving all the meats on sticks right now."

Cal missed my eyes falling as he reached for the door handle. Fariah was still mad at me and showing up at her family's place felt like rubbing hummus into the wound. "What about...?"

The bushes behind me shook. It hit me that it was far too big to be a bunny when two massive shadows leaped out. They lunged for me and I reacted. Lifting my hands, fire spurted from my fingertips. It was little more than a grill lighter but the would-be attackers reared back. They didn't even look at me, and just dove into the bushes.

"Cal!"

A low growl ripped the air. Molding my ass against the truck, I turned to face the new threat. With fists curled up, arms wide and nose high in the air, my fiancé looked about to murder someone. "It's them."

"Who?"

"Werewolves. Eric's pack. They can't get away," he shouted and ran after.

"Cal? Wait!" I beat feet into the bushes, suffering the snapback from three men bending branches. "Is this smart?"

The trees clustered tight here, winding around a narrow creek that'd dried up. I struggled to keep pace, both my fiancé and the other wolves striding like they were eight feet tall. I with my stubbier legs could only manage half their gait.

"Shouldn't we wait for help?" The trees opened into a grassy meadow. Cal froze right on the edge, his claws out. I skidded in behind him hunting through the still grass. Out here it grew above my chest.

Cal began to pace partially hunched over with one hand dropping to the ground. His eyes were wild, the pupils dilated to black saucers. I wove a spell of electricity on my fingers, prepared to fire at the first thing that moved.

"I think I should get Ink. Or Gara–"

A horrifying rhythm sundered the air, like a hundred people striking flesh. The grass parted, and the massive red wolf appeared. Eric grinned at Cal. "Hello, meat."

Pain struck my neck. I slapped my hand to it and plunged a dart tip deeper in. Wooziness swam in my veins and I fought to keep on my feet. The electricity on my palm began to fade until the final spark poofed away.

"Fuck."

The void opened up inside of me and I fell.

Chapter Ten

Cal

"Layla!" Ten werewolves and my monstrous half-brother stood before me, but all I heard was that soft gasp. Her legs wobbled and she looked about to hit the ground. I broke my stance and reached out to catch her.

Eric struck.

He used no finesse, never needing any skill beyond the bulging muscles his moon curse gave him. A fist the size of a bowling ball slammed into my ribs. At the absolute last second, I dodged away, taking only a quarter of the brunt, but it was enough to leave me wheezing. Pain rolled up my chest, but at least my internal organs didn't pop.

Dipping a hand down for balance, I glared up at him. "Is that the best you've got?"

He grinned, showing off the human teeth he'd filed down into fangs. "You wish." Eric placed two fingers in his mouth and whistled.

The winds changed. *No!* Two of the cult's pack leaped from behind the trees and grabbed Layla. She flung her elbow back, catching one. The other grabbed a fistful of her hair and pulled. Her wrenching cry shattered my heart and I froze.

"Bind that one for Mr. White."

"Fuck you!" I let the wolf run free, my bones stretching and shrinking, muscle building under my skin and fur above it. My brain lit up like Christmas. The attackers smelled like recycled air, diesel, the compound and lightning. Thirteen in all. Just before my human jaw stretched into the wolf's, I shouted, "Get your paws off of her."

"Ha." Eric laughed. He slammed his palm around Layla's throat. "Shift, and I'll snap her little neck. It'll be like breaking a twig."

Her eyes glared murder, but her hands were pinned between the two werewolves, and Eric drilled his filthy nails in. In a matter of seconds, he could rip her neck open. "Cal," she mouthed, her body shaking.

Where's the fucking demon? The angel?

I had to stall for time. One of them would hear her pleas and come running. Slowly, I fought back the wolf. It was enraged, demanding we leap on Eric's back, rip his throat and pull his tubes out through the hole until his lungs plopped out. I agreed, but we couldn't do anything until Layla was safe.

As the fur faded and my knees dropped into place, I stood. "Okay. Let's talk about —"

A fist slammed into my head and sparks burst in my eyes. My ear crumpled and I lost all hearing on that side. I lashed out, swinging wildly, but my punch sailed past.

Eric clamped onto my shoulder and laughed. "This was to be our alpha?" he crowed and slammed two punches lightning-quick into my stomach.

Fuck! I hit my knees, vomit spraying from my mouth. The peanut butter struck Eric, spreading down his disgusting shirt. He glared at the mess in horror as if he wasn't rolling around in filth every day. "I never wanted that job," I thundered, then a dry heave crumpled my stomach. Coughing, I reached for my lips, and blood spurted over my palm.

That's not good. Either I broke a tooth or have internal bleeding already.

Eric latched onto the back of my head, ripping my hair as he had Layla's. The nerves were long dead from the years of him doing it to me as a kid. I didn't blanch, just stared into his mad eyes. "You don't deserve it, witch fucker!" I braced myself for another punch, but Eric swung his leg. The pain hit before I could piece together he had kicked me.

The massive boot crunched my ribs and I tumbled backward. The pain drove me to pant, but my chest screamed in agony to stop. My ribs wheezed, and I coughed, more blood dripping down my lips.

"Cal!" Layla cried out for me. "Get out of here."

The bastard laughed with macabre hilarity. He posed in the middle of the ring of his cultists, raising his hands to get them to join in. "Yeah, meat. Run. Tuck your tail between your legs. You coward. You worthless piece of shit."

I shook my head, refusing to give in. Rolling over was the hardest thing I'd ever done, but I managed to get my hands under me. The next step was standing up. I willed my energy into my arms, ordering them to pop me up so I could catch Eric by surprise.

A foot slammed into my spine, ramming me to the ground. I lashed my fingers back, trying to rip apart the skin and pry him off. Eric was a beast, whether by the moon or not. Nearly seven feet tall, three hundred pounds of muscle and malice — the man murdered with his bare hands when he was bored.

He dug his heel in, and my spine cracked.

I screamed.

I lost.

"Cal!"

Fingers clamped onto my hair, wrenching my head up even as he drove his foot down. Scrambling, I reached to claw at his wrist, but Eric didn't flinch as I tore apart his flesh. He kept pulling me up, forcing me to look at Layla.

Her beautiful face was twisted in horror, her mouth trembling and eyes streaking in tears. I wanted to assure her everything would be okay, but I could barely breathe, much less speak.

"Here's what's gonna happen." Eric spat against my cheek. His breath stank of raw meat and blood. "I'm gonna take your fucking greenskin and give her to Mr. White so he'll cut her up into little pieces."

Layla!

Why isn't she casting a spell? What did they do to her?

"There's nothing you can do about it, meat. Because…" He slashed fast. I barely caught the glint of a razor edge before it flew past my eye. Pain burst over my face like white fire. I opened my mouth to scream when Eric hurled my head down. My ripped-open face struck the muddy ground, muffling my cries.

"You'll already be dead," he taunted, standing up and polishing his fake claw.

Blood smeared into my eye and I slammed it shut, doing everything I could to keep it safe. I lost Eric as he moved out of my line of sight, but I could see Layla. He'd take her. White would do...the worst things imaginable.

I can't stop. I have to keep fighting even if it kills me.

"Cal, for fuck's sake. Transform. You have to—!"

Eric lashed his steel claw out and pressed it into Layla's cheek. "Yes, go ahead, meat. Transform. Put on our father's skin and let the wolf watch me gut her here." He slashed fast, ripping open her skin.

"You worthless bastard!" I shouted, the pain numbing to a boiling rage.

Layla didn't even whimper but tears gushed down her cheek. Then Eric turned and aimed his claw right above her heart. "I'll rip it out of her chest and eat it in front of you."

"My alpha," one of the hooded cultists whispered. "Mr. White said we're not supposed to kill her."

"I'll do whatever the fuck I want. Who's the alpha here? Me!" Enraged, he swung his blade back, prepared to prove everyone wrong. Those damn fools knew a Horseman would obliterate them for disobeying, but they were more terrified of the psychopath they worshiped.

I didn't remember getting to my feet, sucking in the pain and running. All I knew was Eric and striking him with every bone in my body. He swung his arm and I hit him dead center in the chest with my shoulder. For a moment he cried out, the torturer getting a taste of his own hell.

Eric tumbled back, striking his head on the ground. None of the other wolves moved to help. It'd be the perfect position for me to pounce, to rip his throat out and show it to them.

My vision filled with a red haze save for the white glow rising around Layla. She lifted her lips in a smile and my body collapsed. It hit the ground like a wet sack, my legs bent under me. I fought to catch a breath, my heart squeezing under my creaking ribs.

Enraged at suffering a tenth of what he had unleashed, Eric rose to his feet. He glared at the others, his hands out like he could call the claws at will. "I'll fucking kill you!"

"No," Layla cried out. "Stop!"

Look away. Don't watch this. Please.

His foot slammed into my spine and I cried out. Eric swung his fake claw forward, digging the sharp end deep in between my ribs. Maniacally, Eric twisted it back and forth and I couldn't stop screaming. I'd taught myself to keep silent for every whipping, every punch to the face, every kick to the gut since I was four years old. The tears wouldn't stop. Not for me, but for Layla.

I can't save her. I can't…

"So long, meat." Eric wound up as if it'd be his final blow. Maybe it would kill me, but I'd watched him long enough to know he'd beat my corpse until my limbs tore off. I stared him right in his mad eye, no longer the terrified child. Eric sneered at the challenge and he swung.

Black. It hit like a blur, slamming into Eric's back and sending him flying. I lay there, the ground rumbling from two bodies smashing together. *What the hell is happening?* With the last of my strength, I turned onto my side.

A wolf blacker than midnight stared Eric down. His lips rippled, showing off the fangs. Eric, trapped in his human form, clung to his arm, but blood spurted between his fingers.

"What the fuck are you doing here?" he shouted at the black werewolf.

He answered with a snarl and leaped, aiming to scissor Eric's throat. The gigantic bastard swung with his claw, throwing off the wolf, but he couldn't get through the thick fur. Eric staggered back, his chest and face covered in claw marks welling with blood. The wolf landed on all four paws and circled.

Without a gun, Eric was helpless. His sneer faded to a panicked frown. "Pack mates," he ordered, "attack!" Swinging his claw out, Eric waited for the real werewolves to shed their human forms and leap after the lone wolf.

The wolf huffed a canine laugh. No one took a step. None of them shed their cloaks or transformed. They watched the black wolf bite down on Eric's leg and shatter the bone. He screamed, trying to fight back against the wolf dragging him by his broken leg. Even with blood spurting between his fangs, the wolf laughed, shaking his head to wrench as much pain as possible from Eric.

Then he let go. He watched Eric turn in a blind panic to try to scramble away. In the dirt, Eric — the man who'd tortured me and my brothers every day of our childhood — cried and screamed for help. He crawled across the grass, trying to kick at the wolf who sat and watched.

Just as Eric nearly reached the edge of the pack, the wolf leaped. Eric lifted his arms, trying to impale the wolf's chest, but he wasn't fast enough. The long jaw clamped around Eric's throat then snapped together.

It wasn't fast. Eric tried to scream, bubbles of blood fountaining from his neck as the black wolf shook his head and tore away his trachea. Spitting it out, the wolf sat on Eric's chest and watched until the final spasm stopped.

Dizziness wrapped around my head. I tried to focus, but one second a wolf sat on Eric and the next it was a naked man with black hair. He wiped off his bloody face, then spat on Eric's corpse. As he turned, his job finished, my mind lit up with one last thought.

"Mark," I cried out then crashed into darkness.

Chapter Eleven

Layla

"Cal!"

His brother stared at the two men pinning me, and they both let go. My knees hit the dirt and I kept going, dragging my legs in the muck and blood just to get to him. As I reached for his still body, his eyes opened and he stared up at me. I expected a smile, but he didn't seem to focus on anything, his mouth slack before a great shudder shook his limp form.

"Go on," Mark said, pacing around completely naked. "Heal him."

"Lay..." Cal whispered and I cushioned his head in my hands. The hot stickiness clinging to my palms almost caused me to shudder, but I kept my smile.

"You did it. I'm safe."

Mark snickered behind me, and Cal closed his eyes.

"Sweetheart? Cal. Come on, you have to stay awake. Someone call an ambulance!" I shouted to the silent werewolves standing around.

"What the shit for? You're a witch. Witch him."

God, his skin was clammy and turning gray. How much blood did he lose? How far away was the closest hospital? His lips quivered as if he were trying to reach over and kiss my hand. I lost it. "I'd fucking love to if these assholes hadn't taken my magic!"

Mark's awkward pacing came to a dead halt. He stared at the hung cloaked heads with a silent accusation. "It was his idea," one piped up, pointing to the disemboweled Eric.

Without saying a word, Mark shoved me away and caught Cal's waning head on his lap. "Come on, Claw. Wake up. You got to focus. Look at me."

A low groan was his only answer.

The sound of a body hitting the floor whipped me around. Ink stood on top of one werewolf and dangled another two above his head by their collars.

"Where the fuck were you?" I shouted. All of my tears, my terror and my impotence winnowed to a single point. If I didn't bludgeon it into someone, I'd scream.

My bodyguard demon flung one of the wolves away and stared down at me. I struggled to get up and he reached out with his hand. I ignored it, choosing to go it alone.

"I see the big bad wolf is no more," Ink said in a soft voice. "Your werewolf put up quite a fight."

Damn it! My useless hands bunched into fists and I started flinging them at him, screaming, "Where were you? Why weren't you here?"

"My bond," he said calmly, taking each blow without flinching. I couldn't stop. If I did then…then I'd have to watch Cal bleeding out on the ground.

Tears fell hard, the salt digging into my cheek wound. I didn't even remember it until the pain sizzled on my skin, but I kept clobbering Ink. He caught me in his arms, pinning me against his chest.

"Layla?"

I sobbed, burying my face into Ink as he held me tighter. "Cal's dying. I don't have my magic. I can't —"

Ink jerked me away. His eyes went black as onyx. "Your magic's been removed? By who?" He thundered so sharply the ground quaked and his human illusion vanished, leaving the demon behind.

"Claw? Come on, man. You've got to transform." Mark was jiggling Cal's body up and down. It caused Cal to hiss, the pain insurmountable. He'd been bleeding since the first punch and that bastard wouldn't let up.

"Leave him alone!" I shouted, reaching for Cal, but Ink swept me up and pinned me against him.

Mark glared at me. "The wolf is stronger. He's more likely to survive in that form. Bro, don't fucking do this to me. You gotta shift. I know it hurts, but there isn't any time. Come on. Why the fuck aren't you?"

Me. Even though they were glassy, Cal was staring at me watching him. Damn it. I gulped, steeling myself for this. *Don't you die on me*, I mouthed to him, and turned away.

I watched Ink while listening to hear if Cal managed it. My demon drew his finger against my cheek and pouted, "You're injured." The touch was soft and tender, but the flash of his claw wrenched my stomach. I whipped my head away, my heart pounding a million miles an hour. He dropped his touch instantly and walked over to Eric's corpse. Ink didn't say a word, only slashed once with his claws. A loud plorp of something wet and heavy hit the ground, then he returned to me, blood splattered over his claws.

"What did you do?"

"Less than he deserved," Ink growled, wiping his fingers off on a silk hankie. "It is all right. He's managed it."

I blinked madly, trying to shake away my tears, and turned to Cal. His beautiful eyes were closed, his thick gray fur tattered and stained with blood, but his chest was rising. "Ink, you have to get him somewhere safe."

"Your lack of magic—"

"He's dying!" I shouted, then slammed a hand over my traitorous mouth. How could I say that? How could I think it?

Ink bowed his head and glanced over at Mark. "Very well, but should anything happen to you…"

"I'm fine," I insisted, doing my best to ignore the hole opening inside of me. I had a few hours before the pain would become overwhelming, and a few more after that until it killed me. Cal mattered more.

With more care than I ever expected, Ink slipped his hands under Cal. My poor boy whimpered—causing my legs to shake—but Ink relaxed, taking his time before he lifted Cal and the both of them vanished.

Mark blinked and rose to his haunches. "The one time his witch is less than worthless."

I sneered, wanting to ask why he wasn't two minutes faster, but blaming him wouldn't help. This wasn't his fault—it was the cult's. It was White's. It was that fucking bastard. There, lying in the grass, was the monster's weapon. It glittered in the sunlight, the tip crusted in blood.

I didn't know why I picked it up, the claw as long as my thumb and surprisingly heavy. Glaring at the corpse, I took a step closer.

"What are you doing?" Mark asked. He'd moved toward me, as had the other wolves.

Answering them was pointless. What I needed was to tear Eric to the same pieces as he had me. Rip his cheek, kick in his ribs, tear out his... Oh, Ink had already done that. Good. I tossed the claw to my other hand, staring into his dead eyes. Vengeance demanded blood. The hole inside of me had to be fed.

I lashed my arm out and a hand caught my elbow. My first instinct was to kick, but Ink tipped me over his shoulder. I didn't stop my attack, the steel claw plunging inside his belly. "Shit, I'm sorry. I didn't mean to."

"I understand," Ink said. He looked once at Mark, then walked to the side and we were back at home.

"Holy shit. Layla?" Daniel ran over, books falling from his lap. "What the fuck's going on? All the demon said was—"

"Cal's dying and my magic's gone." I gulped, the finality of both of those facts hitting me harder than Eric's punch. My hands shook and the claw stumbled from my fingers. I wanted to curl up into a ball and scream, but that wouldn't help him. It wouldn't help me. "Wait. Ink, where's Cal?"

"Upstairs."

"Up..." I shoved him aside and took the steps three at a time. My chin nearly struck the landing, but I got my feet under me and kept going until I reached the bedroom. Stretched out across our bed was a huge gray wolf. The afternoon sun was cruel to him, highlighting every open wound.

Garavel stood beside him, trying to clean off the blood with a rag. "My lady witch…" he greeted me.

I shouted to my demon, "Why the fuck isn't he in a hospital?"

"Would any of your healing centers accept an injured wolf?" Ink asked, appearing behind me.

"No, but he can shift back. We need to get him…"

"I despise agreeing with that selfish fleabag, but he is correct. At this point, I fear the wolf is the only aspect keeping Calvin with us."

Damn it. A vet? Would a vet even try? Cal in wolf form weighed like four hundred pounds. He barely fit on the king-sized bed. *What do I do? What do I…?* I reached for Cal, running my fingers through his coarse fur, praying it never turned cold.

"My bond, our first concern is your magic. You?" Ink stared at Daniel who was huffing in the threshold. "Have you found a solution?"

"I don't—"

My magic was gone, my fiancé dying. I managed to text without looking at my screen, my eyes glued to Cal. His eyelids opened a slit, the bright blue shining back at me. With a heavy stutter in his lungs, he dipped his tongue out and touched my wrist.

Please, god, let someone answer.

* * * *

It was five minutes before the doorbell rang. Five passes of the minute hand that felt like five hundred as I ran my palm over Cal's back and pleaded with him to stay with me. His breathing became more ragged, his tongue dangling out as he kept huffing through his snout. The chirp of the bell rang like the funeral dirge and I leaped clear out of my shoes.

Daniel was the one to catch me. "I'll get it," he said, letting me stay by Cal's bedside. Daniel made it to the stairs before I remembered who could be on the other side.

"Wait!" I shouted, jogging down the stairs and reaching out for the door handle. Daniel was already in place, pulling it open. The afternoon sun flared behind a silhouette and I raised my hand.

The black hair didn't fade and I frowned. "Mark."

Cal's brother sneered at Daniel then stomped inside. "Where the shit is he?"

"Who the hell are—?" Daniel asked, only for the werewolf to spin around and snarl with his full fangs. For his part, Daniel didn't react, which obviously bit into Mark.

Raising his head, Mark breathed deeply. "Got it," he said and took off for the staircase.

I wasn't about to let him go that easy. "Who said you could come in here?" I shouted.

"This was my place long before it was yours, greenskin," he responded, hitting the landing and running for Cal's bedroom. Garavel slipped out to stand in the way, and Mark barreled on past.

I noticed four rips across the chest of his shirt. If my angel weren't made of ebony, he'd be bleeding right now. Garavel stared down at the damage with a thoughtful look. "He requires a nail file."

"He needs a lot more than that." I sneered and dove into the room. My legs locked up.

Mark climbed into the bed beside Cal. He pulled his brother's head into his lap and tenderly stroked the fur as he whispered to him. There was no love lost between me and Cal's only remaining brother. But I had forgotten how those two had been through hell together and forged a bond stronger than anything a shared parent could give them.

"I can remove him if you wish," Ink said. He'd been quiet, watching at a distance. Now he moved closer and wrapped an arm around my shoulders from behind. I clung to his wrist to keep myself upright and shook my head. Cal wouldn't want it.

"Can you help him?" I asked.

"Ain't you the one with the healing power?" Mark taunted. The void inside of me pulsed, my stomach knotting in a huge cramp. I wanted to double over in a ball, but Ink held me safe. This shouldn't be happening so fast.

Mark stared at me with a dismissive eye, but he kept out one hand with his claws. "As worthless as I imagined. I told you to avoid that one," he whispered to his sleeping brother.

I locked my spine in and stood up taller. It seemed convenient for him to appear just as Eric and the rest made a move. Fuck, there were still a dozen other werewolves out there no doubt mad as hell about a second dead leader. "What about the pack? Are they going to—?"

"The pack is mine," Mark snarled. "A few challenged me, but not for long." He smirked with pride and I noticed dark stains on the chest of his black shirt. How many others had he killed today? "Unless you're going to do something to help, I suggest you get the fuck out and leave us alone."

"What I need is my goddamn magic back. Then Cal will be... He'll be..."

Don't think about it. He'll be fine. We both will. Then we'll get married and live happily ever after.

Daniel leaned in through the doorway. "About that. I remember seeing —"

"My question is how your connection was once again severed?" Ink interrupted. His pecs hardened against my back until they felt more like stone than Garavel.

"I don't know..." I groaned. One minute we were chasing after some damn werewolves, the next I fell to my knees and the hole opened up.

"I do."

Oh shit.

My stomach dropped and every man turned at the new voice. With sunglasses perched on the tip of his nose, the ex-witch hunter stood against the far wall with his head quirked to the side. Ink reacted first and not well.

"You!" he thundered, lashing out with his demonic claws.

Raul didn't even blink, only lifted his hand. A symbol flashed on the back and Ink vanished into thin air. The last I saw were his eyes burning in rage.

"What the...what did you do to him?"

"Relax. It's a demon-banishing sigil. He's probably out back."

"Layla, what's the witch hunter doing here?" Daniel asked. He'd taken Ink's place, but Raul didn't do much more than glance at him.

"She invited me to save her. Or perhaps her wolf." Without anyone's permission, he walked right into Cal's and my bedroom. Raul swung around a small bag and dug inside. Holding a tiny blue bottle, he lifted Cal's lip to place the glass against it.

Mark struck, but Raul dodged as if he wasn't even there. "What the shit is that?" Mark demanded.

"Healing draught. Or do you want him to die?"

Mark glared at the unexplained man, then me. He didn't trust Raul and, truth be told, I didn't have a lot of good reasons to either. It could be poison, or something even more diabolical. Maybe it'd give him control of Cal's mind. But we didn't have a choice.

I took the bottle from him and dug my knee into the mattress. The stench of iron billowed off of Mark, but I ignored it to focus on Cal. He'd done everything to save me. Even when... *Please, let this work.*

"Sweetheart, this will help you," I said, dripping the clear liquid through a gap in his fangs. As it hit, Cal began to shake. His tongue stuck out like he was trying to spit out the awful taste. The mystery liquid slipped down his throat. With one great moan, he collapsed to the bed.

"Cal?" I sputtered, running my hands over him. His skin twitched as I ruffled his fur, his heart beating and chest rising. He was alive but not awake. "What did you do? Why isn't he better?"

"He's alive. That's the best I could do with what I had. Here, this should help close the superficial wounds." Raul uncorked another much longer bottle and began to pour thick cream onto Cal's body. With that, he sighed, his tail lightly wagging as the cream matted down his fur. Sure enough, some of the wounds began to close.

"My heart," I cried out, wrapping my arms around Cal's neck and pressing my cheek to his forehead. His eyes stayed closed, but I couldn't hear the struggling wheeze in his lungs.

Ellen Mint

Raul shook out the last of the bottle, then he scooped to catch the contents with his palm. A single drop splattered against the back of his hand, washing away the demon ward. "Damn it," he cried just as a hand slammed into his throat.

"Ink!"

"Allow me to dispose of the trash." He wasted no time and plunged his claws forward to rip out his intestines.

"Stop!" I shouted, putting all the force into that single word. It must have been enough as Ink paused just before he pierced skin. "He came here to help."

Ink snarled. "What help can he provide other than pain? He tried to kill you once. What is to say he isn't trying again?"

"You..." Raul coughed, his voice dropping to a whisper. Intrigued, Ink leaned closer. "You're a fool," the elf shouted, and a massive branch shattered the window.

I yelped, leaping over Cal to protect him as glass rained against my back. The branch split apart, forming smaller vines that wrapped around Ink's wrists, biceps and thighs. He was completely pinned but laughed in response.

"You believe this parlor trick can stop me, elf?" With a simple shrug, Ink ripped the vines to pieces.

"Elf? Where's an elf?" Garavel shouted, leaping to his feet. His wings shot out, upending the lamp and clearing the dresser. Garavel reached for his sword as the sound of crackling wood filled the air. I looked down at my feet to find the floorboards shifting. *Who the fuck's doing that?*

"Before me, but not for long. Let us see how far I can skip this stone," Ink taunted.

"You'd better be sure you can," Raul antagonized right back.

Nails flew, hitting the ceiling. One by one, floorboards rattled in place, ripped free and dashed toward Ink. If he noticed, he gave no sign and reached for Raul's collar. Garavel had his sword out, his wings beating in anticipation of taking flight. And all the while, the floor began to cave below us.

"For fuck's sake!" I shouted, leaping to my feet. "Will everyone stop destroying the house?" I zeroed my glare in at Raul first before the bed and Cal's wounded body went through the floor.

He took a deep sigh and released whatever elf hold he had on the boards. Then I looked to Garavel. "Put that thing away. We don't need it."

"Yes, my lady. Sorry." He slotted the sword behind his back where it vanished into the ether.

I clung to Ink's arm. "Drop him."

He didn't move, so I began to pull. *Fucking hell.* There was no give whatsoever. The demon ripped away his mask, revealing the black and red hissing monster below. "Why is the witch murderer here?"

"I contacted him," I said.

All of my guys except Cal turned to me. "You're in contact with him?" Daniel spat.

Ink shook his head as if he knew this would all happen. "Your foolhardy libido will be your undoing."

"She let you into her bed."

For the love of god. I glared at Raul, trying to get him to shut up before they murdered him. "My magic was taken from me, just like the witch hunters had. I thought he might know a way to bring it back."

"Do you?" Ink pressed and Raul gulped.

Damn it.

"Are you playing coy or stupid? Either way, you will be a stain on the pavement before the sun falls."

Raul raised his hands. "I'd love nothing more than to heal Layla."

Two of my guys growled at him using my name. This was going well.

"Your hanging 'but' could crash a bus," Daniel said.

Raul sighed. "But I don't know how. That was handled by our witches."

"You mean slaves," Daniel fought back.

"They were compensated."

"Oh, that makes it okay."

Ink pushed the two apart. "Step back, mortal stain. I will finish this."

Daniel turned his venom on Ink. "For fuck's sake, I'm not dead anymore."

"Which makes you as fragile as the bones of a juvenile songbird. If you get in my way, I cannot be held responsible for the damage to your innards."

Daniel laughed once, then flung what looked like black spice at Ink. The human flesh burned away to the demon skin and Ink cried out. His eyes aflame, he stepped back from where the black dust had landed.

"I'm not without my resources, demon."

"You'll be without your eyes soon enough, mortal. Sleep with both of them open otherwise."

I tipped my head back and screamed. In my head, lightning shot from my fingertips, giving every bickering man a good jolt. I kept going, covering over whatever Daniel and Ink had left in their tanks until everyone fell silent.

"Are you—?" The void pulsed, tendrils of pain seizing up my chest. I groaned and pitched to the side. Garavel was quick to catch me. As I shook away the red haze, I was surprised to find concern in everyone's eyes. "Finished?"

"Yes, my bond."

"I'm sorry."

"I don't know what was going on, but I beg for forgiveness," Garavel said.

After patting his cheek for being him, I looked to the final holdout. Raul went still, his fingers nervously twitching before his stomach. He must not have meant to as he stopped the second I stared. "In the agency."

"The witch hunters, you mean. The people who'd hunt and kill—"

"Yes, Ink. We know."

"Hm, I like this guy."

Christ, in all that mess, I damn near forgot Cal's brother was still here. He had a smarmy grin on his face and nodded at Raul, who paled at the attention. Tugging his sunglasses lower, Raul stared at me above the frames. "We relied upon the spells provided to us by the witches. Many had the same protection runes, wards against demons and the like, but to my knowledge, only one witch knew how to take magic from others. And she was the only one who knew how to counter it as well."

"Who?" Daniel demanded, but my heart dropped.

Valerie. She'd seemingly rescued me on a lark. She was why Daniel drew breath. I had no damn idea how to find her.

"How do we locate this witch?" Ink demanded as if he could read my mind.

Raul shrugged. "No one knows. She disappeared the same day you invaded the agency."

"You mean when we saved Layla."

Damn it. This hole was growing faster than ever. I didn't have time to dick around and find a witch. How would I? Doubtful she'd be on social media posting about her favorite Rae Dunn cauldron.

Seeming to sense my fear, Raul sighed and looked only at me. "There is another problem."

"It doesn't strike you as strange that dipshit Eric had access to this rare potion?" Daniel voiced what I'd already feared.

"Conquest has all their secrets, doesn't he?" I said. "All their witches, too."

Raul's head dropped. "It's worse than that, I fear. There are almost no witches left."

What?

Garavel laughed. "Witches cannot vanish. They are created by the angels to guard this world."

"They're vanishing, one by one. Every known witch in the hunters' database is gone. I tried to warn a few in time, but I could only get a handful before..." The cold hunter who'd turned my life inside out sighed and dropped his gaze. "I'm sorry."

"I don't understand. How can they be dead? They're witches. They're powerful. They fight off... Oh. The potion. They're being poisoned, like I was. Like they'll all be if we don't stop Conquest."

"I fear it may be too late. The seams are beginning to split."

A loud bang echoed through the house. My heart leaped into my throat. *Is it White? Did he find our house? Is he coming himself to drag me away and use me for his demented plan to rip the universe to pieces?* I hugged tighter to Garavel, feeling like a tiny mouse hiding from a hungry cat.

Then the bang came again — softer, and less demanding. The front door. "I will get it," Ink said. "Better yet, let us make our new elven shield get it." He reached for Raul, but froze, his feet trapped in place by whatever Daniel had thrown.

Bickering broke out between them yet again, every guy wanting to be the one to protect me and stop the others from getting the credit. I doubted they even noticed when I slipped past and down the stairs. With no spells to protect me, I pulled in a deep breath to launch a scream. That'd at least get them all running.

I yanked open the door and steeled my legs.

"Laylee." My mother shoved a water bottle at my chest. "Drink this. Now."

For all our animosity, I trusted my mom to at least protect me. Pinching my nose, I slugged the heavy bubbling liquid back. A cough broke and the bottle fell. Growing dizzy, I tried to take a step toward the couch when darkness hit.

Chapter Twelve

Daniel

Her body tumbled for the floor. I flew down the stairs, arms stretched to catch her just before she hit. Trying to lift Layla and get my feet under me, I glared at the old woman lingering in the doorway. "What have you done? Layla?"

She was breathing, but her eyes were closed and her cheek twitching.

The mother looked at me with a disinterested scoff. "You're still here? Interesting."

"So help me, if you hurt her." I tried to raise the threat. All the old witch had to do was lift her fist. Winds burst from behind me, pushing me closer and dragging Layla with me. I couldn't do anything to keep my feet in place. With a smirk, the witch shook off her spell.

Layla moaned. She ran her hand across her forehead, then sat up.

"Are you okay? What happened?" I asked.

She wiggled out of my arms, damn near launching to her feet. "It's back," she shouted then took the stairs, using the railing to get her body up them. I kept asking her what was going on. Her response was to grit her teeth and keep going. At the landing, she took in a deep breath, placed a hand over her chest then dashed for Cal's bedroom.

Damn, she was fast when she wanted to be. I had to push around Garavel to slip inside as Layla held her hands above Cal's fur. Her lips moved and I recognized the spell whispering under her breath. A ball of light rose from her palm and was absorbed directly into the gray fur.

The dying wolf kicked his leg and strained his head up. I knew he was chasing the high that wiped away his pain, but that dark-haired werewolf leaped toward Layla. Before he could get a word in, the demon caught him by the shoulder and hurled him against the wall. "It does not matter how often you scratch me…"

The werewolf took another two swipes at the demon. Ink sighed, his face splitting open then growing back together. "I fear your ears are clogged with mange. You may wish to have that inspected."

"Layla?" I eased closer. She was casting another healing spell, one right after the other, and her skin had turned a sickening gray. Sweat dotted her forehead, her arms shaking as the last of her energy fed into Cal. "You need to take a break."

"No," she insisted. "It's working."

"You…" The air shifted, not in flapping papers or even a breeze on my cheek. I knew the eddies of energy flowing around us. I couldn't say how, or even point to them. It was a feeling like the hairs on the back of my neck. But as she walked into the room, all the energy snapped from a free-flowing wave to a hard line aimed at Layla.

Her mother stared around the tiny room crammed with too many people. She skipped past Garavel half in the closet, the witch hunter leaning against the dresser to avoid the demon pinning the werewolf, and landed on me. "We should discuss whatever you've found in the dead's memory," her mother said.

"No," Layla interrupted, casting a third healing spell. As this one soaked into Cal's skin, the fur melted away. The wolf might have felt safe enough to return to human form, but seeing all the scars and bruises across his bare skin was stomach-wrenching. One side of his chest looked like it'd been caved in.

The sight did nothing to her mother. "What matters is…"

"Cal. All that matters is Cal." She glared at her mother with a declaration and lifted her healing hands off of the werewolf with a threat. If she tried anything to pull her daughter away, Layla would unleash hell.

"Fine." Her mom slipped off her purse and pulled out a blue leather tome — her spell book. "But this will take time."

"I don't care," Layla insisted. She slid onto the bed to take Cal's head in her lap and ran her fingers through his hair. "I'm here. It's going to be okay. We're all here for you."

Cal stirred. His hand clung to Layla's thighs, his nails digging into her flesh like she was his rock in the middle of the sea. I took a deep breath and stepped back. "You need some space. We don't all have to be in here." I looked at the demon still clinging tight to the werewolf, but his focus quickly turned to Stone.

"Do not believe you are free to wander, witch hunter. You have much to answer for."

"It's no wonder you'd be against me saving his life."

"For fuck's sake, I need to focus. Take all your pissing contests outside," Layla ordered. "Not you, Garavel. I need you to stay and, um…" She glanced over at Cal's brother, then bit her lip. "Protect."

"I will gladly be of service." He bowed then zeroed in on all of us. "You heard our lady. Remove yourselves from the healing chambers."

It was a lot of shuffling to act like we meant to abandon Layla while not catching anyone's eye. The prudent thing would have been for each of us to find a separate room in the house. How we wound up together in the kitchen was anyone's guess.

Perhaps it was my fault. A disquiet feeling rattling in my soul wouldn't leave. I thought it might be hunger. Going without food for thirty years made remembering to eat on the regular challenging. As I dug through the wolf's protein and chocolate-heavy stocks, the witch hunter blazed through first.

"Are you going to disembowel me here?" he asked, facing down the demon.

Ink was rattled. He'd claim otherwise if pressed, but he was struggling to keep his human skin on, and his eyes were black as pitch. Though he couldn't keep his snark in check. "Tile floor, immediate access to knives and fire, extended hose—this appears to be the best room for murder. Now, will you scream, or is your upper lip too stiff from the magic you've stolen?"

The demon made a feigned hint at swinging for him, then he looked at me. "Are you not going to tell me to stop?"

"What the shit do I care if you kill him?" I countered. Layla'd be pissed, but that'd be an Ink problem. Besides, the witch hunter kept crossing his arms, looking as cocky as ever. No doubt he could handle himself.

"Why are you in this house, witch hunter?" Ink demanded.

The first flare of emotion burned across Stone's face. "I am not a witch hunter!"

"You are using magics beyond your ken, are you not? Relying upon their tricks of illusion." In one quick swipe, Ink yanked the sunglasses off of Stone. His body twitched and turned green. More than that, he had quite a few bruises himself that he'd been hiding, both of his under eyes a deep purple.

"What happened to you?" I asked.

"¿Qué mierda te importa?" Stone spat my own words back at me. I stared at him a long time, then took a big bite of an energy bar. "While you grow fat on candy, I'm in the trenches of this war fighting for my life."

"Oh, my poor heart. It bleeds for the man facing the consequences of his past actions. Truly. What a tale of woe. To be hunted by those you once thought friends — kidnapping, murdering, abusive, traitorous friends. So sad."

Stone narrowed his eyes at me. I'd chipped his armor. "Keep speaking of what you don't know, and I will return you to your grave."

It was Ink who laughed. "Endearing yourself beyond measure already, witch hunter." Then he slipped on the glasses. In a blink, a second Detective Stone stood where Ink was. Though the glasses had trouble with Ink's taller height, the forehead doubling as Ink shifted back and forth.

"You idiots!" That blustering façade shattered. Stone lashed out and ripped the glasses off of Ink's nose. The demon must not have cared as he didn't fight back while Stone fumed. "Do you have any ability to understand what's coming? How many billions will die if Conquest gets his way?"

"Billions come, billions go. Mortals show particular affinity at both the comings and the goings." Ink shrugged it off while I went silent. Conquest was why I had died in the first place. He had ordered the hit via a djinn. The question hanging over my head was why.

"You waste your time dicking around over piddly wedding shit while the world burns."

The uncaring incubus snapped on a dime. His voice hardened and he glared down at Stone. "The only reason you are not currently dangling by your hamstrings from the weathervane is because of her. Please, keep dismissing her wishes so I may pull out every one of your tendons myself."

"That's all you have, demon. A creature of threats, of chaos and pain. What can you offer her beyond that?"

"Back-breaking orgasms to start," Ink said.

"And you. The ghost she wasted valuable resources in bringing back from the dead. For what purpose I'll —"

"How do you know so much about me?" I interrupted, not needing to be reminded of my place in this house.

Stone's eyes flared a moment, then he slipped his shades back on. I didn't even care about the tan skin sliding over the true green. I only focused on him doing his best to hide the glimmer of truth. "You're still stalking her, aren't you?"

The witch hunter snorted but didn't answer.

"How else did you get here so fast? It wasn't from her text. You were already prepped and waiting. No wonder you waltzed in uninvited. How often do you do that? For all we know, you came here to take advantage of her weak—"

"You know nothing about me, Mr. Lu. I am providing her protection."

"She doesn't need any protection from a foul-smelling witch murderer," Ink said.

"No? So when a Horseman tries to steal her away again, you will rely upon the, what? Easily broken werewolf? The befuddled angel? Or the demon that can be stopped with a single sigil? Did you even know she was in trouble? Did you care?"

Ink reared forward, claws out. One hand was aimed at Stone's eyes and the other at his guts. I knew if I leaped in between, he would go right through me. It was the smug witch hunter who calmly lifted his fist from his pocket and clenched it. Ink shrieked, his body shredding backward.

"I. Will." Even with every step shearing bits off, Ink kept trying. "Wear your intestines as a scarf!" Ink took one more step, and Stone pulsed his fist. The demon vanished.

Calmly tugging down his suit jacket, Stone didn't even look in the direction where he had banished Ink. I couldn't entirely blame him, but the lack of the demon meant I was alone with a man trained in killing every one of us, especially Layla.

"If you've come to hurt her…" I began.

"Conquest does not have the resources to risk a full-frontal invasion. Yet. His use of the werewolves failed, but he will keep trying. This meager team of fools will not be enough to protect her. I came to warn Layla, but none of you seem to be capable of being civil."

"You were the one to banish Ink." *Why the shit am I arguing for the damn demon?*

"If I were still with the agency, he would have been sent back to hell instead of the garage."

"So that's it. You're this big, bad agent who knows how to counteract every creature and magic, and we're all a bunch of useless morons?"

Stone's face fell, his lips parting and he shook his head. Whatever was going through his mind, he didn't elaborate and walked for the door. "I am leaving. If you try to stop me, I will be forced to retaliate. Understand?"

"I've already been shot once," I countered, not needing to see the gun to know it was on him.

The witch hunter smirked. "And it took an act of creation to bring you back. Do you think anyone will bother a second time?"

Layla would. She'd do it again and again. The problem was we only had one feather left.

I chased after the smug asshole, prepared to argue him to death, but he'd vanished. The front door was still open from her mother walking in, but a chill frosted my arms. Something in my gut told me he didn't have to use doors to leave.

We didn't need him. We had saved Layla just fine. So Conquest and his goons could negate her magic and nearly kill her. And there were spies everywhere, meaning nowhere was safe. Ink should have been able to sense her every breath, but he hadn't been there. It was up to that other werewolf making it in the nick of time.

Bruises splattered across all of his skin. Ribs broken so badly the chest was caved in like cheap plastic in the dishwasher. Eyes rolling back and tongue dangling from the mouth. It wasn't Cal that popped into my mind, but my body broken and dying in that bed.

What use was I to her? The angel, demon and werewolf could fight. The witch hunter was crafty. *After she learns White's secret, what else can I do?*

Would she revive me a second time?

Could I save her?

Fear clenched inside me. Fear I knew — the emotion festering inside of the dead. But it'd been academic as a ghost. A simple matter of weighing the costs versus the benefits and often falling into despair. This was a visceral horror boiling in my gut until I was spitting blood.

What if Layla dies because of me?

"You gangrene-cocked, brittle, micro-brained…! Oh, he's left." Ink shrugged and walked for the kitchen. "I'll begin dinner. Tonight is popcorn enchiladas."

* * * *

Layla

"He's looking a lot better."

I frowned at my mother. She'd been saying the same thing for the past five minutes. Whispering the spell, I leaned closer to inspect Cal's left eye. Both were shut tight, but that was the one Eric had slashed while I watched. The broken capillaries had faded to little more than a hint of red, but that fucking scar straight down his eyebrow didn't even turn pink. Its red strip mocked me, and I zeroed in on it.

Another blast of magic caused Cal to sigh, but it did nothing to the wound. "Why isn't this healing?" I whined, my voice soft to not rattle his ears. "It should be working." I cast it again, my fingers turning cold as the magic pumped out of my empty bucket straight into him.

"I'm sorry, Laylee." My mom cupped a hand around my shoulder. "Some scars can't be healed by magic. They cut right to—"

"The bone?" I could heal bones. I could reset them even while I was fighting. I could knit flesh. I could fix this—fix him. We could sit at the table together, laughing over whatever fresh horrors Ink made, as if none of this happened. As if I didn't nearly watch him die...

"Some slice into the soul. I fear you will exhaust yourself to death before knitting it together. Only time can fade that one."

Tears burned in my working eyes. I bent over and kissed Cal on his warm forehead. Failure seeped from my pores. What kind of witch was I that I couldn't even heal a little scratch? "He..." He almost died to save me. He could have shifted, he should have shifted. But if it wasn't for Mark, Cal would have given up everything for me. *I'm worthless.*

Wiping my eyes, I focused on the task ahead. "He needs an eyepatch to help it heal. I think there's one in the bathroom." I eased my feet off the bed and put pressure on my legs, only for my lower half to give out. Two sets of hands reached for me while the werewolf smirked. He seemed to be enjoying my torture, even if I was tearing myself to shreds to save his brother. I shook away the help and forced myself to rise.

"Lady witch, perhaps you should rest and—?"

"I'll get the patch. Garavel, you…you know what to do."

He gulped as if he didn't, but I was too tired to think of an order. Ignoring the emptiness sloshing in my veins, I limped for the bathroom down the hall. Two wet towels lay on the floor. I nudged one away with my foot, certain if I tried to pick them up, I'd hit the ground.

Digging through the serious first-aid kit, I tried to focus. *Don't think about Cal's blue eye turning red. Don't picture blood pouring from it as he screams and hits the ground. All that matters is…*

The first-aid kit dropped off the edge of the sink. It hit the closed toilet lid and spun, hurling every bandage and alcohol wipe around the small room. "Fuck."

"You cannot keep on in this manner."

"Mom, you can either lecture me or help me," I muttered, easing around on hands and knees trying to find the eyepatch.

"I believe I can do both," she said. She was slower to get to her knees, but she joined me on the wet floor. Despite that, we hunted silently, shoving Band-Aids back into the kit in no order whatsoever. The next time I needed it, it would be a mess.

The next time…

My mom held out the black eyepatch. I moved to take it, then stopped, my head dropping. "Go on. Out with it. Tell me how stupid I am for wanting to marry him. For falling in love. For letting him get hurt."

"Layla, my lamb." She scooped her arms around me and I was five years old, bawling my eyes out over a dead butterfly. I clung tight to my mommy, needing her to make the bad stuff disappear.

But that wasn't how it worked. We never fought the bad thing, just ran from it, over and over, until I was left to confront him on my own.

I pushed out of her arms and pooled away my tears with a wet piece of gauze. "Isn't that why you're here? To remind me how a proper witch acts?"

"I am here because you needed me." My mom placed her hand in mine. "I will always be there when you need me."

I crinkled my hand around the eyepatch. A nice promise, but I'd lived the truth. "Then why did you leave?"

"Laylee, it's…"

"You haven't told me. Was it White? Were you running from him? Was he coming for you like all the other witches? Is that why?"

"I was…" She clenched her teeth hard and sighed. "I was trying to protect you from a dangerous foe. I didn't want you to suffer the way I had."

"Mom?" Conquest's taunting words came back to me. He'd had me trapped, at his mercy, but all he cared about was my mother. "What happened to your coven?"

My mom paled bone-white. "They were…killed."

"By the Horseman?" I knew it without having to say. It made sense.

"By my recklessness. We believed ourselves invulnerable and capable of feats no other witches' coven could manage. We were idiots. I never would have joined them if it weren't for your—" My mom quickly silenced her tongue, her face drawn. She didn't want me to know any of that. "My point is that Conquest is a threat beyond my power, beyond yours.

He is not to be trifled with, and I fear the reason he came for you in the open is because he knows."

"Knows what?"

"That the ghost lives."

"Daniel? But he... Shit." Deep inside, I didn't think much of my excuse to bring him back to life. Conquest seemed to kill people because they got in his way. Outsourcing it made whatever secret Daniel stumbled upon feel even less important. But if he was running scared and trying to stop me...?

"You would do well to find out whatever the young man knows. Then we need to speak of a way to protect you from Conquest's gaze."

I nodded, my skull feeling like it was full of bowling balls. With a grunt, I tried to get to my feet, and my mom held her hand out. I took it and rose.

"For now, you should rest before you drain yourself to nothing."

I gritted my teeth at the idea. Could I do to myself what the hunters kept trying? Sleep sang in my veins, but I shook my head. "I have to check on Cal first," I said, lifting up the eye patch and walking to his room.

My mom breathed deeply. "Do you really intend to marry this man after everything that happened today? And everything that can happen in the future?"

I stared down at the patch. Three hours ago, we were picturing our wedding and in a flash, I had almost lost him forever.

Chapter Thirteen

Daniel

Fingers, this is the dumbest shit I've ever heard.

We were supposed to be rehearsing. We had a huge gig at Tony's tonight. The bar, not the restaurant in the truck stop off the interstate. It was our make-or-break. The rest of the guys were all there waiting for their star bass player.

What was I doing? I slapped my palm against the filthy briefcase. Two women looked up from their newspapers but the bus kept rolling. All I was told was to get on the bus beside some stop in Verona and bring the case to the...

"Shit!" I cursed, catching the glare of grannies. The gated community flew on by like it'd shoot any buses on sight. I leaned over the seat and tugged on the cord. The bell rang out and the bus came to a slow stop. People grumbled as I struggled to slip past. One called me a thug and jerked a hand at the strip of blue in my hair. I gave my apologies, then shot him the one-finger salute and slipped out of the door.

God, this place was a swamp in summer. The water off of the lake hung in the air, permeating worse in the yuppies' section of town. A hint of the fancy mansions peeked out behind a ten-foot white wall. There was a brown roof here, a turret there, but not a trace of graffiti on the bricks keeping the riffraff out. Did they have some high-tech lasers to shoot any kid with a spray paint can? Sounded like the richies.

The sidewalk opened up onto a street blocked off by two huge barriers. I moved to slide around one when a little door in the middle guardroom opened. "Excuse me. What do you think you're doing?" His uniform was tan but he stank of bacon.

With a wide smile, I hefted up the briefcase and said, "I'm here on business. I have a business meeting."

"Funny. Don't move one step or I'm calling the cops."

This hassle wasn't worth the hundred bucks. I was tempted to throw the briefcase into the gutter and wash my hands of all of this. The guard held a hand up and he inched back for his phone. It rang just as his palm gripped the receiver. "Er." He answered it, and his piggy face dropped. "Yes, sir. Yes. Of course. Right away. Sorry, Mr. White."

After hanging up, the guard whined at me, "Why didn't you tell me you had an appointment with Mr. White?"

"Not like you asked," I said. "Can I go in or are you gonna shoot me in the back?"

"Yes, please. Go now." If I was smart, I'd have noticed how the man's power-hungry smile snapped to a panicked frown, or that his face was as white as the class-dividing wall. But all I wanted was to get this over with.

I didn't have a damn clue where the hell I was supposed to take this. As I looked around the little Victorian mansions, I caught one dead center. It was whiter than a polo club, three times as big as the others, with towers on both sides. It looked like someone had dropped a medieval castle in the middle of the city.

Fingers hadn't given any explanation, and I hadn't asked any questions about what I was carrying. All he had told me was that if I didn't do it, he'd wake up without those digits we needed to make music. No way was I letting Tiger Whisper die because of his boneheaded idiocy.

I hadn't cared on the bus, assuming it was either dirty money or more drugs, but the case was light, almost like there was nothing in there. As I stared at the foreboding Midwestern castle, my curiosity grew. *No one knows I'm here. What'll it hurt to have a quick look?*

The security guard was no doubt back to whacking off in his booth, and all the other neighbors were probably busy stealing money from the little guy. No one had noticed me in their wealthy playground. A weird hedge shaped like a corkscrew sat on some dude's lawn. I sidled up to it and slipped around to the back.

In the shadows, I squatted down and placed the briefcase on my lap. *There's probably a fucking lock or a…*

The lid popped right up. Not like the wealthy were known for being smart. I opened the briefcase, my fingers digging into a weird burn spot in the leather. The stench of charcoal radiated from inside, but it wasn't a pile of some snitch's ashes or a mess of coal hiding diamonds. A single piece of paper lay upside down. It was that tobacco-yellow color books got after they'd been at the second-hand store for years.

I looked to both sides, then flipped the paper over.

"You've got to be fucking kidding me."

It was bullshit. "'The balance of creation and destruction are requisite. Remove the shell around the earth? Shatter the very cosmos of the Celestials?'" Some fucking nutball playing wizard dress-up had written down gibberish. That was what I was bringing no questions asked to a rich person?

Were they all insane?

Waste of my goddamn time. I slammed the lid shut and was half tempted to hurl the briefcase onto the porch and book it. But Fingers needed the money, and I needed that stupid bastard.

After I pushed the bell, I expected some Lurch-looking fool to answer. The man was normal-sized but dressed like he had come from a funeral. He didn't ask me anything, just twisted his head to the side.

"I've got this for a…"

"Mr. White. Yes. I shall take it—" He reached for the briefcase, but I balked.

"Eh, I'm gonna need a receipt first. So you don't accuse me of nicking it."

The butler sighed as if I was making his life hell. "Very well. I will…fetch you a paper."

Then he went, leaving the door open. I waited until I heard the creak of his footsteps and eased my way inside. Damn, this place hurt to look at. Every wall, ceiling and piece of stuffy furniture was blindingly white. *Where's the color? It's like living in a hospital in heaven.*

A massive three-story portrait filled the wall of the foyer. In it, a huge horse as white as everything else reared up. Dark storm clouds hung behind with lightning shredding the land, and the seas boiled with lava. Cheery. The banisters were topped by metal horse heads, and sure enough, there were more horse paintings in the next room. *Someone's got a theme.*

"It's not about profit."

My ears twitched, the voice reaching inside my chest and gripping my heart. An exhilarating combination of fear and want boiled inside of me. I was terrified to hear it again but had to know more.

"You're asking a lot. This will take years," a less compelling voice argued.

"Three decades, by my account," the first man responded. I trailed their voices around a corner with a bucking horse statue to a room. The door was open an inch. A fire blazed inside despite it being hot as balls out. As I peered through the gap, I spotted a man in a suit. He looked uncomfortable despite the fancy couch.

"I'll be an old man by then," he said with a laugh.

"I don't believe you'll have to concern yourself with that." Dread. There was no other way to explain the voice. It was an inescapable, ever-consuming personification of dread.

"Why?" the second man asked and the first didn't answer him.

I couldn't see whoever it was inside, but my heart raced. What the hell were they talking about that would take decades? Robbing from little old ladies' pensions?

"Have you made the inroads I requested?"

"The director isn't keen to play ball."

"Then we will find another who shall. It is a dangerous job after all, hunting witches."

Hunting witches? Spells in briefcases? They were all crazier than a sewer rat. None of this made any sense and the sooner I forgot about it, the better.

"What of the spell? Until we have located that, all of our plans will be for nothing."

"Hm. I believe the answer is already here." A shadow moved in front of the tiny gap. I tried to slide away when a beady eye appeared, its iris boiling with lava and lighting.

Fuck. Ducking tight, I hustled back to the front door.

"All we need to do now is flood the world with as much magic as we can." The voice of dread kept talking like it was right beside my ear.

"Then we can talk profits."

"And conquest."

Gasping, I dove back into the foyer just as the butler returned. He glared at me. "What are you doing inside?"

"It's hot as sin out."

He shook his head like that wasn't an answer, then shoved a piece of paper at me. "There. Your receipt. Now, if I may. The master has been waiting for this."

I damn near threw the briefcase at him, wanting it gone. He caught the case and nodded, but as he did, the shadows behind him shifted and two long horns prodded up from his head. *I'm losing my damn mind.*

"Thanks," I said, needing to get out of this weird house. I damn near kicked open the front door and ran across the wide porch for freedom.

"Incidentally, you did not look at the contents, yes?"

"Of course not," I said with a laugh.

The butler snickered, his unnervingly red lips rising. "Of course not, indeed."

The door slammed shut and I bolted upright. Sounds and lights zapped in and out of my consciousness. I clenched over my heart, hot blood dripping from the wound. A hand slipped in under mine and clung tighter to my fingers.

"Daniel?" she whispered and I breathed. *I damn near forgot.*

"Did you see the spell?"

Layla nodded. "Give me that notebook."

I was in the living room, safe, with Layla at my side. Thirty years walloped me in the back of the head. Not just the memories, but isolation and loneliness filled my mind. So too did the pain of my death. I gasped, clutching tighter to my chest while the others crowded around.

"What is that coward using to unravel the creator's hard work?" Garavel asked. He clung tight to the back of Layla's chair and peered over her head.

"Let me guess, Daniel was killed over nothing more than the Horseman's family recipe for olive cake." The damn demon smirked, looking unimpressed by the proceedings.

Layla blew her hair out of her face and wrote like the pen was burning. She only paused for a moment to look over at me, concern in her eyes. I nodded to tell her I was fine, put on a smile then turned away. Death was so much more than the pain of my body failing. Its fingers dug into my brain, freezing apart my soul and shattering the pieces. It had happened every moment when I'd remembered that I wasn't alive.

"I think that's all I saw. All he saw. It was a quick look," she said, then she handed the paper to her mother.

Isabel stared down the writing, then crossed out a word and wrote another over it. Layla did her best to not watch, but she bit her lip as more of her hard work was scratched away. No wonder she hated being called stupid if her mother would correct her like that.

I brushed my cheek against Layla, startling her. "Are you okay?" I whispered.

Her eye sockets were dark after all of this magic, but she put on a smile. "Of course. We need this. It will — "

"This doesn't stop him," her mother pronounced and dropped the notebook to the table with a thud. "It's not even a spell, more academic posturing about the state of the realms."

Garavel reached over and scooped up the notebook. "Let me see."

We all gritted our teeth as he dug in, but Isabel threw her head back in exhaustion and slammed her hands to her eyes. *Did I die for nothing*? I couldn't look at Layla losing her faith in me. Instead, I faced the demon. "Well, let it out."

"Here? With our beloved's mother in the room?" Ink slapped a hand to his chest in fake outrage.

"Go on. Tell her that she wasted her time, her energy, an angel's feather for nothing. That I'm nothing!" I shouted at the incubus who had finally been proven right. I flew out of the chair, hurling it back as I faced off with the demon that could rip my skin from my bones with one pull.

For his part, Ink calmly adjusted his cuffs and peered down at me with an exhausted look. "I was only going to inquire if you'd like seconds of my cinnamon bun nachos."

Like the fuck he was. I whipped around to Layla, prepared to call out Ink for his usual bullshit, but my heart clenched. She'd crumpled in her chair, her body dangling off her shoulders like she was about to fall to the ground. Her skin was gray and dull, her eyelids hung heavy as if she couldn't raise them and she kept nervously tapping her finger against the desk. She looked closer to death than Cal.

Ink saw it all behind me. Was he trying to protect her by being nice? To me?

What the shit is going on with him?

"Ah, I understand now," Garavel pronounced. "This is taken from the Book of the Accords."

"The what?" Layla sat up, looking revived for a moment.

"The Book that was written when the realms were created. When the Accords were struck, all the other species were gifted their own worlds and mages severely punished for their crimes."

"Yes, yes, you hate humans, we know. Get to the point," I pressed.

"I do not hate humans." The big angel pouted before focusing. "This is not conjecture. It is truth. A final piece of the truth. The elemental power that formed the realms required the power of both angel and demon. Nahum and Metatron. Do you not have feasts in their honor?"

"Um." We all looked around, no one having the heart to tell him nobody remembered any of that.

"What does this have to do with White?" Layla asked.

"This explains how a balance of creation and destruction is necessary to create the shield keeping each realm intact."

"So...the same thing could end it?" Layla asked, then she pressed her palm to her forehead. "White said something, something about hunting witches and getting to the director. Oh, fuck."

"What?"

She shot up fast, her eyes wide. "The witch hunters — Raul! Whoa!" Layla's sudden jolt of surprise wracked whatever energy she had left. Both Garavel and I caught her while Ink grumbled.

"The feeble-minded witch hunters will be the cause of their own destruction. Of course."

"We have to, I should contact him and…"

I reached over to take her hand, stopping her from going for her phone. "You're exhausted. You need to sleep."

"The mortal is right," Ink declared. "Whatever help you think the rock can provide will be as available in the morning as it would be now."

Layla nodded without a word causing all of us to panic. She must be in really bad shape. I hooked a hand around her waist and helped her to her feet. The second I got her up, she had to ask, "What about Cal?"

"I will watch over him while also puzzling about this text. There is an inscription at the bottom that is familiar. Did you read any more?" Her mother held up the start of a sentence that I didn't even remember seeing.

It was Layla who shook her head. "No. The rest was covered by his thumb."

Her mom sighed deeply, then shot me a glare. I shook it off, not wanting to get into a witch fight tonight. With an arm around Layla, I helped her up the stairs. Her bed was filled with an injured werewolf being watched over by another one. I guided her toward my little guest room.

As she plopped onto the bed, I scurried around trying to clean it up. "You can sleep here tonight. For as long as you need until Cal's…"

I lived to not care. I died to not care, too. Caring about people had only led to a bullet in my heart. I should think of him as competition, but for a brief moment, having to live without Cal struck me, and I gulped. "Until he's back on his feet," I said, frowning at myself. I didn't like him very much, but I respected him. He had saved Layla with every breath in his body.

She squirmed on the bed, trying to pull off her jeans, but her movements looked so painful, I assisted. Though I wasn't of much help when she slipped her bra out from under her shirt. In just her tank top and panties, she curled up on my bed. I tossed her clothing onto the dresser along with my mess and reached for the light.

"Daniel?" Her soft voice cut through the sudden darkness. "Aren't you going to stay with me?"

"There isn't a lot of room," I said.

The bed's old springs squealed and she patted the side. "I can make some."

Still wearing my jeans, I slipped under the blanket and filled my arms with her. She rested her head against my chest, her breathing slowing almost instantly. For all her bravery and skill, she was as fragile as me. This soft, sweet woman slumbering beside me was as innocent as dawn's birdsong.

Death clenched down my throat until its icy tendrils plunged one by one into my heart. I screamed without sound into her hair, reliving the moment that bullet had shredded my chest.

"I swear to god, Layla. With everything in my power, I will not let you die."

Chapter Fourteen

Layla

"We should take you to a hospital. You're stable. You're awake."

Cal shook his head hard. "No."

"You are as stubborn as a yak in an avalanche," Ink unhelpfully added from the door.

I swept my fingers across his forehead, teasing his hair while staring at the dark patch. "Come on. Your eye."

"Isn't hurting much," he insisted, as he had been since he woke up starving. After he'd downed a dozen eggs and the last of the bacon, I'd been trying to talk Cal out of bed, but he wasn't having it. Despite him insisting he was fine and just needed rest, I couldn't miss the way he winced every time he blinked. The wound was painful and needed proper care, not the kind I could give him.

"What if you lose it?" I insisted, moving to stand up.

Cal took me by the hand. He rubbed both of his thumbs up the palm while staring at me with his good eye. "Then I'll be a pirate," he insisted and pressed my hand against his chest. The steady thump below was the best music I could hope for, but it didn't change the fact that he needed a doctor. The damn future nurse should know that, too.

"You would not last a fortnight on the open seas," Ink said. "Someone would toss a ball and you'd leap right over the gunwale."

Cal laughed, but his voice was strained and he sneered, wrapping a protective arm around his ribs. "You need to work on your bedside manner, Ink."

"My manners on the side of the bed rarely concern me," he countered, though he'd been watching Cal all through the night. Ink had said it was to keep an eye on Mark, but we all knew he wouldn't hurt his brother. Was Ink worried about him, too?

"Sweetheart, come on. We can take my car. It'll be..." I frowned. Saturday at urgent care would take the whole day. But I'd gladly sit in those plastic chairs watching thirteen hours of *Law & Order* if it helped him.

"I'm fine. You don't have to worry."

"He won't move." The dark shadow in the room shifted out of the corner. When I'd woken up to check on Cal, Mark had been sitting there with only a hint of his eyes visible. He hadn't said a word. Didn't even ask for food. Just sat and watched as I'd tried to heal away the scar one last time. "It's a wolf thing. You wouldn't understand."

I crossed my arms. "Enlighten me."

"Why? You're not a wolf, and you never will be...witch."

That selfish prick. I clenched my fist under my arm, wanting to smash it right through Mark's nose. It'd only make everything worse, but I'd at least get to enjoy his surprise.

"He's right," Cal spoke up for his brother. "When we're sick, we're big, furry babies. Hide under the covers of our den, lick our wounds. I just…" He looked past me to the demon propping up the doorframe. "I need time." Then my sly wolf nodded. It wasn't much, but I looked over fast enough to see Ink return it.

"You heard the stubborn canine," Ink jumped in, wrapping his arms around me. "He intends to lick himself clean."

"That isn't what I—" Cal complained, but Ink snickered.

"Best to leave him to it until he is ready to hear reason." Ink pulled me off the bed, but Cal reached over one last time and took my hand.

He gazed up at me, his good eye shining. "I love you."

"I love you, too. So why won't you—?"

Before I could finish, Ink pulled me not just out of the room but into the kitchen. The leap was short through the in-between but my stomach still twitched at the realm travel. I placed my hand over it and glared at him. "What the hell was that for?"

"The wolf requires slumber, something he cannot attain while he is gazing at you in love-addled wonder. I am helping."

"You should be helping me get Cal into the car. Or you take him to the hospital. Get him to see reason!" I couldn't understand why they were all acting like this. Men—obstinate babies in every species.

"He is." Ink sighed and curled his palm over my shoulder. The delicate touch lengthened until he was kneading the worried knot. God, I hadn't realized how badly the stress had built up until Ink was unraveling it. I wanted to curl up against his chest and sleep. Last night wasn't easy thanks to the horrific nightmares. I was sure I had kept Daniel up.

"Ink. He needs — "

"You safe. He nearly ended his existence for such an endeavor. We all would...prefer if you refrain from spiraling down that mortal coil."

"What are you talking about? I'm taking him to a hospital, not a basilisk fighting ring."

He snickered once and collapsed his arms around me. Ink pressed his chin against the top of my head. "My bond. You were in the middle of nowhere, a place no one save you two knew you would be. Yet the wolves found you. Think."

"That resort owner set us up?"

"Think harder," he scolded and I glared at him.

"The reason they found Calvin, the reason that the red menace had an anti-demon ward on him was because — "

"White's tracking you." My mother breezed into the kitchen. She locked eyes with Ink as I tried to wiggle out of his tight embrace.

"What do you mean? Conquest can't..." I gulped and looked at Ink. "A demon ward? Is that why you couldn't help?"

Ink parted his hands and shrugged.

"Fuck. And I was... I'm so sorry. I shouldn't have blamed you. Yelled at you."

"My bond, you were distraught, an emotion that seems to wrack humans. Guilt after the fact will only compound the problem. Release it."

I should have known. Ink would have never served me up like that. He'd be there fighting to save me to save himself. "Why didn't I look for it? I could have removed it."

"How? Your magic was taken."

"With a knife." Break the circle, break the magic. Ink smiled at me with pride, my incubus always encouraging my bloodlust. I reached to hold him tight, trying to apologize again, when my mother's comment hit. "How is Conquest tracking me?"

"There are numerous ways," my mother said, "but at a guess, your blood. I imagine he's had plenty of opportunities to take a drop here or there."

"Shit. Shit, shit, shit. What do I do? Is it safe here?"

"If it weren't, he would not have waited until you were away from this house. He is not powerful enough to risk an attack with all of us gathered together," Ink said with gritted teeth.

"So, what do we do? How do I...? Is that why Cal won't go to the hospital? Does he think they'll —"

"Attempt to abduct you as you wait for him in the lounge of grief and burned coffee? Naturally," Ink said.

I bit my lip, trying to swallow every damn curse I knew. Not because my mom was there, but because I was afraid if I let them out, I'd blow a hole in the wall. "What do I do? I can't go into hiding. You guys can't keep holed up here forever."

"I dare say we'd probably crack each other's skulls open in under ten days if we were confined together," Ink admitted. He was being generous with the ten days.

"Where's my spell book? There's got to be something to counteract a tracking spell." Damn it, I had left it with Daniel again. I needed to stop doing that.

I moved to race up the stairs when I caught my mom staring at me. Fuck, it was learning fractions all over again. She'd stare over my shoulder, watching me do it. If I got something wrong, she'd make that face until I figured it out.

"What is it?" I asked, ripping apart years of weird parental issues.

My mom blinked in surprise. "Blood is a powerful tool. It contains all that makes us who we are."

"Yes, Mom, I know about DNA."

"Then you also know that, with it, a powerful-enough spell caster could control you, harm you, perhaps even kill you?"

"Uh..." I looked over at Ink, wishing Daniel or Garavel were here. They knew about magic shit. They could help.

"Lucky for you, I do know a spell that can counter it...in a way." My mom tugged out her spell book and laid it on the counter. The pages fell open as if it could read her mind.

"What is it?" I asked.

"You will become invisible."

I barked a laugh at the stupid idea. *Can't find me if I'm invisible. Take that, undying personification of humanity's greed!* My mom kept giving me that look and I swallowed. "I know the invisible spell, but I can't keep that up forever."

"It isn't literal. You will remain corporeal, but to everyone else, you will cease to exist. Their eyes will slide past you, their ears not hear you. To the world, you will be invisible."

"So it's become a batshit recluse or fight off White's minions in the grocery store?" I could barely wrap my mind around the idea when I looked over at Ink. "No. What about them? My guys. If they can't see me then…" I wrapped my hand around Ink's, our fingers interlocking. He needed me to eat or else he'd wither away without dying. Daniel was still struggling with what it meant to be alive again. Garavel needed me to be his rock. Raul could turn on all of them if I up and disappeared. And Cal… We were gonna get married. He couldn't stand at that altar alone.

Having to go without their touch for weeks, or months, or…would we ever defeat Conquest?

"Stop being so dramatic, Laylee," my mother chastised. "You can easily grant vision to whoever you wish to see you. But do it sparingly. We have no idea who is working with Conquest. His spies are everywhere."

"That doesn't seem so bad." At least I wouldn't have to worry about going mad with loneliness. My mother pulled a pot out of a cabinet and dug into the spice drawer.

"With that handled," Ink declared, "I shall take Calvin to the barber's for medicine."

I flinched, partially fearing he might dump him at a hair salon. Ink stood taller as if preparing himself, and I reached over to catch his hand. He peered over at me in surprise. A part of me didn't want him to leave me alone with my mother, but Cal needed him far more than I did.

I settled on, "Thank you."

"My bond." Ink smiled warmly and drew his palm against my cheek. "The sooner you cease fretting about the mutt, the sooner I can ravish you in bed." With that, he took a step to the side.

A scuffle broke out on the floor above. I couldn't make out much beyond the occasional shout of "Hey!" Heavy feet hit the floorboards, then the sound vanished. No doubt that was Mark fighting against Ink trying to help his brother. Sure enough, I heard the loud clomp of combat boots down the stairs. The front door was flung open without anyone closing it.

Heat burned down my neck and I turned, catching my mom staring. She'd paused in dumping whatever she needed into the pot. "You're still letting the demon eat from you?"

"Yeah?" *So I have sex with an incubus…a lot. What of it, Mom?*

"And the werewolf, the angel, you sleep with them as well?"

Some daughters could probably talk about their sex lives with their moms without wishing for the pit of hell to open up under them. I was not one of them. Rubbing my shoulder, I stared at the door, wishing Daniel or Garavel would come running inside. "What of it?"

"Do you love them?"

It wasn't the same accusing tone she'd used when I mentioned my wedding. Instead, it was full of pain and concern. I closed my eyes tight, trying to shake off the memory of Cal—bloodied and broken—just before Eric had sliced his face. After taking a deep breath, I said, "Daniel, too."

"And the elf?"

Raul? I curdled my face, wanting to vehemently shake my head. He cared for me as much as I cared for him. Enough for him to show up to save Cal's life. "I don't know," I confessed.

My mom set the burner to high and calmly dumped in all of the ground sage. Only the hiss of the water filled the air. I was tempted to leave her to it, maybe find Fiona or ask Daniel how he slept.

"Didi's scar. Did she ever tell you how she got it?"

I wasn't expecting that. "Uh, no. I didn't... You told me not to ask."

She grimaced and banged the spoon against the pot. "I wasn't much older than you were. Not even a year into it when I joined what I thought was to be the greatest coven in the world. Ten of the strongest witches with the longest lines. Some of them stretched back to damn near the first. All killed. All except for Didi."

"Because you went after White?"

"We thought we were unstoppable. That we'd bring about a revolution. Save this world from pain, famine, greed and death. We were fools, storming his stronghold, thinking nothing of what we'd face. It was a slaughter."

The few times I'd faced off against White, I'd been pants-wettingly terrified. I'd only escaped by the skin of my teeth, and—I feared—because he let me.

"If we'd been smart, we'd have known that you cannot kill an idea. As your lust can never truly die, neither will greed, pride nor conquest. He is eternal."

"So how do we stop him?" This unstoppable killing machine wanted me dead? How was I supposed to ever sleep?

My mom whispered into the pot, then she looked back at me. "It needs a few minutes to simmer. Didi's scar was a reminder of the graver cut done to her because of me."

"Mom?"

"Witches need to preserve the line with a daughter. She walked into that den with her future in her womb and limped out empty."

Christ. Auntie Didi had never said anything about losing a baby. Of course, I was nine and I'd barely learned what a penis was, so I wouldn't have been the best counsel. "But she could have had another?"

My mom pressed her lips. "It doesn't work that way for witches. You get one chance. Thanks to the magic, the first one is strong and teeming to enter the world, but…they can die just as easily as any baby. You could have died…" Her eyes teared up and she clutched tight to her arms, nails digging in.

"So you left me." *To keep me safe, to keep the line safe.*

"Laylee, this universe is a mess. The magic is wild, untethered, with only one conduit to control it — us. Each time a witch dies, or her line runs out, the magic has nowhere to go. It feeds back, splintering the seal and letting the worst of creation in."

I nodded grimly, hating to accept what made sense. Angels didn't let witches keep access to magic for shits and giggles. We were to be the guardians, the wardens of this world without end. *Thanks for that.*

Turning her back on me, my mom faced the pot. "But that isn't why I left you. It's why I left your father."

"Mom?"

"Love is dangerous, not because it makes us vulnerable. If a witch loses her daughter, if the worst out there comes for her, everything is gone and the world becomes a deadlier place for the next one. You damn near learned that the hard way."

"So we're back to this. You think I shouldn't marry Cal because of some future child..."

"I think—" My mom wielded the ladle like a sword, then she softened. "I think you need to be protected by more than what those bumbling fools can provide."

"What does that mean?"

"Drink this." I accepted the ladle but stared down at the off-green liquid sloshing inside.

Was she going to force me into some witch witness protection plan? Knock me out, stuff me in her car and I'd wake up in another state away? Could I trust my own mother?

"Where was I?" I asked.

"What?"

"You told me witches get knocked up when they're twenty-five, but you said you took on Conquest a few years older than me now."

My mom swallowed hard and nodded. "You were left with a babysitter, unaware of what I was. Or what could happen."

I had nearly become an orphan then and there. At best one or two years old, never knowing my mom or my dad, left behind with some random lady who had answered an ad. All because my mom had to be a hero and take on the big baddie by herself.

How many other daughters didn't see their mothers after that night? How many grew up never knowing what they had lost?

I threw back the potion and tried to keep from retching. It tasted like the time Ink had done the laundry in the same pot as dinner. For a beat, my skin tingled from my forehead to my toes. I stared at my hand, expecting it to go transparent, but there were my fingers and the bruises from the werewolves.

"I don't think it worked," I said, tossing the ladle back into the pot. My mom wasn't looking at me.

"Layla?"

"Maybe you missed an ingredient. Or Garavel switched around the spices." I couldn't be certain, but I suspected Ink was the one to talk him into dumping all the spices into one big pile then pouring them back into random containers.

My mom looked around the room, then she tugged on the pot and finally her book. "Layla? Are you still here?"

"Where else would I...? Oh. Holy shit, it worked. Can you hear me? Mom?"

My voice sounded no different to my ear, bouncing off the tiny kitchen walls, but my mother looked like she was in a near panic. She kept flipping the pages of her book back and forth, cursing at it.

I'd never seen her so frazzled. It wasn't that I didn't think she ever got stressed—she just kept me away from it. If things got bad, and they always did, she'd call for Didi to take me away. My mom was a rock, a statue, a gargoyle standing up against evil. Now, she was a human in a panic about losing her only daughter.

"Mom, I'm so angry at what you did. You could have told me you were leaving. Contacted me, helped me through this witch shit. I thought puberty in a trailer was rough. Having to share a bathroom with two thirteen-year-old boys was nothing on facing scroungers."

I pressed my ass tighter to the counter, the pressure proving I was alive. My mom kept hunting for me.

"I missed you and…I love you. I just wish you'd…" I sighed. "I wish you'd understand that I love them, too. Let my mother see me," I said.

Like flipping a switch, my mom's panicking eyes focused on my hand. Her gaze traveled up my arm before landing on my face. "Laylee," she damn near squealed in relief, before the storm set in. "What the hell were you playing at? Why'd you take so long?"

"I…I wasn't certain how to make myself visible."

She nodded as if my stupidity made more sense than me not wanting her to see me. "You're going to have to do that to every person you interact with going forward."

"Until when? Until I die?"

"Or you counteract the spell. It's relatively easy. Here." She pointed to her book that I couldn't read. As I stared at her, my mom blushed at her fumble. "It'll be in your spell book, too."

Duh. I should have known that. "Is the antidote to the witch hunter poison in here? Do I have it?"

My mother didn't answer right away. She dumped the potion down the sink. Hopefully, it wouldn't get into the city water. "Possibly," she said, suddenly clamming up. *What the hell's that mean?* "I suppose this means the wedding is off the table."

"What? Why?"

She closed her book shut and sighed. "Do you not see the danger you put them in? How close they come to death while you are being hunted? It would be best to let them go, remain vanished until they move on and forget you. If you'll excuse me, I'm going to keep studying this ancient Accord spell to try and save the world. Real work instead of silly frippery about veils and flowers."

167

What the fuck? Did she do all of this just to keep me from Cal? I wanted to throw her out of the house, out of my life. I raised my hands, my fingers invisible to anyone who didn't get the special blessing. The beautiful amethyst Cal gave me was bent, the gem leaning inward from the grip of the werewolves that had nearly killed him.

As I tried to straighten it out, the prong nicked my skin. A drop of blood dripped around my ring finger.

Chapter Fifteen

Cal

"Shame I'm only going to have to wear this for a month." I adjusted the eye patch, doing my best to avoid the eyebrow gash the clinic had butterflied up. Layla had worked too hard to heal away the rest of my hits, leaving me looking fine if not dangerous.

"If you'd like, I could stab your other eye," Ink offered, extending a claw.

"I'm good. Have you seen Layla? I want to give her the good news." Taking one last look at myself in the mirror, I turned to face the demon.

Ink propped himself up on my bed, one hand aimlessly picking at the comforter. "When last I was in her presence, she was collaborating with her mother."

My happy smile dimmed. "You left her with her mom? Is that smart?"

"Already on the outs with your future mother-in-law?"

"That's not it. I just… I don't trust her. And I worry she's going to hurt Layla again."

With a belabored sigh, Ink twisted off the bed like he was about to fall, then he spun and landed on his feet better than Fiona. Wiping down his shirt, he stared at me. "Yet you never concern yourself with the hurt you could cause her."

"What?"

"Once again you place your neck on the chopping block as if it will not split her heart in half when the ax falls."

I turned away from him, not needing the demon's nonsense or his sense. "That isn't what happened. I was biding my time until you showed up. What's the point of being in a pack if…?"

Shit.

The demon's ears perked up, his eyes shining bright. "You think us a pack? The wandering spirit, the fatherless angel, the debonair and daring incubus and the broken werewolf. At last, the tiles align to reveal the full picture."

"It's a slip of the tongue."

"I always found them to be more a slip of the foot, especially when in the bathhouses."

Moon take me, I had too deep of a headache to deal with Ink. "Can I trust you to have my back?"

"Provided the enemy does not employ a ward to keep me a hundred feet away from said back, I suppose so. Assuming I am not attempting to swipe a starcraft from Emperor Merino." The witch hunters were trying too hard. All they needed to stop a demon was a copy of Sheep Wars.

Ink wandered out of the room as if he was tired of being in it, but paused at the door. "So you intend to continue with the wedding despite the imminent threat?"

"Eric's dead. One less danger to both of us."

"My concern lies more in the ancient personification of conquest who's taken an unnatural interest in my bond. Would it maim him to not buy her dinner at the very least?"

I mentally boxed away Conquest and his minions—none of that mattered right now. "I love her. I want to marry her. Whether it happens once we finish off the damn Horseman or..." *Fuck.*

Ink homed in on the 'or' right away, his brows peaking. "There is a secret wedged upon your tongue, wolf. Shall I try to pry it free?"

She was right—planning a wedding in three months was lunacy. We should put on the brakes and take our time. Let all of us get used to Daniel being physical before changing the dynamic again. It made the most sense, but the logic part of my brain melted at the idea of Layla in a white dress standing below that rose window.

"I'm gonna marry her, end of story."

"Strange how often the wedding is the end as if the love affair expires the moment the vows are made." Ink smirked at his jab and sauntered away. I shouldn't have expected the sin of lust to get it. Love was counter to his very existence, after all.

I took one last look at myself in the mirror, then shouted out through the doorway, "The next time you whisk me off to the hospital, will you let me put some damn pants on?"

"No."

As I changed out of the indecent gown to proper jeans and a tee, my bedroom door pushed open a touch.

I lifted my head, trying to smell whoever had moved it. Usually, I got a strong whiff of cat, Fiona enjoying my bed for her mid-afternoon naps, but there was nothing. No, it was odder, a lack of scent, as if a black hole moved through the room.

The hair on the back of my neck stood on end not out of fear but confusion. Every heightened sense told me I was alone, but my heart pounded faster like it knew someone I wanted was here. I closed my eyes and reached a hand out, expecting to feel a warm body, when the stairs creaked. "Claw? You here?"

I jerked at the sound of my brother. "Yeah," I shouted back and finished my hair.

"Doesn't matter how much you mess with it, you'll always be ugly."

I stuck my tongue out at him through the mirror and he laughed. Like he owned the place, Mark prodded into my stack of books on the dresser. He read over one of the anatomy ones.

"Thanks for saving my ass."

"It's what I do, protect my baby brother at all costs."

I was imagining the accusation that I had failed to protect Eli. At least I hoped I was. "The pack's still out there."

Mark answered with a shrug.

"You aren't worried they're gonna pick a new alpha and come after you?"

He slammed the book shut and stared at me. "No."

I was up and vertical. This couldn't wait any longer. "I'm glad you're here."

"'Cause otherwise you'd be kibble? Fuck Eric. He deserved a slower death. I dreamed of trapping him in a bear pit slowly starving to death while his legs went gangrenous."

Eric was why Mark's leg had never healed right. He'd done far worse to all of us, even Eli. It was a plus for the world that Mar had ripped out his throat.

Taking a deep breath, I faced my brother. "I'm getting married," I announced.

Mark didn't look at me.

"We don't have the full details worked out, but I was hoping you'd be my best man."

I expected a laugh, for Mark to slug me on the shoulder. Maybe even for him to taunt me about a bachelor party or the old ball and chain. I never anticipated him to stare up at me from below his wide brow and growl.

"Are you out of your fucking mind? I told you to stay away from that witch. The greenskin nearly got you killed."

"Eric's the one that tried to kill me. Layla" — I shouted her name at him, expecting some respect for my fiancée — "saved my life."

"She was a whimpering puddle when I showed up." Mark snarled, picked up one of my textbooks then slammed it to the ground. "Fucking hell, Claw. You're getting your life together. You're gonna be a nurse. Why are you throwing it away on a moon-damned witch?"

"Because I love her."

"You love… You can find anyone else. Someone that isn't being hunted, someone who won't get you killed! Stay the fuck away from her. That's an order."

An order? I snarled at him, my muscles rippling in anticipation of a shift my body couldn't handle. Mark answered in kind like we were kids about to tear each other to pieces over a scrap of food. "You can't order me around."

"Because you think they'll save you? The demon? The angel? The witch? You think they won't leave you to die the second it's their ass on the line?"

I lunged, the wolf in me wanting to clench around his throat and spin onto my back. The human settled for gripping onto the collar of his jacket and hauling him closer. Mark was always pissed about the few inches I had on him. His eyes blazed as I pulled him onto his tiptoes. Staring him down, I ordered, "Get the fuck out of my house."

His knee bent like my order clanged through his blood, but he shook it off and smashed into my arms. I let go, too exhausted to fight him. "She's going to get you killed. Use your goddamn brain for once, Claw."

"I am."

"No, you're thinking with your dick. Fuck her. Use her, then get the hell away. She's dangerous."

I snorted, clenching my fists. "No, she's my mate."

Mark answered with a derisive laugh. "You're...? That shit ain't real."

"I love her."

"You used to love licking peanut butter off your hand too."

I closed my eyes, unable to look at him. "I cannot live without her. She's my light when the darkness creeps in. My center when the whole world spins. I need her more than air." Taking a deep breath, I stared Mark down. "And I'm going to marry her. I'm asking you to be my brother and stand beside me on the happiest day of my life."

He shook his head. "No. No, you're...you're gonna get yourself killed. I can't be a part of this." Mark flung my offered hand away. He marched down the hall, every step a slam against me. All the while he kept shouting "No" and "You're going to regret this."

I didn't move, listening to the front door open and slam. Rage percolated under the wolf's skin—he was our kin, he should support us—but inside my heart broke. My last brother couldn't get over his own damn prejudice for me. I glanced at a picture on the wall, one of the three of us posing in front of a huge rock. Mark and I had tried to climb it while Eli had begged us to not get hurt. I couldn't remember who was the first to reach the top, but no matter how much we fought, we always made up in the end.

"Cal?"

Holy…! I leaped in the air, my heart racing. As I landed, I swung wide-eyed to find Layla standing next to our closet. "Wow. You snuck up on a werewolf, that's…impressive."

She smiled sadly and my heart lurched. Had she heard Mark's shouting? He was an ass with a bullhorn for a mouth. Of course she had. "Babe…" I reached for her, my arms outstretched.

Maybe it was the patch cutting off my depth perception, but it seemed like for a second Layla hesitated. Just as I was about to drop my arms, she leaped for me, crashing my ass into the vanity and tipping the mirror. Holy hell, my heart pounded hard with her against my chest—like I had run five miles on my paws.

I didn't know why my body was acting like we had just survived a fight that didn't happen, but I clung tighter to her and breathed in her scent. How did I not notice it before? The longer I was with her, the more she smelled like safety, hope, love. And often three other men, but that felt like home, too.

"I'm sorry about Mark, he's... He's a stubborn son of a bastard."

Layla didn't answer me, her fingers pressing harder into my back as she buried her face against my chest.

"Good news, I won't lose my eye. Though I'll be this roguish scoundrel for a few weeks, so I hope you're into pirates."

"I've been thinking," Layla said in a tone that should have come with a bass drop. "About the wedding, about you almost...about you getting hurt."

"It's not that bad. I feel right as rain now. What does that mean? Can you be left as rain?" I didn't want to hear what she'd been working herself up to say, so I kept talking. "Eric's dead. It wasn't easy, sure, but we knew it wouldn't be. What matters is that the Horseman's lost his champion. He's on the ropes and soon we'll take him down. So...we can celebrate?"

"I keep going over how I almost lost you. I watched that..." Layla shut her eyes tight, her lips fluctuating as if she couldn't speak the horrors. "How he split open your face." She swept her hands around my cheeks, barely touching my skin.

"It could have been worse," I said to assure her, but she shuddered and I realized what the worse was. *Damn it.*

"I keep thinking that we'll survive this megalomaniac's plan. We can't really get hurt. We'll all walk away unharmed, happy, alive. It's the dreams of a naïve idiot."

The disappointment tried to whimper in my throat, but I swallowed it down. Instead, I pretended to push back a fallen hair just so I could trace her face. "Babe, I..." Fuck, Eric's punches had hurt less than this. "I understand."

"Let's do it."

I blinked, shaking off my fake smile. "What?"

Layla hooked her hands around the back of my neck and pulled herself higher. Moon take me, but I could swim in her gorgeous brown eyes. "We could all die tomorrow, or in six months or a year. All I know is I don't want to face Conquest with regrets on my head. Let's get married in three months."

"Yes!" I cried, then jerked back. "Are you sure? Ninety days is—"

"I don't care." She sounded near tears, her eyes shining. "I know it's stupid, and we're gonna go mad from stress, but I love you and I want us to be together forever."

Cinching my arms tight around her waist, I plucked Layla clean off her feet. "Yahoo!" I shouted, not spinning her around but slightly swaying back and forth. She laughed and I kissed her.

I kissed her for today, for tomorrow, for next year, forever.

"I love you," I told her over and over as I kept kissing her. She started to giggle from my madness before her roving fingers snagged on the eye patch's elastic. Her smile didn't fully drop to a frown, but she turned contemplative, and I placed her back on her feet.

Layla pulled me to her, forehead to forehead. "Whatever happens, whoever comes for us, promise me... Swear that you'll make it. That you'll stay alive. Do you promise, Cal? Please."

Curling around her, wishing my body could be her shield, I closed my good eye and whispered, "I do."

Chapter Sixteen

Layla
Two months later, three weeks to the Big Day

Dragging my tongue across the glue strip, I stared at the clean desk and breathed a sigh of relief. "There," I declared, dropping the last of the invitations onto the pile. Three stacks loomed around us like a city about to fall.

Cal finished writing out the address with one of my casting Sharpies. I tried to shift my leg in anticipation of breaking free when a pair of sad puppy eyes landed on me. "Babe?" was all he said as he hefted up a box. Purple and white cardboard rained down across the table. I slumped into the chair and groaned.

"How are there so many?" I whined, tapping my fingers in exhaustion. I lost all feeling in the tips if I stopped.

"Because we're inviting that many to our wedding," Cal said with a soft laugh. He was enjoying this far too much. I glared at him and he winked. His eye was so much better, only having issues in low light, but the scar remained. It folded in half from his huge grin, and he returned to the addresses his mom had sent us.

I fanned the invitations out in front of me and flexed my hand. "Why can't we send them an email instead?" I closed my eyes.

It left me vulnerable to the hand that clamped onto the back of my chair. I yelped just as Cal pulled me into his lap. He brushed back my mess of hair to plant his chin on my shoulder. "Do you need a little incentivizing?" With his panting breath on my cheek, Cal swept a palm over my belly and pulled my ass back until I knocked against his cock.

"That's only going to wear me out, not wake me up." I groaned at having to do the adult thing. Focusing, I whispered the incantation across the invitations. Anyone who received one would be able to see not only me but the venue. Hiding the resort was my mother's idea. She wasn't happy about the wedding going forward, but at least she wasn't threatening to kidnap my groom to stop it.

The spell was simple, but each time it drained me. Giving one person the right to see me was easy — gifting it to a hundred was worse than Ink in a banana split bikini. I reached for my mug of coffee and lifted one CC of caffeine.

Cal caught on. "Need more?"

I shook my head. There wasn't time. There wasn't time for me to complain either. "These should have gone out...months ago."

"Blame Iowa," he said. They'd been stuck in shipping hell for days to the point we were freaking out that they wouldn't get here.

"We should have upgraded," I said, even though we were already scraping the bottom of the bank to buy these. Nothing frilly, no fancy tissue paper, no cutouts. Just a single piece of nice cardstock with some printed purple flowers. We were doing the best with what we had.

"You know, we could take a break." Cal pulled aside the tight neck of my sweater to place a kiss, but when his lips touched, he kept going until he nipped against my tender skin. I leaped in surprise at the force, my heart beating faster. He nuzzled lower, his paws finding their way under my sweater.

One day off from wedding shit would be wonderful. It'd been a constant headache since we had set the date. The second I had locked in that I was a bride, a billion things I never gave a shit about before needed a decision. Flowers, dresses, food — that made sense. But the size of candles? Tiny candy almonds in organza bags? White plastic carpets for people to walk on? An official wedding monogram? The only reason I hadn't gone mad was the help.

"Here." A hand grabbed mine, then pressed a cold energy drink into my palm. My survival instinct cupped it and raised it to my lips before I nodded my thanks to Ink. He crossed his arms and stared down at the mess of stationery. "The wolf is draining you to your last drop."

"Jealous?" Cal asked with a laugh.

Ink pushed two of the invitations around with his pinkie. "All for a morose party in the forest."

"Weddings aren't morose."

"Of course they are. A wedding is naught but a funeral for your sexual freedom. You gather at a church, speak the sacred texts, cry tears for the loss then congeal over cold meats and drab speeches by men you barely speak to. They are the same."

I ignored my whining incubus and stared into Cal's eyes. "Do you know any funerals that end in hot naughty sex?"

"Depends upon the proclivities of the widow." Ink smirked, proud of his joke, but I bit my lip. He'd been MIA a lot lately. If I called him, or if I had a slightly elevated heart rate, he'd be there — either to disembowel or disrobe. But I didn't find him as often. He wasn't sitting in the living room watching infomercials at all hours of the night. He hadn't even swiped my phone in weeks. It held a charge longer than a day.

As if to prove my point, he turned to leave, but I reached over to take his hand. "Hey? Are you — ?"

"I have crafted the perfect floral arrangement for your joining!" Garavel cried. He ran into the room extending a crown woven out of yellow flowers and leaves. "A multitude of these were across the green spaces near us."

"That's because they're dandelions," Cal said diplomatically.

"Ah, a lion is an auspicious token to have before a battle," Garavel declared and dropped the crown on Cal's head.

No matter how many times I tried to explain it, Garavel kept falling back on his battle metaphors. What was he going to do if…when we defeated Conquest? I had never found the nerve to ask him exactly what oath he had sworn to me. I just knew I didn't want to lose him. Any of them.

"All we need is — "

"Son of a bitch!"

I smiled at the familiar crash of the front door and the heavy clomp of boots. Daniel was hunched over, his left side bowing from the case in his hand as he stomped past. He swiped back his longer hair and turned. The frown didn't vanish until he spotted me and a soft smile rose in its place.

"Problems?" I called to him.

"No. I was…" Daniel walked toward the dining room, then paused and stared at the other men. "I finished the lesson early. For my sanity's sake and their health."

I winced, uncertain of what to say. It'd been Daniel's idea to make a little money on the side teaching kids piano and guitar. He also came home wanting to smash an amp after every one. This wasn't a permanent solution, but it gave him a chance to play. We'd been worried that Conquest would come after him, but it seemed like the Horseman had ceased caring. Once the secret had been revealed, it was as if Daniel didn't matter.

At least it kept him safe.

"What are you up to?" Daniel asked before he caught the invite pile. "Ah. Wedding shit." Then he looked at the dandelion crown on Cal's head. "Weeding shit too. I'll be in my room if you need me."

I almost reached for him to help with the invitations, or just to sit and talk, but the other guys took up a lot of space and Daniel seemed to prefer the quiet. He jerked his head once, inviting me to follow, but I had to say no. These invitations had to go out tomorrow or no one was coming to the wedding. With a sigh, Daniel patted his bass and turned for the stairs.

"Calvin, I understand the limitations of a paw, but your handwriting is abominable." Ink rifled through the finished envelopes just waiting for stamps. Which I was supposed to get. *Fuck.*

Cal yanked out a blank one, then handed Ink the pen. "I'd like to see you do better."

Ink snickered. "You are attempting to chip away at my ego to trick me into doing your chore." Even as he said that he bent over and—with a quick flourish—wrote out the next address. We all gawped at the stunning calligraphy.

"That's beautiful," I said, causing Ink to shrug. "People'd pay like thousands of dollars for that."

"Yes, people are often offering up trinkets and coins for my services." He sounded unimpressed but his eyes shone with pride.

"Would you consider...?" I extended the second list toward him and Ink sighed.

I expected him to roll his eyes or vanish, but he took the paper. "At least find me a proper quill. This tip is far too plump to be of any use. A bit like your *pen*, wolf."

Cal snorted, but he didn't bite back. If Ink was willing to help, we'd both take it. While Cal sat down with the stack, Ink stood beside him. He groaned about having to use yet another goose feather but set to work addressing all the envelopes I'd sealed. Taking a deep slug of the energy drink, I cast more spells over the invitations themselves.

Garavel picked one up as it finished shimmering to read, "*Cum hac invitatione tibi concedo aditum ad nuptias?*"

"Just a little spell to invite people to the wedding," I explained.

"This is a powerful artifact," Garavel whispered, holding the cheap paper reverently in his hands. "A written witch's spell must be guarded at all costs."

"Most of these are probably gonna wind up in a dumpster." I didn't know more than a quarter of the people we'd invited, and those were in our class. The bulk was made up of Cal's family — a whole lot of werewolves about to be invited to a witch's wedding.

Nope. I didn't have time to think about that.

"My lady?" Garavel looked at me and he took my hand. "I shall protect it with my life."

"Cool." I reached over to gather up the next round to stuff them into envelopes when my phone buzzed. Twisting the screen around I read the single text. "Crap. I've got to go."

"Where?" Cal asked.

I slotted my spell book into my purse and picked up my light jacket from my chair. "War meeting," I said, checking the phone once more.

"Oh. Well, have fun doing war…things," Cal muttered.

Ink snidely whispered to himself, "Well executed."

I kissed Cal. "I'll be back soon. And I'll get stamps."

"We don't have stamps?" He hunted through the boxes that I knew were empty. I had no idea how I was going to afford the stamps for a hundred and fifty invitations, but that was what credit was for.

I gave a quick peck to Garavel's cheek and he burned hot, then blushed. "Be well, my lady."

"Ink?"

He didn't look up, just kept writing out the names as if he was cursed to do it. I tried to ease closer when my phone beeped again. "Damn, I've got to go. Dinner?"

"We'll think of something," Cal called to me.

I got a bunch of waves from everyone except my gloomy demon.

* * * *

"Are you even listening?" the smug asshole asked.

I began to roll my eyes when Raul fisted my hair and pulled my head back. His eyes burned like emerald fire and he kissed me. I expected him to back off and repeat himself, but Raul kept pushing me not onto the hotel bed but the dresser. My ass bounced off the edge and I gasped, my panties failing to keep away the chill.

"Why's it so god damn cold in here?" I could nearly see my breath in the air.

Raul broke away from my lips while keeping a hold of my hair. The scars across his bare chest glowed like a firefly. "Because." He punctuated that statement with a snort that puffed from his nose like a bucking bull. I lifted my feet, caressing them up his legs. His eyes rolled back and his mouth parted as I teased his inner thigh.

"That's not an answer," I said.

He jerked and gripped both of my legs. I expected him to tug my feet up, but he yanked me off the dresser and spun me around. A dingy mirror reflected the elf rolling his hands over my hips to pull me into place. Raul began to wind his fingers around the straps of my panties, tugging the band to the point of no return.

"Because," he snarled, nipping my shoulder. "The agency." Raul hefted me by my panties, raising my hips until his cock grazed my covered buttocks. "Uses." A soft plink told me I had lost yet another pair of underwear. I didn't have much time to mourn them as Raul scraped his nails down my spine.

I arched my back, lost in the flush of sensations flooding my body. A hard slap struck my ass and I gulped. He hooked onto my thighs, lifting my legs off the ground. I slammed my hands to the dresser so I wouldn't fall, and he thrust inside of me.

"Heat signatures." Raul groaned as he entered me.

"What?" I cried out, chipping plywood off the cheap dresser.

He sank his cock straight to the base, his balls swinging up to slap against me. Thrusting hard, Raul pressed his thighs into my ass, spearing me higher. I started to rise, getting a sense of balance, when he shoved on my back. My cheek hit the cold dresser and I yelped.

"Do you ever listen?" he argued, his voice flustered as he kept drilling me harder than before.

"It's hard to pay attention when there's a dick in me," I fought back.

"Excuses."

I reached my hand around and plunged my nails into his bobbing ass cheek. "How well do you remember Latin with a cock in your ass?"

Raul grumbled and the wall shook. I turned my head and the cheap plaster shattered. Two vines ripped through the hole and latched around my wrist. I tried to pull, but they sucked back into the wall, stretching my arms out in front of me.

"Sensitive subject?"

He bent over me, slipping most of his cock free. Heat burst down my ear, but he didn't say anything, just kept breathing heavy while the vines tightened. "I could tie you up until you can't move."

"You can try," I countered, tossing my head back and forth but unable to catch his eye.

Raul drew his palm down my back, sweeping it back and forth. Vines sprouted from my wrist shackles and wrapped twice around my chest. They met in the middle and braided together before shooting up my cleavage and back over the top of my breasts.

"Is that all you've got?" I asked. A bit of fire'd get me out of this.

His hand drifted off my back and I couldn't hear anything. I tossed my head around trying to see him before I looked in the mirror. He watched me through it while stroking his palm up and down his shaft.

Raul raised his chin and smiled. "No." Four more holes burst through the wall. The vines circled my waist and flipped me around to face him. At least the ones on my arms slackened enough I didn't dislocate a shoulder. The second they let up, I tried to rip the vines apart to prove my point, but he beat me to the punch. Two of the new vines curled around my upper thighs then snagged onto my wrists, pinning them right against my belly.

The tips of my fingers dangled just above my vulva. I fluttered them, drawing Raul right to it. He groaned and the vines wrapped faster. The other two worked on my legs, of course, binding down my calves and ankles until I couldn't move them an inch. He raised his hand and my legs spread apart. My bound ass slid down the dresser.

"Well?" he challenged me.

Fuck. I was teetering, unable to shift my legs to catch myself. The vines were the only thing keeping me from falling onto my face and my legs cried out. They weren't used to this kind of punishment.

"Well…?" I stared defiantly into his eyes even as I kept sinking to my knees. "Are you gonna fuck me or what?"

Raul laughed and he dove just as I fell onto his cock. Bound and helpless, I landed on his lap. He thrust harder, watching my breasts jiggle between the vine's harness.

"I thought you were a feet man," I taunted.

He stared hard at me and growled. "You don't know me."

"More than anyone else…oh, fuck!"

He leaned forward enough to lap his tongue over my nipple. The vines tightened, hefting my breast higher. He sucked on it. Raul kept spreading my legs farther, stretching me to the breaking point. I pulled back, trying to rip free, but there were too many. The force kept prying on my legs until I was damn near doing a split on his dick.

Raul clutched the mess of foliage circling my spine. He dug his knuckles into my back and thrust harder than ever. All the while, he stared me in the eye, daring me to challenge him.

I groaned loud, and he broke eye contact to find I was able to swirl my finger over my clit. He let loose a growl that rumbled up my chest. "Did I say you could touch yourself?"

"Try and stop me," I taunted in his ear.

Rather than pry my arm off, which he could easily do, Raul pulled me back by the vines, then reached between my legs. We battled for my clit while daring the other to stop. He bucked, his breath catching and lip rising in a sneer that told me he was close.

"Give it up. You'll never win," I said.

"You're struggling yourself there, witch."

"Only because...be...fuck." I lost control. I was fucking a man who'd bound me in plants on the floor of a cheap motel. My brain had been fighting my body, but staring at Raul not as a competitor but a hot man under me, my body seized the moment.

I tipped my head back and screamed. All the build-up, the foreplay, the angry sex slammed together into a back-breaking orgasm. If anyone was listening, it probably sounded like I was being murdered. It was a long, unbroken scream from the bottom of my lungs.

Raul didn't stop, but he smirked, knowing he had won. He kept thrusting, enjoying his victory when I leaned forward and kissed him. The cocky smile fell to a soft press of his lips. I drew my tongue in, tasting him, just as Raul's jaw dropped.

His body snapped rigid as he gushed hot, slightly green cum all over my belly and down my thighs. The bastard could go for hours if it was hot, wild sex, but the second I was tender with him, he came apart. Raul sneered, seemingly annoyed that I knew him well enough to know how to get him off.

The vines broke off my legs and I thudded back, my ass hitting the cheap carpet. *Oh yeah, there's the pain.* I tried to flex my knees to get blood back in them, but my calf seized up. I reached for one, only for my arms to snap back to my chest.

"Are you gonna...?" I asked, tugging on the vines.

Raul, with one hand around his still spurting cock, stared at me. "What if I don't?"

With a long sigh, I cast a very handy herbicide spell. The vines blackened around my fingers and crumbled to dust. I reached for my aching leg to massage it, but he beat me there. Of course, the calf got a few seconds before he wound up at my feet.

"Is it true?" I asked, flailing my foot out while Raul worked the balls with his thumbs. "About the heat signature? Are they using Predator tech?"

"No," he admitted. "Your nipples get hard when the room's cold."

I grabbed the first thing I could and flung his suit jacket at his head. He easily dodged, then picked up my other foot to rub it. I wished I could close my eyes and ignore the reason I was here. Nothing more than a random tryst in a hotel with a stranger who made my blood boil. That'd be easier.

"How many?"

His thumbs paused and he took in a deep breath. "Seven."

"Is that including the other five from —?"

"Yes."

Twelve more witches gone, most likely dead because they had trusted the hunters to not turn on them. I shivered and pulled my legs back under me. Raul let them go, his hands thudding to his naked thighs. "We should get to work," I said, hunting for my lost clothing.

I didn't look back as I dressed, but I sensed he wasn't moving, just sitting there watching me. For a moment I looked into the mirror. He caught my eye, that cocky expression melting to one of complicated concern. I didn't have time to worry about him. It was his choice to keep at this, even if we weren't getting anywhere.

"Where are the teeth?" I asked. Raul jerked his chin to the briefcase on the bed.

The first time he had asked me to do it, I had worn winter gloves to handle them. After two months, I emptied the bag into my palm like they were pearl marbles. Raul staggered to his feet while I got to work.

"Dead." There wasn't even a hint of life in the first tooth. "Dead too. And again." Only two remained.

Raul extended his hand next to mine, the skin back to its tan hue. I dropped the three dead teeth into his palm and he scowled. The sunglasses hid most of his expression, but he was terrible at keeping a poker face. "Even this one. Are you certain?"

I shrugged. Dead was dead.

"But she was an elemental who kept to herself. I'd thought if anyone would have..."

That could have been me. If I hadn't gotten lucky, if the agency hadn't been breached and I'd escaped, they'd have done the same to me. Kept my name in a file, assigned an agent to check up on me and ripped a tooth out of my jaw for easy tracking. And, once they had aligned with Conquest, killed me when my back was turned.

"Dead." I dropped the next one in his hand.

"¡Oye! Do you have to be so morbid?"

"Would you prefer me to say 'has passed from this mortal coil thanks to a bullet to the brain'?"

He full-on shuddered, causing the teeth to hop like popcorn. I turned away, a familiar scowl rising up the back of my neck and into my brain. "What do you even care?"

"I knew some of them, worked with them. They were kind."

"Which is why you and your old buddies imprisoned them and ripped out their teeth. Because they're just so darn nice."

I expected a fight. God knew we'd had a ton of them since this began, but Raul went quiet. He clenched his fist, sealing away the teeth of witches who had never seen their end coming. "It wasn't supposed to happen like this. There were fail-safes in place."

"Which means jack shit when powerful people who don't give a fuck about the rules are in control. That's when the bodies pile up." Unlike him, I had never met any of these witches — all of them scattered across the continent. But who was left to speak for them as they were being cut down in their beds?

"I know." Raul stared past me to the curtains drawn tight over the window. It was less for what we had just done and more out of fear of anyone spotting a green-skinned man. I almost never saw him outside of dark rooms or in the dead of night. I wondered sometimes if he got to see the sun.

Another one was long dead, the life drained from the tooth. I didn't say it, only handed it over to him and concentrated on the last hope. It wasn't feeling good. Just before I listened in, he sighed deeply.

"Why *do* you care?" I asked again.

"We need them to help against Con —"

"I mean why do you care about them? About each one like she's a person?"

"She is. Was. I..." Raul swallowed deeply and pressed his closed fist to his chest. *"No sé qué decir."*

I didn't expect an explanation. Half the time he wanted the agency gone, the other half he shouted back at me that they had to be upheld to protect against dangerous magic. I closed my hand tight and listened to the life. It was a spell so old it was barely words, but I got the gist.

There wasn't... *Wait.* A spark shivered in the heart of the tooth like a single match struck in the middle of a blizzard. "I'm getting something."

Raul leaped into action. He flung a pile of papers onto the bed, then dug out a goose feather. "Find her," he demanded, as if I didn't already know the point.

I held the tooth up, then stopped. "It's very faint," I said, trying to keep his hopes level.

"She is no doubt on the move. I will find her before they do."

He'd said that each time I got a hit, and each time he had come back empty-handed. "Why do you keep doing this? You're one man against...how many witch hunters?"

"Fifteen hundred."

"Great." One thousand five hundred people who'd been trained to eliminate witches wanted us dead. And he thought we could take them on? "There's almost no chance you'll get to her in time."

"Be that as it may, I have to try."

"Why?" *Why keep risking your ass for some witches?* It'd been a close call a few times, once requiring me to patch him up. Each time he clashed with the hunters under Conquest's control, there was a good chance he wouldn't come back.

Raul took a deep breath. I expected a brimstone speech against the backstabbing of his director and the other turncoat witch hunters. Instead, his lips drooped and he brushed his palm against my cheek. Holding me tight, he whispered, *"Porque lo hago."*

The tooth crumbled to dust and, as it fell, the feather began to draw.

Chapter Seventeen

Raul

She watched me hunt for transportation to intercept the living witch. I shouldn't have even noticed. The agency had used an open office because sometimes we needed a lot of room to move large creatures. At least Kevin had escaped into the great lake before everything had burned. People would often look over my shoulder and comment on a case. It encouraged bonding.

But I couldn't stop scratching my neck from the way her eyes kept staring. I'd swear she was mentally peeling my clothes off — if she hadn't done that a half hour before. "There," I said, hoping to pull her attention off of me and to the fight.

"Will you be leaving soon?" she asked.

"I have to catch a bus tonight from the next town over so I'd best move quickly." It'd been my life since I had come back from the elf lands, never staying more than a night in a location. I hadn't spoken to my mama in six weeks. It was logical, even if the constant pizza and taco nights were hell on my heartburn.

She was watching again, biting her lip to keep herself from saying whatever was on her mind. I paused in packing up to catch her gaze. "Why? Do you want me to stay?" The laugh slipped out at the ludicrous idea. It'd put not only her but especially me in serious danger. I would be a fool to linger.

Leeland scratched her forearm, lifting her sleeve. "How long will you be gone?"

"Hard to say. Depends on if I find her or not." Why was she staring at me like that? Did she miss me? Or did she want to come with me? Just me and the obstinate witch, the two of us alone striking out against the world. For as bullheaded as she could be, her mind was sharp and her body...

Cogeme con esas tetas.

She stirred off the bed, sliding her bare foot to the floor. I peered down at her little brown toes with the peeling polish when she handed me a card. "It's not even my birth—" I began until I caught purple and silver flowers around the word wedding. "What is this?"

"I thought you might like to come."

"To your wedding, where you're marrying an *aburrido* werewolf."

She tossed her head back and groaned, "He's not boring."

"His profile says otherwise."

"For god's sake, stop profiling us. It's weird. Normal people don't make psych evals of their friends."

I stared at the date at the bottom, October thirtieth. It was coming up so soon, yet she was here with me instead of holding her werewolf's leash. "Since when are we friends? I thought you called me your adversary."

"You're a fucking *cabrón* right now," she grumbled, but her eyes blazed. Every time I'd ask for her help, she'd call me that or worse right before I bent her over the bed. Before I could make a move, Layla sighed and wrapped her arms around her chest. "Look, I just…if you want to come, you have to have an invitation."

"Yes, I can see the spell. As would any witch hunter who happens to get his or her hands on this."

"They won't. Besides, the place is gonna be full of werewolves."

"You'll be lucky to see your deposit again. The stench of wet dog alone…"

She scoffed at me. "You sound like Ink."

I bridled at the attack. As if I could have anything in common with a lowlife sin. All they did was take and kill. I glared at her, but she tossed her hair my way and walked for the door. It was hardly the first time we'd left on harsh words, and I doubted it'd be the last.

"You don't find it awkward?"

"What?"

"Right after I gave you the best fuck of your life—"

She laughed at that and shook her head.

"—you invite me to your wedding. Whatever will the groom think?" If it came to it, I knew I could take a werewolf in a duel. Though, if the others joined in, I might be in a sticky situation.

Layla didn't blush with guilt or turn rabid in rage. She stared at me dumbfounded. "I told him I was going to. He knows I'm here. They all do."

"They know that we're fuck—"

"Yeah," she interrupted. "They all know about each other. What? Your profile of me didn't reveal that?"

I gulped, uncertain if she would attack with her spells or claws. She looked ready to pound me to dust and, for as hot as she was, fear licked the back of my neck that I might not survive. "You are an ever-evolving enigma."

"And you're in snob mode, so I'm done. Come to the wedding if you want. If you miss it —"

"You won't miss me?"

Once again she threw me off balance by stating, "I wouldn't be inviting you if I didn't want you there." Pulling her purse tight to her side, she stared me up and down. "If you'll excuse me, I need to go pick up my wedding dress."

While my cum dried on her soft skin. I snickered at the idea, though for all I knew, the wolf got off on it. Maybe the angel too — the holier in the streets, the kinkier in the sheets. She'd tired of me and yanked open the motel door. A trio of roaches scuttled by and Layla shivered.

"I'll think about it," I said. She looked back and I thumbed the invitation. "Though there is a greater chance I will be too busy trying to keep the world from shattering to pieces."

"Yeah, yeah. I get enough of that from my mother. Raul?" She paused just outside the door. "Good luck. I hope you find her."

"*Gracias*." I bowed my head to check my timeline and the door closed.

Eres un menso.

Whatever I had going with a woman who half the time despised my green ass couldn't last. I knew that as surely as I knew the best way to catch a centaur was a bag of oats and porn. She was as bendable as rebar, challenging me every step, reminding me of what I was and had done. Like I'd ever forget.

I slipped into the shower, paying no attention to the bugs scattering from the light. Keeping the sunglasses on would be unwise, but I hated having to stare down at the green. It was a reminder of what the agency had stolen from me, of the debt I owed Director Zimmerman, but also that I came from the kind of people who'd abandon their own children. That stole from other worlds because they could, and forced undying loyalty on their family.

She had seen it all. More than that, she had saved me from the brainwashing. For all the times she'd dig into me like flints under the nails, she was also a delight to be with. I had never taken the time to talk with the witches, because if we stopped to see them as they were, it'd be a hell of a lot harder to collar them.

The water shifted from polar ice caps to lava in ten seconds. Rather than reach for the faucet, I let it hit my skin. Burn away the impurities, wash off the sin and leave my soul squeaky clean. Drain every lingering remnant of who I was and was supposed to be.

It never worked. My skin glowed like a neon Gatorade sign. I shut off the faucet and stepped out. Staring through the wards I'd written on the mirror, I looked myself in the eye. Steam circled the glass, highlighting the mess of a man.

My first thought was to shake my head to see if the green elf staring back was really me. Three months on and I dissociated every time I looked in a mirror. If I couldn't find the solution to erasing this elven curse, if there were no witches who knew how, then what? Would I have to face that gaunt alien face every time I looked in a mirror?

I was reaching for a towel just as the water began to bead up and streak down the glass. "Oh —"

The no died in my throat as a hand clamped under my jaw and lifted me off my feet. I was pushed back, my legs slamming into the toilet. When my head hit the towel rack, I snarled and met the demon in the eye.

He'd kept up the delusion he appeared human with wild black hair, but his eyes burned an unnerving red. "Forget something, witch hunter?" he taunted.

I clamped both my hands around one of his forearms. He wouldn't release me, but I managed to pull myself up enough so I could talk. "Aren't you growing tired of this cat-and-mouse game?"

The incubus grinned. "Who said I'm playing?" He tightened his hold around my neck, but I lashed my foot out. A normal person would have been huddled on the floor, fighting against a deflated diaphragm. For the demon, it was like kicking a boulder, but I needed it for the leverage. Planting my foot into him, I tugged my head back. His fingers sank deeper into my throat, moving from a threat to making good on choking the life out of me.

Damn that demonic strength. The vines came on their own. Two ripped through the old tiles and wrapped around the incubus' legs, thickening to rope as they coiled. Still, he wouldn't let go.

I don't need their help. I have this.

Flailing my hand out, I tugged for the towel.

"Trying to disguise your shame, witch hunter? As if your kind is capable."

Yes! The second the towel ripped free, I flung it at the demon's face. He batted it away, missing me aiming my gun at his temples.

"Put. Me. Down."

"You think I'm afraid of your little piece? Or your weapon?" He raised his eyebrows with a smug flick and blatantly stared at my exposed crotch.

I knew better than to rise to any demon's bait, especially one of lust. "This is loaded with the ashes of an angel. We both know what that does to demons."

He sneered and opened his hand. I forgot my leg was still planted on his stomach and I smashed onto the toilet. My back hit the tank and my tailbone the seat before I nearly landed at the damn demon's feet. For his part, he watched as if he found it all hilarious. Then he calmly sliced away the vines cutting off his legs.

"Did you really believe a handful of flowers could stop me?"

I bit down on the shiver that struck me with each slash of his claws. I didn't want them in the first place. They kept popping out whenever they felt like it.

Holding the gun as steady as I could, I tried to rise in the tiny bathroom filled with an enraged demon. He didn't make a move but kept his hands out in anticipation of striking again. Something hot dripped down the back of my neck and I feared it wasn't water. Checking in front of the demon would show weakness that he'd quickly exploit.

I was trained to keep my emotions in check, to never let the creatures get the better of us. But my ass ached, the back of my head was bleeding and I had to face another twelve-hour bus ride while he would go right back to her bed. Snarling, I pressed the barrel of the gun to the demon's chest. "Why are you here?"

He stared me dead in the eye. "Because I don't like you."

A laugh rose in my throat at the simple explanation. "*Tú puta madre.* Why should I care if a sin likes me?"

The demon extended his claws like he was a cat threatening to shred my couch.

I checked that the gun was cocked and stared him dead in the eye. "She wants me."

Sure enough, that human illusion shuddered. Just the mention of her was enough to cause his tail to whip around in rage.

"She comes to me. She comes *from* me."

"You wear that as a badge of pride? The angel can accomplish that with his feathers alone. You have to use rage and bondage to pull off what the werewolf only requires his tongue for."

Damn it, he was fucking with me. I tried to shut it down on my face, but the demon's eyes burned with fire. He'd caught on to that weak point. "Shall I tell you every touch, kiss and hard thrust she's enjoyed without your unnecessary presence? There have been many with the sullen musician as of late, and once she bedded both the wolf and angel with minimal bloodshed."

"Is that why you're here? Trying to get me jealous to break us up? Jesus, you sound like a teenage girl."

The demon's smile turned my stomach. He should have been petrified of this gun. It was the only thing in creation that could kill a demon. But he didn't even care that I had it pressed to his chest, my finger on the trigger. "What my bond chooses to lie with is rarely of my concern. Should she take up with an entire troop of traveling troubadours, I shall provide the lyre music and mercury."

"Then why the fuck do you keep harassing me?" It wasn't every time after, because I usually kept my demon wards up. But the second one failed, or I got too far from it, there he'd be, trying to choke me out.

"I am protecting her from you. If you so much as think about betraying her, I will gut you before you blink, much less reach for your pea shooter."

Protecting his investment, more like. Demons didn't care about humans beyond what they could provide, and she gave him a lot. I squared up, slipping my balancing hand off the butt of the gun to reach for the mirror. "And what would Layla say if I told her you're trying to kill me?"

He tipped his head in thought. "She would be incensed and scream at me until her voice ceased to work."

My finger paused in digging through the steam and I stared at him. No doubt he was right. If she really had told them about our meetings, then she'd have had to also told them to back off. "You'd risk her cutting you off just to enact your vengeance on the witch hunters that wronged you?"

Mierda. His eyes went black. Wings of shadow erupted off of his back, blanketing the bathroom in darkness. I blinked against the boiling smoke as the demon rose, his horns sticking into the drop ceiling.

"Of course I know about your past, incubus. We record the exploits of all of the sins. You're not half as clever as you think you are."

He growled like a mountain cracking in half. Damn it, my finger slipped. I reached for the ward when the demon clamped onto me. Ten claws pierced my skin. He clung to my collarbones from inside and lifted me off my feet.

"If you harm her in any way, I will tear your flesh from your bones and toss your bleeding body into the darkest hole."

"She won't like..."

The demon snarled. "I don't care what she'd want. I will protect her no matter what you and your ilk would—"

My finger swooped through the circle, closing off the ward. The demon's eyes opened wide for a second before the magic ripped him away. I batted my hand through the air, trying to breathe through the fading bitter smoke. The one-inch wounds he'd gouged into me began to heal. The elven skin was hard to break, harder to kill, but I could hear it in his voice. He'd rip my head off if I so much as made Layla cry.

I should warn her how fucking unstable her demon was, but she'd never believe me. Shaking off the near-death experience, I dropped my gun to the counter, washed the sweat off my face then got dressed. I had a bus to catch.

Along the way, I tossed the invitation into the trash can.

* * * *

Ink

If that feckless waste of elven hide believed his few tricks would work on me, he'd...

"Ahhh!"

A man's piercing scream distracted me from swooping down on the witch hunter and showing him his own colon. The stranger flung himself onto his bed while pointing at me. He took a deeper breath to aid his louder shriek.

I shook back my wings and caught myself in the ceiling-to-floor mirror. All pretense of humanity was stripped from my bones thanks to the cursed hunter.

My hooves clopped on the worn carpet and my tail swung from between my buttocks, barely covered by a layer of black fur. There was no hiding my best trait swinging haphazardly from my loins and the bed man seemed to notice. His eyes went white and rolled back into his head just before he fell backward and hit the floor.

A single low moan broke not from the possibly dead man, but a woman sitting awkwardly in a chair. She held her head and kept muttering, "Not again," while staring at me.

I shifted my head, accidentally catching my horns on the ceiling. As they punctured the plaster to pieces, a spark of fire caught between them. A great whine burst and the interior rains began.

The only thing worse than an enraged incubus was a soggy one. The falling drops hissed to steam on my flesh. I shook much like the wolf after he'd climbed from a bath.

"Excuse me for the interruption. Please continue with your transaction. I'll remove myself from your room post haste." Bowing my head so I could turn around without ripping out more of the internal pipes, I backed for the door.

The man gurgled from behind the bed and the woman kept bemoaning her state while I slipped into the hallway, far from any human eyes. A shiver crawled up my spine and I shook again, trying to remove the last of the chilled water that stank of peat bogs. It wasn't surprising a human would react as they did to my true form. Even the most lustful eye would shift to panic at the sight of me.

All save one.

"This is a surprise."

I jerked at the poisonous voice hidden below a scarlet umbrella. She lowered it, revealing a smile deadlier than an asp. "I thought you never showed your real form to them, Eros. What's the matter? Problems controlling it?"

"Lust." I sneered, the emotion slipping free after this trying day. Even as my voice betrayed me, the monster obeyed. The demon flesh vanished, my handsome features returning, proper knees and no horns. I wiped a speck of plaster off my chest, doing my best to give her no mind.

"What? You're not going to ask what I'm doing here?"

"You're hunting, naturally." She hadn't changed much since that night on the beach, though the red dress had been replaced with a black leather suit cut far too tight to be breathable in any weather.

Lust swung her umbrella over her shoulder and smiled. "But who is the question."

"There's a witch hunter a few doors down you can feed off of," my spite said and I frowned. It would rid us all of this kidney stone, but if Layla found him drained after a night of hedonism with a sin, she'd have questions. And she'd be upset.

When did this become so complicated?

Snickering, Lust draped an arm around my shoulder. I turned to her with surprise. "Are you showing affection? I thought you allergic to such an act."

"Eros, you wound me."

I picked up her hand via her finger and flung her arm back. "It only seems fair, given all the blades you've left in my vertebrae."

Rather than respond, Lust snapped open her umbrella and hid under it. She walked away while calling to me, "You can either run back to that witch with your dick tucked between your legs, or follow me."

Find Layla. Tell her the dangers that the witch hunter poses. Try to calmly talk some sense into her for once about not only Stone but this wedding and the ever-pressing thumb on her scales.

Lust paused at the end of the hall, her hip swung out. She stared at me below the shade of her umbrella, her eyes glowing red. "Eros?"

"Why are you here?" I asked, striding for her. Layla wouldn't listen to me anyway.

She smiled and stepped back into the elevator. Ah yes, a confined space that could send someone to their death—the exact spot to never be trapped with an incubus. I entered it willingly, surmising if Lust intended to harm me, she'd do it somewhere public.

As the doors closed, she shook back her long blonde hair. Her skin glistened as if it'd been fondled by Midas. "How many?" I asked, crossing my arms.

"Three men away from their wives believing no one would ever know. I suppose they are right in that regard." She dotted her mouth as if fixing lipstick that wasn't there. The bright red hue was all her doing.

"Whatever you've come to bargain for, Lust, I'm not interested. I know the company you keep and find them rather unseemly."

She chuckled at the idea but kept her claws sheathed. "I work for no one, Eros."

"Ah yes, because nothing decries independent employment like carrying out the bidding of a powerful master."

I didn't even see her move, just knew the all-too-familiar stab of five daggers piercing through my ribs. I had almost missed that sensation.

"I answer to no one," Lust snarled while spinning her claws around as if to capture my heart. "Unlike you. I'm surprised the witch doesn't keep your cock and balls under lock and key."

"She could if she so desired," I said calmly.

Lust expunged her fingers from my chest cavity. Black ichor dripped off her shaven-down nails. She calmly licked one off while staring at me. No doubt she'd used that same trick on the first businessman while the other two watched with painful erections.

"If you're here to torture me, I get my fill from the ex-ghost." I reached for the button to open the door as if I couldn't walk out of here on my own.

Lust clamped onto my wrist and I let her. "I'm here for your sake, Eros. I'm concerned about you."

"What an interesting time to start."

She slapped me on the cheek, embedding a diamond from her ring into my flesh. I pushed on the dent with my tongue, popping it free. "All I've ever done is protect you, teach you—"

"To be as you are," I said.

"You're my protégé, the greatest of the incubi below me, yet here you are sucking on a witch's teat." She slowly brushed her hand over the cheek she'd slapped while staring into my eyes. "What has happened to you, Eros? In our days, we'd hunt entire villages until none but a single priest remained."

I breathed deeply, trying to not think of the stricken faces left in their beds—towns where every adult was taken by our benders and the children left orphaned to fend for themselves. If I were mortal, I'd have forgotten the horrified screams embedded on their lips as they realized what was happening. Instead, I carried each one with me no matter how far I walked.

Lust eyed me up. "Did your time in hell unman you?"

I laughed at that. "Perhaps you should spend a few centuries down there and see how you fare."

"If you're scared of hell," she said, tightening her hold on me as if she could hear my thoughts through my skin, "then why are you yet bonded to that witch?"

"Jealousy does not become you, Lust."

I tried to shake her off again, but she held tighter. The life force of three men powered her in ways I could never hope to reach. Her eyes darkened to a sickly green as she stared at me. "He has his eyes on her. He will kill her."

"He can try."

"Don't be a fool. Do you think there is any power on this earth that can stop a Horseman? Has a human ever defeated Death, War, Famine?"

I clenched my teeth, refusing to look at her.

"What hope does yours have against Conquest?"

"If you are trying to get me to deliver Layla to you for your boss —"

"I am trying to save you," Lust thundered. "She will die. It is as written in stone as the Accords that began this mess. The Horseman requires her for his plans, and nothing can stop the march of Conquest."

I would be a fool to ignore the centuries of history. A Horseman was indestructible, an idea, a virus of humanity's creation. As long as one of them harbored dreams of conquering their fellow man, he lived. The chances of us protecting Layla for her entire life felt impossible.

"So you admit you work for the Horseman."

"I work for myself. Conquest is changing the rules. Think what will happen once the realms collapse."

"Death, destruction, tears, rains of fire, demons running rampant. The extinction of cake."

Lust scowled at my flippant response. "Who do you think will come out on top?"

"At a guess, the djinn. That is assuming Conquest isn't foolish enough to puncture through to the Celestials' retirement home. Then they'd wipe us all out with a bat of their luscious eyelashes."

"We will. The ones who prepared for this. While the other realms are in chaos fighting over their scraps of land, those of us who knew what was coming will already be prepared. It will be a new world order."

"Ah yes, because no one proclaiming new world orders has ever been proven disastrously wrong."

Lust shoved me back against the elevator wall, much in the same way I had the witch hunter before. She stared at me for a long time. "Why are you fighting me on this? I'm trying to protect you. To help you."

"Help me or get yourself a little plaything for the apocalypse?"

"What has the witch done for you, Eros?"

I quirked my head up at her dodge. As if I didn't know exactly why Lust wanted to keep me around, collar and all.

She drew the back of her finger down my cheek in a soothing manner, but her power didn't abate for a second. "She keeps you chained up, far worse than I ever did. I gave you decades to yourself, but can you get a moment free of her? She tethers you to that house overrun with barbaric simpletons."

"The wolf can be entertaining at times."

"Each of them taking what should be only yours. And now she dallies with a hunter, much like the ones that banished you to hell."

I breathed too deeply at his mention. My mind yet churned with questions of how Stone had learned of my past and what he'd do with it. He had as much animosity toward me as I did toward him. It wasn't beyond the realm of possibility for him to use that against me in order to earn Layla's trust. But she was too smart for that. She...

"She is wedding herself to another. What use can a married woman have with an incubus?" Lust's wicked words poured into my ear. "How many nights has she refused you for another? How often does she turn your advances down because her interests are taken up in earthy matters? Are you nothing more than a puppet, a toy for her to pull out when her real love is busy?"

None of that mattered. We had a contract. Besides, every time one of the others brought her desires, I feasted. Even if I would prefer to spend a night with her, to sit beside her and feel her slow breaths against my chest as she slumbered...

"Enough!" I shouted, slamming my hand into the stop button. The elevator jerked to a halt and I flung Lust's hand off of me. She let me go, and she let me know she did it. "I've had quite my fill of you today."

"Think upon it, Eros. You are risking your very existence if you stay with her. But what do you have to gain?"

The answer was so foolish even I laughed it off. I shook my head and prepared to step into the in-between.

"When you wake up and realize that she cannot care for you the way I do, bring me the witch. Have fun with your betrayal. Deliver her on her wedding day. Let the whole world know what truly lies at the heart of Eros — ice."

Holding my head high, I walked away from Lust, but the ghosts of the dead lingered in my wake.

Chapter Eighteen

Layla

"Frank?" I called to the gruff man behind the counter. He didn't answer, just nodded and began work on my usual. He'd been the first person I had granted the ability to see me after my guys. While he could be grumpy, I doubted he was some secret monster on Conquest's payroll.

Grizzly's was busier than normal. A flock of college students gathered around outlets fretted about midterms. *That should be me.* I tried to shake the sinking feeling away, but my stomach twisted at the reminder of what I'd had to give up to keep safe.

It's only for a semester. We'll whoop Conquest's butt and I'll be right back on track.

"Layls, over here!" Dana waved. I dodged around the mess of spilling backpacks to join her.

"Working hard?" I asked, pointing to the mess of textbooks on the table. "How are clinicals going? And tests must be coming up soon."

With a wide grin, Dana swept her arm shoving all of the study material onto the bench by the window. "Enough of that. We need to talk wedding shit."

"Dana, you didn't..." I dropped my small binder to the table, my shoulders shrinking in at her abandoning everything for my problem. Then I caught her look and laughed. "You're using me to get out of studying."

"Duh. Now, make with the goodies. Is it in?"

I leaned in closer to whisper, "Yes."

"Well? How's it look?"

"I don't know. I just picked it up." It was her brilliant idea to try on a few high-end dresses at the boutiques and buy a cheaper lookalike online. Without that, I'd be a naked bride. "Can I leave it at your place for now? I wouldn't put it past Cal to peek." Or all of them to put on a fashion show critiquing it. *I want my dress to be a surprise.*

"No problem. I'll lock it in my closet so Angelo doesn't get any ideas."

"How's school going for him?"

Dana sighed and Frank dropped my praline latte in front of me. I nodded in thanks. He gave a single grunt and returned to his domain. "He's settling in okay. But you should see him in that ring bearer tux. A-dor-able. Bet Cal's scorching hot in his."

She elbowed me to agree and maybe show pictures, but I gulped. "I don't know." I took a long drink and said fast, "They haven't picked them yet."

"What? But you've only got..."

"I know. I know the timeline. It's...we're fine. We've got it. Invitations are almost done. Just need the stamps.

Got the dress in my trunk. Location's figured out. Food."

"Are you certain you wish to inflict speared meat upon your guests, my bond?" Ink's curious question wafted around me. He rubbed my shoulders before perching on the table.

Dana took him on. "What have you got against kabobs?"

He shrugged. "Foods of spice fed to packs of northern werewolves seems as if it could be a rather messy affair. Have you considered more menial delights? Those small balls on sticks? Or the bound wieners?"

"Bound…?" I asked, before shaking my head. "Ink, it's fine."

"I'm only considering the state of the lavatories after their —"

"I said it's fine! We don't have time to change it, we can't afford to change it and we're both looking forward to a gyro station. Okay?"

Fuck. I didn't realize I'd slammed my hands to the table and shouted until the busy café fell silent. Worse still, my incubus didn't have a biting response. He stared at me sullenly, his lips pouted in thought. Then he bowed. "As you say." He walked off.

"Wait, Ink…" I didn't have time to chase after him. Sinking back into my chair, I burrowed my head into my hands. "I don't know if I'm going to survive this."

"So I shouldn't ask about the other thing you're doing?" Dana leered over my open binder. One side was crammed with fabric swatches and floral arrangements. The other had cryptic incantations and ingredient lists for poisons. Be a really interesting wedding if I got the two mixed up.

"It's fine," I said. For two months we had puzzled over the old spell and what it would mean. In that time we'd come up with nothing useful. At least Raul was bringing in reinforcements. Sort of.

"Well, the sky's not spitting fire yet, so may as well focus on the wedding instead."

"Here are two of the photographers who agreed to find an opening for us." I opened up their websites on my phone and let Dana have a look. Neither was a great option, one too expensive and the other just getting into weddings.

She pursed her lips at the same problem I ran into and I sighed. "I'm tempted to give Ink a camera and let him have a go at it."

"Only if you want the world's first erotic wedding album," Dana said. "Oh, look what I've got." She pulled a bundle of purple flowers and lace from her bag. "For the broom, ya know. My cousin did something similar with hers. Maybe add a silver brooch to the middle or a wolf fang."

It was beautiful, but my tongue stuck to the top of my mouth. "Jumping the broom," I said.

"You're gonna, right?"

"I don't know if I should. I wasn't really... My mom didn't tell me, still won't tell me anything about that side of...me." I brushed my thumbs up the spray of flowers, watching the little heads dance. My father was an enigma, a black hole in my existence. Most of what I got from that half of me came from Didi, then a handful of kids in the foster homes and finally Dana. She was the first person to take me to a beauty parlor that could work with my hair.

"Layls." Dana wrapped an arm around my shoulder pulling me closer. "It doesn't matter if you never knew your dad. If you want it, you have just as much right to the broom as any of us."

One foot in, one foot out. That'd been my life for as long as I could remember. People would demand to know what I was all the time — black or white. Witch or mortal. My entire existence was in flux, my being decided not by me but by whoever I encountered that day.

What would my father think? Would he have jumped the broom at his wedding? Or did he get married after my mother? Could he be trapped in some witch-induced limbo? Anything seemed possible in a world with centaurs and unicorns.

"I'll think about it," I said, slipping the flowers and lace into my purse.

"Now we get to the good stuff, Calvin Rollin in a tuxedo." Dana cracked her knuckles and dove into her laptop. We didn't get far in dressing up my fiancé, though the app she found to let me add anyone's picture to the model was far too much fun. I tried Garavel, who looked best in all white, then Daniel. That one took some time before I found a suit without a tie and vest, the shirt barely buttoned. Ink was the hardest of all. Nothing really fit. Maybe he'd show up to the wedding in that tiny red G-string from Halloween. That'd get the photographer snapping.

"Excuse me. I hope I didn't miss much."

I leaped at the soft voice and glanced over as Fariah delicately placed her huge woven bag on the table.

"Nah. We're dressing the boys. Which one of us is gonna have to walk with Jared?" Dana asked me.

"I hadn't figured that out." I scratched my head nervously. I'd asked them both to be co-maids of honor, unable to pick between the two. But I guess someone would have to go last.

"Not it!" Dana shouted.

"I don't much care," Fariah said and she pulled piles of fabric from her bag. "Which hijab do you think would best match, Layla?"

"Wow." They gleamed like gemstones under the café's industrial lights. She had an entire spectrum of purples from lilac to plum, some with a shiny outer layer, others in rich cotton. I was drawn to the one in satin with a silver trim over its royal purple color. "This one's perfect," I said before looking up at Fariah. "But whatever you think would be best."

"No, I think you're right. That will work." With that, she folded back up all of her scarves to put them in her bag. Dana reached across the table to tug on the end.

"Where do you get them all?"

"Some come from my aunts overseas, but most I buy off the internet," Fariah said with a little smile. "With that decided, I'm going to order." She stood up and left the bag at her place.

Dana very loudly returned to adding other hot men's photos to the app. She'd made her stance on the cold war between me and Fariah's girlfriend very clear—keep her out of it. I shifted nervously in my chair, took a deep drink—forgetting the coffee was boiling—then reached into my purse.

"Fariah," I said, waving to her. She'd just finished paying for her coffee because she never used the tab system. After calmly putting away her card, she looked at me.

My brain went dead. I'd been running over this speech in my head for weeks. This was my only chance before school and the wedding took away our last seconds of free time. "Here!" I shouted and thrust the envelope at her.

She took it but her lips curled in confusion as she pulled out the wedding invitation. "I don't believe I need one."

"Not for you, for…Maram. She won't be able to get in without it. Ya know, because of." I touched the tip of my nose and wiggled it back and forth.

"Ah." Fariah nodded that she understood, then she dropped her eyes. "I'd assumed she would not be welcome, considering…"

"I mean, we're gonna have a demon and an angel and so many werewolves. What difference does an ifrit make?"

Frank coughed loud and stared me dead in the eye. Right, there were normal people around who didn't know about all this magic shit. I lowered my voice to the point I was quieter than Fariah. "I'm sorry. I just… No excuses. If you trust her, then it doesn't matter what she is. She's your girlfriend and she should be at my wedding."

"Are you certain this is what you want? It's your day and I don't want to start a commotion."

"Fair, come on. There's gonna be like forty werewolf cousins at this. No chance any djinn can out-commotion them."

She dropped her head and thumbed the invitation farther out of the envelope. "Very well. If you're sure. Thank you."

I locked my arms around her for a big hug. "Thank you for…being a surprising rock in all of this immortal-creatures-from-another-dimension stuff. It's tricky."

"Quite." Fariah chuckled to herself. Whatever her fire genie girlfriend got up to, it had to be a challenge. God knew I had my hands full with my five.

Four.

Four and a *cabrón*.

"Layla, are you aware this invitation is covered in black paw prints?"

I sighed. "Yes. Like half of them are."

Chapter Nineteen

Daniel

I didn't care what the hell the commotion was in the kitchen. I had to get this damn song finished. Being alive was a lot more work than I remembered. The constant breathing, the eating, the bathroom breaks, oh, and that ever-pressing need to earn a wage to pay for it all.

I caught sight of myself in the mirror, a damn pimple rising on the end of my nose. "Sometimes I miss the grave," I muttered. Fifty years of experience in a twenty-year-old body was less fun than anime made it seem. Despite being wise enough to know that Layla was stressed from her upcoming wedding, my body's raging hormones wanted to kick in a door the second I saw her with the wolf or the angel. The less I thought about the demon, the easier it was on my cortisol levels.

"Fuck!" A string snapped on the old bass. I dug into my case, hoping there was an extra the previous owner had missed. My cash reserves weren't exactly at the point I could waltz into a store and buy a new Fender.

"Hey, Daniel?" Cal knocked after peering into my room. I stared at him, waiting for whatever he wanted. "We're eating cake in the kitchen."

"Is it someone's birthday?" It wasn't Layla's, I knew that, but as for the others, I wasn't sure.

"Nah." He blushed and fiddled with the gap in his eyebrow. "Wedding cake, for the wedding. You know, picking the best option and all."

The wedding. Of course. I shook my head, not in the mood to deal with the happy couple. A loud groan rose from my stomach. Right. I needed to eat. Again. Sighing, I put my bass away and joined him. "So, what flavors are we sampling?" I asked as the kitchen door swung open.

Small plastic containers covered the entire counter. A two-layer cake slice with enough frosting to give a rabbit diabetes sat in each one. Garavel held one of the orange cakes, his eyes closed as he licked off the fork. "This one's really good."

"Carrot cake?" I read the label. "Who the fuck wants carrot cake for their wedding?"

"Bugs Bunny?" Cal said and he went for a yellow one. "This is banana cream. There's a lightness there. Here, try it."

My famished stomach was what pushed me to take the half-eaten slice from him. I dove in, at least excited about the sugar rush, then frowned. "Damn it!"

"What's wrong?"

"I hate banana!" I shouted, the fact hitting me like a semi.

He stared at me. "Then why'd you take it?"

I scraped my tongue and took a long drink of water. Between guzzling, I said, "Because I forgot."

"Oh. How do you feel about raspberry?"

I hated to admit that I couldn't remember, so I took the chocolate cake with raspberry filling and dove in. "It's fine. A little tart."

"This one is so good." Garavel cheered while holding a plain white cake.

"He's said that about every single one. Ink!" The flustered groom abandoned his chai cake to rush over to the entering demon.

"Calvin, you seem quite flustered," he said.

"We're trying cake."

The demon patted him on the shoulder. "I'm certain with enough practice you shall master it."

"No, not... I need to pick one for the wedding. Can you help?"

He snickered. "Once again, you fear you cannot anticipate the desires of your bride. Very well, I shall save the day from a most foul confectionary disaster."

That was how all four of us wound up eating cake in the tiny kitchen. Garavel pushed for every flavor except lemon. That one he declared an abomination in the creator's eye. I worked through the stranger offerings. "Olive oil cake?"

"I dunno. The lady just handed me a big box full of samples." Cal shrugged.

Eh, I'd eaten worse.

The demon combined a pear and nutmeg cake with a green tea and jasmine one, his lips smeared in green goo. "They are rather pedestrian options. Where is the salmon and pimento offering? Or a cake made of pure gold?"

"Pretty sure that'd break teeth," Cal said as if the incubus wasn't fucking with him. He did that a lot, always trying to be a peacekeeper.

The demon quirked his head to the side and stared Cal down. "Is that not the end goal of a werewolf wedding?"

What? Confusingly, Cal turned red and looked away. They didn't really break teeth, right? That was... Dear lord, what did Layla get herself into? I put my fork down, needing to warn her, when the demon announced, "As you seem to intend to keep within the confines of the limited creativity of your cake woman, the champagne and raspberry cake. Elegant and sweet on the outside with a mysterious and occasionally acerbic bite inside."

Cal grinned ear to ear. "That's perfect. Thanks, man." He draped an arm over the demon's shoulder and both took another bite of the winner. "Damn, you're right. Garavel, what do you think of this?"

With that problem solved, I wasn't needed. Not that they had any use for me anyway. I put down my fork and moved to return to my bedroom when the air grew still.

"I just wanted to thank you all for helping with the wedding."

"You would be firmly trapped in shit's creek without my assistance," Ink said.

"I am always happy to assist with easing in the folding of new troops," Garavel chimed in. Either he still didn't get what was going on, or he preferred to keep pretending.

Cal nodded to both of them, then he looked right at me. "It means the world to her."

Fuck. My head dropped and I nodded. Yeah. For as exhausted as I was with this, Layla was ecstatic. It gave her an outlet away from the doom and gloom of everything else in her life. And, for some stupid reason, she loved the idiot.

Loved all of us.

"No problem," I said noncommittally and backed up for the door. Warm hands pressed against my back and I shot straight up. Those palms curled around my chest and her chin landed on my shoulder.

"What are you all doing?" she asked in a soft voice.

"Babe! This is… It's a surprise." Cal overreacted, running around scooping the loser cakes into his arms.

"There shall be cake at your nuptials," the demon said. "Surprise."

Layla laughed, her warm breath dancing against my cheek. "I suspected that might be the case. Cal, all the stamps are in the dining room."

"Thank the moon. We can finish addressing the invitations and then have dinner?"

"I wish I could. I've got to get changed and meet with my mother."

Every man in that room went rod straight.

"Are you certain?"

"Lady witch, your day has been rather exerting."

"I suppose I shall be peeling you off the pavement once you've finished your session arguing with her."

I was the only one to keep quiet and rub my hand up her forearm. They weren't wrong. Casting that spell wore her down, and it looked like her day of errands hadn't exactly refueled her. No doubt the elf had a lot to do with that, but she needed us to believe in her.

"Maybe she plans to pick out her mother-of-the-bride dress," Layla said with a bitter laugh. It pained me how accurate the demon was on the raspberry.

I turned in her soft embrace and wrapped my arm around her waist. "I'm certain you can handle whatever your mother throws your way," I told her.

The light caught in her eyes and she smiled. "Thank you, Daniel," she declared before kissing me. The others groaned at missing their opportunity to be in her corner.

"Come on, there's something I wanted to show you."

Holding her body tight to mine, I took in every flush of her heartbeat through my palms as we worked our way up the stairs to my room. It didn't happen every night, but the few I got to spend with her in my arms were bliss.

As she walked through the doorway, which I was tempted to close behind us, Layla paused and stared at the bed. Hot girl in my bedroom, fuck yes. And there went those fifty years of experience yelling at my erection that she was too exhausted.

"Are you going to play my song?" she asked.

That'd get her right into bed. Hell, we could fuck in the hall while the rest of them listened.

I shook my head. "Sorry, it's not finished yet."

"That's okay. All good things and whatnot," she said with a laugh and perched on the bed next to my case. I moved the bass guitar to the side to sit next to her.

"About the wedding, I've been thinking…"

Her eyes began to waver as if she was hiding back a mess of tears. It could be from stress or exhaustion, but I knew it was everyone else trying to talk her out of this.

This is insane. You haven't even been with him for a year. What about the rest of us? What about the world ending?

"I've been playing with some dudes. We're not a band yet, but I was thinking we might be able to make our debut for the reception."

"Really?" she gasped, the tears gone.

"Do some covers, work the crowd. Lead the dances. I did a few weddings back when I was alive...before."

"But I don't want you to be stuck up on the stage all night."

I brushed off her concerns. If I wasn't playing, I'd probably be drinking, and after taking a forced thirty-year hiatus, I was a lightweight. "We'll figure something out. And now you don't have to worry about picking the music."

"Oh, crap, am I supposed to...?" She looked about to pull out her binder and inspect that dreaded list. Then Layla laughed and leaned back on my bed. "Thank you, so much. You're...you've been wonderful with all of this."

Have I?

The werewolf and demon were thick as thieves — even the angel would hang out with them, forming a demented three musketeers. I, however, found any excuse to avoid socializing, or worse, doing wedding shit. "I just want you to...to be happy." I brushed my hand against her cheek.

She softened those sexy lips of hers and I went in for the kiss. Layla reached around to hold my face and my body shifted, needing to guide her back. Then she had to give a cute little giggle gasp against my mouth and I was gone.

Not caring that she'd worn herself to the nub with wedding shit and the ex-witch hunter, I straddled her tempting body on my knees and she fell back onto the bed. *Fuck.* I forgot the drawback to tight pants and erections. There was no hiding my cock suckered down my inner thigh as I bent closer to kiss her.

"Daniel?" she whispered, raking her fingers up my back.

"Yeah." *Why does that feel so good?*

"What about the ceremony? Do you know how to play the *Wedding March* or *Canon in D*?" As she asked, she bit my earlobe. Layla was the one to cry out. Damn, I needed the jaws of life to get my cock out now.

"We can play a cassette, no big deal."

Layla paused and stared at me. "What's a cassette?"

There went that fifty-year-old man again, dumbfounded at her not knowing what a tape was. The years weighed on my heart without touching my body and I shook my head. "Stream it, then," I muttered, intending to slip off to let her rise.

The loud pull of a zipper froze me in my tracks. Biting her lip and staring at me, Layla worked open my fly.

"Holy shit," I cried as my pants gave way and she wrapped her palm around my throbbing cock.

She giggled and I lost it. Diving back to her, I sucked on her neck as she circled her palm up and down my shaft.

"Sounds perfect," Layla whispered before we got down and dirty on top of my sheet music for Pachelbel's Canon.

* * * *

Layla

"You're late."

I didn't know why I'd expected a warmer greeting. Placing my bag on the table and pulling out my spell book, I looked around the library. The urge to tell my mom I'd gotten tied up fucking the ghost that used to haunt the place perched on my tongue, but I swallowed it at her look.

"Sorry."

"Well, just...try to keep focused. We've got a lot of ground to cover."

I sat across from her and peered down at her book. To my eyes, the pages were blank, but I knew they were full of old spells. In fact, the same ones I'd bookmarked in my book. My mom was busy jotting down whatever spell I had to master next while I kept looking from her blue tome to my red one.

"How come my book's bigger than yours?" I asked. "Didn't all of my magic come from you and your mother?"

She dropped her pen and closed her eyes tight, her lips barely moving with what I once thought were swallowed curse words. Now I recognized a spell weaving in the air. My mom shrugged it off and resumed writing. "Because you don't just have my spells. Whatever lingering magic may have been in your father's line is included in there."

"So, a witch's magic isn't lost if she doesn't have a kid?"

Oh crap. My mom dropped her pen, threw her shoulders back and stared at me. Then she tented her fingers. "If a witch does not have a daughter, all of her line is lost. But if she dies before the daughter inherits her magic, the spells linger in the...I don't know, DNA or something, until another witch is created. So yes, you have to have a baby. All that time you're wasting on an overinflated party could be put to that instead."

I pursed my lips, fighting to keep my voice level. "So we won't be going shopping for dresses? Something matronly with lace sleeves and a modest neckline?"

My mom, dressed in a leather jacket and T-shirt, glared murder at me. Being on the run hadn't aged her hard. She barely looked like she was in her forties, never mind her fifties. At least that'd bode well for me.

"Here." She handed over the first spell, something to create a barrier that'd disintegrate a person on contact. *Eesh.* I studied the spell, the words simple and direct, but the magic felt wrong—like being served a plate of broken glass.

She asked nonchalantly, "What about lilac?"

"I need lilacs for the spell?" I didn't see that anywhere.

My mom shook her head. "No. It's a simple enough incantation but draining, as you can hopefully sense. Still doable, assuming your demonic leech hasn't sucked you dry."

There was the dig at Ink I knew was coming. Then my mom went quiet and she turned away. "For the wedding. I don't want to clash with the other people you have standing up. Girl servants or whatever they're called."

"Bridesmaids," I said automatically, then blinked. "You…you want to come?"

"Want to? I think you're wasting time and valuable resources, but I should. To at least keep an eye on you and your flock of cocks."

I dropped my hand in front of my face, hiding my frown. I should have been happy. This was the first time she'd shown even a hint of wanting to come. What did it matter why? Just as long as she was there the way normal mothers were.

"So, should I bother with lilac or try something else?"

This was the only olive branch I was getting from her. "Lilac's good," I said, keeping my voice flat.

"This part's tricky. You have to finesse the words with a long A." She ran right past her offer and back to working on the spells. I dove in, locking the mess with my mother deep in my mind. She couldn't be like Cal's mom, who was happily helping with decorations and coming in early for setup. That'd be asking too much of her. I'd be an idiot to expect anything more.

"*Layla?*"

I sat up and looked around. "Did you hear that?"

"No," my mom said.

"*Layla, your presence is required.*" The voice danced in my brain without making a sound. I knew the words without hearing them and stumbled to my feet with my book in hand. Scratching my forehead, I stared down the empty shelves.

"No. There's something, someone's calling to me." Just like in the forest. I reached for my spell book and the voice seized control of my legs.

"*Walk to me, child. Don't be afraid.*"

My body took off on its own, launching me down the aisle and for the door. I tried to reach out to catch a passing shelf, but my hands locked to my side.

"Where are you going?" my mother called.

I tried to shout back, but my jaw was locked. I couldn't do anything but walk and watch in terror for wherever this voice was leading me. All the while, it cheered me on inside my head. "*Yes, child. Down the stairs. Not much farther.*"

"Laylee?" my mom cried out from behind. "Layla!"

My body took off running once it hit the street. Not into direct traffic, thank god, but around the darkened church and into a small wood between two suburbs. All the while, my mother kept shouting for me to stop. *I'd really fucking love to.*

It couldn't be Conquest—he couldn't find me. Unless he'd figured out a way to get to me, in which case I was fucking dead. *Ink? Come on, you're always here when I need you. Except when Eric attacked. What if…?*

No. He'd come. He'd have some smart-ass remark and stop whatever was dragging me around the trees. My body took a hard left and an eerie blue glow punctuated between the shadows of the woods. That couldn't be good.

I have to break free, I have to… My foot dropped, my toe digging into the dirt. It wasn't much of a rebellion, but it was enough. The voice cried out as I hit the dirt, hard. Mud and wood splinters shredded the knees of my jeans and smeared my palms, but I was free.

"Layla, where are you?" my mother shouted from behind.

"I'm here," I called to her. *And I'm angry.*

When I picked my spell book up, it flipped open to one of the bigger fire spells—it read my mind better than my incubus sometimes. I steadied myself, flames rising off my muddied palm as I walked for the strange glow.

"You want me." I cursed. The flames grew high enough they could take out a neighborhood. The neon blue light erupted around me, bleaching my vision. I kept going with my lips twisted into a maniacal grin.

"Here I am!" I shouted and extended my hand.

A little old lady stirred a huge cast iron pot on a camp stove. She banged her spoon on the edge then looked up at me. "You made it."

"Valerie?" I called. She had saved me from the witch hunters and gave me the spell to bring back Daniel. "Holy crap, you're alive. I was worried that…"

"It will take a lot more than some young whelp of an agent to finish me off. Never you mind." She beamed at me in that friendly old lady way as if she had invited me into the woods for tea and cake.

"Wait, you can see me? How?" All I got was a knowing smile and a wink for an answer. I eased closer, curious about what new potion she had brewing.

Hurricane winds burst from behind. They flowed around me but merged to strike Valerie. Her cottony hair blew back. The light on the stove flickered out, and her pot flew off the hook. She remained perfectly still against the force, only clucking her tongue at her potion soaking into the dead leaves.

"Get away from her," my mother fumed from behind me. She clamped a hand to my shoulder while extending her palm high.

"Mom? What the hell? Valerie's a…"

"I told you to stay away from her," my mom screamed, not at me but the old stranger crossing her arms.

A painfully familiar smile crossed Valerie's lips. "Good evening to you too, Bella."

My mom held up both hands, her power doubling until the air crackled in rage. "I told you to stay away from me… Mother!"

Chapter Twenty

Layla

Before I could open my mouth, my mother launched a crackling ball of lightning at the old woman. I reached out to warn Valerie, but she wasn't there. The lightning burrowed into a tree, tearing off bark before it evaporated.

A slow laugh echoed out of the woods and, for a brief second, the darkness parted. Blue fire flew through the air like horizontal meteors. My mom whipped her hands in a circle, winds rising high enough to stop the fire dead in its tracks.

"I could have given you everything," Valerie taunted from nowhere. I stared around while my mom kept two hands extended. "But you were such a petulant brat, preying on my generosity."

"Generosity? All you wanted was —"

The trees ripped apart, an invisible force the size of a rhino rampaging through the forest right at my mom.

She spun and held her palm out. Electricity crackled through the nebulous air, tearing out the trees. "Control," my mother said as the attack sputtered into puffs of smoke.

"I knew better than you, Bell," Valerie shouted. One by one, fires struck in a ring around us.

"How many of our sisters' blood is on your hands?" my mother screamed, picking up the wind. Instead of putting out the flames, it caused them to dance outward, threatening to set the whole area on fire.

"How many mothers watched their lines end because of your pride?" Valerie shrieked back.

"Enough!" I pulled the threads of magic lacing up both of their spells into myself, collapsed the power into a single mass and launched it away. The wind died instantly and the fire vanished. Goosebumps rose up my skin as the cold and silent October night raced in to fill the void.

Only the looming moonlight remained to reveal Valerie and my mother standing awkwardly with both hands out to kill the other. My mom looked at me first. "How did you do that?"

"She is growing in her power. No thanks to your pathetic teachings."

"Here it fucking comes." My mom threw her hands in the air like she was an exasperated teenager. "This is Gryla all over again."

"I told you to wait before lighting the flame, but no, you knew best."

"She was going to eat him!"

"Better one than all." Valerie and my mom circled each other like hissing cats, their faces gnarled up in disgust.

"What the hell is going on?" I shouted. "Why did you call her 'mother'?" I put to mine.

"Of course, Bella did not tell you. She rarely shares vital information until it's too late."

"Don't you fucking start that again," my mom threatened before noticing me. "Layla, get away. She's dangerous."

I looked at the woman with skin as fragile and wrinkly as crepe paper. A small pair of bifocals were perched on her nose and she wore a shawl over her long prairie dress. "Is she really your...my grandmother?"

"Hello, dear." Valerie smiled at me in what would be a comforting way if it wasn't for the hunger in her eyes.

My mom locked onto my hand like I was five years old and pulled me toward her. I gave in for a second before pulling back and digging in my feet. "No. She's not dangerous. She saved me from the witch hunters."

"She's the reason you were captured by the hunters," my mother said darkly.

I shook my head. "Only because they forced her to be. Like they do with all witches. She saved me from their wicked draining spell. She got me out before they...before they got their fangs in me."

Valerie smiled with pride while my mom kept her hackles up.

She bunched her fists and snarled. "You've got it wrong. She didn't work for the witch hunters. Did you, Mother?"

My grandmother sighed in exhaustion.

"They worked for you." The accusation struck Valerie right in the chest, but she harmlessly wiped it away.

I was the one bowled over by it. "What? No. That doesn't make any sense. They collar witches."

My mother barked a laugh. "At her behest. It was her idea. Since I was little, she'd been scheming with the hunters to find a way to get all the other witches in line."

"It was a convoluted mess. Men murdering us in our beds while our daughters cried in their cribs," Valerie thundered. "You don't remember the before times. You were a child."

"I saw what you did!" my mother shouted back. "The experiments. The potions you brewed and forced down the gullets of witches."

Oh my god. My mom knew the potion to reverse the magical drain because it was in her book, because… "Did you…? Did you do that?" My breath caught and my knees began to bend. I feared I might hit the ground, but who could I reach for? They'd both lied to me.

Valerie sighed the same way my mother would when I'd say something dumb. "I found a solution to a problem no one wanted to address."

"Slavery," my mother challenged back.

"Safety. Protection. We were too scattered, most lines as likely to fall from an errant demon as they would to the hunters. The foolish witch hunters were in no better shape, so I offered a solution for both." Valerie closed her eyes tight, then she glared at my mom. "You should have been the first to lead them, to teach them and build an alliance for generations to come. Coward."

"Still sore that I outsmarted you," my mom crowed, raising her head.

"Stabbing me in the back is not outsmarting me."

My mother laughed. "Way I hear it, your new buddies did the same. Or are you on the Horseman's side, too?"

Valerie fumed. "Zimmerman was always weak-willed and power-driven. Only a fool would believe the lies of a Horseman."

"They turned on you," I said, then groaned. "You broke out all the creatures and sabotaged the hunters' weapons." I didn't think anything of it at the time, just glad to get out of their sewer dungeon, but that made sense. Except… "Why did you stay?"

Valerie wrinkled her brow in confusion. "To save you, of course. I could not let them have you, not Zimmerman. Not a witch of my blood." She held her hands out to me. "You're becoming quite an impressive witch, Layla Monvoison."

"It's Leeland," I said.

Valerie shook her head. "No, it isn't. Though, would it hurt you to put on proper clothing? Your blouse barely covers your stomach, young lady."

"Fuck off," my mother shouted.

"We're talking, Bella," Valerie said and waggled her fingers. My mom's head snapped back and her eyes went white.

"Mom?" I called, my lip wobbling when Valerie picked at my hair. I recoiled at the unexpected touch, but she kept going.

"You should pull this back to show off your pretty face."

"What…what did you do to her?" I stared at my mom even as Valerie knotted my hair back. Isabel wasn't moving except for a noticeable tic on her left cheek.

With a little laugh, Valerie waved away my concerns. "I put her in a timeout. If she's going to behave like a child, she should be punished like one, too."

Jesus Christ. My mom wasn't going to win mother of the year any time soon, but she'd never done that to me. I swallowed and watched Valerie circling me from the corner of my eye.

"You've risen the young man from his grave," she said.

"Yeah...yes. How do you know?"

"You used my spell. Now here, drink this." She pulled out a metal flask. Even with the cap screwed on, it stank of grease and lighter fluid.

I shook my head hard. "No, thank you. I'm good."

Valerie opened it and stared me dead in the eye. "You don't have a choice, dear."

She placed the flask in my hand and whispered something. My hand jerked, lifting the flask toward my mouth. I tried to turn my head, but it wouldn't move. Closing my eyes, I searched for the thread of magic to rip it away and free myself, but there was nothing to be found. My mouth opened and the flask's lip smacked into my front teeth. I groaned and thick gloop poured down my throat. It stank to high heaven but tasted like nothing. The metal of the flask bit into my mouth as the final dregs poured down. When my hand fell, the cold metal ripped the skin on my lip and I yelped.

"What? Do you need a lolly for taking your medicine?" Valerie asked as she took the flask.

I closed my hand, once again having control. "What was that? Why did you do that?"

"For your own good, child. Goodness knows you need some actual parenting in your life." She glanced over at my mom, then gave a satisfied *humph*.

The air cracked and my mom lashed out a fist. She aimed for Valerie, but the woman moved at the last second. "You abusive bitch."

"Bella! Watch your language."

"Fuck you," my mom thundered and I was rocked off my heels. I was so confused, it took my mind a minute to realize it was my mother holding me. She pulled me closer, away from Valerie who was picking up her things. "You have no right to her, no right to me."

"You are my daughter. I created you, which means I own you. But I did not bring you here to fight."

"Like that's going to save you." My mother wound up like she was about to throw a baseball.

"Conquest," Valerie said, stopping my mom from blasting her face off. "You've learned what spell he found."

"And you knew the whole damn time, didn't you?" my mom said.

Valerie shrugged. "We have an opportunity here."

"I know what you do with opportunities, Mother."

"Ask your coven how they feel about the ones you take, Bella. Conquest intends to use the angels' creation against them and unravel the realms, but I say we use it to finish what they started."

Valerie pulled out her spell book. It was bound in tan leather. From between the pages, she pulled out a sheet of paper. "We were always meant to close off the realms. It was why they allowed witches to exist. But our foremothers were greedy. They kept that magic for themselves and left us in an unending loop."

"You can't be fucking serious. Close the realms? That's impossible," my mother challenged her.

"No, it isn't," Valerie said and she handed me the sheet.

My mom reached for it, ready to tear the paper to pieces, but I tugged it back to protect it. *If this could stop Conquest...*

"Perhaps cooler heads will prevail in this matter," Valerie said.

"Layla, you can't trust her."

"And you've given her no reason to trust you either, Bella."

My mom gritted her teeth. "I hate that fucking name."

Valerie shrugged as if she didn't care. "Prepare yourself. Once Conquest makes his move, you will have to be ready."

I stared down at the sheet, the words total gibberish. "To do what?"

With a soft voice, Valerie said, "To make the world a better place." Smoke poured up from the ground, obscuring her. My mom lashed a hand out to cut through it, but she was too late. My grandmother was gone.

In a flash, my mom ran in a circle around the area. She dug a stick in the ground, drew a rune and whispered a spell of generic protection before casting it. Even in the bubble, where the air stilled unnaturally, my mother kept quiet and watched.

"Why didn't you tell me?" I asked and her watchful glare turned on me.

"My mother is..." She frowned and formed a triangle with her fingers. "I'd hoped you'd never have to meet her."

"None of this makes any sense. When I was in the witch hunter's lair, she worked for them. They treated her like a servant."

My mom laughed once. "I'd have fucking loved to see that. It was either a ruse on her part, or she'd seriously miscalculated." She smiled to herself at the idea of her mother being controlled by the hunters, then shook it off. "You heard it from the gorgon's mouth. Before her interference, the hunters were disjointed. Little more than a pack of men looking for an excuse to murder women. She organized them, taught them how to counteract magic."

"The witch hunters were controlled by a witch the whole time?" It sounded farfetched.

"I doubt they knew it. Had to keep reality hushed up from the rank and file so they didn't realize they were being pulled by the whims of their real puppet master. My mother is horrifying."

"But she saved me then. She risked her position for me." They'd been hunting her ever since. I thought she did it to escape, but it was all to save me.

"That's what she does. A random good deed, a helping hand to the downtrodden. And none of them have a clue that it comes with strings attached. Sometimes they aren't pulled for years and always to her benefit."

Fucking hell.

"Give me that paper," my mom demanded all of a sudden.

"Why?"

"Using another witch's spell is dangerous. You never have total control of the magic you unleash. She does."

I got the spell for Daniel's resurrection from her. I used it without a second thought. I...

"Laylee?"

My head shook while my mind buzzed with what my grandmother could have done to me. Was it all to get me to drink the potion? To come out into the woods? Or was she planning to do much worse? "This is the best hope we have for stopping Conquest."

"No. My mother twists logic into a snarl of barbed wire. You think it makes sense, but if you try to get at the heart of it, you'll bleed." She reached for the paper, but I swung it away.

"What if it works? What if we...close the realms?"

"That would be the end of magic."

"It's what the angels planned," I said.

My mother cocked an eyebrow. "And you think they wanted what was best for humanity?"

The only angel I'd met was a selfish dick who had treated Garavel like a Roomba. But what choice did we have? We hadn't gotten any farther in our research to stop Conquest. This might be the only way I could get my life back.

Seeming to sense my decision, my mother dropped her hand and sighed. "At least it's from the Book of the Accords and not a twisted spell of hers. That's...something."

My mom paused in her feral wanderings and fell to her ass onto the soggy leaves. With her eyes closed tight, she took a deep breath. "I'm sorry you had to see that. I did everything I could to keep you from her."

"Why?"

"She forced you to drink one of her potions and you ask me...?"

I stared at my feet, my sneakers smeared in mud and the blue potion she'd been brewing. "Did she do that to you?"

"Every night. Made me sleep. Kept me docile. It took me a few years to figure out a counteragent, and another witch helped me with it. Not many liked my mother, for some *strange* reason," my mom said sarcastically.

She sighed deeper and stirred through the leaves before looking up at me. "I ran a year before my magic came in. It wasn't easy. It would have been fucking impossible without the other covens hiding me."

"Why?"

My mom held out her wrist. "Blood is thicker than water, right? She can track me with just a pinprick of her finger."

"Is that how you found me?" I asked, cold seeping up my bones.

I didn't know what I'd expected as a response, but I'd never anticipated my mother's face crumbling. She hung her head low and whispered, "I'm sorry. I just… I tried to be better than her. I hated that she was turning me into her duplicate, just there to follow orders. I grew up in the coven system—random women showing up at all hours, staying for months, then disappearing. When I ran from her, I thought I had left all of that behind. I didn't want the magic, I didn't want any of it. But we…"

My mom wafted her hand around causing a small vortex to form. A leaf caught in it, spinning round and round until she let it go. "We can't escape it. Though, if it wasn't for my magic, I'd never have met your father."

I sat on the ground next to her and tugged my knees to my chest. "What happened?"

Every time I had asked that, I'd gotten silence. I had been told to forget about it. That the answer didn't matter. But this time, my mother stared at the autumn stars, and the dam shattered. "There was a gremlin having a bit of fun with a city's power grid. Your father was a lineman."

"He played football?"

My mother stared at me. "No. He worked the lines, the power lines. The gremlin caused a blackout. I was chasing it down on my own, trying to keep undercover while also protecting my home. I never expected to run into this thick-headed, brilliant, protective man." Her harried voice softened and she glanced her palm against her cheek the way a lover would.

"After that night, I did the worst thing a witch could do."

God, that was a long list of potential atrocities. I clutched tight to my locket.

She smiled wanly and met my gaze. "I fell in love. Hard. I wanted to give up on magic, forget my past and live a normal life."

"What stopped you?" I asked, wanting the same, aching to be normal for once.

"You. Despite everything I did to be careful, magic found a way through all the birth control."

My heart lurched. *I kept her from the love of her life? It was my fault that she fell back into it?* "I'm sorry," I whispered.

"Laylee, no. I… Once that test turned blue, I had a choice to make. Either stay in my happy bubble of denial or have you. I'd pick you every time."

Tears burned in my eyes. I fought to keep them in. "Why? Why didn't you stay with him? We could have been…" I pulled in a hard breath that nearly swerved into a sob. "Happy."

"No, we couldn't. Not if I wanted to keep you safe."

"Why the hell not?" I screeched, my voice scraping at the layers of trauma built in my throat. "We'd have been a family. A normal family with love. I'd have had a mom and a dad, and… Why?"

"Because I had to protect you. I had to protect —"

"The fucking line. Again. I'm sick of it. I'm more than some goddamn spell receptacle, Mother."

"Don't you talk back to me. I know you're more than that. I raised you to be," she shouted.

Somehow we both shot to our feet, as ready to do battle as she had been with her mother. My hand reached for my spell book, but as my palm brushed the leather, I stopped. I couldn't spend my life fighting her. If she couldn't stop fighting me, then I didn't need her either. I'd gone fifteen years without just fine.

"Maybe I should find my father. He has the same blood as me, after all."

"Don't you fucking dare!" my mother shrieked. "You'll ruin everything. He's safe because I…because…"

"What, Mom? What did you do to him?"

"I didn't have a choice. If they found him. If *she* found him… I erased his memories of me. I pulled every second we had together out of his heart."

"What the fuck!"

"The alternative was killing him to protect you. If you contact him, then I might have to."

She's as bad as her mother. Maybe worse. Both of them trying to convince themselves that the ends justified the means. "You can't tell me what to do. I'm not your puppet."

"I never wanted you to be," my mom argued back, despite all the evidence in my life.

"I'm going to marry Cal. I'm going to stop Conquest. And I'm going to meet my father," I shouted at her, cutting whatever cord remained between us.

My mother reached out. Maybe there was a spell on her fingers, maybe nothing. I didn't have time to wait and see if she'd control my body like her mother did. With a quick jerk, I ripped the magic clean out of her. She gasped at the force and plunged to her knees.

Pain shot through my heart at the sight of my mother weak and vulnerable. I wanted to reach a hand out to help her back up, but I had to be strong. I couldn't let her control me or anyone else. With my head high, I walked out of her protective bubble and into the real world. The cold hit me fast and I shivered.

"Laylee…" My mom whimpered, her hands digging into the dirt. "Please."

"We're long past that, Mother. You took my childhood from me. You left me to fend for myself, and you've never told me why. I'm done."

With that, I turned on my heel and walked toward the lights of the neighborhood full of normal kids lost in happy dreams of love.

"I did it because of her." My mother's soft voice barely cut above the motorcycle roaring past in the distance. "She was getting close and I knew, I knew she'd take you from me. Do to you what she did to me. Faking my death was the only way I thought to protect you from…from turning into me."

A solitary gasp broke the air and my mom whispered, "I'm sorry."

Chapter Twenty-One

Layla

Ten days until the wedding, and I should have been working on tying ribbons to sticks, but my eyes kept drifting to my spell book. I'd tried to figure out what the hell Valerie gave me, but it looked like nonsense. Some parts were in Latin, the incantation at least, but at the bottom was a sentence that read like gibberish with every translation spell and app.

"Mi àm la'atzu eretu nam-tar."

Whatever it meant, it was written in block letters at the bottom like a warning. Do not get this parchment wet after midnight, maybe?

The doorbell rang and I slid the box off my lap. Cal came bounding down the stairs, his eyes wild. He ran so fast, his palms smacked into the door.

Ink snickered. "Your mutt is in need of an outdoor excursion."

"Funny," I said.

"Perhaps you should consider clipping the announcement bell. I've heard that can reduce a canine's stress."

I stared at Ink who'd been sitting in the chair quietly all afternoon reading a magazine. Where he had gotten it was anyone's guess. He slipped it down just enough he could peer over it and gave a wink.

"Holy shit!" Cal cried out. I turned as he flung his arms around whoever was at the door. "Marcus, man. It's been forever."

A handsome, dark-skinned man with tight braids and both sides of his head shaved walked in. Or tried to, as Cal kept exuberantly hugging him before letting go. "See, the house is still standing. That's good," the stranger said and he peered around inside.

"Oh, Layla." Cal dashed over and took me by the hand. The stranger glanced around confused and I granted him the ability to see me. His glazed over eyes focused on me as Cal said, "This is my cousin Marcus."

"Um..." It was a little hard to see the family resemblance.

Marcus laughed hard and slapped Cal on the shoulder. "It's like looking in a mirror, no?" He pulled Cal next to him, both wearing the same smiles, even if every other feature was different.

"He's the son of one of my mother's first pack's members, which makes him a cousin," Cal explained. "And this is Layla, my future wife."

Marcus' gray eyes shined as he took my hand and shook it warmly. Then he whistled and said to Cal, "*Elle est vraiment belle.*"

My cheeks burned at the compliment and I whispered, "*Merci.*"

At that, Marcus' face lit up and he elbowed Cal, "*Elle est trop bien pour toi.*"

"*Oui, je sais,*" Cal whispered, his pale skin turning beet red fast. Then he looked at me and his smile ticked upward like he was the luckiest man in the world.

"Are you taking in Gaulish strays now?" Ink asked as he rose to his feet. "Or is he to be a wedding present?"

Marcus breathed deep and his brows shot up fast. He lurched for the incubus, but Cal placed a calming hand on his chest. "Don't worry, this one's fangless."

"Are you certain of that, wolf?" Ink didn't flare his teeth or claws. Instead, he wrapped a protective arm around my waist and pulled me to my feet. He smiled possessively and leaned to nibble my throat.

I didn't have time to deal with this and pushed my palm against Ink's lips. "Marcus?" I asked, ignoring the demon nipping on my finger. "Are you here for the wedding?"

Cal answered, "He's going to marry us."

"So it is to be a three-way ceremony? Now I'm intrigued," Ink said.

"No, I mean…" Cal began before catching on that it didn't matter.

"Wow, I didn't even think about— But that's good. Great to have you help us out."

"I've done a few of these in the past," Marcus said with pride.

With a slow sigh, Cal said, "Not many would do a mating ceremony for a packless wolf."

Marcus shook his head and clapped his hands once. "Shall we get started?"

"Don't you want to get settled in first?" I asked. "We could, um…" Oh god, where the hell was he going to sleep? "Daniel might not be against sharing his room." The second the words left me, I could feel him shuddering somewhere in the world.

Luckily, I was saved by Marcus laughing. "Nah. I brought my tent. Gonna do some roughing it old-school style in the woods. Haven't let loose in months, damn crunch time."

"He's a developer on Sheep Wars," Cal said.

That caught the instant interest of the Sheep Wars addict. "You are one of the minds behind a game where Sheep are the dominant species of the galaxy?" Ink asked. "A wolf."

Marcus gave a little shrug and smiled.

"Tell me all that you know of the Mythical Llama."

"Ah, no shop talk this trip," Marcus said. "Game's gold, I'm free. Let's talk about the future newlyweds."

Ink instantly grew bored and wandered off, though he promised he would have much more pressing questions for the bestower of the Sheep Wars trilogy. Marcus took up the armchair while Cal sat beside me. He held my hands and sweetly brushed his thumbs over the backs.

"What do you need from us?"

"Well, I guess first thing is vows. You guys gonna do them yourselves?"

Vows. The most important part of a wedding, probably the only necessary part. Standing before friends and family, swearing to forsake all others while I was sleeping with four other men. How the hell was that going to work?

"Yeah," Cal said for me. He curled his arm behind my back and pulled me closer. "That's more our speed."

"Makes my life easier," Marcus said. "Now, how traditional of a mating ceremony are we talking? I assume there won't be the battle of servitude."

"The what?" I asked.

"No."

"What about the testing of fertility?"

My eyes shot open. "Excuse me?"

"That's not necessary either," Cal said. I clenched tight to his knee, needing an explanation but he kept plowing ahead.

"Nontraditional. Got it." Marcus jotted all of this down. "What about the bite?"

"Oh, yeah," Cal said with a big grin, then he stared at me. "We have to do that."

Biting? Fights? Fertility? "What the hell is he talking about?" I shouted. "Who's biting what?"

"The groom and bride bite each other to cement their union," Marcus said like it was no big deal.

My mouth dropped open and I struggled to form words. In front of all my friends on my wedding day, in a fancy gown, I was supposed to let Cal bite me? "No." I shook my head hard and leaped to my feet.

"Babe?" He sounded genuinely shocked at my response. Couldn't he hear himself?

"You want to do that…!" I blushed, remembering Marcus. "That…in front of people. No way. I can't." I stumbled into the coffee table, taking a hit to the shins. The other men stood in concern, but I kept twisting away, making a break for the hallway outside the dining room.

"Give me a second," Cal said to Marcus and he dashed after me. "Layla, I don't understand. What's the problem?"

"The problem? What does biting me have to do with a wedding?"

Cal's whole body crumpled in, his head drooping against his chest. He whispered, "Everything."

Damn it, what am I missing? I reached out for his hand before he had a chance to flee away. Cal let my fingers thud against his before he locked his around mine. "I knew a traditional wedding wouldn't happen, and I'm fine with that."

"Because I'm a witch," I said.

He shook his head, then sighed. "Because I'm packless, because you're not a werewolf, because a lot of reasons. It doesn't matter. All of that doesn't matter, but I just… I wanted to do the bite. But I get it, you're not used to it. It's silly. Forget it."

All of his excitement had deflated to nothing in an instant and I felt horrible. "Can you explain what it is?"

"After their vows, the couple will take the other's hand, swear to protect and love their mate with their whole heart, then seal it with a bite."

"Where's it done?"

"Depends. I've seen some nip on the wrist, others the cheek, occasionally the shoulder."

I frowned at the idea of him clamping onto my clavicle in front of everyone. "Why didn't you tell me about this?"

"I don't know. I guess I just thought you knew. Stupid. Of course, you wouldn't, it's a wolf thing. You don't have to, Layla. It's not a part of who you are."

"But it is a part of you," I said and closed my eyes.

"You think it's disgusting."

"No, it's just…" I got turned on by biting and being bitten. Should the bride be super horny at the altar? It was barely a kink, but my skin prickled at the idea of anyone catching on.

Cal released my fingers and moved to walk away. "I'll tell Marcus that we can keep it simple. No werewolf stuff."

"What if it's my wrist?" I asked, holding my arm out to him.

He curled his palm around it and traced my veins with his thumb. Delicately, he leaned closer and placed a soft kiss there. I sighed at the touch and ruffled my fingers through his hair, but Cal shook his head. "If you don't want to do this, I don't want to make you."

"I...I may not get it, but you do. And it matters to you. It's your wedding too, right?"

Cal's enthusiasm inflated beyond limits and he pulled both my hands behind the nape of his neck. "I love you," he said then kissed me. "I want to be with you. In the legal sense, in the wolf sense, in all the senses. That makes no sense."

I laughed at him and pressed my forehead against his. "It does sound romantic in a way."

He softened and drew his fingers down my forearms. "The bite's supposed to symbolize the pain of the relationship. You swear to the moon and the gods watching that from that moment on everything you do is so she never has to feel a pain that sharp again. I don't want anything bad to happen to you."

"Me either," I whispered. Cal kissed me sweetly as he swept his palms over my hips.

"Is there anything from your culture you want to add to the ceremony? Maybe a spell or a potion?"

I pursed my lips hard, my heart churning. "Yeah, there's something, but... I've got to talk to someone first."

* * * *

The yellow bungalow was nestled next to a stand of avocado trees. I stewed in the sweater I should have left back at home while doing my best to not creepily watch the older man resting on the porch. *This is so stupid. What am I doing?*

"You are aware of the unwise nature of your actions?" Ink asked like it was a fact.

"I don't need your approval," I said.

"I would hardly expect you to begin requiring it now."

Run across the street right up to this stranger and say... Say what? "Oh god, what do I say?"

"There is the truth if you intend to be hurled into an asylum."

"Those aren't a thing anymore," I said.

"Really? Has humanity ceased using the criminally insane as cheap labor? Surprising."

I didn't have time to explain the complicated for-profit prisons. The man shifted in his lounge chair and I sank lower to the ground. Ink came with, one palm planted between his hunched legs as he stared out. "There is no reason we cannot return home. Perhaps in time to stop the werewolves from marking every errant stone in the garden."

"No."

"You're correct. The spray bottle has ceased to function."

I shook off Ink's nonsense and focused. The spell was easy enough. I'd used it to track down my mother and never once thought to try with him. Why?

There has to be a reason, an explanation why I...why I'm the way I am. Maybe he'll be happy to learn I exist. Accept that witchcraft hid me from him but we could be a family. I could learn all about him, he could learn about me. Walk me down the aisle. Be a father.

I stood.

"My bond." Ink cupped my arm. There was no pressure in his fingers, but I knew I couldn't move until he let go. "Think upon what you are doing."

"I'm going to meet my father," I said, my voice straining in disbelief. All those years of me asking and hoping and wishing, and all it took was a simple pinprick.

"Then what?"

I blinked. The rosy images of me bonding with my father cracked into a man ordering me off his property. This could go horribly wrong. But I'd always wonder if I didn't take the chance. What if I lost him before I tried?

"What are you getting at, Ink?"

He stilled his lips, a rare event, and stared across the way. "You discovered him via magic, yes? The blood of your blood. The flesh of your flesh."

"You make it sound so creepy."

"What if an unsavory person, Samuke or worse, were to do the same?"

I stared at him, waiting for his point.

Ink scratched his chin in thought. "While I find your mother's beliefs and actions abhorrent in the best of times..." He slipped his palm down my arm until his fingers curled around mine. "I know that she would drain the oceans dry to keep you safe."

"She lied to me."

"I suspect for the most ignoble of reasons a being can give," he said cryptically.

"What's that?"

Rather than answer, Ink lifted our joined hands and kissed my knuckles. "You already know. I will not stop you, but I only wish you to weigh the consequences. If you can find him through your blood, they can find you."

He let go.

I took two steps, then looked over my shoulder. A part of me expected Ink to leap forward, sweep me into his arms and rush back home. He hadn't been happy when I asked for his help in getting to California. But he did it. And he let me go.

Nodding once to him, I pulled my purse tighter to my side and walked across the road. A small wooden fence circled the gravel yard and I stopped at the gate. Closing my eyes, I whispered, "Let my father see me." The man in the chair shifted as if the air changed without him understanding why.

"Excuse me?" I called out. "Are you Curtis Pierce?"

He placed his glass down on the table beside him and sat up higher. "Yeah. Who's asking?"

"I'm Layla…Monvoison."

"Never heard that name before."

"It's French," I said as an excuse. "I was wondering if I could ask you a few questions about your work as a lineman."

He could throw me out so easily, but the man shrugged and leaned back in his chair. "A'right. Head on in. The latch sticks a bit, just wiggle it."

I eased my way through while taking in the house to find any hint of who he was. A basketball hoop without a net hung above the one-car garage. There was a flag in the far left window for a team, though I didn't know who. I did appreciate the bright purple color.

"Have a seat, Miss…Mono-something or other."

I laughed at his charming fumbling and perched on the chair next to him. "You can call me Layla."

"Curtis, though most call me Curt. You wanted to ask about my time working the lines? Any reason?"

"I'm doing a paper on electrical grids through the ages. I thought it'd do wonders for my grade if I interviewed people who were there." *What the hell am I talking about?*

He stared at me with the same dumbfounded look I had to be wearing. "Okay. Who am I to turn down a nice chat with a lovely young lady? Shoot."

I reached into my purse as a distraction and pulled out my damn wedding binder. Hiding away the checklist with my elbow, I flipped to the spell portion and pulled out a pen. He looked at me with curious patience and my mind blanked. *What do I say?*

You're my father.

You don't remember my mother because she erased your memories of her.

Surprise!

"I...I, um, I love your slides," I said, pointing to the royal purple slippers on his feet.

He lifted one and smiled. "Thanks. Good to know they're still cool with the kids."

Wow, that was cheesy. Oh my god, my dad's cheesy.

I had to fight off the stupid grin at learning something about him. "Can you tell me a bit about yourself, Curtis? Mr. Pierce? Um."

He laughed again and tipped back in his chair. "Let's see. Born in Oakland, the third of five kiddos."

I have aunts and uncles?

"Did not great in school. Never had the head for it. But electricity just calls to me. I can't explain it. It's like I can almost sense where it's going and when it's not. Worked pretty well for me, for a while anyway. Uh, do you want any specifics about my time as a lineman?"

I blinked, my heart racing with the idea that my dad and I both suffered from dyslexia. We had so much in common. Could he sense it too? Was he already wondering if there was a child out there looking for him?

"Ah, anything you want to share?"

"Well, you got to have nerves of steel to do that job. Hundreds of feet in the air, being batted around in blizzards and hurricanes while live wires spark near your hands. Maybe not be quite right in the head too, putting your life on the line so people get to keep their lights on."

Curtis placed his hands behind his head and stared up at the electricity poles running along the street. "I loved it. There's a freedom in the work, a wildness you don't get much anymore. Moving from job to job, helping people. Facing the worst of it so they don't have to."

"Do you...?" I coughed and tried to shake off the weight in my heart. "Do you remember a blackout about twenty-six or twenty-seven years ago in—?"

"The one in...? Yeah. That was a doozy. No one could figure it out. The grid was lit up like Christmas but nothing was getting out. I..." His once forthcoming mouth turned down and he squinted. "I remember I fixed it. There was something on the roof. Like a wire was wrapped around a little garden gnome? No, that can't be it."

"Were you alone?"

"No," he said quickly, then shook his head. "I mean, yeah. Least I think so."

Maybe the memories weren't gone. Maybe she'd just hidden them. I could pull them free, let him remember Mom. Remember the love they had, and we could become a family.

Curtis turned his head and stared at me. "Why do—?"

The front door flew open and two sets of legs stomped down the stairs. I heard the stampede of giggles and only saw a flash before Curtis sat up and said, "We don't slam the front door."

Two young girls, the eldest at most ten, said, "Sorry, Daddy."

Daddy?

"Kids," he said with a shrug as they ran to the pavement and started to draw with chalk. "You got any?"

"No." I shook my head, my heart reeling. *I have sisters. He has… Of course, he has another family. He was free of this magic that keeps taking it from me.*

"I won't say they aren't a handful, 'cause they are, but…you look into those big eyes that are just like yours, that sweet smile, and you know… They're about to ask for twenty bucks." He laughed at that. "Course my wife always gives in, she's such a soft touch. Probably why I fell for her."

"Your wife?" I tried to keep my voice level but a squeak broke through.

He looked over at me with wary concern. "Yeah. She's a nurse."

"Really? I'm studying to be a nurse!" I shouted, excited to find another shared trait.

"And you're doing a paper on electrical grids from the nineties?"

"The school wants us to be well rounded, so…"

"It's a fine profession. Wearing, though. Got to be tough as nails and gentle as a river for it. But that's my Toya, always needing to help people, most of whom don't want it." Curtis snickered and slid in his chair. Suddenly, he hissed in pain.

"Are you okay?" I asked, partially standing.

"It's fine. Don't worry about it," he assured me even while gritting his teeth. "Accident at work. Laid me up good. Best I can manage is a few hours in a chair here or there."

"I'm…I'm sorry."

"Not much can be done about it. Back stuff's the worst to get fixed. Anyway, you had questions for me."

"I…"

Curtis Pierce had a nice life. He had two adorable girls in braids and a loving nurse wife. If I told him the truth, if he welcomed me with open arms, then… Then what?

One of the girls covered her palm in pink chalk then slapped it on her sister's cheek. The pink handprint glowed against the brown skin. Instead of crying, she did the same to hers and went after her sister who was wily enough to run away. *Happiness. Family.*

My mom could have taken this from him. She could have been as selfish as hers, as every other damn witch. But she let him go.

I have to do the same.

"I think I've got enough," I said, closing my binder.

"Oh. Well, that was quick. Good luck with your paper, Miss Monovision."

"Monvoison."

"Each time I hear it, it sounds wrong. Like it should be something with an E."

I couldn't stay any longer. He might begin to remember and that would bring my enemies to him. I held my hand out. "Thank you for your time, Mr. Pierce."

He clenched his fingers around mine, and I whispered fast. The magic glowed for a half second, lighting up his face, before it sank inside. Curtis stared at his hand in confusion while I walked down the sidewalk. At the gate, I heard him stand and sigh with a loud stretch.

"Holy…!"

"Daddy?" The two girls, used to their hobbled father, paused and watched as he dashed down the porch steps and scooped both into his arms.

"I'm a great Tyrannosaurus Rex, and I'm going to gobble you up."

"No!" they squealed in happy delight, chasing each other around until they'd fall into a pile.

I stopped looking back, but as I approached Ink he kept watching them. "You did not tell him."

"No."

"But you gave him a parting gift."

It wasn't much, just a little healing magic to chase away the pain. If I was lucky, it'd be permanent. If I wasn't, at least he'd get a few hours of freedom.

A finger swept over my cheek and I blinked in surprise as Ink wiped away a tear. A smile twisted up his lips, but his eyes were crinkled at the edges. "My bond, I believe it's time I take you home." He bent over and swept me up into his arms.

I locked my hands behind his neck and gazed into his eyes. "Happily," I said, giving my father the same gift my mother did — peace.

Chapter Twenty-Two

Layla

One week before the wedding and I was finally trying on my dress. Dana had gotten a bottle of champagne for the occasion. My stomach seethed with butterflies, but as I ran my fingers over the fabric, those butterflies turned into wasps. Instead of the soft silk I'd imagined, it felt like a cheap Halloween costume.

I closed my eyes while stepping into it, praying that the loose threads and dangling parts would all magically transform into the fantasy wedding dress of my dreams. "Damn it. I think it caught on my ass."

"Hang on, the zipper's... Shit." Dana kept yanking it and me up into the air. "Maybe if we grease you down first. There we go."

Just before I could start to panic, the unforgiving fabric slipped over my hips. Dana pulled on the zipper, only for it to get stuck halfway. "This damn thing's so tiny I can barely get the teeth to..."

Please don't rip it. I don't have time to fix anything right now. My backyard was full of werewolves, my dining table covered in unfinished favors, my bedroom crammed to the brim with decorations. If I added one more task to the list, I was going to explode.

The teeth raked against my bare spine and I shivered, but the zipper went all the way up. Dana placed a calming hand on my shoulder and she gasped in exhaustion. "There we go. All good, and..."

Her silence caused me to open my eyes.

Oh no, a lumpy marshmallow monster broke into Dana's apartment and replaced the mirror! The creature lifted its arm the same way I did and reality crashed around me.

"Oh my god," I cried.

"Wait, there's a tie back here. Maybe that'll make all the difference." Dana got to work knotting what was supposed to be a beautiful purple ribbon around the waist. In reality, it looked like a scrap of leftover fabric they'd barely sewn over to hide the frayed ends. The bodice, which in the picture was beaded with white crystals, had a handful of sequins randomly sewn in place. Worse than that, the top bulged below my breasts, then cut straight across right above my nipple line. If I so much as breathed, I'd spill out of it. The waistline hit just below my second rib so I looked like a potato in a skirt.

I raised my foot and the hemline brushed against my upper ankle. The floor-length silk gown with crystal beading and a purple sash was in reality an ankle-length polyester and sequined costume. It cut so tight to my hips, instead of flowing like a bell, the skirt bulged awkwardly before cutting inward.

"No." I didn't know what else to say. I was supposed to walk down the aisle in this? "I can't wear this. I can't... What am I going to do?"

Dana pursed her lips. "Maybe if we take it to a seamstress? They can do something to fix this." She hoisted up the bodice and my boobs fled into my armpits for safety. Jesus, it made me look even worse than before.

I wanted to cry, but I was so far beyond tears, a string of mad laughter grew in my throat. "Oh my god," I shouted, damn near cackling in horror at the abomination in the mirror.

Dana gave a more careful laugh, her eyes darting around the room as if she was looking for help.

"I...I'm terrifying. I look like a blobfish in heels." The laughter hit harder than ever, my stomach seizing along with it. "It's like I'm wearing a white trash bag with the drawstring still on."

"At least you're finding the humor in this," Dana said.

"If Cal sees me in this" —I gasped for air between my laughs—"he's gonna turn around and run the hell away."

Everything hit me at once. I would have to walk down the aisle wearing this on the one day I was supposed to be the most beautiful woman in the room. "Gah!" The tears gut-punched me and I tried to crumple in half, but the tight dress wouldn't let me bend more than twenty degrees. I wrapped my hand around the standing mirror and planted my forehead against the glass. The tears fell so hard my eyes stung with salt, but I couldn't stop.

"What. Am I. Gonna. Do?" I couldn't stop sobbing except between breaths.

"We'll get you a new one," Dana said, as if it was easy.

"It's in seven days!" I shouted at her. *Why didn't I try it on earlier? It's my fault for waiting so long.* "I'm sorry."

"Layls, there's off-the-rack ones out there. We could hit up a few boutiques. Maybe get lucky. Anything's gonna be better than this."

And buy it with what? Our credit cards were already belching smoke. Any off-the-rack dress that fit me was going to cost extra—thousands of dollars I couldn't have afforded before we had to buy cupcakes to supplement the cake or get another tux for Marcus, and god knew we needed a fancy acrylic sign. Couldn't have a wedding without that!

"Do you got a fancy weaving spell in your book? Maybe a fairy godmother you can call up?"

I wished. I shook my head and stared at the mess of a woman in the mirror. Who did she think she was, believing she'd get a happy day, a real wedding? She'd never deserved that.

"Girl, let's get that off of you. It's probably gonna give you a rash."

"Dana!" I cried as she pulled on the zipper, but she was probably right. Maybe my wedding dress was full of bedbugs.

"Why does this wedding feel cursed?" I asked the universe.

"Forget all of that. Here." Dana passed me not a glass of champagne but the full bottle. I took one look at the unnervingly shiny dress, placed the bottle to my lips and drank. "We're gonna find a replacement, something cute. It might not be show-stopping, but anything's better than that." She kicked the dress and it slid across the floor like oil.

"How?" I asked. It was October. All the cute dresses were in autumn colors—burgundy and orange and plum. The only way I'd be able to afford a white one was by paying with a kidney.

Dana picked up her comb and clips. "Let's put such gorgeous braids in your hair, no one will even see your dress."

I sat in the chair as she parted down the left side and clipped my hair back. "What am I going to do without a dress?" I asked.

"If I can get my sister to fork over her extensions, we could Lady Godiva it. Just a few carefully placed braids over your nipples, and boom. How do you feel about walking down the aisle naked?"

I laughed hard at the idea. "Ink would love it."

"That perv would." Dana got to work while I did my best to look at my face and not the dress lurking on the floor.

What am I going to do?

* * * *

I knocked on Daniel's door and it shuddered open. Instead of my punk rock boyfriend, my big marshmallow lay on the bed. Garavel was twisted up with his back against the wall and legs along the side so a little black body could nap in the sunlight.

"What are you doing here?" *In Daniel's room, on his bed.*

Garavel looked up from the sleeping kitty and smiled. "She has chosen this spot as her preferred destination for a morning slumber."

"Cats go where they want, but you don't have to…" I began, before catching the loving way he watched over the cat who didn't have a care in the world. Easing across the room, I did my best to sit on the edge without disturbing Fiona.

"How are you doing?" I asked, reaching for him. He smiled with his whole face and my palm slipped inside his huge hand.

"There are a great many werewolves around."

I winced. "Yeah, I didn't expect the whole crew to show up a week before the wedding. That's, uh…" I peered over at the angel who'd sworn a blood oath against all werewolves. "Challenging?"

"You are concerned that I will obliterate them to dust," he said softly and drew a single finger down Fiona's back.

"Uh…no?"

"I understand they are here at your discretion. My sword will remain sheathed until such a time that arrangement changes."

That sounded like something Ink would say, not Garavel. Using his hand for leverage, I pulled myself across Daniel's bed. His comforter came with my ass but I managed to lay my head against Garavel's shoulder. The gentle grinding of stones inside his chest was soothing.

"They'll be gone soon," I assured him. Or maybe myself. It wasn't that I didn't like having Cal's extended family around, they were just…

A loud howl ripped from the backyard, shaking the windows, and ten followed suit.

"Are you sure you're okay? You've been hiding up here a lot." As had Daniel, and I didn't think I'd seen Ink in two days. Everyone was just elsewhere. Or maybe they were all bunkered down together waiting for the wedding hurricane to blow over. I wished I could join them.

"Fiona does not enjoy the exuberance of the numerous wolves. It puts her on edge, and reminds her of..." Garavel held his tongue and turned away. "It is easier to keep to my rookery."

"I'm sorry." I draped my arms around his neck and rested my cheek on his chest. "I swear, once this wedding is over—"

"Everything will return to as it once was?" he asked.

Except I'd be married. "Yeah," I said. "Least, I...I think so. Hope so."

"You will be joining your forces with Calvin. No matter how smoothly a transition is planned, there will be chaos among the ranks."

Oh, boy. I sat up higher. "Garavel, that's not what a wedding is. It's—"

"A merging of one person with another. A declaration given before the world that they are to be a united front in all matters of life and love."

"Yes, how did you...?"

Garavel swept his large hand over my cheek and traced down my smile line with his thumb. "Lady witch. I am—"

"You're in here again." Daniel's loud groan broke from the doorway.

"Fiona is—"

"Yes, the cat loves my bed, I know, but that doesn't give you the right to..." He switched his bass guitar and spotted me laying on the right side. "Layla. Wow, your hair is...?"

I nervously touched the braids, my scalp a touch sore and in desperate need of coconut oil. "Is it too much?" I fiddled with the purple ribbon Dana had woven down the right side.

"It's beautiful. You're beautiful and in my bed."

"Oh, sorry." I began to scoot away when Daniel laughed.

"You can stay. The giant rock angel shattering every spring, however…"

Garavel mumbled under his breath and swung his legs out. The floor shook as they landed and he stood. At that moment, the bed heaved, nearly throwing me into the air. I gulped and clung to the brass headboard, my heart pounding. Daniel caught my eye, then he looked at my hand and smiled.

"If that's why you came, I'll be happy to oblige," he said, taking off his backpack.

Fiona gave an angry meow as Garavel picked her up from her coveted spot. He didn't hold her long, the cat quickly climbing up his arm and launching for the door. "I should leave you alone, lady witch. Um…" He stared up to the only hatch into the attic, then out of the window where the werewolves played drunken horseshoes.

Everything grew extremely awkward fast. I too slipped to my feet and nervously tossed my new braids around. "I'm here for your help, Daniel."

"Oh?"

"I still need to write my vows…"

"And you thought I'd have the wherewithal to spew lovey-dovey poetry about the werewolf?" he challenged me, and I frowned.

"It's just, you know, you're so good with words."

Daniel stared at me like I was out of my mind when a new voice broke from the door.

" 'Upon my word, I tell you faithfully, through life and after death, you are my queen'."

Ink leaned against the doorframe, his head tipped down. Instead of a cigarette, a sucker stick perched on the side of his lips as he spoke. " 'For with my death, the whole truth shall be seen. Your two great eyes will slay me suddenly. Their beauty shakes me who was once serene. Straight through my heart, the wound is quick and keen'."

"Wow, that's...beautiful," I whispered, feeling every lovelorn pain in his words. Ink didn't look at me, just kept staring ahead.

"That's Chaucer," Daniel said. "Do you have a single original bone in your body?"

Ink pulled the sucker from his lips and stared at it. Then he smirked at Daniel. "I know of one my bond enjoys quite vigorously." After the groans at his pun, Ink rubbed his hands together. "Now, to the nuptial vows. I assume the state of Calvin's wolfish member will be required—both the functionality and performance rating."

"What? No. No, no one is talking about his penis at the wedding."

"Is not the chaining of genitals the entire point of the affair?"

"What is the point of this wedding?" Garavel asked, so quiet I was almost able to shrug it away. Then he reached a hand out to me and pleaded, "Lady witch?"

"Tis a question that hangs upon the heads of lovers and the lovelorn alike," Ink said.

"You know," I said. "Come on. It's why everyone gets married."

"I've been wondering too," Daniel said. "You live here. You've got all of us. What more do you need?"

"Security."

We all spun around to find Cal standing just outside the room. He tried to get around Ink still in the doorway, but the incubus didn't move. "Maybe you guys don't need it. Maybe you don't want it." He looked at Ink who finally uncrossed his arms and slipped inside. Then Cal held out his hands and I took both.

Staring into my eyes, he said, "But I do. Safety was a luxury I didn't know for decades. In my heart, I know that you love me, that you'll be with me until my muzzle turns white."

I laughed as tears misted in my eyes.

"But my brain needs to know it so I can be the best person, the best husband for you, Layla."

I flung my arms behind his neck and kissed him. "Cal, I..." My declaration of love rammed into three other men watching. "That's why. Okay?" I said to the others who had enough decency to nod along.

"Now that that's settled, babe, look what just came in." Cal popped open a familiar little black box. Inside rested a silver band with six tiny amethysts embedded into it. "How do you feel about wearing that for the rest of your life?" he asked.

"It's beautiful. I can't wait to..." The happy tears warped to a discordant note as I stared down at the wedding ring. "Oh no. Oh, shit."

"What?" Cal looked at the ring in concern.

"Is something the matter?" Garavel piped up.

"Did he pick a cursed ring?" Daniel asked.

Every man reached over to either comfort or protect me, but I kept slipping farther away in shock. As I dug my nails into my cheeks, my mouth fell open. "I didn't get you a wedding ring. I completely forgot. What the fuck is wrong with me?"

"Babe..."

"I've been obsessing over caramel apple sticks, purple candy and little mason jars crammed with candles, but the one thing that lasts past the wedding is what I forgot. I'm so sorry." *How could I do that to him?*

Cal stepped forward away from the others. "Layla, don't cry."

I bit my lip to try to obey, but everything hit at once. My wedding dress was unusable, the flowers were a pile of weeds, I had no family coming to see me marry and I had forgotten his ring. Tears gushed down my cheeks.

At once, all of my guys leaped toward my side. Cal got there first. He should have been fuming at me. Instead, he curled his palms over my cheeks. My tears caught and ran down his fingers, and I couldn't stop crying.

"It's okay. I swear, it's okay." He pulled me into his arms. A hand brushed against my upper back and another on my shoulder. I couldn't guess who, only that they were all trying to comfort me as I came apart.

"I. Am. The. Worst."

"No, you're not. You are sweet, adorable and stressed to the breaking point." He sounded concerned, then kissed the top of my head. "It's my fault. I should have told you werewolves don't do rings."

"What?" I pulled my face off of his chest to look into his eyes.

Cal held out his bare hand. "Forget to take it off when you shift and there goes your finger."

"Oh." I hadn't even thought about that. I tried to shake away the embarrassment blazing on my cheeks, my skin red hot to the touch. "What do married werewolves wear?"

Instead of answering, Cal took my flaming hot face in his hands. "It doesn't matter," he said and kissed me.

"A tooth."

Cal popped away and glared at Ink. He started to move his hands over my ears as if to protect me, but I pushed myself away to look at my chatty incubus. "A tooth?"

"Taken from the jaw of their mate. Dipped in silver, if I remember properly. Am I correct, mutt?"

Cal's lips pulled back and he growled. "Don't start this shit, Ink."

"You're not taking Layla's tooth," Daniel insisted.

"Of course, I won't. It's not... It's a stupid old ritual. I'd never expect her to—"

"Cal?" I pressed my hand to his chest, the steady beat of his heart thumping up my palm.

He sighed as if he really didn't want to get into it. "Fine. During the mating ceremony, a werewolf will remove a fang as a sign of devotion, then dip it in—yes—silver. You anal prolapse. They wear their mate's fang on a chain."

"Why?"

Groaning, Cal rubbed his palms over his face and mumbled below them. "To show that they would never turn their fangs on each other. It's...stupid."

"You said that previously," Ink chimed in.

He glared harder at him. "Barbaric, then. I don't want to do it. Layla, please don't think you have to pull out a tooth to make me happy. I don't need a ring, I don't need a necklace. I just need you." Cal wrapped me up tighter than ever and placed his cheek on the top of my head. While rocking back and forth, he begged, "Please?"

How stupid would I look saying my vows, then doing nothing? All those werewolves waiting for me to pull out a tooth and give it to him. What would we do? Move on to the next part? I closed my eyes, wishing the wedding was over. That every problem was solved, the dress burned, the guests gone—until it was just me, Cal, Ink, Daniel and Garavel in a big bed together.

"You always will," I whispered, holding him tight.

Chapter Twenty-Three

Layla

"The dogs are ready!" Cal shouted from the huge rented grill. He clacked his tongs and a mass of werewolves converged on him, plates at the ready.

"What are you doing, man?" Marcus sidled in beside him. "The groom doesn't cook at his own rehearsal dinner."

"I like doing it," he said, then shimmied a burger off the grill and placed it on a bun. "For my bride." Cal grinned with full cheese as he handed me the plate. "There's a little something extra in there." He winked at me.

"You're in a good mood," I said, lining up the ketchup bottle.

I damn near sprayed a mass of red goo across three werewolves when Cal wrapped an arm around my waist. "In twenty-four hours, I'll be married to the hottest woman in the world." He stared down at me and growled. "I love the dress."

"That's good." Since it was all I had for the wedding.

"Ice your loins." Ink stepped in between us and pried Cal's arm off.

"Since when do you try to stop me? Or any of us?"

Ink tipped his head and tapped a finger to his chin. In place of the red shirt, he'd put on a white one. All of my guys were done up nice for the rehearsal, but only Ink's outfit screamed money and power. "The night before the ceremony is a time for embracing purity. You wouldn't wish to be drained before the consummating, would you?"

Cal frowned like he'd planned to pull me away for a quickie, though our house was bulging with guests so I wasn't sure where. "Fine," he complained, then he pulled me close and kissed me. I began to break off when Cal palmed my ass and rolled his tongue in my mouth. "I love you."

"I love you too," I whispered.

"Hey, where's the meat?" a werewolf cousin shouted.

"Coming up."

As Cal busied himself with feeding the hungry masses, I walked away to talk to the non-furry people at the wedding. Ink was right on my heels. "I'm surprised you aren't trying to take over the grill."

"My talents would be wasted on the rudimentary palate of werewolves," he harrumphed.

It had been a good rehearsal. Everything had gone well—no one had broken through the windows and tried to murder us. Angelo was adorable, slinging the ring pillow on his back like a turtle. There wasn't a single bad omen, but I couldn't shake a feeling in my stomach.

Or maybe it was the fact I hadn't eaten all day.

"Cal, Marcus is right. Let him take over. You're the guest of honor," Cal's mother called. She was the only one who could pull him away from the grill.

I stopped beside her. She was sitting in one of the few deck chairs. "Hello, Cat...erine. Catherine." My face flexed with a hundred different attempts to seem nonchalant.

She smoothed back her white hair and looked up at me. "How are you holding up, Layla?"

"Good. I'm...I just want it to be over," I confessed.

Cal's mother chuckled, and she graced her hand on mine. "I don't blame you. It's a lot."

"I'd have been content with eloping, but..." *Oh god, why am I saying any of this to her?*

Her caring smile shifted and pain warped her features. "You want to make him happy. You do make him happy. This is the most open I've ever seen him." She gazed up at me like she was waiting for me to say something, but I didn't know what.

Of course I want him to be happy. I want all of them to be happy...even if it's a balancing act that would test an acrobat.

"Layla!" a voice from my past squealed. I barely had a chance to turn before arms flew around my shoulders and shoved my burger toward my chest. Ink took it before ketchup and mustard smeared my boobs.

A flutter of golden wings made me smile, and I reached over to close off the hug. "Mikki. You made it."

"Barely. Fucking airline diverted us to Texas, then Boston, then Texas again. I could have fucking walked here. Oh my god, you are so cute in that hair. That ribbon is perfect. How's Cal? Shitting himself?"

The nymph I'd been kidnapped with talked a mile a minute. "You look wonderful yourself," I said, taking in her beautiful gold dress cut at the knee.

She gave a little curtsy like a fairy in the woods, then unleashed her mouth. "I'm sweating like a fat pig in a butcher shop in this. I thought it was supposed to be freezing cold up here."

Even if it wasn't unseasonably warm for two days before Halloween, the mass of werewolves and their unnatural body heat would keep this place toasty. "How are your people?"

"Nymphs gonna nymph. Things are…" For a second, her exuberance dimmed. "This is a party. Who cares about some dusty old nymphs? Cal! Are you ready to get neutered in a church?"

Mikki moved to Cal's side and Dana wandered by to mine. "Who's that with the wings?"

"She's a nymph," I said and Dana's eyes bugged out as Mikki threw her arms around Cal for a big hug. "She's cool."

"Better question, who's that fine brother you've got marrying you off? Please don't say priest."

I laughed as Dana openly drooled over Marcus. Though, as he expertly wielded both tong and spatula with a tight apron over his suit, I couldn't blame her. "That's Marcus. He's one of Cal's cousins."

She stared dumbfounded at me, and I pointed to the other horde. "Just like all of the other…"

"Oh, so he's a…? You know, with the fangs and claws and dangerously ripped abs and tight ass. Hey, Marcus!" Dana waved to him, then she whispered, "Is he married?"

"Nope," I said with confidence.

"You handle your meat like a pro," Dana shouted, striding toward him. I caught Marcus laughing at whatever Dana said before she shot me a thumbs-up.

In the corner of the garden, next to an old gnome, Fariah and Maram spoke softly together. I took a moment to duck away from the action and joined them beside the mums. "Thank you for coming," I said to Maram.

She jerked her head up like a startled deer. "Thank you for inviting me." Fariah held her hand to form a united front and my heart clenched.

"No thanks necessary. I'm just glad that you feel comfortable enough to be here for Fariah."

Maram nodded, her head drifting lower so she stared at my shoes. "I wouldn't want to be anywhere else." The two lovebirds gazed into each other's eyes. A sharp howl broke from the werewolf clan and a chant to drink broke out. "Are they always this loud?"

"Be glad you missed the full moon," I said. It'd been like a frat party during an old monster movie. I had half expected to see Dracula doing a keg stand.

"All right, everyone. We're Gods of Death and we're here to play this evening," Daniel announced over the mike. The band stood on a scrap of plywood to keep them out of the mud. Though they'd taken the time to put up a banner. It had not only their name but the word death in various languages.

"I cannot decide if it is ironic or apropos to have a musical act named for death entertaining a matrimony." Ink crossed his arms, but his foot started to tap as the first earworm played.

"Is that your way of trying to get out of having to dance?" I asked.

"My bond." Ink caught me by the hand and, in one swift move, spun me right into his arms. "I would never dismiss an opportunity to sway my body with yours." He hoisted me up until I was partially resting on his leg, then waggled his eyebrows.

"I thought you said the night before the wedding was for purity."

"Only the contemplating of. And you are contemplating how badly you wish to dirty your purity."

"Laylee?"

With a weary sigh, Ink released me. "I shall go and attend to the groom's needs. At least keep him from receiving any obvious injuries. Your dinner." He passed me my burger from I didn't know where, then sauntered off. As he went, his tail swayed back and forth with the music.

I fiddled with the bun, then turned to my mother. "I didn't expect you to be here." Even after I'd texted her about my father, she hadn't responded.

"I felt that I should tell you that..." My mom suddenly hugged me. "I'm proud of you."

"For getting married?" squeaked out of me even as tears threatened to test my waterproof mascara.

"For standing up for what you love. It's not an easy path to take."

I clung tighter to her back, struggling to calm the rolling in my stomach. She'd walked away from the man she loved for me. I had done the same to protect him from this world. What would happen if I got pregnant? Would I have to choose? "Does it get easier?" I asked, swallowing down sobs.

"No," my mother said and she framed my face in her hands. "But it gets better, fuller, happier. And also harder."

"Thank you for...for coming back."

"I was wrong to leave you. I don't want to control you. I want you to live your life...even if it involves all of them." She looked at Cal and Ink both nodding along to Daniel's song. My guys.

Wait? Where's my – ?

The air flattened back my hair and a streak of white plunged to the ground. "Lady witch," Garavel said, his voice in a panic.

"What is it? What's wrong?"

"I was traversing the perimeter when I spotted someone."

Oh god. This is it. Conquest is coming for me while I'm in a white sundress and heels. I wasn't ready. We weren't…

The garden's little gate swung open at hip level. He'd pulled his hair back into a slick ponytail and left off the tie. Two buttons were undone, revealing a hint of the scars below. The black lenses reflected back at me as he stopped just out of my reach.

"Evening."

"Raul? You… You're here? But I thought —"

He adjusted his shades keeping the green skin at bay. "Things are heating up with Conquest. Surely you can sense that the barrier is weakening."

I placed my hand over my stomach that hadn't been able to chill for days. Was that why it kept twisting just like when I was forced into the in between? "If you think I'm going to abandon my wedding to help you fight off —"

"I was walking the wedding grounds putting up defenses. Your spell of invisibility was weakening on the east gate so I shored it up for you."

He did? "Th…thank you."

Raul nodded once while staring at Cal. "Does that fool have any idea how lucky he is?"

"I think so," I said before taking a bite of my special burger. He'd hidden chopped-up mushrooms and blue cheese inside. How sweet.

"Lady witch, I shall return to —"

I stopped Garavel by holding his hand. "Stay. Go to the party. There's lots of people who aren't werewolves here. And I bet Fiona'd like a sausage or two."

Garavel stared longingly at the makeshift stage with a strobe light, then the grill. "But I am required to protect—"

"You are required to be happy. Have fun. If anyone tries to come after us tonight, they'll be in for a big surprise."

"Very well," Garavel said and he bowed his head before racing off after Ink.

"The world could end tomorrow. Do you really want to spend that time at a stuffy wedding ceremony?" Raul asked.

"Yep."

He sighed in exhaustion. "Then I shall be there too."

"Really?"

He slipped his hand inside of mine and squeezed. "Really." I knew it wasn't a good idea for him to be there. Ink would probably try to kill him twenty different ways. But I also knew I wanted him there, along with everyone else in my life I cared for.

"My bond," Ink shouted with a wave. I dropped Raul's hand, but he didn't rush over and attack, so that was good. Instead, he clamped both his arms around Cal. "Now is the hour when we embark upon the celebration of his final night of freedom."

"What?"

"Bachelor party," Daniel said. He handed his bass to one of the other band members.

"I shall entrust your care to the wiles of Miss Manaliki and the terrifying glare of Miss Dana," Ink said with a nod to the two women. "We shall see you on the morrow." With that, he began to drag Cal out through the house.

At the last second, my fiancé shouted, "If I don't see you again, I love you."

All four of them vanished from the party as I worked my way to the dance floor. So too went Jared and Scott, Cal's groomsmen. Raul followed me. "An incubus bachelor party. Do you think they'll survive?"

"I give it fifty-fifty," I said before giving in to the party. Tomorrow I'd be a wife, but tonight I had my girls and a pack of wild werewolves.

Chapter Twenty-Four

Cal

A screeching monster blared in my ears, wrenching me from sleep. I struggled to unstick my eyelids and the moment I did, I regretted it. Light slammed into the back of my head causing me to whimper and bury my head under a pillow. All the while, the monster kept screaming.

"Up and at them, sunshine." A hand ripped away my dark solitude and I stared dumbstruck at the far too-happy smile on the damn incubus. "Breakfast?" he asked, holding out a plate of runny eggs and cheese.

Oh god. Last night hit in a series of confusing vignettes. I couldn't piece it all together but at the heart was… "Ink?"

"Your phone is demanding attention," he said before dipping a slice of melon in butter and eating it. "I suspect it is your blushing bride."

Layla? Crap. I snatched up my phone to answer it and smacked into a bed leg. A mysterious arm dangled from below the covers. *Why am I on the floor?* I turned my back on it all and answered, "Morning."

"Cal, are you…?" Layla's worrying voice calmed and she laughed. "Ink?"

"Pretty sure that bastard did it on purpose."

"Of course he did. Are you okay?"

"Yeah. Got the hangover of all hangovers but that's what greasy food and a hot shower are for. Mm, at least the hotel has a good breakfast."

"Oh, you texted me about a hotel. I thought you guys were going to a harbor," Layla said. "I hope you didn't get any new tattoos last night."

"No," I assured her, then I tried to stare at my own back.

A low groan rose and the bed behind me rocked.

"How are the others?" she asked.

"Well." I peered up as the blankets tumbled off of a half-naked body. "Daniel's still alive."

He groaned in response and doubled over in pain. "Are you sure? I wouldn't put it past the demon to poison us."

"If I wanted you dead, I'd tell you to your face," Ink said.

A vague memory tickled the back of my mind and I stood up. "Garavel? Is he…?"

"Slumbering like a baby." Ink patted the angel's back as he lay face down on the second bed. A great snore broke and Garavel's wings shot out, hitting Daniel right in the stomach.

Layla snickered at the multitude of groans, then she said, "My poor boys. I hope you'll make it today. I wouldn't want to walk down the aisle by myself."

I'm getting married. Even though my tongue felt like shag carpeting in a gas station bathroom, I smiled wide. "Babe, you are the best hangover cure. I love you."

"Love you, too. See you soon. All of you. Bye." She ended the call and I looked at the clock. Oh shit, it was already ten. She'd probably been up for a few hours doing the impossible to make herself even more beautiful.

I ran my fingers back through my hair and hit something sticky. "I call the shower first," I said.

"For the love of the Celestials, will someone silence the wolf?" Garavel grumbled from the bed.

"Good to know you're still with us, 'cause I'm getting married." There was a skip in my step as I worked around the bags toward the bathroom. When I got close, my foot kicked into a wad of blankets, and a green hand popped out. Rather than reach for my ankle, he grabbed the blanket and wadded himself deeper into the blanket cocoon.

As I reached for the door, I caught Ink staring down at the sleeping elf with a gleam in his eye. "Hey," I called, hoping to keep him from doing anything stupid.

Ink looked at me like the dog caught eyeing up a cookie.

"Thanks for last night. It was a blur, but a fun one."

He smiled widely. "You are welcome, Calvin. And I believe our beloved will quite enjoy the ink upon your backside."

What?

* * * *

Daniel

I placed a cool washcloth over my eyes and leaned back against the headboard. I hadn't had that much to drink in thirty-something years. My new liver was working so hard my skin smelled like rubbing alcohol. Why had I let the damn demon talk me into any of that?

"Good morning!" Garavel boomed as he waved to people walking past the hotel window to get to the pool. He'd been doing that for the past half hour.

"Have you tried the whipped cream on the omelet? It's quite a journey of delights." The demon was right beside him, as chipper as ever.

I did my best to shut out not only the idea of anything they were eating but the concept of food. Vomiting today would fuck up my vocal cords, and I had to get this right.

"Ah, fuck!" Light seared my brain as I sat up. I fought through the pain and fell to my feet. "I need to get back to the house."

"Whatever for?" Ink asked.

"I…" *I didn't finish the song.* They didn't need to know I'd dropped the ball on my one thing. "I forgot something. I'll call a cab."

"I can take you," Ink offered in a highly suspicious way. I stared at him, waiting for the joke, but he kept holding his hand out.

"I'd rather walk," I said, then doubled over as I tried to defeat gravity.

Ink bent clean down so he could stare into my face. "Then I shall follow behind laughing and pointing."

"Mm, I can ferry you," Garavel offered. He dabbed a napkin to his lips and dropped it on the plate, then he held out his arms, waiting for me to leap into them.

Great, so my choices were demon, angel or walking two blocks then passing out face-first into concrete. "Fine," I said and caught Garavel by the forearm. He dug in tight and spread his wings.

"We're not flying out of this room. We'll go out through the lobby."

It wasn't an experience I would have ever liked to have again, but at least he didn't hold me like a baby. We didn't say a word, thank fuck, and he set me down outside the house. I took a second to get my feet under me and stared up into the window. Somewhere in there was Layla, probably in lingerie, putting on makeup and doing her hair.

"Daniel, may I ask you something?"

'You just did' hung on my tongue. "Shoot."

Garavel stared around like he expected to find archers. "Do you believe this joining of assets is a wise idea?"

No. They'd been together for a year. Cal was using it to slap a Band-Aid on his trauma. The chances of it working seemed impossible.

The upper floor window flew open, and Layla poked her head out. She wore a white silk robe that partially opened as she waved smoke out of the house. "I told you not to use that outlet."

"Sorry," Dana called from deeper in the house.

I gazed at her in her own world. Even as she fought to clear a small electrical fire, Layla was beaming from cheek to cheek. She was so damn happy it almost hurt.

"Yes," I said to Garavel. *Because even if it does fail, we'll be there to help her pick up the pieces.*

"Thank you for your honesty, Daniel. Now, I should arrive at the resort to decorate. Goodbye."

"Wait!" I turned just as I realized what he was up to, but the angel flew high into the air. His large shadow passed over the street and he was gone.

So much for getting a ride back. *Maybe I'll call Tyson to get me on the way to set up.* I needed to focus. Jogging up the stairs, I made a beeline for my room. I just missed Layla laughing as she slipped into Cal's room.

I took a quick peek inside mine fearing to find a pile of werewolves sleeping on my bed. The comforter was on the floor and a mess of clothing sat beside it—just how I'd left it. I picked up a box of binders on the desk. Rifling through my drawers, I tried to find my notebook, but no good.

Where the hell is it?

I switched to the box of binders but they were all nursing shit. *It's got to be here somewhere. I wasn't stupid drunk enough to...*

My fingers brushed against familiar leather. I expected to feel a jolt rush through me, but it'd vanished since I came back to life. Pulling out Layla's spell book, I asked the universe, "How the hell did this get here?"

She hated being more than a few steps away from it most times. For no reason, I opened the book. Blank pages flipped past. I'd once been able to read them all, was able to help her save the world, stop the bad guy. Now, I was her wedding DJ. The guy she kept in the spare room. What could I do to help in the upcoming apocalypse?

I let the book flip to the end when a strange paper fell out. It was covered in Latin, telling me it was a spell, but one she must have gotten from her mother. "Hm." I skipped past the bits I could read to the last line. Something in it felt familiar. Where had I seen *'nam-tar'* before?

"Ah!"

A woman screamed and I looked up just as a girl tied her robe tight. "Sorry," I muttered, holding a hand over my face.

"What are you fucking doing here?" she shouted.

"Just looking for my notebook." I patted my pocket to explain when I felt a familiar heavy thud. It was on me the whole time.

"Mikki, what is it?" Layla's sweet voice called.

I booked it out of my room, sprinting past the fuming woman. "Here," I said, handing Layla her book. She caught it and pressed it tight to her chest. I reached for the stairs to bound down them, then paused and kissed her on the cheek.

"Happy wedding," I said, then ran for freedom.

* * * *

Ink

As the rush of water striking naked skin rose from the bathroom, I sat and waited. The mortal had fled off with Garavel to waste more of his limited time, no doubt. I was supposed to be keeping track of Calvin to make certain he got to the church on time. But as the man believed he could handle washing himself alone, I was left with only one task.

The lump at the door shifted. I stood. Rather than fling off the covers, the worm inside dropped its limbs to the ground. The deep groan would have no doubt moved some to tears. I crossed my arms and waited.

"Alas, you did not die in your sleep," I said.

He jerked at the sound and flung himself over. With one arm extended like he could fire lasers from his palm, the witch hunter fell on his ass. The last of the blanket went too, leaving him half-naked and shivering on the cold floor.

"Is this when you betray me?" the hunter asked. He spun around trying to keep his eyes and palm trained on me as I walked.

"Of course not. In order to betray you, I'd need to have felt a bond of loyalty first."

He was without his many tricks, his stolen spells and potions abandoned with his trousers on the chair. It left him vulnerable, a fact that was quickly dawning on the mostly-mortal hunter. I unbuttoned my cuffs and rolled my sleeves to my elbows. Goosebumps trembled up his verdant skin, his eyes burning as he realized how poorly he'd calculated. The prey was alone with the hunter.

Smirking, I reached forward.

"Layla!" he shouted.

I froze, my face knotting into a sneer at her name on his lips.

"She wouldn't want this, would she?"

If he had intended to appeal to my better nature, he should have aimed for the angel instead. "Are you scared, hunter? Is urine drenching your leg now that you've been stripped of all your power?" I reached for him. He swung with his bare hand, the elf stronger than a human but not by enough. His nails bounced off my skin and I dug into his wrist.

On a human, it'd have left deep bruises. For the elf, it must be a touch painful judging by his contorting face. I yanked him across the ground, hopefully causing numerous rugburns on his naked flesh. "You know it, don't you?" I taunted in his face and extended my claws high. "Fear. Alone, abandoned by all you'd count on, you face death."

I yanked him up. He struggled but could do nothing against the force as he nearly planted against me. I drew my claws to fillet his handsome face off his skull. "How does it feel, witch hunter?"

"Uh...?"

Hot steam and the scent of an Irish countryside rolled out of the bathroom. I did not bother to turn to the werewolf gawking at us.

"Should I leave you two alone?" Calvin asked. "Cause Layla'd either be mad you kissed him or really mad she missed it."

I snorted at the idea and released my grip. The hunter had enough grace to not tumble like a sack of potatoes. He rolled and dashed for his clothing.

"We have a truce," the hunter snarled while leaping into his pants.

"He's right, Ink."

"Do you wish to have the man that nearly killed your bride at your wedding?" I put to Calvin.

For a flash, the wolf roared in his eyes. He stared daggers at the hunter, but it washed off his body. "Layla wants him there."

"And we all must do whatever she wants," I cut back.

I expected him to argue, but Calvin deflated. "Man, please, just one day, can you let it go?"

Ignore every honed instinct, every hard-fought truth inside of me all because Layla let her heart be bamboozled by an emerald scepter? I glared at the elf, who'd already dressed and was prepared for another of our showdowns. A wise man would cut him down here. *She's so distracted by wedding paraphernalia she wouldn't notice – possibly for weeks.*

Calvin draped a bonhomie arm around me and pleaded, "For her?"

The wind sucked out of my sails like a reverse typhoon. I lowered my chin and gave a barely perceptible nod. A single sharp laugh broke from the witch hunter and I bounded toward him. He extended his little dagger that'd punctured me before—proving he held to this truce as much as I.

But I paused before he could reach me. "Remember that fear of death's fingers on your spine and know until the end of your short days that you did the same to her."

He blinked. Perhaps there was a dawn of realization on his face. I did not care. I turned from the mess and walked for the door, needing an escape.

"Ink, wait. We need to get to the resort."

I brushed past him and said over my shoulder, "You may wish to dress, Calvin, unless you intend to consummate the marriage on the altar."

In the haunting stillness of the hotel, I walked alone. It was as it had always been, as it should always be. Incubi were solitary tigers, chasing their prey until the life drained from their eyes, then moving on to the next. They did not have to suffer the impunity of witch hunters or the incessant groveling of werewolves. They were free to take where and when they wanted.

I was free to…

The exit door swung open and a man in utility garb glanced over at me. "What're you doing here?" he grumbled.

"Enjoying a smoke."

"Where's your cigarette?"

I crossed my arms and smiled. "Don't need one." Smoke wheezed through the cracks in my real skin, the acrid white fog blanketing me. The man waved his hand around as if to confront me before he must have realized it wasn't worth the hassle.

Solitude. I had craved it once. After the hunt was finished and the prey drained, all I wished was the freedom to be as I was. To never apologize nor answer for my very existence. When did that change?

"Got a light?"

I should have expected this. Despite closing my eyes, I extended my claw toward her. Flame caught on the tip and she pressed her cigarette into it.

"Thanks, love," Lust purred and she took a long drag.

"You're not supposed to..." The guardian of the back stoop started up before he got a good look at her, then his brain ceased to function. A bit of drool built up at the side of his lips and he muttered, "You can do whatever you want."

"Of course, I can. Now shoo. Your betters are talking."

The man nodded dumbly and he walked in the direction Lust pointed—right off the edge of the platform. It wasn't a neck-snapping fall, but judging by the groan, he wouldn't be dancing for a few weeks.

"It's almost time," Lust said.

"If you expect me to betray—"

"Eros, you are betraying yourself right now. What makes you think you can play the role of devoted househusband? You are a predator. You are designed to take, not give, and you know it in your heart."

I did once. I had walked the world caring nothing for those left in my wake. I'd embraced what Lust had taught me to be. What had once seemed second nature warped upon my escape from hell.

"You do not know me any longer," I said.

Lust snickered, the edge of her scarlet lips rising from below the brim of her black hat. "I know you better than yourself, Eros. It's your pet witch who lives in the dark. She does not know the rush you feel draining the final drop of life from your prey. The families, the destitute villages left in the wake of our hedonistic hunts."

I'd put all of that behind me centuries before I was banished to hell. I stared at Lust, my heart stone.

She put out her cigarette on the back of her hand. "Of the witch you betrayed to her death."

My heart lurched and I clenched my fists tight.

Lust drew her palm down my arm. "Admit it, Eros, you're a monster. A creature just like all the others that good witch fights. And once she learns your truth, your whole truth, she'll turn on you too."

I tried to shake my head, but how could I deny Lust's words? I was a sin born of a weak man to tempt others to their doom. There was no heart to find in that, no love to be given to such a monster. I would be a fool to believe otherwise.

"Help me save you, Eros," she said. "Bring me the witch tonight. Pull her away, give her to Conquest and wash your hands clean."

I closed my eyes tight, trying to not think of the werewolf, the angel, the ex-ghost, the damnable elf or the witch. I tried to think only of myself.

Lust purred in my ear. "I will set you free."

Chapter Twenty-Five

Layla

The mirror enthralled me. Dana had done a wonderful job pulling my braids back and adding purple and white flowers to the side of the updo. My makeup was perfect thanks to Fariah's skills, leaving me dewy and the kind of natural that required twenty different products. I was beautiful in every way except for the dress.

At least it didn't have a mustard stain on it.

I placed my hand to my chest, wishing the neckline was less square or the waist higher. A palm swept over the top of mine and locked our fingers together. My heart pounded fast in surprise, but I caught the flash of black hair and smiled. "I thought you were keeping Cal in line?"

Ink draped his other arm around my baggy waist and pulled me tight to his chest. "He is contained within the four walls of the church. He and his fellow groomsmen discovered a game of marbles and are playing in the vestibule. They should be entertained for a few hours at least."

I smiled at the idea of Cal in his full tux trying to shoot a marble across the floor. Then I caught my reflection and frowned. "That sounds nice." Better than what I'd been up to today.

"My bond?" Ink looked at me through the mirror.

"Lots of little things coming up." Like my breakfast, and lunch. *It's nerves.* A whole lot of things could go really wrong today. But it wasn't a Horseman unraveling space to bring about the destruction of the world. I wasn't on the edge of vomiting because the realms were breaking apart. *Nope.*

Ink didn't say anything, though he could probably hear my panicking thoughts, or maybe just my desire for crackers and ginger ale. His gaze drifted off of my face and down the dress. There was the pickled disgust I knew to expect.

"Is this what you intend to marry in? Plain peasant garb?"

I raised my shoulders, causing the straps to dig in and make my bra bulge from below the neckline. "I don't have any other choice."

A flicker of a smile rose on his lips. "Are you certain?" He let go.

I craned my head back to find my incubus holding a white garment bag practically bursting at the seams. "Ink?"

Pulling on the zipper, he said, "If you would indulge me with a moment of submission on your wedding day…close your eyes?"

I did as he asked. Warm fingers caressed under my chin and pivoted my head back toward the mirror. All

I heard was rustling, my demon never grunting unless I desired it. When a blazing hot palm landed on my exposed back, I held a breath. He tugged down my zipper.

Was I really going to have sex right before I walked down the aisle?

"Just don't mess up my makeup or hair," I said as my dress hit the floor.

He drew his palms down my calves and picked up my feet one by one. "Your lack of faith wounds me."

I knew I had to look like a mess, standing in inhumane shapewear to get my boobs to defy gravity and my hips to denounce their existence, but Ink didn't care. "You will step up." He said it just as he was the one to pick up my feet and place them. I could sense a great mass circling my legs, but didn't feel anything until a soft and slippery fabric graced my sides. Ink guided my arms. I expected my palm to clench around a cock or two, but he let both fall to my hips.

Then I touched it. A skirt puffed out wider than anything I'd had before, made of fine tulle with finer embroidery overlaid on top. I kept tracing over the appliqués, trying to discern them as Ink drew two caplet sleeves up to my shoulders. He worked quickly, cinching up the back.

Ink drew both of his palms across my bare shoulders and whispered against my ear, "You may open them."

"Holy fuck!"

A sweetheart bodice with beautiful lace flowers and amethyst crystals in the center cupped my breasts and flattened my not-flat stomach. Beautiful and fragile lace sleeves caressed my upper arms. At my waist, the skirt exploded into a waterfall of lace and tulle. There the flower appliqués turned into a mix of lilac and royal purple. The hemline kissed the tips of my silver shoes. Instead of the same blinding white of the dress, it was a purple ombre rising like a magical flame toward my knees.

Oh my god. I wanted to spin in this dress. To stand at the top of a balcony so the spotlight caught on every crystal and I glowed.

"I'm a princess," I cried. "Shit. Fuck!" I waved my hands fast at my eyes, trying to dry off the tears before I tested the strength of my mascara.

"Is this preferable to your other garment?" Ink asked.

"It's…" I'd never seen anything this beautiful in my life. I'd never imagined I could feel this beautiful on my wedding day. A dress like this had to cost thousands of dollars. "I can't wear this."

Ink's prideful smile darkened. "Why not?"

"You have to take it back. If I get a stain on it. Ink, you can't steal something like this. It's—" Fuck, I did not want to take it off, but this looked one of a kind. The rightful owner would trace it back. "It's a felony."

"My bond…" He reached a hand around my waist. "All is well."

"This isn't like the bikini or the dress to the ball. It's…" I couldn't do it. I couldn't wear a stolen dress to my wedding, even if it was perfect.

"I do not steal." He drew his fingers along one of the lace flowers. "I made this as I have all the other clothing you've required."

"What? How? When?" The lace alone had to take hundreds of hours. He was one person.

Ink shrugged. "I admit your length of engagement did make it a challenge. I only finished two nights prior with the final dye. I would avoid the rain just to be safe."

"You...you made this, for me?"

"Alas, Arachne was unavailable, so it fell to me. I hope you can accept my amateur talents."

"Ink." I thought I'd never seen him because he didn't want anything to do with this wedding. But he'd spent all his time making me the perfect wedding dress. "I don't know how to thank you."

"It's all right," he said, cupping a hand under my chin. "I do." Ink kissed me softly, his lips warming over mine. The intoxicating fever rushed up my body, and I tossed my arms behind his head. But Ink backed off and dotted the tip of his pinkie to the side of my lips. "Not even a smudge."

I laughed, giddiness threatening to overtake me. I didn't realize how much I'd been dreading walking down the aisle until Ink had taken all that fear from me.

"Layls, we need to get into place," Dana called, poking her head into the dressing area. She stared at Ink first, then her eyes shot out at my dress.

"I'm coming," I said.

"Don't need to know what you and Tattoo are up to," she said with a laugh and shouted for Fariah.

I'm a bride, and soon I'll be a wife. Hope bloomed in my eyes brighter than any I'd seen in fifteen years.

"Ah." Ink caught me by the arm and kept me in front of the mirror. "We must not forget the *pièce de résistance*." Into my hair, he placed a silver comb shaped like a tiara with a long veil trailing behind.

My heart gasped at the picture-perfect bride in the mirror. "How did you do all of this?"

Ink turned me around. As he pulled the veil over my face, I caught the bottom was dyed the same as the dress. Staring me in the eye, he said, "It's not difficult to borrow extra reams of fabric and lace as a famous clothing designer."

What?

"It's time," Dana called.

Ink extended his elbow to me. Together we walked out of the cabin set aside for the bride and toward the church. Red maple leaves tumbled before my feet like a fall of rose petals. Dana and Fariah both stood on the steps just outside the church's closed doors.

Dana gave a quick glance over at Ink, then handed me my bouquet. The doors opened and Garavel and Daniel ushered Dana and Fariah inside. I barely looked at Scott or Jared in their matching suits and focused on my guys. Garavel was in black just like everyone else, but the white shirt glowed. Not just in contrast to his ebony skin—it was literally radiating light as he beamed at me.

If anyone could make a rented tux look punk, it was Daniel. He'd left off the vest and his tie was loose. Instead of cufflinks, he had used safety pins to hold together his cuffs. His hair was tousled to the side, then held in place with gel. He nearly ruined his whole no-fucks aesthetic when he saw me. "Damn! Layla, you look like…"

"A queen," Garavel whispered in awe.

I blushed hard under my makeup. "Thank you."

"I always pictured you in a hot skater dress, with a slit up to your hip and some platform shoes," Daniel said. "But, shit, my tongue's a knot looking at you."

"You pictured us getting married?" I asked him. Daniel's eyes went wide and he gulped. I pulled him close and kissed him on the cheek. "Maybe one day."

"I'd be a lucky fool for it," he said, then he turned his head. "Okay, that's the cue." Daniel picked the next song on the wedding playlist. "Go."

Dana and Scott, then Fariah and Jared both walked toward the main doors, then down the aisle. Quickly, Garavel and Daniel joined them inside and shut the door. I was left alone with Ink, both of us waiting for the doors to open.

"There is yet time for you to flee," he said.

I laughed at the idea.

"I could take you to any exotic location you wish. Vanish into each other for a fortnight or more. Forget our obligations, imagined or otherwise, and just be. What do you say?"

"Ink." I patted his warm cheek. For a flash, the human illusion faded, and I stared into the eternal hellfire of his eyes. "I'm gonna go get married."

He sighed a moment, then turned fully human again. "Very well. Let us commence with the long walk to the ball and chain."

I stopped and looked over at him. "What are you doing?"

"I thought, given your decision with your father, that I would be the one to guide you down the aisle."

"No." I shook my head and slipped out of his arm.

Ink's mouth drooped and pain rattled his features.

"You're not giving me away, you idiot. I'm keeping you. Remember?"

The edges of his lips ticked up. "How could I forget?" he asked and kissed me. Unlike the polite peck of before, he plunged his lips to mine and cinched his hand around the back of my waist.

I pulled back, placing my forehead against his. "Go on in and get a good seat."

"I have the best in the house," he said. Rather than opening the door, he vanished.

The harp song finished and I raised my shoulders high. Holding my bouquet, I stood in the center of the aisle and took a deep breath.

Chapter Twenty-Six

Cal

For a moment, I caught Daniel and Garavel's eyes. They both stood beside the door ready to pull it open and reveal...her. *Shit, are my palms sweating?* I clenched both tight, then thought how bad that looked and shook them out.

Jared chuckled. "Getting cold feet?"

No, they were on fire. I wanted to run down that aisle, kick open the doors and pull Layla into my arms.

"Shut the fuck up." Dana threatened him with a long glare and he did just that.

The music changed and the doors opened.

"Holy fuck..."

My peripheral vision noticed there was a skirt and other dress parts, but all I saw was her. Those big, beautiful eyes, that generous, caring smile, her damn nice tits. That dress cut right down her cleavage, leaving my wolf howling.

"Easy." Marcus clapped a hand on my shoulder, pinning me in place. I didn't even realize I'd moved toward her.

The music swelled to a romantic crescendo and Layla took a step closer.

"You saved the galaxy as Commander Sheep."

What the...? An announcement blared through the speakers, causing all the guests to pause in rising. They stared around confused while the game ad kept going.

"You've protected the Island of Rookery as Lieutenant Merino. But are you ready to conquer the world as Viking Roslag?"

I met Layla's gaze as she cracked up at the other end of the church. I couldn't help it and started to laugh, too. They were going to remember this wedding for a long time.

"Download *Sheep Wars: Ragnarok* today and get a free Emperor Merino masthead."

The game jingle ended and Pachelbel's Canon began. On cue, all of our friends and family rose and turned to gaze in wonder at Layla. A hand slipped into my pocket and I nearly broke away from her until Ink said, "That's a bargain." He wandered off with my phone to stand just to the right of Marcus. Daniel and Garavel somehow worked their way back to the left.

We all waited for Layla, but I was the one to extend my hands and hold her. I leaned in to whisper to her, but she beat me to it. "You're so hot it's not fair."

Lifting her veil, I gazed into her beautiful eyes. "I was going to say that."

Marcus gave a soft cough to shut us up. "Friends, family, packmates and colleagues, we are gathered here today to celebrate the love between Layla Leeland and Calvin Rollin. And judging by the way they're looking like they want to devour each other, we better wrap this up fast."

Everyone laughed and I looked back at them. It was only supposed to be for a second, but the door opened. Dark hair snuck in through the gap. Mark stared around, then he looked up at me and nodded.

"Cal? What's wrong?" Layla asked.

Beaming, I held both of her hands and faced Marcus. "Nothing. Everything's perfect."

* * * *

Layla

Daniel finished the last of the song then nodded at me while I struggled to keep the tears at bay. After gathering his sheet music, he stood by Ink.

"You were flat on the eighteenth bar," Ink whispered. Daniel turned on him, looking about to argue, before he stopped and smiled it away.

Marcus took over once again. "Now we get to the good stuff. The couple has decided to write their own vows. Cuz?"

Cal's eyes shined as he took both of my hands in his. "Layla...whew." His leg began to shake with nerves.

"You've got this," I said softly, brushing my thumbs over his hands.

He beamed at me. "All my life, I've run. I thought if I never stopped, then the past wouldn't reach me. Then I met you and..." Cal laughed. "All of my past smashed into me, into both of us, like a freight train. For the first time, running away didn't feel like freedom. The thought of losing you —"

Cal stopped and turned away. His voice cracked as he coughed out what sounded like a sob. "I love you. I love the way you tuck your cold feet under me when we sit on the couch. I love the way you smear peanut butter on half the bread and then fold it over. I love the bonnet you wear to bed and how you never have two toenails painted the same color."

The tears began to glisten in his eyes and he pulled me closer, guiding my palms to rest against his chest. "I love your heart so full of compassion and need to help. Even if it drags you into dark places, and we're all worrying ourselves white."

Ink, Daniel and Garavel all nodded in agreement.

"It's who you are. You're a vengeful goddess, a glorious healer, a protector of the innocent and..." Cal drifted his gaze down my body. "So fucking hot," he whispered in my ear.

My cheeks warmed at the low growl he punctuated at the end. Cal reached back to take the ring from Scott, then he held my hand. "I swear, until my dying day, to protect you with my last breath, to shield you from the pains of the world, to honor your wild and compassionate spirit and to love you with every beat of my heart."

He lined the ring up at the tip of my finger. "Layla? Will you be my mate?"

"I will." My voice cracked as Cal glided the ring onto my finger. The second it was on, I had to wave my hands over my eyes to stop the tears. It caused him to smile, then reach over and run his thumbs against the top of my cheeks. I folded into him, nearly resting my forehead against his as we breathed together.

"Ah, not quite yet," Marcus interrupted, getting a laugh from the audience. "Layla, your turn."

I breathed from my diaphragm and lost myself in Cal. The hundred people faded away. Marcus and the bridal party vanished into nothing. "For so much of my life, I didn't think I was worthy of love. That something inside of me was broken, and no matter how many shapes I bent myself into, I could never be good enough. Never deserve it. You taught me..."

I let my gaze drift over Cal's shoulder to the others. "Some days I wish I could be perfect for you, to finally be worthy of love. But then I wouldn't be me, and you..." *All of you.* "Wouldn't be you."

Daniel jerked his head once, his lip quivering. Ink folded his arms and tapped a finger against his mouth, hiding most of his expression. Garavel openly sobbed on Ink's shoulder.

"Cal, even though you've fought through a darkness I can never fully understand, you are my light. You brighten every room you walk into. You're the calm in the middle of a hurricane. My pillar, my home base. Even when the world's going to hell, I know I can count on you to be there by my side."

"No matter what," Cal mouthed.

"You're sweet, you're fair, you're dedicated to helping and healing the smallest person." I leaned close and whispered, "Plus, you fuck like a god."

He blushed up to his blond hair but grinned ear to ear.

"Cal—" I reached back and picked up a necklace from Dana's hand. The chain unraveled and a crescent of silver dangled off the end. I'd cut off the longest of my nails, dipped it in silver and hung it so it looked like a little moon.

"I swear to love you with everything inside of me and do everything I can to be worthy of your love every day. To keep you safe when the monsters are at bay. To make certain you never run out of Whooseits."

Cal and the rest of his family laughed hard at that.

"Most of all, I promise to stay by your side with every beat of my heart no matter what this world throws at us." I draped the necklace over his head, and he placed a hand over the small pendant. "Cal, will you marry me?"

"Of course, I will!" he shouted, scooping me up and almost kissing me. The low, exhausted growl from Marcus stopped me and he put me down.

"These two lovebirds have decided to participate in the sealing ceremony. Layla, you may begin."

God, my hands shook as I took Cal by the wrist. Nerves jangled up my spine while I kept tracing my nails back and forth over his throbbing veins. Then he cupped his palm against my cheek, calming me with a look.

"I promise, that as my mate, you shall never feel a pain more biting than this," I recited. Lifting his wrist to my lips, I took one last look into Cal's eyes, then I bit down. He didn't even flinch—just stood there misting up as I pulled my teeth back. Two white crescent welts rose on his skin as Cal nodded at me.

"What the hell's going on?" Jared whispered to Scott, who shrugged. Shaking his head, Jared sighed. "Canadians are fucking weird."

"Layla." Cal raised my wrist. First, he swept each finger down my forearm, then he framed the bite spot with his thumbs. "I promise, that as my mate, you will never feel a pain sharper than this."

I steadied myself, prepared to keep even the deepest bite from showing on my face. Cal lifted my wrist to his lips and he kissed me. Looking me deep in the eyes, he barely pressed his front teeth against my skin before pulling back. It wasn't even a sting. I held my wrist, confused, but he bowed his head and whispered, "I swear it with all my heart."

Cal?

"You can finally kiss the bride," Marcus declared.

We both reached for each other. Cal swept his hands around my waist and I held his cheek as he kissed me and I kissed him back with my whole heart. At that moment, the sun set through the window, wrapping all of us in its rosy glow.

A great howl broke from the pews. I laughed, holding tight to my new husband. Dana dramatically pulled the reed broom from a package beside her and laid it at the base of the stairs. Holding Cal's hand tight in mine, I looked at him. He silently counted *one, two, three*, then we both jumped. Our love was sealed by both his people and mine.

I couldn't stop myself and reached over to kiss him again. Arm in arm, we escaped down the aisle as all the scary monsters began to clap for our love.

Chapter Twenty-Seven

Layla

Instead of entering a bare-bones barn, Cal and I walked into an autumn paradise. Green vines covered in purple and red leaves were wrapped around the crossbeams. Swags made of purple and yellow mums dangled beside our acrylic monogram sign. What made me gasp were the stars floating above our heads.

"How?" I asked, spinning in a circle to take in the bursts of purple from flowers spilling out of every open space. I spotted my angel standing next to the cake table. "Garavel, this is amazing."

He beamed at me and pointed across the way. "I had help."

Raul had traded in his witch hunter suit for a fancier tux, but he still wore the sunglasses. Touching his forelock, he gave a little bow. "The demi-angel's flowers could barely finish off the banquet table," he said with a shrug. "It wasn't difficult to encourage the local flora."

"What about those?" I pointed to the ceiling where small orbs of light circled each other, casting an ethereal glow through the shadows.

Raul gazed up, then he stared at me from the side of his glasses. "You deserved the stars."

"I didn't think you'd show," I said. Or that the other guys wouldn't try to murder him if he did.

"A witch and werewolf wedding? I'd be a fool to miss that once-in-a-lifetime engagement." He swept his gaze down me. "You're beautiful."

"Thank you." I blushed.

"I was stating a fact. No thanks necessary."

"For coming. I...I'm glad you're here."

His closed stance opened and he reached for me. Just before he could take me by the waist, Raul paused. "In the event that I need to stop any drunken werewolf outbursts?"

"Babe, they need more pictures!" Cal called.

I shifted my bouquet and waved back to him. Just before I joined him I whispered to Raul, "Because I wanted to see you." As I walked away, I lifted my skirt high enough to reveal my feet in high-heeled silver sandals with an ankle strap. Vines clenched around the beams as Raul stared at my nearly bare feet.

"Okay, now, kiss your husband's cheek," the photographer instructed.

"Gladly," I said and leaned in just as Cal turned his head and caught my lips.

The pictures went so fast, the two of us marionettes to our very expensive photographer's whims. I only insisted on one picture of me and all my guys. Rather than have them stand awkwardly behind me, I sat on the floor. Cal, Ink, Daniel, Garavel and even Raul all sat around me, their hands extended out toward me. I stared up at the photographer on a ladder but they all looked at me despite being told not to.

"That's perfect," our photog cheered on Cal and Catherine, then he turned to me. "What about the bride and her mom?"

My mother jerked in surprise, nearly dropping her falafel. "It's all right. I don't…"

"Come on, Mom." I cheered her closer to stand next to the flower wall. Perfumed hydrangeas and lilacs hung from the vine trestle — the only touch of spring in the autumn world.

My mom stopped beside me, and I raised my chin.

"Shoot, I've gotta change cards. Give me a second."

"It was a beautiful ceremony," my mother said.

"Thanks. We made a lot of it up. Seems witches don't do weddings."

"No, we don't." She shook her head, her voice heavy. "But if we were to start, yours would be a lovely template."

"All right, give us a smile." The camera went off, stealing our image and possibly a piece of my soul. Anything seemed possible anymore. "Mom, put your arm around your daughter to show how proud you are."

My mother awkwardly shifted closer and raised her arm like she had been ordered to hug a grizzly bear. "What you said, about feeling like you don't deserve love…?"

Damn it. I wrote those vows when I didn't even think she'd be there. "I don't want an argument right now."

"Smile."

We both did and the flash went off.

"I'm sorry," my mother apologized, "for making you feel like that."

"Mom, it isn't—" I wanted to argue it wasn't from her abandoning me, but the truth knotted my tongue.

"Laylee, you are a brilliant, wonderful girl. I couldn't be prouder of the woman and the witch you've become."

I shook my head, unable to believe this. "Even if…?" I looked over to my new husband introducing his brother to his groomsmen. I had done the one thing witches weren't supposed to do—I fell in love and I kept him.

My mom shook her head. "You're forging a new path, and if anyone should appreciate how hard and trying that is, it's me. Despite my best efforts, you grew up to be a better woman than me."

"Mom." I flung my arms around her in a huge hug. She collapsed her face to my shoulder and we ugly cried together. We mourned the time we'd lost and celebrated the future memories we'd make.

A bright flash went off, catching us with our cheeks stained and noses snotty. "Beautiful," the photographer called before wandering off to take some candid photos of Cal squeezing Mark tight.

"You've always been loved, Laylee." My mom let go of me and looked at my men standing around the gyro station. "And you always will be."

I'd wanted to remember every detail of my wedding, but the reception became a blur. I think I ate dinner. There was certainly cake, which Garavel offered to cut before he tried to take the top tier for himself, then Cal's mom took over. Rather than sitting in the rows of tables, the werewolves pushed them back so they sat in a circle, often chanting and stomping their feet. Cal joined in on occasion while I watched with Fariah and Maram. Dana went missing during the speeches, but once I realized Marcus was gone too, I called off the search party. It was the perfect evening for fun and insanity.

"Gentlefolk and not-so-gentlefolk." Daniel cut over the music. The lights above the dance floor dimmed. He strummed one chord. "It's time for the bride and groom to have their first dance."

Cal swooped in behind me, placing a hand on the small of my back. With every eye on us, we stopped dead center on the dance floor. He took my hand and held me close. "Are you ready?" he whispered as hundreds of phones came out.

The floating orbs began to descend, small pinpricks of diamond light dancing around us. I raised my palm to catch one and it tickled. Smiling, I stared up at my husband. "Always."

The music started sweet like a love ballad from an old musical. Cal swept me in a circle, the two of us not so much dancing as sway-walking. I didn't need the theatrics of a choreographed dance. I just needed him.

"You're my magic," Daniel sang in his rough but heartfelt tenor. I peered over my shoulder to find him clutching tight to the microphone, his eyes closed. "One touch and I soar. You're my magic."

"Oh my god," I gasped as Cal spun me. *He's singing my song.* There went the tears again.

"One kiss..." Daniel let the note hang before he whispered into the mike, "and I'm yours."

"You leave me in awe, hanging by a claw."

I blinked in shock as Cal sang along with Daniel. He was quiet, far more uncertain than the seasoned veteran, but he couldn't stop smiling.

"My heart beats anew." Cal pulled me close to whisper, "With love just for you." He kissed me as the chandelier lit up bright as the sun. Everyone clapped and roared, flashes going off like fireworks. I staggered back like it was a dream.

The tempo kicked up with an instrumental solo. Daniel called into the microphone, "Everyone, get on the dance floor." It took a moment before people grabbed hands and dashed to join us.

Cal kissed my hand, raised it, and spun me faster than before. I lost my bearings, letting my feet lead me. A hand caught me and I blinked up into black sunglasses.

Raul rested his hand on my hip and began to sway back and forth.

"What are you doing?" I asked, chuckling.

"It was their idea," he said with a sigh, then tipped his head back and sang. "My past had been born, with a heart of thorns." Raul stared at me from below his glasses, his hand less-than-innocently caressing my ass. "But you overcame the curse of my name."

Daniel's chorus picked up. For a moment, Raul carried it, but as it approached the end, he paused. "You're my magic," he said, then pulled me flush to his taut body. "One kiss and I'm yours."

I puckered my lips, expecting him to take me on the dance floor. A huge finger tapped him on the shoulder. "May I?" Garavel asked. He was the only one still dressed to the nines, his bowtie straight as an arrow.

Raul tipped his head and handed me over. I strained to reach Garavel, my giant angel nearly engulfing me in his embrace. "Hm," he mused, then he bent over. I locked my hands behind his neck and Garavel stood, lifting me off the ground.

Dangling off of him like a necklace, I lost myself in his eyes. He smiled brighter than heaven itself and swept me off my feet. Then Garavel opened his mouth and sang. I expected to hear a voice that'd shake mountains, but his was soft and delicate—like a silk thread catching the morning light. "A voice inside sings, on angelic wings."

Garavel laughed hard and he spun so fast, my legs lifted. He caught me in his arms and pressed his nose into mine. "To hold you tight...ly? And become right...ly?" He shrugged at fumbling his lyrics and I reached up to kiss him.

"Hold this." Daniel passed over his bass, and he leaped off the stage. Singing into a lapel microphone, he carried on the chorus while approaching me. Garavel set me down and I wrapped my hand around Daniel's shoulder. My angel kissed my palm and placed it on his chest before he bowed out.

Taking my hand, Daniel led me around the floor. His lips trembled as he sang the lyrics closest to his heart. "Trapped as a drifter, only a whisper. I'd lost all my drive..."

"Whoa!"

Daniel dipped me. My locket struck my chin as my head tilted back. He held me so safe, I let go and reached back to trace my fingertips over the floor. The music stopped dead. Daniel snapped me up. Gazing into my eyes, he said, "Till you gave me life."

The cymbals crashed and the beat picked up. Daniel gave me one last turn before he drifted away. I stared at the last man standing. Ink didn't rush in to take me the way the others had. He crossed his legs and carelessly rolled up his sleeves.

The other members of the band sang the chorus. As the last lines of, "One kiss and I'm yours," rang out, Ink clasped a protective hand to my back. He nearly yanked me out of my shoes. I stopped with my breasts pressed to his hard chest and my legs straddling his knee.

Ink gave his trademark smirk and raised an eyebrow. "Mrs. Rollin," he said with a little bow, then he began to sing. "In simply one blink, your life spilled with ink."

He leaned back, taking me with him until his throbbing cock pressed against my belly. When Ink caught my flush, he snickered and spun me out fast. I barely had a chance to catch myself when he locked both hands around me from behind. "Sweet and sometimes tart, you taste..." He moved his palms, one sliding higher up my bodice and the other parting down my thighs. With a heat that'd rival my core, Ink breathed against my neck, "...Of my heart."

The band sang the chorus one last time and I spun in Ink's arms to face him. He locked his arms in tight with unbreakable incubus strength. "My bond, there is a secret I've been keeping from you." Ink's eyes burned red hot and he stopped dancing.

"What is it?" I asked.

He smiled and whispered in my ear, "You'll see."

My stomach lurched and the world went dark. The band, the clomping of feet and the drunken laughter of our friends vanished to nothing. I clutched my fingers, hoping to feel a warm body, but they found only chilled air.

"Ink?" I said, laughing. "Where are we?"

"Ink?" Shivers ran up my flesh as I felt another moving through the darkness without speaking.

"Ink!"

Chapter Twenty-Eight

Layla

A flame sparked in the darkness, the red light splintering through the black to reveal the sly grin of my incubus. He danced the fire on the tip of his finger while staring me down, and I wrapped my arms tighter to my shoulders.

"Ink? Where are we?"

"Forgive me for this. I was asked to whisk you away." He raised a candle to his finger and lit the wick. With a cheeky smile, he handed it to a pair of hands lurking in the dark.

The candle rose through the shadows to reveal a bright blue eye. It winked at me. "Babe."

Fire sprouted from the candle, each baby flame zipping to light another wick until the entire room glowed. Five men stood in place. Daniel was by the bed, which was covered in rose petals. Near the vanity stood Garavel, his wings brushing against the mirror that sparkled like it'd just been cleaned. Cal reached over to take my hand while placing the candle on an end table. Far in the back beside the window with drawn curtains lurked Raul, nervously scratching his wrist.

In the center of it all stood Ink, looking like the cat that caught the canary. "It took us some time to think of a proper wedding gift."

"The idiot wanted to get you a ram," Daniel cut in.

"Two sheep and a ram, as per tradition." Ink snarked a moment, then he tugged apart his tie. "But what in our strange and foolish partnership has been traditional?"

"What is it?" I asked, my brain slowly noticing that all of them had lost their jackets and nearly all their ties. Ink was the final holdout and, as he slipped it off his neck, he bound his hand in the silk and smiled. Cal cupped my cheek and kissed me.

I was about to kiss him back when he pulled away. White feathers brushed up my arm. I reached for Garavel, but he slipped in behind me. "My lady." He kissed down my neck while curling his wings around me.

"Exotic comfits, rare gems and spoils of war...all seemed too pedestrian for you," Ink said. He hadn't moved, and was standing there watching as Garavel ran first his feathers, then his hands over my body.

"So we decided," Daniel said. He stepped closer, walking past Cal to take my hand. Staring deep into my eyes, he placed my palm against his chest. The heat of his body sizzled through the thin shirt.

"You mean you yelled at each other until you couldn't think of anything else." The once stone-silent Raul spoke. He rose from the window but didn't approach. Instead, he placed his foot on the chair…his bare foot.

"We're giving you us," Cal interrupted, his eyes blazing like the wolf was just below his skin.

"Don't I already have you?" I asked. Garavel slipped to my right and Daniel claimed the left. The two of them kissed and nipped down my neck while rolling their palms over the lacy bodice.

Ink stepped forward. "For one night, you get all of us."

"All of…" I stared past Ink and Cal to the oddest man out. "Are you…? Are you gonna kill each other?"

Raul raised his hand as if to show he didn't have any wards. It was Ink who answered. "Tonight, no. Tomorrow…"

It wasn't just Ink and Raul. There were Cal and Garavel, who could swing wildly at the drop of a hat. Or Daniel and pretty much anyone. He'd been so reclusive lately, I didn't think he wanted…

"My bond." Ink caught me by the chin and stroked his thumb down my cheek. "Put aside your fretting for their fragile egos. Tonight, you are to think only of yourself."

A low moan rumbled in my ear and a long cock pressed against my hip. Lips kissed from my shoulder down to my hand, then feathers traced after. Electricity sparkled inside of me. Five very different men wanted me tonight.

"Fuck me." I groaned and my incubus smirked.

"As you wish." He raised my chin and pressed a kiss of devouring on me. My knees melted and I slid toward the floor. Daniel and Garavel clung to my belly, keeping me aloft.

"Layla." Daniel moaned. "The second you walked down that aisle, it took everything in me to not pull up your skirt and fuck you on the altar."

Ink gave up his possession and I turned to take in Daniel's desperate kiss. Every touch of his teemed with life and an exuberance to never miss a single moment. He darted his tongue in my mouth and a hint of mint lingered as he pulled away.

"Shall we unwrap your gift?" Ink asked, reaching for my bodice.

Yes. The beautiful wedding dress that'd kissed my skin like rainwater all day became a constricting potato sack. *I want out of it now.*

"Ah." Cal interrupted. "That's my job." Both Daniel and Garavel walked away to stand by Ink while Cal slipped in behind me. Working on the buttons one by one, he breathed in my ear, "I've been aching for this for weeks." Cal traced the tip of his pinkie down my spine as he went. "Lying in bed, thinking of your gorgeous, sensual body slipping out of your wedding dress."

The bodice began to bow out, but Cal slapped a hand over my stomach. He pulled me tight to him and, as his cock pressed through the layers of tulle against my ass, he growled.

One by one, each of my guys pinched their thumb and finger around the bodice. Even Raul walked over beside Garavel to join in. They watched in rapture as Cal undid the corseted bow at the back. My beautiful dress slipped down my body and five men went with me. Cal muttered and yipped as he swept his hands from my naked back to my stomach. The other four took a varying path down my breasts. Hands circled, then under, hefting them up before racing to my nipples. The competition was fierce and I feared they might start fighting, but they worked together. Garavel and Raul both teased one while Ink and Daniel pinched another.

I shivered deep to my core, my mouth quivering at the sensations. Then Cal popped open my bra. Greedy fingers tugged on the straps. I didn't catch who threw it, just that both Daniel and Raul dove in to suck on my tits.

"Holy fuck," I cried out, threading my fingers first through Daniel's gelled locks, then tearing down Raul's ponytail. He grazed his teeth against my nipple at that, so I pulled on his hair. He bit down. "Yes!"

I was so lost in the throes of those two, I didn't realize that Ink and Garavel had thrown their arms over each other's shoulders and dropped to their knees. Behind me, Cal kept nibbling on my ear and running his hands across my body. "Babe…" He panted, pressing his thick cock between my clothed buttocks. "Moon, I love you," he cried out and thrust his palms down my panties.

He fingered me fast, teasing my clit with a dangerous hunger. "She's so damn wet." Cal moaned in my ear.

"The dam is breaking," Ink declared. He and Garavel both took a side of my panties and slipped them off my thighs. Digging his nails into my legs, Cal widened my stance as Ink split his tongue in half. My demon smiled mischievously, showing off his talents, when feathers brushed up my clit.

I squealed at the soft touch, nearly pulling away from the two men sucking on my breasts. Cal locked in like a brick wall behind me. "Not yet," he rumbled, pressing his nails tight.

Two slippery tongues glided over my clit. I whimpered at the heat shooting through my body. "Babe?" Cal asked, the beast drawn back.

I reached behind to hold on to him and tell him I was fine when Ink tongue-fucked me. He plunged his serpent's appendage in hard, somehow twirling the split halves to sweep around inside of me. My assuring fingers clamped onto Cal's hair and I hung on for dear life. Garavel bowed to me, his wings sweeping back. My head started to return the sentiment when he pressed his juicy lips around my clit and sucked.

Ink swung onto his back and wrapped his hands behind my ass. Greedily, he tugged me lower, threatening to send me toppling onto a pile of men. As my stance slipped, I fell onto his twirling tongue. He'd gotten more creative, letting one half slip out to lap over my taint. I tried to focus on Daniel and Raul sucking on my nipples, but the damn incubus knew every button to push. He grunted and slipped his thumbs over my anus.

"Fuck!" I shouted, the orgasm hitting like a freight train. My body jerked in shock from my nerves overflowing. Luckily, Cal wrapped me up in his arms, holding me safe. His cock pressed against the small of my back as every other man wiped off their mouths and stood to watch.

I struggled to breathe, air catching in my chest.

"Layla?" Daniel asked. "Are you okay?"

"Yes," I panted, vehemently jerking my head. It was amazing, fantastic and way too short. I shouldn't have felt disappointed, but...

It was the low chuckle of my demon that gave me pause. "My bond." He pushed aside Daniel and Garavel to reveal he was naked. As he reached for me, he shed more than his clothing. The black and red skin of the demon steamed in the candlelight. He swished his tail back and forth, the fire in his eyes. In his vagina-quaking, end-of-the-world voice, Ink said, "That was merely the appetizer."

One by one, each of them reached for their clothing. Hands that pulled apart buttons would stop to caress my body. Lips plunged to mine so fast I couldn't make out who was kissing me, while another sucked on my neck or bit my thighs. Jackets, shirts and belts hit the floor with a thud. Ink gave me one deep kiss, the heat of his body inflaming my skin like a hot tub.

A hard slap struck my ass and I stared behind to catch his tail sneaking away. Ink grinned wickedly, then he turned to Daniel. "It's your course."

Daniel wasted no time in scooping me up into his arms. He stared with thigh-quaking certainty at me. "You are going to fuck me harder than you ever thought possible," he commanded.

"Is that so?" I teased.

Daniel smirked and cupped his hand over my asscheek. "Yes," he ordered, then picked me up. We didn't go far, just to the foot of the bed. Daniel kissed me hard, roving his hands down my curves before he hooked onto the back of my thighs. As he pulled, I had no choice but to go with him. He fell back onto the bed, taking me with him. I climbed over his eager body. His cock slapped against my belly and I tipped my hips so I could rub my clit on his shaft.

His groan of pleasure made me smile. "How's that?" I asked.

"Not enough." Daniel snarled. He clenched his palms under my buttocks and hefted me up. "When I tell you to fuck me," he demanded, lifting me until I hovered just above his eight-inch cock, "you fuck me."

I plunged deep, the whole of my body shaking as he bored through me. Shivering and gulping, I meditated on every meaty inch pulsing inside of me. He was so goddamn long, I struggled to lift myself. Daniel smiled at my attempt and he ran his hands over my swaying breasts.

"Good, keep going," he said. I tried to, but someone clenched my ankles together.

I plummeted forward, my palms slamming into the bedspread. Soft silk wrapped around my ankles, trapping them. It tightened me around Daniel and I nearly yelped as he thrust with his hips.

"You can handle this, Layla," he assured me. "You're amazing."

The pinch shifted to an overwhelming flush of pleasure. *Damn right I am.* I raised my hips and thrust down on him. From behind me, fingers danced up the soles of my feet, nearly on the edge of tickling, but the owner knew the right pressure to keep me from losing it. *Raul.*

I smiled at the man massaging my feet, then I focused on Daniel. He drew his hands down my vulnerable arms while smiling. "You're beyond beauty itself. Aphrodite is a troll in comparison. Fuck!" He groaned and jerked his hips, pushing deeper into me.

Raul pulled my legs higher, tipping me closer to Daniel. I leaned up to kiss him when something both pliant and hard slipped in between my locked feet. I pushed my soles closer together in curiosity. The low groan from Raul told me I was right. He fucked my feet slowly, lifting his hips to do it while massaging my calves.

"You've stopped fucking me," Daniel said, staring me in the eye. "Is it too much for you to handle?" I almost laughed when he lifted an eyebrow. "Do you need incentive?"

The way he asked made me shiver to my cock-clenching toes. I licked my lip and nodded, curious about what he had in store. Daniel circled my forearms, then he clenched my wrists and yanked me down. My ass shot up into the air and warm heat breathed against it.

I tried to lift my head to see, but Daniel strained me tighter and he began to jerk his hips. I struggled to meet him when a slippery tongue glided down my asscrack. Boiling hot hands clamped onto my buttocks, spreading them to the breaking point as he licked rapidly around my anus.

Holy shit! My body flooded with so much pleasure from both behind and in front, it was like a wave battled inside of me. I leaned back, giving in to the slowly ramping licking on my ass. Teeth bit into my calf, muffling a moan, but Raul kept fucking away between my feet. Both were distracting, keeping me bouncing from one sensation to the other.

Daniel released my wrists and cupped my face. "Fuck me, Layla. Fuck me how I've dreamed of being fucked for thirty years."

"Yes," I shouted. Ink and Raul moved with me as I flexed my hips up and down. Raul let go of me, letting my feet slide over him while I rose off of Daniel. Ink shoved his tongue in time with my thrusts, giving me more force.

"My lady," Garavel cried. I looked up to catch him and Cal watching intently. Both held their cocks and the sight sent me into overdrive.

My body began to tingle, but I fought to keep on the verge of collapse. *No. This one has to last longer. I'm not done yet.* "I. Fucking. Love. You!" I shouted, bounding faster as Daniel squeezed my tits.

With one hard thrust, I lost control. A squeal ruptured from my lips and I tossed my head back. The orgasm ricocheted up my spine, hitting every crumple zone. It sent me lifting off the bed. Hands caught me, holding my arms up as I came over and over on Daniel.

"Yes, Layla. You're all I want! I love you!" He groaned at the sight of me splayed out above him and jerked once. His cock bounded inside my vagina, pumping cum into me.

My head spun, my vision blurry. Safe arms lifted me away, and I turned to find Raul holding me. His green skin was flushed and tiny red dots covered his chest. How many capillaries had he blown trying to not come all over my feet?

I staggered up on my toes to kiss him.

He laughed darkly. "That's not how this goes."

Curtains blew in as massive vines sprung from outside. One thicker than sailor's rope knotted around my wrists. Before I could catch my breath, it hoisted me into the air. My shoulders popped at the strain as my feet left the ground. Below me, five men watched while Raul crossed his arms. "You knew it would always end this way," he said, then clenched his fist.

Chapter Twenty-Nine

Layla

The vines splintered, each one taking a wrist. They snapped my arms straight out parallel to the floor. I tried to wiggle against the foliage, but a single thorn pricked against my wrist and I paused. How many of those could he command at will?

"What do you think you're doing?" I shouted at him.

He twisted his hand and the vines obeyed, climbing down my body. Only they didn't just stretch to the ground. They wrapped over and under my breasts, corseted up my stomach and sprouted between my ass cheeks. My righteous indignation faded as Raul traced my skin between the vines. They'd trussed me up, spiraling down my thighs and leaving me helpless — exactly how he liked his witches.

"Is that all you've got?" I taunted, my heart pounding faster. Raul stared up at me. "I can take more."

His green lips quirked up. "So you think."

"Ah, fuck." The vines tightened, squeezing my breasts and tugging on my ass. Instead of thorns, small leaves unraveled from buds, brushing over my skin in mind-numbing patterns. They kept teasing my nipples, ass and vulva, the touch barely there but constant enough to drive me mad.

"This..." I gulped, fighting to keep focused. "Is nothing."

Raul smirked. "Then how about—?"

"Elf." The word was a warning right before incisors scissored arteries. Ink stared at him like he was about to smash Raul through the wall. I braced myself for the worst, but Raul looked to Garavel.

"Go ahead."

Wings erupted from Garavel's back and he took off. With his hands sweeping up my body, he hovered behind me. I tipped my head back to catch my angel. Garavel swept a protective hand against my belly, and he held on to me. All the while, his wings kept pumping, the steady whoosh keeping him airborne. With each flap, the feathers caressed my skin, only to be teased by Raul's leaves. Both were having a hell of a time torturing me.

"My lady," Garavel whispered. He ran his hands over my breasts then tugged on the vines down my cleavage. They tightened against my taint and inner labia. I gulped at the forceful touch from him. "May I...?" he asked, sweeping his palm down toward my crotch.

"Yes!" I cried out, then softened my voice. "Please, I want you."

"I want you, too," Garavel said.

The vines tightened around my ankles. In one quick jerk, they spread my legs. A handful of gasps caused me to look down. Cal, Daniel and Raul were staring up at me hanging in the middle of the room on full display. Cal crossed his arms so tight his veins bulged while Daniel toyed with his spent cock. Raul was bold as brass, stroking himself and meeting my eye as he did.

I shivered at the intensity when Garavel thrust his dick inside of me. He was sucked right in, my vagina greedy for more punishment. Garavel moaned against my shoulder as he used his wings for leverage. Each down flap pushed him in, but when his wings rose, he'd slip out. I couldn't stop my frustrated growl.

"Angel, do as we discussed prior," Ink called to him.

"Okay." Garavel pulled out, then hooked onto my vine snare to spread my asscheeks.

"Are you...?" I asked, trying to turn over to see him.

That sweet, innocent angel smeared his wet dick around my anus. "Do you wish me to stop?" he asked.

The only one I'd let back there was Ink, who—true to his word—never hurt me. Garavel didn't have that penis flexibility. But the way his face glowed in excitement, and the rush in my body, I ached to feel him try.

"Keep going," I said.

"But first," Raul interrupted. He caught a bottle of lube from Ink and walked below my spread legs. After coating his finger, he reached around my backside and coated my anus. God, it felt so good, roaring back up the tingling rush that Ink had started with his tongue.

My eyes closed and I started to whimper, which was when a hot tongue lapped against my clit. The second Raul sucked on it, he plunged his finger deep into my ass. I thrust back on it, wanting more. He kept toying with me, sucking harder on my clit and thrusting his finger in.

"Never go in dry," he said, pulling away.

Garavel nodded at the sage wisdom, then he placed his hand on my shoulder. "My lady?"

I wanted to hold his fingers and tell him it was all right. He looked so innocent, his sweet face framed by his feathers. I nodded. "Please, take me, Garavel."

His eyes lit up and he kissed my half-turned lips. My neck couldn't take the strain and I had to face ahead just as Garavel gripped my hips. His wings flapped low, scattering a feather to the ground. Pressure pushed against my anus and — for a moment — doubt crept in.

But as I looked down at my guys, knowing all of them would stop at a single 'ouch', I relaxed. Garavel thrust in. It was hard going, but he took his time.

"My...witch. My Layla. I am... This is... Mercy!" Garavel shouted with every half an inch. His imposing body rose up and down with his wings, widening me with his dick. I kept breathing steadily, doing my best to enjoy the sensations building in my lower half.

Instead of the quick spike of need, a deeper ache rolled through my loins. Garavel's thighs pressed against mine, and his belly molded around my back. He clung tight to the vines and breathed in my ear. "May I?"

"Yes. Take me," I cried out.

The release of his dick set off a pang of exquisite loss, only for it to be filled as he thrust again. He wasn't jerking his hips. Instead, he relied on his wings to do the motion while I partially sat on his lap. It was delicate, and soft, and so fucking dirty.

"I have wished to be with you like this for so long." Garavel panted.

"To do anal? What sites has Ink been showing you?" I tried to laugh, but a combination of pleasure and danger thundered inside of me.

Garavel gripped the vines around my shoulder blades and pulled me back. "To take you in the air." He thrust deeper and spots burst in my eyes.

"God." I moaned, rolling my head.

"My lady?"

"It's good, so good, I just want…" My first instinct was to shut up and be happy with what I got. But this was my gift after all. I stared down at my men and caught the green eyes. "I want more."

Raul ran a hand back through his hair, then he reached out. Vines caught his palm, lifting him into the air. "You know, I'd had other plans to —"

"Just fuck me already," I growled at him.

His gaze flared at my challenge. Raul hooked a hand around my waist, pulled me to kiss him then thrust his cock in. I groaned against his lips, half of my body crying out in pleasure or pain. Maybe both.

Raul took my lip in his teeth and bit down. I answered by doing the same, pressing harder than he did. "You're so damn wild," he taunted.

"And you're a wet blanket," I teased.

He quirked his throbbing lips. "Is that so?" Raul leaned back, thrusting his cock to the hilt. At the same moment, Garavel did too and I wanted to cry out. But that damn wily elf had a trick up his sleeve. Even panting, with his hair falling around him, he quirked his finger. Two small vines split off my thighs and wrapped around my clit.

Staring me in the eye, he thrust and the vines squeezed. I yelped in shock, but my body pounded harder. "You don't have the balls to do that again," I cried out.

"Do you think your childish taunts affect me?" he asked, thrusting faster than before.

Garavel flapped his wings in time with Raul, both of them boring me out until I was nothing but cocks all the way down. I pushed my ass back with all my strength, then swung forward to meet Raul. "Yes," I said, staring him in the eye.

He kissed me and the vines squeezed my clit again and again. It was the most painful suction I'd ever felt, but exquisite. I needed more. "Harder, you fucking bastard," I ordered.

Raul clamped a hand to the back of my head and yanked me to him. Garavel hung on for dear life, his breath catching as he came along for the ride. Staring me down, Raul stopped his hips for a second that lasted years. "I hate how much I love you." Raul snarled. He thrust, squeezed and kissed me.

I cried out against his lips. This orgasm ripped my legs off and stopped my heart. I sputtered for air, clenching tighter to the vines while Garavel's frantic flapping stilled. He groaned against me, shot his load and plummeted.

The entire cabin shook when he hit the ground, but my angel called out, "That was fantastic."

"Yes—" Raul drew the back of his hand against my cheek and his eyes rolled back. His lips shivered and he pulled out just as his green cum shot out and struck the wall. Panting, his skin flushed and eyes wide, he whispered to me, "You are."

I smiled at the sentiment and tried to reach for him. My arms and legs were still stretched in his foliage.

"Um, little help?" I asked my elf, who was sitting cross-legged on the ground.

Black slashed through the air so fast, I didn't realize my wrists were free until I started to pitch downward. I fell into my incubus' arms. He held me like the monster rescuing the damsel, his red and black skin hissing with steam while his cock teased against my weary ass. I nestled my cheek against the rocky cliffs of his chest when I caught a pair of watchful blue eyes.

My werewolf, my husband, paced back and forth. His lips were tucked up into a half growl and he looked about to plant a knuckle to the ground. Instead, he used the bed to bounce himself over and wrap his arms around me. Ink didn't let go.

"She's reaching the end of her tether," Ink said to Cal.

"She can handle more than you think," I sniped back.

Ink stared down at me with a foreign sense of curiosity in his eyes. "It's not enough to bring three men to their knees?"

I shook my head, then leaped up. Locking onto his horns, I dragged Ink's face to mine and kissed him. Cal growled, his chest rumbling against the side of my body. He pulled back on my braids, scattering the last of the flowers. His lips twitched and eyes narrowed as he stared at me hanging off of Ink's horns.

"I fucking love you," Cal declared and kissed me, rattling his tongue in my mouth like an auger. He clung to my skin, coated in sweat from sex with three other men. I lashed my hands around the back of his neck and he lifted me from Ink's arms. Cal carried me bridal style toward the bed.

"You are the most entrancing woman I've ever... We've ever known."

One by one, Daniel, Garavel and Raul all stood. They took their turns kissing me. Daniel's was hard with an edge. Garavel's caused me to sparkle to my toes and Raul's ground me to my core. I drifted away from him and looked to Ink. "What about you?"

"Encouraging an incubus to join your marital bed? I believe there are folktales warning against such a thing."

"Get the fuck over here," I said, reaching for him. Cal lowered me to the bed. My occasionally obedient demon followed. He climbed on top of me and kissed me. With his forked tongue, he licked both above and below mine, then he flicked the tip against my nose.

"My bond," was all he said as he stepped to the side.

Cal was dancing back and forth on his feet staring down at us. "I meant it, Layla."

My brain was running on too many orgasms and cocktails to have a clue what he meant.

My husband raised his wrist and declared, "You will never feel a pain sharper than my bite. I swear it with my last breath."

"Let's try to keep everyone breathing, at least for the night," Ink interrupted. He sat down behind me, lifted my head then laid it on his lap. I expected to feel his cock knocking into my skull like an obstinate salesman, but all I knew were his soft legs.

Cal swept up my calves, pushing the soles of my feet against the bed. He took a knee and climbed closer, his eyes swearing the same promise he had at the altar.

"Layla, my heart," he whispered, massaging my exhausted thighs and spreading them. Ink reached down and teased my nipples. The ache barely took a break before starting up again.

"My lady," Garavel said, bowing his head. He deployed one of his wings over Cal's head, hiding us below a heavenly canopy.

"My love," Daniel said, then began playing the acoustic guitar version of the song they had written for me.

"My challenge," Raul added, sprouting his vines up the bed, creating four thick posts that sprouted flowers. The air grew heady with jasmine and sweet pea.

With romantic music, surrounded by white feathers and flowers, my husband approached me. Cal lifted my hips higher by holding the small of my back. He stared into my eyes as he lined up his cock. "I love you." He sighed, then thrust himself in.

Ink clung to my grasping hands, holding me tight as I took on Cal's massive cock. He stopped with only the head inside and gazed down at me, the worry growing. Could I handle what the last boss was throwing at me? Had I put my lady parts through too much?

"Breathe," Ink whispered so softly I knew only I had heard it.

As I pulled in a steadying breath, the pinch vanished. Heat sizzled up my spine and I leaned back on Ink's thighs. "More!" I cried out. "I need you, Cal. Please. Give me all of you."

"Always, forever." He pushed his hips, spreading my weeping vulva as far as it could stretch. "Babe." Cal began to thrust agonizingly slow. I gave in to the force, working with, then against him for more delectable pressure.

My leg lifted and landed my ankle on his shoulder. Fuck, the angle was good, but I was ravenous for more.

Risking it all, I placed my other ankle across from the first. Cal wrung his hands around my calves, his eyes closed as he thrust deeper inside. I kept inching my ass off the bed, meeting his cock with all I had left. The orgasms that'd been left to simmer started boiling fast.

I dug into Ink's hands, giving all that I had left to Cal as he panted, his balls slapping against my ass. He hadn't been this deep since our engagement and I cried out for more. I didn't know how he managed, but he nearly pulled all the way out, then rammed his mega-bus dick in hard.

"Fuu—!" was as far as I got before my tongue turned to gibberish. Squealing in delight, I fucked him deeper and harder than we'd ever dared before. I was not going to be able to walk tomorrow, and I didn't care. My ears rang, my vision began to whiten and my lungs were about to burst. I hung on to that moment of impossible pressure by claw and fang.

"Yes," fell from his lips and I focused on those blazing blue eyes. "You're my wife," Cal groaned.

"And you're my husband," I said.

His mouth slackened, and he threw his head back. A howl from the bottom of his chest erupted free and I spiraled out of control. The orgasm to end all orgasms shattered my body into pieces. My hearing popped and I was flung backward. Instead of falling, I floated, drifting on an impossible cloud of perfection and love.

All I knew was the pleasure dancing with every nerve in my body. It reached into the depths of my soul and caressed my heart. If I died in this moment, it'd be the perfect end.

"Layla?"

My name punctured through the pink haze and I winced. Light broke in next bringing with it the outside world. I felt my legs, then my arms — all dead to the world. My chest ached and lips buzzed like I'd been panting to the point of hyperventilating. I blinked away the final vestiges of orgasm-land, even as my body continued to shiver with aftershocks. Cal's worried face came into view.

"She is yet with us," Ink said.

"Thank god," Cal cried out and he ran a hand back through his hair.

"You fucked me so good, I passed out," I said, my voice croaky. Ink helped to lift me and I looked over at the other concerned faces. "All of you."

Pride shined on four of my men, but I wondered about the last one. Instead of tossing me over his shoulder or ravaging me against the window, Ink dabbed a cool cloth over my burning skin.

"What about you?" I asked, trying to catch his eye. "What do you have planned?"

He smiled and dipped his head. "My bond, you have been wracked, penetrated, bound and sucked in nearly every orifice available tonight."

"So? It's my wedding night. Don't you want to join in the fun?"

Ink turned me in his arms. While looking into my eyes, he swiped a balm over my nipples. I nearly hissed at the touch before the cool ointment took effect. I didn't realize how hard they'd been bitten in the throes of all of that.

"What I wish is to ease away your rather vigorous pains." Ink circled his fingers around my wrists where the vines had left red welts. Then he stared daggers at Raul, who was trying to chase his foliage out of the honeymoon suite.

I sighed as more balm did its job and nestled against my incubus. "Not even a blow job?"

"No," he said, tending to my lady bits instead of taunting them.

"You know I could cast a spell and heal myself?" I asked.

"I do." Even with that, he continued massaging me.

I swept my hands around the back of his neck and held him tight, happy to let Ink take away all the pains he could. When he reached for my ankles, I turned to whisper in his ear, "I love you."

He couldn't respond as I kissed him.

I couldn't guess how long we all snuggled on the bed before dressing and heading back to the reception hall, but everyone cheered like we'd finished a trip around the world in a hot air balloon. My mother fussed with my hair, then handed me my bouquet.

"They've been howling for you to toss it."

"Oh." I gulped, realizing a roomful of people knew just what I was up to. *Don't think about the fact they can smell five men on you.*

Cal's brother snuck in beside him and punched him in the arm. "Here I thought you'd skipped off to your honeymoon." He didn't sound pleased or angry.

Cal laughed at Mark. "Not yet. Just had a gift to give."

"Furs, feathers and fiends," Ink announced from the stage. As the lights hit him, I realized he'd left off his shirt. The tattoo of chains in the shape of a heart gleamed off his chest like it was fresh. "Please join us on the dance floor as our blushing bride shall bestow her bouquet on one lucky sot."

"Will you get the hell off?" Daniel fumed close enough to him that the mike picked it up.

Ink smirked. "I often do, at her discretion."

Bodies began to form around me, hands pushing me toward the stage. I bounced on my feet, expecting to see a handful of women out there. To my confusion, all of the werewolves stood, their arms outstretched to win. I looked at Cal, who'd sidled in close to me.

"They love a game of catch," he said, then spun me around.

A snare roll began and Ink counted. "One...two."

"Three!" Garavel shouted.

I hurled the flowers as high as I could and turned. The bouquet bounced off hungry hands, werewolves leaping to be the one to snag it until it sailed over the crowd. From behind the mass of bodies, a single palm lifted into the air and caught the flowers. Brown rot crept up the stems.

The mob parted to find the winner. Light struck the white hat, then the blinding suit. "Good evening, Miss Leeland."

Chapter Thirty

Layla

How?

Hands held me and Cal growled.

The werewolves sensed the unwanted guest and took a step back. Conquest didn't move. He tipped up his hat with his cane and stared me dead in the eye.

"You're not wanted here," I said, as if that'd work.

The Horseman smiled, his features warm and pleasing, but the cold of death radiated from him. "Your invitation says otherwise," he countered and lifted one, the spell still glowing.

"Thief," Garavel shouted. "Murderer!"

"There's no reason to prolong this, witch. Give me what is mine, and I shall spare the rest."

Ink launched off the stage, landing in front of me. "If you touch her, you will learn if a Horseman can die." He put all of his fire into that threat, but Conquest didn't blink. His laser focus fixed on me—the damn prize he'd been hunting for.

Where did he get an invitation? How did he learn about this?

With a swivel of his head, Conquest looked directly at Mark. He curdled his lip into a cruel laugh and ordered, "Fetch."

Fuck! Mark nodded and black fur erupted through his suit, tearing the seams to pieces.

"Mark?" Cal shouted even as he tried to herd me back. "What the fuck are you doing? Mark?"

His brother finished his transformation and stared him down. He couldn't talk, but he rippled his lips in a snarl and snapped them at me.

"Mark, stop that right now," their mother shouted, rushing for him. The voice caused the werewolf to jerk. Fur sprouted off her jaw and down her throat as she shoved closer.

"You must make life a challenge." Conquest sighed. "Have it your way." He slammed his cane to the ground and the world exploded.

Nausea wrenched my stomach in half and I almost hit the floor. At the last second, I stretched my hand out and prayed this would work. The in between crackled from Conquest's cane. The barrier keeping the trash dimension at bay burned away in a wave. When it touched the others, they gasped at the sudden chill and froze. Anyone left in the in between would die. Anyone except Conquest and Ink.

I closed my eyes, guiding the magic, when a warm hand took mine. Raul yanked his glasses off and the power of the elves surged between us. It strengthened the spell I'd appropriated from the realm-striding thieves. The barrier snapped back, reality fighting against the in between. Floorboards ripped to pieces. The ceiling vanished to a sky of melting glass.

"Push it back," I shouted, my insides twisting into a pretzel. The agony was too much, and I lost sight of anything other than the exploding barrier.

Mark leaped. White teeth, red tongue and black fur. They all came snapping for my throat. I didn't have time to change my spell. I lifted my hand, terrified of the pain, when a massive gray blur plowed into Mark's side. He spun out on his paws, smashing into the other stricken werewolves. Only Mark managed to avoid falling into the in between as if he'd been protected by Conquest.

Rather than race in and finish him off, Cal paced in front of his fallen brother. He growled, his eyes burning like winter. Mark rolled to his feet and launched at him. Cal met him bite for bite, the two rolling across the floor. Somehow, Cal got the upper hand and pinned Mark under him.

A high-pitched whistle burst the air. All the werewolves screamed and the door burst open. I stared through the in between to a sky of blood. A woman on wings careened through the entrance. She dive-bombed to clamp her talons around Cal.

He snarled and spun to tear them off, but she dug in and he whimpered.

"No!" I broke from the spell to fire at the damn harpy. My mother caught my hand.

"If you stop, they all die," she shouted and pumped her magic into me. "Trust he can handle it."

Cal was twisting in her talons, the massive wolf giving her problems. He snapped his jaws, nearly hitting her chest. Gray feathers scattered across the ground, but he couldn't tear into her skin.

"Once again Calvin requires my assistance," Ink said. He walked for the two tussling a foot off the ground. A shot pierced the air. It just missed Ink, who glared at the Horseman. He was holding a gun.

"Your services are no longer required, Sin." Conquest aimed the barrel at Ink's chest and I wanted to laugh.

Nothing could kill demons.

Red bubbled on the back of Ink's hand. I thought it was his real skin at first, but there was no hissing black. The wound looked like a third-degree burn. *Oh god.* "Ink, that's—!" I tried to warn him it was the witch hunter gun, but Conquest fired.

There was no time to react, the cocky incubus standing still for the bullet. My heart clenched, my eyes too slow to close as I had to watch, had to feel him bleed out in my arms.

The floor shattered to pieces and a massive tree burst from the ground. It took almost the entire shot, scattering sparks to both sides. As they touched, reality reformed itself. Ink placed a hand to the tree, then stared at Raul, who was panting hard.

"Do not think this gives you leverage over my body," Ink shouted.

The harpy screeched and took to wing, dragging Cal with her. Blood dripped from his chest down his paws.

Ink leaped up the tree. He shouted, "I'm a taken incubus," just before launching for the harpy. The bird woman couldn't go fast and there was no chance she'd hold up against the demon. He'd tear her to pieces faster than a bucket of chicken.

I cheered in anticipation, missing the black shadow lifting off the ground. Mark plowed into Ink, knocking him off course. Shrieking in glee, the harpy woman took off through the door, stealing Cal. Mark snarled at Ink, who'd been tossed into the drum set. Then he turned and leaped for me.

"Stop, traitor. Or I will cleave your head from your neck." Garavel dropped in front of me, his sword gleaming. He heaved it toward Mark, who had enough sense to dance away.

"Ink?" I shouted.

"Yes, I will collect him. Keep your tears at bay." His words were flippant but his tone said he was going to murder everyone in the way of reaching Cal. I only caught a vague blur as Ink dipped into the in between to save my husband.

The barrier began to recede. I willed everything I had inside of me to it. One by one, the guests emerged back into the real world. Eyes of fear became rage. They tossed off earrings and shoes to shift. I clung tight-fisted to both my mom and Raul.

"It's working. We've almost got it!"

"Laylee, I don't know how…"

"Thank the elves," I said. My mom looked surprised.

"There is a first time for anything," Raul said.

The bubble was closing in on Conquest. He hadn't moved since his spell, and stood there watching as we countered everything he had. Was he worried? Did he have no other plan? Could I save the world and my wedding tonight?

I have to try.

A painfully familiar ache opened in my stomach, but I kept going, draining all I had and then some. "Layla," Daniel shouted from behind.

"Get the humans out of here," I said. The barrier slipped away from a lot of our classmates, their eyes wide as they faced a whole lot of new shit in ten seconds.

"I'm not leaving you to this monster. We need to get you out of here." Daniel jumped off the stage. He held my spell book and reached for my hand. Magic struck back like static electricity, setting his hair on end.

"I can do this."

"He will kill you," Daniel shouted, near tears.

"It's now or never, Laylee," my mom interrupted.

All three of us took a step closer. The barrier was almost down, freeing the last of those he'd trapped. Mikki shook frost off her wings and cursed with every swear word in existence.

Garavel swung hard for Mark. The bastard darted back at the last second. His sword slammed through the remaining wedding cake, spraying frosting everywhere. It wedged into the table. Garavel grunted, fighting to break it out when Mark slammed his paw down on the blade. It had to hurt, but the werewolf grinned with full fangs.

He's made of ebony. He'll survive.

I had to close my eyes to push the last of the barrier back. The final vestiges didn't go easy. A tear formed between both realms and a terrifyingly impossible chill radiated out. "Mom?"

"I've got an idea to stitch it up. Stay in place," she said, then began to weave a new spell.

"Raul, Daniel? Help the others?" I clung tight to my mom's hand, gifting her what little remained of my magic.

The stalwart agent nodded and took Dana by the arm. Thank god Angelo and the werewolf kids were back home with the sitter.

"What about Fariah?" Dana shrieked, just as a streak of fire shot by with our friend in her arms. "Okay then. Let's get the fuck out of here."

Only Daniel remained, his eyes bulging with panic. "You have to get out of here. Now. Layla, if you... He's going to kill you."

"I can't leave." *Why didn't he understand this?*

"Then I won't either," my mortal boyfriend stated, as if he wouldn't be tissue paper to White.

I pulled him close and kissed him, slipping my hand around my spell book. "I love you," I said then flung him out of the door.

"That was stupid." My mother chastised me for wasting precious magic. "But it probably saved his life."

I nodded and steeled myself. She'd nearly closed it, putting an end to Conquest's plans. Garavel had Mark on the ropes. He'd abandoned his sword and had taken to swinging his fists at the werewolf. Mark hopped back, avoiding a blow that'd crush his skull. He landed right beside Conquest.

Why's the man so calm?

"Garavel!" I shouted.

Conquest shot his arm out, catching Garavel by the head. "Clay soldier, thank you for being so predictable."

Garavel's arms dropped and his eyes sank into the back of his skull. He slumped to his knees, his jaw dropping with a silent scream. "Let go of him!" I shouted, trying to distract Conquest.

The cat smiled at his mouse. "You think all of this was for you, witch? The universe does not spin around your thumb." He closed his eyes and Garavel began to shake.

I took a step, only for my mom to hold tighter. "If you let go…" she said.

"He's hurting him. I have to stop this!"

A gut-wrenching scream tore from Garavel. *I can't take it.* I didn't even think of a spell until I was two steps away. As I pulled away from my mother, the magic snapped back like a fire whip. The pain was distant. All I focused on was saving my angel.

"Conquest!" I shouted.

He popped open one eye. Like an exhausted kindergarten teacher, he asked, "Yes?"

"Fuck you." A ball of hissing magic burst off my fingertips. He reached out to catch it like it wouldn't melt a normal person's face off. Conquest laughed and tossed the magic to his other hand, which was when I clenched my fingers. Vines burst from the ball and encased his arm. As they climbed, they embedded multitudes of thorns into his flesh. He looked more annoyed than in pain, but the vines quickly consumed him.

I reached out to take Garavel's hand, but he wasn't moving.

"Come on. You've got to get up. I can't carry you. Garavel. Please."

His lips wobbled in a confession. "I did it. I couldn't fight. I'm—"

"We have to get out of here." I couldn't pull him, so I tried to slip closer and shove him away.

Oh no. I turned my back on the Horseman.

I looked just as he swung. Silver split the vines like bean sprouts. His sword elongated—the blade thin with black ichor burned into the metal. "A mere party trick," Conquest snarled, his chest heaving.

Dipping into the last of my magic, I popped a barrier out just in time to shield Garavel. Conquest chuckled and swiped his blade. The magic thick enough to stop bullets didn't even slow it down. The black sword sliced right through my barrier and across my palm.

"Fuck!" Pain lanced up my arm into my brain. I clamped a hand to Garavel's head to keep from passing out. *Heal it. Heal it now.*

Gritting my teeth, I started to whisper the spell. Conquest grabbed the back of my hand and forced my fingers apart. "I will bleed every drop of you. I will tear your bowels free and spread your lungs to the dirt until you feed the touchstones. You will destroy the world, witch. Think on that in your last minutes."

Oh god. My blood rose off my palm. It danced in the air to Conquest's whims. He guided it toward the small tear in the realms. I fought to close my palm, but I couldn't. My stomach ripped in half, and I screamed. The void tore through the slit, its ravenous fangs eating me alive.

"Let her go." My mother's unflinching voice broke through the darkness.

"Are you offering yourself in her place?" Conquest asked with a laugh. "It was never you I was interested in."

"I don't fucking care. Get away from my daughter!"

He had everything he needed. I couldn't even flex my fingers, the pain unimaginable. But Conquest stopped bleeding me dry and looked at my mom. "Or what?"

My mother clasped her hands and a wave of energy ripped free. It washed over me, repelling every ounce of cast magic. Feeling returned to my body and, with it, the weight in my other hand.

Conquest laughed. "Is that all? The only reason you survived that night was because I let you. You're nothing more than a gnat I swat away."

"Swat this," I shouted then swung my spell book at his face. The leather spine, thickened by generations of women, cracked the Horseman's nose. White liquid gushed down his face. He let go of me to touch his injury.

"You cur!" White snarled, looking like the impotent businessman he masqueraded as. He lunged for me when huge feathers broke out. Arms locked around my waist, and I clung onto Garavel.

"Nice try," Conquest said. His blade snapped through the air, the black sword streaking to cut through Garavel's wings and me. The speed of it cracked the air in half. I held my breath for the blow we couldn't escape.

Vines burst out of the ground, wrapping around Conquest's arms. Raul's face was contorted in pain as he fought against a raging Horseman. It wasn't for long as Conquest got control and swung...only for my mother to step in the way.

The blade bit through her shoulder. She didn't even take a knee, just kept walking toward him while blood stained her lavender dress crimson. "Mom!" I cried out in confusion and fear.

"Laylee." She stared back at me, tears in her eyes, her hand clenched tight.

She needed me to do something. To save her. To stop this monster. I raised my shoulders high.

"Run."

"What? No. Mom!"

Her fist plowed into Conquest's nose—and the world exploded into white.

Chapter Thirty-One

Cal

Layla!

The forest tore at my skin, the fucking bird unable to get higher than six feet. I kept trying to get my jaws around anything. She shrieked in rage while flapping toward a break in the trees.

I had to get back to Layla. I had to save her…somehow.

There was one very stupid idea left to me. I shifted, shedding the protective fur and heft of the wolf. It let the damn harpy get higher, but she didn't even look down as I grew opposable thumbs.

"Hey." Taking a talon to my kidney, I crunched my core muscles, ratcheted my hands behind my head and wrapped them around the harpy. I managed to catch her wings. With all the strength in my body, I pulled both of them down hard.

She screamed in pain...or rage. I got what I'd wanted, and the only thing keeping me afloat plummeted toward the ground. In her panic, she let me go, but I wasn't about to do the same. I clung to her damn wing as she fought to flap.

"We're both meeting the ground tonight." I snarled into the wind whipping against my cheeks. The autumn air froze my body as I forced her head toward the dirt. She fought me like a mad chicken, but I had the power now.

If I go down, at least I'll take you with me.

Layla in her wedding gown, letting me promise she'd never feel pain again flashed in my head. *I can't do this. I can't risk my neck for one harpy.*

Just as the rocks and grass came into view, I let go and transformed. It wouldn't be pretty, but the wolf could take the hit better than the human. The harpy squawked and tried to fly away, but we were too low. She got a few flaps in before her neck and chest plowed into the dirt. I extended my paws out, hoping that'd cushion the fall.

Gritting my teeth, I counted down the inches before all of my ankles snapped. What I didn't count on was the pair of arms wrapping around me from below.

"Calvin, I fear you've been enjoying too many of those Whooseits," Ink said, deadlifting me.

I squirmed, my ribs aching where he'd caught me, but not broken. He let me down and I took off after the harpy, fangs out. She'd dropped into the dirt, her face half buried, and feathers were strewn about behind her. I leaped up, landing both paws on her spine. The muscles didn't twitch. The breath didn't catch. I sniffed the back of her still head.

Iron.

"Do you intend to paw that corpse all night or can we return to saving our beloved?" Ink asked.

She's dead...? It didn't matter. She was going to kill me. She'd tried to kill Layla.

I dropped back to my haunches and transformed again, needing to be as far from the stench of death as possible. It wasn't until dirt scraped over my palms that I looked up at Ink. "What the fuck are you doing here?"

"Keeping you from becoming wolf tartare. It would clash horribly with the Persian menu."

I slammed a hand to his shoulder, my rage building. "What about Layla?"

"I'm here to take you to her. She will need our help." No smart-ass remark, no chiding me for being useless. He didn't even stare at my naked ass. Ink was all business. It should have assured me instead of striking fear in my heart. I nodded and reached for his hand.

"Let's go," I said, waiting to be whisked back to the reception hall. Ink began to shake his head. He tried to take a step, and his body vanished. A cold wind wiped the demon away from my grip.

"Ink? Where the hell are you?" I spun around, trying to find him. The bushes parted. A full moon caught on the jet-black fur and I clenched my fists.

"What did you do?" I shouted at my brother.

Mark wasted no time in shedding his werewolf coat. He stood and stared me down across the open grass. "I fucking told you to stay away from the green skin. You should have listened to me, Claw."

"I don't understand." I kept shouting, the pounding in my head too strong to let thoughts in. "You killed Eric, the Horseman's champion. Now you're working for him?"

"You think that rotten asshole was his—?" Mark snapped his head back and laughed. "Eric was a means to an end, nothing more."

"Whose end?"

"You know who." Mark began to pace back and forth, moonlight landing on his white shoulders. They'd been covered in scars, his entire chest ripped to pieces and sewn back together. Some of them were over twenty years old, some I'd never seen before. He clenched his fist, reveling in the feel of his claws. "He gave me a chance to put the bastard down and I had to take it."

"This is about him?" I shrieked, my heart flipping at even thinking of our shared father. "The world's going to end. Do you understand that?"

"Maybe. Or maybe it'll get the good shake-up it needs."

He was out of his mind. Conquest must have poisoned him, twisted the rage and guilt in the three of us until all Mark knew was vengeance. For all of his bite, Mark wasn't this.

"I don't have time for this," I shouted at him. I had to save Layla. My brother would... I'd figure out how to fix him later.

"What are you doing?"

It wouldn't be an easy walk, nearly naked and back through the trees, but I could see the resort through the woods. Strange lights pulsed from the windows. I hoped it was Layla's magic saving all our friends and family. Sneering at him, I turned to run out of the meadow.

"You think I'm gonna let you go back to your bitch?"

His hand landed on my shoulder, and I swung. It wasn't pretty—all of my fighting was usually saved for the wolf. My knuckles slammed into Mark's jaw, snapping his head back. My skin split open, the pain a distant memory as I reached over to club him again.

"You goddamn, stubborn son of a bitch!" I shouted. Mark dodged, weaving back on his feet. "You're the reason Eli's dead!"

My final brother's eyes went wide, then a sneer climbed up his lips. He hunched over and slammed into me. I tried to smash my bleeding fists into him as he drove me into the ground. My already aching ribs screamed at the force, but I wouldn't give up. Neither did he. We both kept swinging, kicking and biting anything we could reach.

Mark and I had been wrestling since we were pups. Sometimes at the encouragement of the asshole, but as often for fun or to prove who was the bigger wolf. This was nothing like those times. When Mark cried out, I dug my thumb in deeper. If my bone creaked, he tried to snap it off. We were going to kill each other while we screamed into the night.

"You killed him!"

"No, I fucking didn't! You and your bitch witch did."

"Stop calling her that." I lunged out to punch Mark in the throat, hoping to silence him, but he wrenched his head back and I caught his eyes. They were starting to turn.

Fuck that. I slammed my hand up against his jaw, knocking his sprouting fangs into his tongue. He coughed in shock, spraying me with blood, but it stopped his wolf.

"I tried to keep you out of this, both of you, but you wouldn't listen. No, not Calvin, the golden child."

"He hated me, too."

"You got a smack, I was whipped. He breaks your finger, he snaps my femur. You were destined to be the alpha from the second you hit the ground."

"Are you fucking kidding me? Did you seriously start the apocalypse just so you could control a pack of cultists in the woods?"

"It was supposed to be me!" Mark roared and lunged for me. I tried to smash my knee into his chest, but he stepped on my thigh and wrapped his hands around my skull.

My brother, the only one I'd been able to count on when shit got hard, shoved his thumbs into my eyeballs and squeezed. "Get the hell off of me!" I thrashed, trying to break free as he kept pushing to make them pop like grapes.

"I did this for you. I took on the pack for you and Eli, so you'd have a real life. You fucked all of that up, you bastard!"

My leg swung and, by pure luck, smashed my shin into his balls. For all his bravado, the alpha male shriveled into a mewling kitten. He let go and my head snapped back. White light burned in my eyes and I struggled to blink, tears building as Mark fell to the side. He huddled to protect himself while I fought to get my vision back.

The wind shifted and I breathed deep. *Death.* It wasn't just the harpy's blood spilling from her broken neck. The grim collector was all around us. I struggled against the vast white sea, terrified it might never recede. A black cloak unfurled on the horizon. A shadow stood alone in the endless void, its form obscured but—as it raised its head—a crown of silver spikes glinted off the black. The creature raised its bone-white hands and red dripped from the palms. It raced over the field, covering the entire area in crimson except for a massive huddled form.

Eric. This is where he died. Am I going to die here too?

I looked toward the specter, but it vanished. The white was replaced with the indigo of a midnight forest, except I could still see the lake of blood if I blinked. If Death wasn't here for me, then…?

The air pulled from my lungs. The world bent inward toward the reception hall. I struggled to breathe when the dark sky lit up. A massive sun rose from the darkness, hanging above the resort before it exploded.

"Layla!" I shouted. Flames danced through the night. Pieces of the reception hall rained down from the trees. Fire strained out of the windows.

"She never stood a chance."

I reached over to kick Mark in his lying face, but he rolled and began to transform.

"Our friends, our cousins were in there!" I yelled at him.

"I warned you not to do this." As the last of his human mouth shifted, he sneered. "This is your fault."

My brother faded into the darkness, and I took off running toward the light. *Layla's smart. She'll have found a way. She'll be okay. She'll…she's…*

Sticks impaled my bare skin but I didn't care. I just kept running until I came face to face with the beginning of the end. Our guests lay on the lawn, covered in soot and nursing wounds. Those that could stand were staring in horror at the inferno while others huddled on the ground for help. I ran around trying to find anyone.

"Layla? Babe? Ink? Daniel?" Every face was familiar but unwanted. "Garavel?" I tried, then my heart lurched. "Mom!"

She was limping to the point of dragging her foot behind, but she kept helping one of her cousins away from the wreckage. "Cal?" My mom turned to me and I threw my arms around her. "Oh, thank the moon you're okay. What happened?"

Mark is behind all of this. It's his fault. He…

I shook it off. Right now my brother's betrayal didn't matter. "What happened? Where's Layla?"

"I…I don't know. She was holding him off so we could escape." My mother spun her head back to stare at the building that burned so hard it cratered into the ground.

No. She wouldn't do that. She'd find some way out. Ink would save her. Except he had been with me until Mark had banished him. Daniel was mortal. What about Garavel or the fucking elf, surely one of them could—?

"Cal?" I didn't know how long he had been repeating my name, but judging by the pained look on Marcus' face, it'd been a while. He held Dana's arm, and she was holding her phone out to me.

"It's for you," was all she said.

I placed it to my ear, fearing I'd hear White cackling about how he'd killed her. "Calvin?" Ink's voice was stricken and flat. "Get to the hospital, immediately. Time is…fleeting."

Chapter Thirty-Two

Cal

The first time I called Layla my wife was with tears in my eyes and a confused hospital attendant staring at me. No one seemed to be able to help, their confusion rising each time I asked. Years passed as I dashed from reception desk to reception desk pleading with anyone to find my wife.

I ran through a fog, only the glowing red lights of the hospital puncturing through the gray smoke. My wife was somewhere in this building, possibly dying, and I couldn't fucking find her.

"Calvin."

My legs stopped dead and I turned at the soft voice. Ink stood calmly next to a door he'd just exited. Unlike me, he'd changed out of the bloodied tux for his usual. I'd slapped on whatever my cousins could loan me and run as fast as I could.

"Is she…?" I tipped my head to the door where all the blinds on the windows were closed.

Ink pursed his lips and gave a curt nod. *Damn it.* I shoved past him. "Wait, you should know —"

I didn't care what he had to say. I needed to see her. Pushing open the door handle, I led with my hope.

White struck me first—a haunting glow from the bed where a body hid below the blankets. It yanked me back to the explosion, the moment of eerie quiet before the world tore itself to pieces. Machines whirred and beeped, covering the silence and smell of death.

Fuck. I tried to pinch my nose, but it dripped down my throat and clenched to my heart. Death was here, waiting to claim what it'd missed before.

A soft sob broke me from the bed. The haunting moonlight caught on a body in a chair. She was so small, her legs tucked to her chest as she huddled up, fingers digging into her bare, torn skin. She'd bent her face to her knees but her braids scattered to the side.

"Layla?" I whispered, terrified I'd lost my mind, that she was in the bed and I was making up what I wanted to see.

The head rose off her knees and I gasped. Her beautiful face was pocked and red from the fire, but she was breathing. She was alive.

"Cal?" she cried and I raced to her. My hands wrapped around her cheeks, needing to feel her. Layla hissed and I mentally smacked myself for touching her burns.

"Oh god, babe, I was…are you? Jesus." She collapsed against my shoulder and I tried to hold her while on my knees. Layla kept crying and rocking back and forth. *If she's here, then who's in the bed?*

"Her mother." Ink quietly closed the door and stood guard.

"She..." Layla shook in my grip and all I could do was hold her. She went silent save painful gasps of tears and a whimper that gouged out my lungs.

"She is dying," Ink spoke for her. "They do not believe she will make it through the night."

"Wh...?" I stared back at the demon. "What happened?"

"It's my fault." Layla bawled. She almost fell out of the chair. I caught her and lifted her in my arms.

"No, babe. Shh, come on. It's not your fault."

It's mine.

Layla began to cry again, her sobs dry and her throat wheezing. I tucked her into my lap and sat on the chair. She snuggled in my arms, holding on to me like I could protect her from the evils of the world.

"Ink?" I tried to get him to come clean, but he bowed his head.

"There is time enough for retribution. For now...tend to her." With that, he slipped outside, leaving me alone with Layla.

I held her for as long as she needed. Hours. Days. It didn't matter if my legs lost all blood flow and had to be amputated. I wasn't letting her down, not again. She didn't talk about what had happened, but she kept staring at her dress. It was burned up to her ankles. A black char line circled the hemline and the top was speckled in blood. What concerned me more was the blood welling up on her palm.

"Can I ask about the bandage on your hand?"

She shook her head hard and bundled her face back against my chest. 'Why aren't you healing it?' died on my tongue. She'd tell me in time. Right now, all that mattered was holding her.

"It's okay, babe. I'm here. I've got you." Every word rang hollow, a false promise that I'd protect her. That I'd keep her from pain.

I had invited the big bad wolf to our wedding. Her mother's death was on my head.

* * * *

Garavel

It's my fault.

The denizens of the healing ward kept staring at me. I'd had nowhere to go, but someone had pushed me toward a small alcove far from my lady and her agony. Bells and inhuman voices called through the ether, but I no longer had the strength to move.

"Sir? Do you need help?" Another one of the nurses stopped.

"No one can help now," I said solemnly. She blanched at that, then scuttled away. I lifted my eyes from nowhere and watched her run. "Why do they keep doing that?"

"Probably because your arms are slathered in blood." Ink approached from the side. He rested his hip on the half wall keeping me penned up. Instead of looking at me, he stared at the blue sign above the large metal door.

I hadn't looked at my hands since the implosion. There were screams, I thought. The heat was real. What of the chaos of nothingness inside of my heart? All I could remember was the weight of Layla in my arms driving me to fly as fast as possible.

"I don't know where it came from," I said.

"Might want to keep that fact to yourself. The nurses are on edge about our cavalcade of survivors."

I'd been in the eye of the blast — a power I hadn't felt in hundreds of thousands of years. It should have obliterated me to dust. It had done so to many of my fellow demi-angels from both our enemies and our creators. "How did we survive?" I asked the demon.

"Her mother." My friend slipped from his lean. He staggered around and slumped onto the plastic chair beside me. "I nearly reached you, had my hands around her waist when the realms blew."

Tipping his head back, Ink closed his eyes. Smoke twisted from below the lids. "I have been disemboweled in more ways than there are organs in the body. Drowned. Suffocated. Stood against the swipes of djinn, werewolves...Lust. I've never blinked as they tore me to shreds. But that power..."

He snickered. "I'd almost think it frightened me."

"It was angel magic."

That caught his attention. "How? Isn't the last one dead?"

Dead by my hand. Cleaved from this earth by his sworn protector. In trying to save what my dear friends had died for, I'd set the end in motion.

"Every realm was created and sealed away by an angel."

"As we already established."

I tipped my head and admitted our most sacred lore, a secret none should reveal. "By the sacrifice of an angel."

Ink sat up higher and turned to me, but I couldn't look him in the eye.

"That explosion, while an effect of the Horseman or Mrs. Leeland trying to counteract what he did, was not caused by either. It was an ancient trap left behind should any mage try to break free of the prison."

"A magical land mine?" The elf approached us. He'd been patched up by lesser doctors who weren't employed in saving Layla's mother. Though he'd kept the sunglasses on over top of the bandages around his head.

"Getting ideas, witch hunter?" Ink asked.

"I'm thinking. You should try it sometime, sin. If there are landmines powerful enough to strip the earth to dust, then Conquest has no chance to break through. His plan will fail."

"It would, except…" If I closed my eyes too long, I felt him. The slam of his cane inside my mind, the pierce of his voice shattering my veins.

"What happened when the Horseman grabbed you?" the elf asked.

I fought. I ran for centuries, never stopping, refusing to give in. But like a gentle rain wearing down a mountain, I stumbled and gave in just before she saved me. "He knows."

"Knows what?" Ink placed a hand on my knee as if to comfort me, though his eyes pierced through the realms as if to steal my thoughts, too.

I leaped to my feet and began to pace. "It's my fault. If I hadn't… I shouldn't have brought her there. She was safe. She should have stayed above. It's my fault. It's mine!"

"Whoa," the elf said. "Calm down."

"Ah yes, telling an agitated subject to 'calm' always works wonderfully."

I was too weak. I had partnered with her, needed her, relied on her because…because I wanted to keep her. To no longer return to my creator's side, to lose everything I was for him. My selfishness had killed her mother.

"I cannot stay here."

"Where are you going to go? The house is full of recovering werewolves," Ink said.

No, I could never return there. To my bed, to her. "Please, tell Layla that…that I am sorry."

Ink stood and reached for me. "Garavel, you're not making any sense. Sorry for what?"

"For starting the apocalypse," I shouted through tears and took off running.

Conquest had pried apart my brain, his incessant voice demanding one answer—where was Ramiel's body? And I had told him.

* * * *

Daniel

Juggling two coffees, I approached the hospital door. The demon and witch hunter both stared through me, eyes blank like they were waiting for someone to tell them what to do. I nudged the knob open and slipped inside.

"It took me three floors but I found a machine that worked," I said and raised my eyes to the chair.

The heartbreaking sobs had stopped. All of us had put in a pound of flesh to try to soothe Layla, and all of us had failed. It had been the demon's idea to call in the werewolf. I ground my jaw at how easily he held her, running his hand against her head as she rested without sleeping. Why did that come to him and not me?

"Here." I handed her the mocha that was probably just coffee mixed with powdered hot cocoa. The cup thudded against the back of her hand before she reacted and took it.

Her glassy eyes drifted up to me, her cheeks deflated and sunken in. Black soot stained her face, which she didn't have the energy to remove. Layla's lips moved, but no sound came out. Instead, she took a quick sip while I slunk back.

I'm sorry. I should have done something. Helped. Been there for her the way the elf or the angel were. Instead, I was leading my band out when it all went to shit. That explosion seared across my mind. If she died, if she suffered the agony of being nothing to no one in this world because I couldn't stop it, I'd never forgive myself.

Layla froze, the cup jerking in her hand. Her eyes bugged out and she covered her mouth. "'Scuse me," she muttered behind her palm as she leaped out of Cal's lap and ran for the bathroom. I caught the werewolf's eye at the sound of retching echoing off the tile. He looked down like this had happened before.

Had Conquest done something to her? He was the Horseman of pestilence. He could have poisoned her.

The vomiting paused, but she didn't come out of the bathroom. I eased near the partially open door and tried to knock without looking inside. "Layla? Are you…?"

"I'm fine," she said then pulled the door back. Her face was a terrifying gray but she forced on a smile below her smeared lipstick. "I think the coffee's gone bad." Then she winced. "But thank you for getting it."

Jesus, I didn't need her gratitude right now. None of us did. I reached over to hold her when the room's door flung open. Instead of the demon needing to make a grand entrance, an old woman with scraggly hair pinned back in rolls strode inside. Layla stiffened.

"What are you doing here?"

The old lady didn't even look at her, and just walked toward the woman dying in the bed. "Can a mother not see her daughter?"

Oh shit, this is...

Valerie didn't seem to care about Layla's obvious discomfort. She walked right up to the bandaged face of Isabel and gazed down.

"Now that you're here, maybe we can heal—"

"Child, no magic can save her. You know this."

My hackles shot straight up at how Valerie talked to her. "Hey." I wrapped a comforting hand around Layla's waist, taking her weight in my arm. "No one invited you here."

"I would not be here if you weren't so cavalier with your invitations," the old witch said with a smirk.

She's so damn much like Ink they'd either get on like a house on fire or kill each other. I hoped for the latter.

Layla whimpered and stared at her feet as if she were due all the blame. I should tell her it was my fault. If I hadn't been so worried that she'd toss me aside the second she learned Conquest's spell, maybe they'd have gotten it soon enough. Maybe she could have stopped him and saved the world before all of this.

"Why did you come?" Layla whispered, her arms crossed over her chest. She wouldn't look at her grandmother or her mother. Instead, she stared at a pile of belongings on the floor. I followed her line of sight and spotted the familiar red leather resting on top of a blue book. "She wouldn't want you here."

Valerie snickered. "What does it matter what she'd want? She is not long for this world."

Layla's hackles rose. She lifted her palms as if she were about to start throwing fire, but her chin dropped and she slammed her hands to her thighs. She pushed off of me to stand next to her mother beside Valerie.

"For all your rebellions, Bella, in the end, you did as a proper witch should."

"What's that?" Cal chimed in. He'd stood, ready to whisk Layla away.

Valerie didn't even look at him. "She protected the line."

Layla wrapped her hands around her stomach and folded inward. I didn't have a clue what that meant, and judging by Cal's dumb look, he didn't either. Standing next to the bed, Layla began to shiver. I dove for the mess of discarded clothing and found a suit coat. Whose it was didn't matter. As I tugged it out from under the books, Layla's spell book slid off.

That mysterious page fell out and slid across the ground to her feet. She bent down to pick it up, which was when I draped the coat over her shoulders. Valerie looked too, her withered lips pursing. "That spell is the only chance of salvation that remains. Do you really think it wise to leave it so unprotected?"

"No," Layla muttered, looking chagrined. She extended her hand and her spell book leaped for it. Rather than open it, she held her book tight to her chest, her fingers flicking over the blood that dried into the embossed grooves.

"What's that spell?" Cal asked. He had the kind of innocent face that'd play dumb to the most cynical of people. The crone stared at him a moment, then returned to watching her daughter die.

"It's going to close the gaps in the realms," Layla said. "Forever."

"That sounds...dangerous?" He looked at me, but Layla shrugged.

"Can I...?" I eased the piece of paper out of her fingers.

Valerie watched. "You allow common eyes to read your magic? Not as if he'll comprehend it."

I hadn't looked closer before, but yeah, the Latin was simple—as all her most devastating spells were. But that damn final phrase at the bottom struck me. What did it mean? And why was 'nam-tar' biting at the back of my head?

"I assume the senior witch will be casting it," I said.

"No. It must be a balance, a witch of both creation and destruction, otherwise the world as we know it would end."

I didn't trust a damn word from her mouth. I hadn't read anything about a balanced witch in her book. God, I wished I was dead again just so I could comb through her literature to see if Valerie was lying. No other spell of hers came with this final line. It looked like another instruction or a warning.

"My bond." The demon appeared beside her, causing me to jump. He took Layla by the elbow. "Forgive me for interrupting, but..."

The door flew open and the elf strode inside. "You're going to want to see this." He walked to the outside window and pulled on the blinds.

It should have been a cold, gray parking lot, with only pockets of yellow light breaking up the night. Flashes cut through the sky, tears of green, red and blue breaking up the black. Even more damning was the parking lot. Where the streetlight once stood was now a massive tree, hundreds of red eyes hanging from the branches and a giant snake with arms wrapped around the trunk.

Layla hustled over to look. I stood behind her shoulder as we all gathered together. "It's like the elven realms," she sputtered.

"It's far worse than that," Raul said and he pointed to the horizon.

Where there should be no sun, three rose in varying positions. The light cut in varying rays, the unnatural sunrises shades of green and purple. A horrifying screech shattered the air and a flock of harpies flew straight into the windows of the building across the street. Car horns blared and pockets of orange fires rose from the city.

Ink took a deep breath. "The apocalypse has begun."

Chapter Thirty-Three

Layla

My mother died on my birthday.

The world ended on Halloween.

Failure hung off of me like an oversized coat. Eyes would watch me, then dart away. Tongues would still whenever I walked into a room. I'd been through my mother's death before, but being at the epicenter of an apocalypse was new.

It could have been days since my mother's heart monitor had bottomed out. Or maybe it'd only been a few hours since the sky had split open and very confused monsters had poured into our world. I had no way to know. A mass of testosterone and concern converged upon me and ferried me back home.

Even if I wanted to crawl into bed and hide until my brain stopped aching, I couldn't. The rooms were crammed full of Cal's surviving kin, many of them needing treatment. He ran himself ragged administering first aid while also joking, "Other than that, how was the wedding?"

At the sight of me shuffling through the room in his hoodie, Cal stopped trying to stitch Marcus up. "Babe?" he asked. "How are you feeling?"

What answer could I give? My mother had died and the world had ended. The world was ending. I had to keep reminding myself that even though the realms were splitting apart, they hadn't collapsed yet. Whatever plan Conquest had begun, we could still stop it—or so my grandmother claimed.

"You should eat to revive your strength," Ink said, swooping in from behind. "I have prepared a sustaining bowl of caramel refried beans for you."

Cal placed a hand to Ink's offered one. "There's a sandwich instead of...that. Layla? Please. You haven't eaten since—"

The wedding. That fleeting moment when everything was wonderful and perfect. They were getting worried, having shifted from politely offering me a bite of their dinner to requesting it. With every split of the barrier, my stomach twisted. I couldn't eat even if I wanted to, but Cal looked at me with so much pain that I meekly nodded.

He handed me the turkey and Swiss he'd made for himself, then he cupped my cheek and brushed down my braids. "We're going to get through this. I swear."

I wanted to ask how, but he smiled for the first time in ages. "Okay."

Cal kissed my forehead, then he stared at the sandwich. I humored him by nibbling on the bread. A pained mewling broke him from me and Cal scooped up the perturbed kitten. "I'm sorry about all of this," he cooed to Fiona. "He'll be back soon. I think."

I darkened and looked to Ink. My incubus stood up straight. "The witch hunter is chasing him."

"Can you stop calling him that? He's not a witch hunter."

"No? He out-of-hand knew precisely how to track your angel. Does that sound of a hunter of witches?"

"We should set up another perimeter to keep the worst of the monsters at bay." Daniel approached from the living room, not noticing me hiding between Cal and Ink. When he did, he paled and ran his fingers through his hair. "I mean, I'm sure your magic is holding, it's just…"

"Shall you compare her face to a warted frog and voice to a dying mule next?" Ink teased.

Daniel tipped his head down instead of challenging my incubus. "Layla." He took my hand and ran his fingers over the back of it. "Right now, we're beaten down. We're regrouping, but we've had Conquest on the ropes before and we'll do it again."

The doorbell rang and ten werewolves leaped to their feet. "Knock, knock," Dana said, pushing the door open while holding Angelo's tiny hand. Beside her stood Fariah and Maram, both of them cloaked under long hoods.

"Layla?" All three of them asked how I was doing by saying my name.

I nodded to my old friends, then caught Maram's fiery eye. "Thank you for coming."

"This is the safest place right now," Dana said. "So, where are we putting our things?"

Cal walked over and took their bags. "You'll all be in my room."

"Will we now?" Dana sounded excited.

"With Layla. I'll stay in the yard with the rest of my family."

"Oh."

Poor Dana's hopes of a wild threesome had collapsed quickly. I almost wanted to laugh at the idea but my humor couldn't get further than noticing a joke right now. "You haven't eaten his bread pie," Ink said to me.

"I'm just not hungry," I admitted and handed him the sandwich. Ink didn't look happy, but he accepted it. "Ink, you can't lie."

"True."

"And caring about someone else's feelings will give you a rash."

"What are you driving at?"

"Can we do this? Everyone's got differing ideas on how to stop Conquest, but I...I want to know if you believe any'll work."

We both watched Cal try to heal our little werewolf army and Daniel speak about magic with Maram. Mikki sat on the couch riling up the other nymphs to help, but we were at most fifty people going up against a Horseman. *I don't know what I'm doing. Would it be better if we run? If we hide away from all of this, hoping to survive the end of the world in our private refuge?*

"My bond." Ink took my hand and ran his thumb over the top. "There are few things in this world that I would put my faith in. Cities crumble, empires fall. Even seas vanish into the sky. But you..." He stared into my eyes. "Conquest will rue the day he ever challenged you."

"Thank you," I whispered.

He wiped his thumb under my eye then stepped back. "If you will excuse me, I need to release the hose on a pair of randy werewolves." Ink bowed his head, then he shouted, "This is a house of healing, not debauchery. If you wish to fornicate, please save it for when the camera's battery is charged."

I didn't believe in myself. I wanted to run, to bury my head in the sand. To forget about White, about magic, about my mother. But Ink having faith in me, Daniel and Cal helping, Garavel and Raul fighting — it gave me hope.

"Pst, Layls." Dana slid away from Cal's half tour. "Here. I got you what you wanted." She passed over a plain brown bag that I stuffed into the hoodie's pocket. "You sure?"

"I don't know. Thank you."

"Well, whatever happens, we've got your back. Now I need to get Angelo before he pets the wrong doggy."

I slipped away from the mess of people to the bathroom. There I could lock the door and bawl my eyes out. With the noise of so many werewolves, no one could hear me, not even myself. I slid the brass lock into place then slumped onto the toilet.

Everything spinning around me was balanced on a needle — White, the apocalypse, the witch hunters, my grandmother, Daniel, Cal, Garavel's guilt, Raul's vengeance, Ink. One wrong move could collapse everything.

Taking a deep breath, I opened Dana's bag and pulled out the pregnancy test.

Want to see more from this author?
Here's a taster for you to enjoy!

Coven of Desire: Death
Ellen Mint

Coming September 2024

Excerpt

The wall had fallen. At long last, the exile's end was upon them.

Conquest inspected the city from his perch in the endless office. Skies of green and red drifted through the inky black. Moons rose and fell without a care for the orbit of the planet.

It was the end for some...and the beginning for all.

"Mr. White?" The call from his secretary pulled Conquest's mask back on. His sharp crown of black and blood red sank back into his balding head. The robes of empires flattened to a simple white suit. He tapped his cane, calling the horse back to the top. The crackling apocalyptic air followed, returning his primordial battlefield to a bland conference room.

"Yes?" he asked, his voice drenched in the mundane. Soon, he'd no longer have to dance to the ever-conflicting tune of mortals. There were only two pieces yet to collect, but one was proving to be a nasty challenge.

"There's a...er, Miss Pale here to see you?" his secretary said, her voice quivering as if she'd just faced her brief mortal candle.

Conquest smiled, his mouth splitting open to his ears. "Please, send her in."

She moved without a sound. Dressed in a smart black suit with her bone-white hair pulled back into a ponytail, she no doubt struck fear into the hearts of all who saw her. He glanced at her through the glass, seeing not what she projected but the truth below. The reality would drive men mad.

"Th...there's wa-wa-water over — "

"That will be enough, Natalie," he interrupted his trembling secretary. She was needed to answer phones, and he didn't have time to find another. Nodding hard, Natalie scuttled back and shut the door tight. Conquest waited for the eldest to speak.

She did not move. Despite being as slender as a skeleton, she filled the doorway, her presence leeching across the floor. The shadow bore a hood and cloak, its bony fingers clinging to a scythe. She, however, held only a purse and a single black pen with a silver cap. That, she kept twiddling between her fingers while staring back at him.

While they could stay like that for days, he had bigger empires to conquer. "This is a surprise. Don't you have dire business to attend to, sister?"

She jerked her chin, the closest she came to laughing. "You've seen what's occurring?"

"It would be impossible not to." Conquest gazed out at the world beneath him. Creatures of unimaginable horror were walking into this world without any possible way to return. The mortals were responding in their usual way, with fear and violence. It would keep his dear sister overbooked.

She moved toward him without so much as her clothing rustling. A bolt of lightning struck from the sky and half of her face reflected a skull. "The realms are splitting to pieces. Who is causing this?"

Conquest shrugged. "Have you spoken to our brother?"

"He has entrenched himself in the far north. This does not seem to be in either the purview or skill of our sister."

"There will be many more mouths that go hungry because of this mess," Conquest said carefully. He feared nothing in this world, because nothing in this world could kill him. Though, there was always the question of the eldest who was destined to also be the last.

Placing a hand to the glass, Conquest peered over his creation. "Perhaps it's finally come to pass. All those sages and madmen crying for an apocalypse have their wish."

His sister clicked her tongue. "Prophecy is a blanket against the cold truth of life and..." She stopped twitching her pen and tapped it against the glass, making her point.

As far as he knew, there'd been no orders from the Celestials to form them. The Horsemen were birthed and thrust into this life with as much understanding to their why as every other carping mortal. While his sisters and brother preferred to follow the script laid out by their creators, he'd chosen to break free.

"Perhaps this is what the celestials planned all along," Conquest said. "They created the realms, now they destroy them."

She didn't answer, her black eyes sinking into her skull until the sockets were empty. A ringing caused her to reach for her bag. She pulled out a shaking hourglass tipping out the last of its sand. The ringing continued.

"I believe that one is mine." Mr. White picked up his phone.

One of his lieutenants spoke before he said a word. "We've found it."

"Excellent. You are certain?"

"Yeah. Davey thought to take a little peek and…"

Conquest did not care what had happened to a mortal foolish enough to give in to his curiosity about an angel. "I gave you ample warning what would happen."

His lieutenant took a moment, sounding like he was swallowing back his gorge. Even a dead angel could cause complete internal explosion if gazed upon by a mortal. "We know, sir. We should be able to get it fully extracted from the concrete in an hour."

"Wonderful. Before you put it in the truck, pluck two feathers."

"Sir?"

Conquest caught his sister's abyss-like gaze burning into his hand clutching the phone. The trap the celestials left behind had torn the flesh clean off. It'd taken him days to stitch it back together and the scars remained. Having Death's attention caused a shiver to run down even Conquest's spine.

"Do you think it wise to question me as Davey did?" he fumed into the phone.

"No, sir. All will be done."

He dropped the phone onto the table. Despite a few setbacks, everything was going to plan. There was one small piece to collect, but that one would be foolish enough to come to him.

"I'm afraid I'm needed elsewhere," his sister said.

Conquest parted his hands and bowed to her. "Don't let me keep you." She vanished in a heartbeat, leaving only the lingering scent of myrrh. Striding for the windows, he gazed down at the world corrupting before him. "You'll have your work cut out for you, sister."

About the Author

Ellen Mint adores the adorkable heroes who charm with their shy smiles and heroines that pack a punch. She has a needy black lab named after Granny Weatherwax from Discworld. Sadly, her dog is more of a Magrat.

When she's not writing imposing incubi or saucy aliens, she does silly things like make a tiny library full of her books. Her background is in genetics and she married a food scientist so the two of them nerd out over things like gut bacteria. She also loves gaming, particularly some of the bigger RPG titles. If you want to get her talking for hours, just bring up Dragon Age.

Ellen loves to hear from readers. You can find her contact information, website details and author profile page at https://www.totallybound.com

Home of Erotic Romance

Sign up for our newsletter and find out about all our romance book releases, eBook sales and promotions, sneak peeks and FREE romance books!